ALTERED DESTINIES:
EARTH REBORN

YVONNE HERTZBERGER

Copyright Yvonne Hertzberger 2019

Cover by Rebecca Poole at dreams2media.com

All rights reserved. NO part of this book may be reproduced without the publisher's prior consent in any form of binding or cover other than that in which it is published and without a similar condition including this condition being imposed on the subsequent purchaser.

The moral right of the author has been asserted in accordance with the Copyrights, Designs and Patents Act 1988

ISBN: 978-0-9948825-4-7

ACKNOWLEDGMENTS

I would like to express my profound gratitude to all those who supported me in the creation of this book. Special mentions go to my beta readers: Laurel, Leslie, Liz, Kim and Carolyn. You all made this a better book by far.

To Ed, thank you for all the insights, suggestions and encouragement as I struggled.

To the members of my critique group, Jane Ann, Ed and Ash - I may not accept all you say but it made me think and that's priceless.

To my spouse, Mark, who understands that writing is "real work" even though it adds little to our budget.

To all my readers, without whom I would have no reason to write.

Finally to all those who took the time to write honest reviews on my previous books. Every author depends on that kind of support. You keep me writing.

CONTENTS

CREDO	1
Chapter 1	3
Chapter 2	9
Chapter 3	16
Chapter 4	22
Chapter 5	26
Chapter 6	33
Chapter 7	43
Chapter 8	49
Chapter 9	55
Chapter 10	62
Chapter 11	67
Chapter 12	72
Chapter 13	82
Chapter 14	86
Chapter 15	93
Chapter 16	97
Chapter 17	102
Chapter 18	105
Chapter 19	109
Chapter 20	117
Chapter 21	124
Chapter 22	133
Chapter 23	140
Chapter 24	147
Chapter 25	156
Chapter 26	163
Chapter 27	171
Chapter 28	179
Chapter 29	185
Chapter 30	191
Chapter 31	203

Chapter 32	211
Chapter 33	219
Chapter 34	225
Chapter 35	233
Chapter 36	239
Chapter 37	244
Chapter 38	252
Chapter 39	256
Chapter 40	263
Chapter 41	268
Chapter 42	273
Chapter 43	277
Chapter 44	281
Chapter 45	285
Chapter 46	289
Chapter 47	293
Chapter 48	299
Chapter 49	305
Chapter 50	310
Chapter 51	315
Chapter 52	320
Epilogue	327

CREDO

It is told that in the time before time, the time before memory, before our people populated the earth, others covered all the lands. They built fantastical cities, from materials we do not understand, filled with numbers of people beyond comprehension.

We know this is so, because from time to time, strange objects emerge from the soil, objects made from things no one has ever seen, nor can fathom the uses for.

It is told that, at the end of the time of the others, there was a great war, conflagrations that consumed whole cities and poisoned the land. These created a cataclysm such as none can imagine. It melted the earth as far as a man can walk in a week.

We know this is so, because we have mined the molten rocks from which we now create our most precious amulets and jewels. We wear these to remind us of our duty to govern well.

It is told that the smoke and ash from the conflagration spread over all the lands and waters, blocking the sun. The earth grew cold. Nothing grew, not the grass, nor the trees, nor the animals of the earth, nor the creatures of the waters.

We know this is so because we find strange animals and plants we do not recognize in the molten rock and in the deep layers of ashen soil.

The people died, leaving only a few, our ancestors. These are the ones from whom we are all descended. It is they who have carried the account of our beginnings so that we may remember and be thankful. And that we may not repeat the errors of those who went before.

Our numbers remain few, our cities small, much knowledge lost.

CHAPTER ONE

BAIN

Bain nudged the man next to him with his elbow. "Who is that woman, that beauty in blue?"

His companion gave a derisive snort. "You won't get far with that one. She is Lord Danza's daughter. They call her the Ice Queen. Every man who vies for her attentions gets frostbite."

Bain's gaze followed the back of the raven haired beauty with the alabaster skin, transfixed, as she glided out the door at the far end of the hall. When she disappeared from view the man who had made the comment held out his hand, breaking the spell.

"I am Kort, third son of Norston, advisor to Lord Danza."

"I am Bain, son of Lord Makin." Bain took the hand and shook it. "I am pleased to make your acquaintance, sir."

Kort chuckled lightly as he accepted Bain's hand. "I am aware of who you are. I warrant very few here are not. Welcome to Kinterron."

"And who was the man the, uh, Ice Queen, was escaping from?"

Kort frowned. "That is Mathune of Belthorn. He imagines himself a ladies' man but has a reputation for cruelty and deceit. I dare say he has his eyes on that prize. She obviously wants none of him. Stay clear of him. He is dangerous."

Bain took a long look at Mathune and nodded. "Yes, I have seen his type."

Bain felt out of place in this great hall. Kinterron was more wealthy than Marston, his home fief. Every candle sconce on the walls bore one of the Jewels of Fire. They glittered in the flickering flames. The women wore gowns of brilliant colours, made from the rare silk of the Jewel Spider, reflecting the colours in the jewels they wore. Even the men wore such jewels in pins on the shoulders of their dress tunics.

The wealth of Kinterron was brought into full view by the artifacts fastened to the walls of the hall, strange objects for which no one could discern a purpose, partly encased in molten rock, or occasionally carefully cleaned to reveal twisted metals that could no longer be made. These had been found in the tunnels where the jewels were mined. Bain was glad that his father and Lady Flor favoured less ostentatious décor.

Bain had not been raised as heir to his father Lord Makin's fiefdom. This event was his first important social occasion since being legitimized and named heir. He had been at court occasions in Marston but none compared with this. Lord Makin had sent him to this annual spring court gathering on his own to learn and to observe. He rolled his shoulders and did his best to look relaxed, though the glitter and opulence made him uncomfortable.

Had Bain been born to Lady Flor, Lord Makin's Lady, this, and all court life, would be familiar. He would have been raised to it. But Lady Flor had borne no children, leaving Lord Makin with no legitimate heir. He was painfully aware of the disdain with which the other heirs, and indeed their families, regarded him.

Two years ago, when all hope of a legitimately born heir faded, Lord Makin had summoned Bain and his mother to court. That order had turned both their lives upside down. Lord Makin had declared Bain, his only bastard son, as his heir, and begun the rigorous training that would prepare him for the role he would inherit.

These two years had been a whirlwind: training in arms, history, strategy, and not least, court etiquette and political gamesmanship. These last two would teach him how to navigate the intricate relationships between the lords of the lands and their advisors without stepping on toes, at least until he had established his position and been accepted in court circles. The present gala was the first of the rotating, twice annual gatherings he would attend as heir. Eventually he would be expected to find a bride at one.

Bain did his best to recall all he had learned about the histories of each fief and its place in the hierarchy of power. With the descriptions he had been given he tried to connect the many faces with names. Which sons would be heirs, and which ones were looking for suitable brides? The effort was fatiguing. *Who is that man, now? And that young woman, whose daughter is she?* To say the situation was delicate would be a gross understatement.

Bain remained painfully aware of how precarious his position was, making him once again forget his companion.

A prod in the ribs by Kort brought him out of his reverie. "… that one is looking your way. Ask her to dance."

With effort Bain pulled his attention back and tried to spot the young woman indicated. "Where?"

"There, in red, the dark haired one, with the ancient jewel pendant. Nice curves."

"Hmmmm." Before he had to commit himself, another man approached the lady in question. He was off the hook … for now. "Perhaps later. I think I need some air." He maneuvered his way between the guests, past the rows of benches and trestle tables, to the huge, carved, double doors at the end of the great hall, grateful that no one seemed to take notice of him.

Once he left behind the bright lights, the music, the jostling and noise of the festivities, he drew in long, deep breaths of the crisp night air. *Of course they pay me no notice. I am a bastard. They will not accept me as the heir to Marston simply because my father has declared it.*

He did his best, and failed, to recall the name of the young man who had answered some of his questions before he met Kort. *Father, I am not ready. You have sent me here too soon.*

The doors behind him burst open and two young revelers, arms entwined, spilled out, almost tripping on the last step before fading, still laughing, into the darkness. No doubt other hopeful couples had already left for their own trysts.

No hope of my enjoying a tryst tonight. He allowed himself a wry snicker, and then sighed deeply. Duty called. He must go back into the fray. He squared his shoulders, gave them another roll and headed back into the great hall. His lessons in history and politics had taught him who was who but now he needed to put more faces to the names. By the time this week's event ended he needed to know them all.

His stomach did a lurch as he passed the banquet table laden with all manner of rich food and drink. In his current state of anxiety eating was out of the question. While the wine tempted him he knew better than to imbibe on an empty stomach. This would not be a good time to make a fool of himself.

The musicians had stopped playing and the guests drifted away from the centre where they had been dancing in search of more food, drink, and seats. Bain could see that many of the youngest guests engaged in serious flirtation or conversation with someone of the opposite sex. Many wore the ancient "jewels of many colours" mined from the molten rocks said to have been created in the "Great Conflagration". Some thought the story to be myth. Most believed the ancient tales of a time before time when the world looked much different – a time before great balls of fire fell from the sky, melting mountains and creating a darkness so long almost all the people starved and history had to begin again.

Bain did believe. Aside from the jewels he had been shown a number of strange artifacts taken from the mines, things for which no one could fathom a use and of materials so strange he could only wonder at them. He thought that those who denied the history were foolish for refusing to see the evidence before their eyes.

A careful look around told him the woman in blue had not reappeared. *Is she with someone? Or is Kort right and she spurns us all?*

Bain took a quick tally of the remaining guests and found that he could put names to most of the older men - the lords and eldest sons. It was a start, not a bad one if he was honest with himself. Many lords were absent from the event, leaving, as Lord Makin had, their offspring to find their own path.

Thankful that no one took notice of him he found a chair in a darker corner and sat down to observe. The evening was drawing to a close. Many of the older men and women had already gone, leaving the hall to the young, those who had not already paired off and left. Here and there another young couple drifted away, no doubt to a more private spot. How many of those hopeful young ladies would have their dreams shattered by the end of the week, he wondered? And how many reputations would be destroyed? No, that was a game a bastard heir could not afford to play – not that he had any desire to. He'd leave that to the spoiled sons of the more powerful lords, the roués who felt themselves above the rules.

The image of the woman referred to as the Ice Queen kept intruding into his thoughts, making it impossible to concentrate on learning names and faces, so he stopped fighting it. He still had not learned her true name. She had a singular beauty, rare in his home fief. The women at home had mostly olive skin and various shades of brown hair, though some blondes and gingers could also be found.

Perhaps that was what had struck him. He shook his head at his own folly - to lose his balance over something so shallow. And yet, he could not get her out of his mind – how she carried herself with such grace that she fairly glided across the floor, head held high on her slender neck. The rich blue had accented her jet black hair and fair complexion. Though he had not been close enough to see them he imagined her eyes as the colour of cornflowers.

With a rueful shake of his head he brought himself back to the present. *Forget her. She is out of your reach.* By now the hall was almost empty of guests. Only the servants still bustled about setting the space back in order and preparing it for the breaking of the fast next morning. The contrast between their toil and the freedoms of their masters was not lost on him. As the son of a peasant healer he remembered only too well. *I must never forget that.*

He heaved his tired body out of the chair and made his way to the barracks where the single male guests lodged. Before falling onto his cot he noted that a few other cots had discarded clothing draped on them but were unoccupied. No doubt their owners had found a warmer, softer welcome elsewhere.

In spite of his fatigue sleep eluded him. Each time he closed his eyes the vison of the beauty in blue intruded. The first hint of dawn already crept into the small barracks windows before he finally shook himself and rolled onto his side away from the light. His last thought was a decision to meet the woman face to face, perhaps to introduce himself. *Maybe when she gives me the brush-off I can let her go.* With that thought he drifted into a fitful doze until the sounds of the young men returning from their revels or waking from sleep roused him.

CHAPTER TWO

MORNING

*B*ain declined an invitation from Kort to join him in the Great Hall for some food. He needed to be alone – and to find out more about Lord Danza's daughter. He needed to learn her name. That thought occurred to him too late to catch Kort and ask him. *Wake up, idiot. You need your wits about you.*

He had no wish to mingle with the others but his stomach growled loudly telling him he did need something to eat. Knowing that the kitchens in most castles were in the level below the main one he sought out a stairway and made his way into the cellars. The aroma of fresh bread led him to the kitchens. Since he had thrown on the old breeches and tunic he'd worn before being summoned to his father's court the servants took little notice of him. He was glad, now, that he had not discarded them. They lent anonymity when he needed to escape the critical eyes of the court. A serving maid passed him with a huge tray laden with fragrant loaves of warm bread. He snatched one off the top.

When the maid began to scowl and shake her head he gave her a conspiratorial wink and a grin. She rolled her eyes but could not hide the dimple that told him he would not be scolded, before she scurried off. He broke off a big chunk and chewed it as he trolled the kitchen for some cheese. Knowing better than to snatch it off the trays so carefully sliced and laid out, ready to take upstairs, he kept on until he came to the cold pantry. There he found not only a huge wheel of cheese but a keg of ale with a mug beside it. Apparently the servants helped themselves. *Just like at home. As long as they do their duty no one says anything.* He filled the mug half-way and drank it down before slicing himself some cheese and taking his booty away up the stairs, down a hall, and out the back doors into the castle gardens. There, though it was still spring, he could see early greens and herbs growing. He recognized a few from the salads served the evening before. In other plots the first sprouts of the later vegetables poked through the earth. The familiar, fresh smell of newly turned soil and growing things refreshed him. He located a three-legged garden stool and lowered himself onto it to enjoy his bread and cheese in peace.

The cheese made him thirsty and he found himself wishing he'd brought a mug of that ale with him. Going back might attract a little too much attention so he decided against it. He left the garden by the side gate and strolled around outside the castle wall to familiarize himself more with the area.

A short way around he came upon a deep, cool, stone chamber. Though unoccupied, the door stood open. A familiar aroma of dried herbs drew his attention. A closer look inside revealed a long, coarsely hewn table covered with bottles, bowls, and mortars and pestles of many sizes. The rafters hung with dried herbs and flowers, most of them familiar to him. The walls were lined with shelves and he spotted a cot along a wall, and three chairs. Though this chamber was much larger than his mother's at home he recognized it as an apothecary, where a healer would store and mix the potions and powders used in the healing craft.

Bain had spent many hours as a child helping his mother gather and prepare remedies, so the chamber drew him in. He spent some pleasant moments sniffing at this bottle, that bowl, another hanging bundle. The tension began to seep from his shoulders and he forgot for the moment that he was a stranger and might not be welcome here.

"Put that down. What do you think you are doing?"

Bain almost dropped the sac he was sniffing. "Forgive me, I ... " He stopped midway in his turn; his apology froze in his throat. It was her, the woman in blue, Lord Danza's daughter. But how? How here?

"Who are you? I have not seen you before. If you are in need of my services ask now. If not explain your presence." She stood in the doorway, hands firmly on her hips, feet planted apart, lips pursed and eyes – eyes that seemed to pierce his very mind.

Bain took a deep breath. *No point in dissembling. She will see through that.* He spread his hands, palms out, by way of apology. "I am Bain, heir to Lord Makin of Marston. I sought to escape the formality of the Hall and found myself here."

He watched a flicker of confusion cross her face, followed by a disbelieving shake of her head, seeming even more angry than before. "Lord Makin has no heir ... " She stopped, eyes widening slightly then narrowing again. "Oh, I see. You are the bastard he has named heir."

The disdain in her voice rankled him just enough that he regained some composure. He squared his shoulders, then sketched her an exaggerated bow. "Indeed, I am he. My mother is a peasant, the best healer in all of Marston. I claim that heritage with pride." He faced her, tall and straight, prepared for further insult, growing more indignant with each breath. "I would know your name as well." He wondered if his bluff would work and she would assume he did not know her identity, dressed as she was like a common peasant woman.

She studied him in silence, eyes still narrowed but no longer quite so accusing.

Bain took the opportunity to return the appraisal. If anything he found her even more desirable in this plain garb and with her hair plaited in a single braid hanging down her back. His forefinger itched to reach out and tuck an ink-black, stray curl behind her ear. He closed his hand into a loose fist to hide the impulse, then tucked both hands behind his back and stood at ease, deliberately matching her stance but without the challenge hands on hips would imply. *Easy, or she'll have me thrown out of the fief and send me crawling back home in shame.*

But backing down was not an option either. When she began to relax a little and looked about to speak again he plunged in ahead of her. "It was my interest in the healing arts that drew me into this apothecary. My mother taught me a good deal as I grew up." He took a deep breath and repeated his request. "May I know your name? You have me at a disadvantage." *True, as it happens. I know whose daughter you are but not your name.*

She ignored the question again. Instead her chin rose in challenge and she reached for the sac he had been holding. "Tell me what this is."

"A mixture of chamomile for calmness, sage for strength, and raspberry leaf to support the womb. Women drink it as a tea, especially when they are with child."

"Hmph."She took it from him, set it down, and reached for a glass bottle filled with roots. Taking out the stopper she handed it to him. "And this?"

He sniffed the contents and wrinkled his nose. He made a quick decision to meet her challenge as an equal and not a trespasser. "I would add mint to this, and honey to disguise the taste, though even with that it will still taste foul. It is valerian root, for sleep." He handed the bottle back and watched as she replaced it in its spot on the shelf behind her. She began to reach for another bottle filled with what looked like tiny black seeds, then seemed the change her mind and drew back her hand. She turned to face him, still stern but somewhat softened in her stance and gaze. "I am Phaera, Lord Danza's daughter." Then, as if expecting a challenge to her declaration she resumed her initial posture, hands on hips, eyes challenging. "I am a healer and this is my apothecary."

Bain recovered quickly from this revelation and gave her his best courtly bow. "I am honoured, milady," then resumed standing at ease and waited. This was her sphere and he an unwelcome guest. He would not presume to take the lead.

She eyed him sideways, eyebrows raised. "I saw a child this morning with a cut on his leg. It festered and a red line was beginning to travel upward from it under the skin. What would you do for it?"

"I'd lance the wound at the point of the worst festering, press out the pus from the top of the red line, and follow it with hot compresses of salted water to draw out the remaining pus. Then I'd wrap it in clean bandages. That needs to be repeated daily until the red line is gone and I see no more pus. By then the swelling should have gone down. When the redness and swelling are gone it will no longer be necessary to repeat the treatments and his mother can check daily to see that it continues to heal. She can replace the bandages with clean ones."

"Hmmm, perhaps you do know something about healing." Before Phaera could say more a figure appeared in the doorway, a woman holding a limp child in her arms.

"My Lady, please help my son! He burns with fever."

As if Bain were no longer there Phaera turned around, took the child from the frantic mother, and laid him on the table. She felt his forehead and checked his pulse with two fingers on his neck, her brow furrowed. Not even glancing at the boy's mother she tugged his tunic up to look at his belly, asking, "When did the fever begin? Were there other signs of illness?"

"Yestermorn he would not eat. I hoped sleep would have it pass and he would waken well."

"Has he drunk anything? Has he passed urine since yesterday?"

"No, milady. He refused all drink." The mother wrung her hands as she looked anxiously on.

Phaera had by this time pulled the boy's tunic back down and opened his mouth to peer at this throat. "His throat is very red.

The pain is the reason he will not drink." She pinched the skin on his hand and watched to see how long it took for the white colour to disappear. "He needs to drink." She handed the boy back to his mother.

The lad's head lolled onto her shoulder. He uttered a delirious moan.

"We need to bring his fever down and soothe his throat." As she spoke she reached for the kettle already heating on a brazier and poured some water into a large cup. "This is chamomile," she said as she dropped some dried flowers into it before adding a good dollop of honey. From behind her on a shelf she took a jar that held a powder and added a pinch of it to the tea. As she began to replace the stopper she spied Bain still standing, watching her. She thrust the bottle under his nose before closing it.

"Willow bark, for fever." Bain told her.

A curt nod was her only response as she poured the cooling tea through a reed sieve into a cup with a long, narrow spout on one side. "Hold him," she instructed the mother as she took the boy's jaw into one hand, forcing the lips and teeth apart. With the other she inserted the spout into the child's mouth and tipped a small amount of tea into it. The boy sputtered but was forced to swallow some of the liquid as his chin was too high to spit it out. When it looked like he might choke she withdrew the spout until he breathed normally again. This was repeated until all of the tea had been swallowed.

Phaera held up the spouted cup. "Do you have anything like this?" When the mother shook her head Pheara turned and filled a large jar with more of the medicinal tea. She handed that and the cup to the mother. "Then take these and bring them back tomorrow. Take care that he does not bite too hard on the spout or it will break. Bring the lad as well. Until then see that he drinks half a cup every hour or so. He need not eat but he must drink. It will help the fever and prevent him from drying out too much. Come back in the morning and tell me how much he has drunk and how many times he has passed urine. If he is not better I will have more tea for you. Also, keep cool wet cloths on his head and behind his neck to help bring down the fever."

"Will he recover, milady?"

"I am hopeful," Phaera answered, "but you must see that he drinks this."

"Thank you, milady. I will." The woman gave an awkward curtsy with her son in her arms, took the jar and cup from Phaera and left.

"How bad is the lad's throat?"

As if having forgotten that Bain still watched her she whirled to face him. "It is very red and swollen."

"Then we must pray he does not worsen."

Instead of accosting him with more anger she let her shoulders sag and her face fall. "I fear for his life. His fever is very high."

"As do I, milady." He gave her bow. "I can see that you have work to do and I have no wish to delay you so I will take my leave."

She gave a distracted nod, but as he exited the doorway she called after him. "I would like to learn more of your mother. You may return in the morning, early. Perhaps you will even be of some use."

Bain struggled to hide his elation as he turned to face her. "Thank you, Milady, I would be honoured."

CHAPTER THREE

HEALING WORK

*B*efore Phaera could give more thought to Bain a young girl ran up to the apothecary. "My lady, come quick. It is Mama. The baby comes."

Phaera looked up and gave the girl a reassuring nod as she reached for her midwifery basket, always ready and filled with fresh supplies. "Run ahead and tell your mother I come."

She smiled as she watched the lass run off. This was the part of her work she loved best. In the six years since she began assisting mothers with births on her own she had lost only one baby and no mother. The delight of seeing a new babe's eyes open for the first time, of hearing its first cry, always warmed her. She loved showing first time mothers just how to help their babe latch on to the breast and see the mother's face soften with tenderness as the little mouth found the teat and began to suckle. Even those mothers who had no need of yet another mouth to feed almost always had this reaction.

Had it really been that long since Mergana, her old mentor, had become too frail to accompany her? And almost that long since she had died? *I really must find an apprentice to assist me and pass on what I have learned. This work ought not to be done alone.*

She knew where all her expectant mothers lived and so strode with confidence to the poor cabin where the woman in labour waited. The husband, banned from this women's work, looked up from his hoeing in the small garden, his expression full of worry.

"Magda will be fine Jordie. This is not her first and she did well last time." At the man's anxious nod she ducked her head and entered the open door of the cabin. As expected, she found the woman inside, her small daughter at her side.

"Bennis, do you know how to boil water?" At the girl's eager bob of her head Phaera added, "Good, then fill that kettle and set it on to heat. Then you may watch. I may have other things for you to do."

The girl beamed, grabbed the kettle and flew out the door to fill it.

Phaera turned her attention to the girl's mother, pacing the floor and grabbing the edge of the table as a new contraction assailed her.

"So Magda. Let us take a look to see how far along you are." Phaera indicated the cot along the wall. "Have your waters broken?"

"Yes, Milady. That is when I sent Bennis to fetch you." Magda lay down on the cot as she spoke and lifted the hem of her gown to her waist, her knees apart. Just as Phaera knelt beside Magda and reached between her knees another contraction made her pull them up. Phaera waited until it subsided and resumed her examination, speaking calmly as she did. "It seems this one is coming quickly, Magda. It is eager to see the world. The pains are coming close together." She removed her hand. "Three fingers already. You are doing well."

"I have been walking as you instructed, Milady."

"Good. That will help. Have you eaten or drunk anything?" Phaera took a listening horn from her basket, put one end to Magda's swollen belly and the other end in her ear. As she listened the next contraction came. "This one is strong, Magda.

The heart barely slowed down with that pain." She lifted the horn and sent Magda an encouraging smile as she replaced it in her basket.

"Will it be a son this time, do you think, Milady? Jordie would so love a son."

"We will find out soon, I think." Phaera reached her hand out to help Magda up. "Now, you haven't told me what you have eaten or drunk." As she spoke she spotted a large earthen mug on the side of the hearth and reached for it to sniff its contents. "Ah, good, raspberry leaf and honey." She handed it to Magda.

"I drank a full mug earlier and ate a small bowl of porridge, but when I knew the pains had begun I left off the goat's milk. I did put some honey in the porridge, though."

"Very good. Now have some more tea." Phaera held the mug while she waited for Magda's next contraction to pass.

Bennis piped up, "The water is hot, Milady." Her little face looked up into Phaera's eyes, questioning.

Phaera handed Magda the mug and went to check on the water. "Well done, Bennis. First we must both wash our hands. Hand me that bowl. Now, do you remember where your mother put the clean cloths I left for the birth?"

Nodding eagerly, Bennis scurried to the only shelf with a door on it, opened it and pulled out the small pile of clean cloths. "Here, Milady."

Magda set her empty mug on the table with a thud as the next contraction came.

"Bennis, come stand here and watch carefully. Remember what you see and hear. Soon you will be a big sister." As Phaera spoke she motioned Magda to lie down again and bent to examine her. "Yes, this one comes quickly. You are eight fingers already. It will not be long now." She turned to Bennis and took the girl's elbow, drawing her close and down until her head was next to her own. "See Bennis? Look. It is time for the birthing stool already. Pull it out and set it in the middle of the room."

Bennis peered wide eyed between her mother's legs and gave Phaera a frightened look.

Phaera patted her arm. "There is nothing to fear, Bennis. Your mama is doing well. That is where the baby will come through. Watch and learn. But first go fetch the birthing stool."

By the time Phaera had once more helped Magda up the stool stood ready. Magda groaned and grabbed the table again.

"I think it comes, Milady." Magda gasped and another groan escaped her as her grip on the table tightened.

Phaera took Magda's arm and helped her down onto the stool. "Hold back on the next urge and let me see if you are ready to push." She reached between Magda's knees and found the birth canal. It still felt tight so she began to gently massage around the perimeter. When she felt the beginning of the next contractions, she said, "Hold back, Magda. Do not push yet. Wait until the next one. Make the short puffs, like I showed you."

Magda obeyed with moderate success as Phaera continued to massage the opening. It softened under her skilled touch so that, when the next contraction came she said, "You may push, now, Magda. You are ready. Hold my shoulders to lean against."

Bennis stood at Phaera's shoulder, clutching one of the cloths she had brought out as if her life depended on it. Phaera made sure Bennis could see between her mother's legs. With the next contraction Phaera took Bennis' hand and guided it between her mother's legs. "Feel, carefully. Do you feel hair?" When Bennis nodded, awed, Phaera added, "That is the baby's crown." She drew Bennis' hand away when the next pain began. "Now open out that cloth. We will need it to wrap the babe in as soon as it is out."

Phaera had no time to see if Bennis obeyed as the head emerged with the next contraction. She heard a small gasp from the girl and knew that she saw it, too, but had no time to explain. The next contraction brought the slippery babe out into her waiting hands. Without looking behind her she said, "The cloth, Bennis. There, onto the floor right here." Bennis obeyed with alacrity and Phaera lowered her wriggling charge onto the blanket.

With the sudden cold air the babe let out a lusty cry. Phaera looked at the wide-eyed Bennis. "Well, Bennis, boy or girl?"

Bennis' fear seemed to flee and a delighted grin spread across her face. "'Tis a boy, Milady."

With the cloth under him so he wouldn't slip, Phaera held him up so Magda could see her new son. "A fine, strong babe, Magda. " Then she lowered the child to the end of the cot. "Now watch closely, Bennis. This is important." She took a thread of silk, preferred over linen as it was less likely to cause festering, and tied it around the cord. Then she pulled a clean knife out of her basket and faced Bennis. "Would you like to cut the cord? Just here, above the thread?"

"Does it not hurt?" Bennis had tears ready to spill over her lids.

"No, Bennis, he feels nothing. This is the final step in separating him from his mother. "

Bennis still looked uncertain but reached hesitantly for the blade glancing back and forth between the babe and Phaera.

"Here, I will help you." Phaera placed her hand under Bennis' and guided it. There she wrapped her own hand around Bennis' small one and pressed the sharp blade against the cord, where it easily sliced through. "Well done, Bennis." She retrieved the knife from the awed girl, wrapped it in a cloth, and placed it back in her basket.

Phaera returned to the babe, swaddled him, placed him in Magda's arms and bent her attention back to the stool. "Now, Bennis, watch carefully."

As Phaera moved over to make room for her Bennis hunkered close to see. Magda bent forward with a small grunt and a bloody mass slipped into the bowl waiting under the birthing stool.

"See Bennis? This is the afterbirth. This is what fed the babe while in your mother's belly. It is no longer needed so it came out. See how it is attached to the cord you cut? When it comes out we know the birth is finished. But we must always let it take its time. Pulling on the cord to make it come quicker can make a mother bleed to death." As Phaera spoke she examined the afterbirth carefully.

"It looks like liver," Bennis murmured thoughtfully as she bent close to see.

"Indeed it does. You are a clever girl. Perhaps, one day, you will learn enough to help other mothers when they give birth. You have done well today."

Bennis' eyes grew round and her little mouth mirrored that shape. "Oh, I would like that."

Phaera allowed herself an inner sigh of satisfaction. Perhaps this girl would keep that wish and find an opportunity to earn the skills that could help her rise above the poverty that almost certainly awaited her otherwise.

"Obey your parents and stay strong and brave. How old are you, now?"

"Six, Milady."

"If you still wish to learn to be a midwife you may come to me when you are ten years old. Perhaps I will have a place for you to become my apprentice. Now run and tell your father he has a son and that he may come in and meet him." She put her arms around Magda and helped her back to the cot.

While Bennis scampered off Phaera dipped another clean cloth in hot water, quickly began to clean Magda off and cover her with the blanket. "You have a fine son, Magda. Jordie has his wish. But Bennis is a brave and clever girl. I am in earnest in my offer to her. Please do not discourage her in this."

"Thank you, Milady. I shall let Jordie know. He will be proud of her as well."

Jordie strode in, followed closely by the proud Bennis.

CHAPTER FOUR

DREAM

Bain returned to the castle with wild hope in his heart. She had asked him to return. Could she actually see something of interest in him? Or was she only interested in his mother and her healing knowledge? And if so, could he somehow parlay that into more contact, more time to kindle a greater interest? He hurried to the barracks to dress for the midday meal. When he emerged he spied Kort making his way to the great hall.

"Where have you been?" Kort had spotted Bain as well and turned to join him.

Bain almost blurted out his good luck but at the last moment stopped himself. It would not do to allow rumours to start. That would put an end to any hope he had of impressing Phaera.

"Just getting the lay of the land. I needed some quiet time. It has been a challenge to learn all the names and faces of the guests."

"You missed breaking the fast. And your name came up in conversation, much of it questioning your right to be here. Disappearing does nothing to change that impression." Kort raised one eyebrow at him and shook his head in disapproval.

Bain sighed. "You are right, of course. Thank you. I suspect you risk censure for you friendly overtures to me."

"Oh, I am not so much in demand that it matters. As third son I have no influence. Besides, I have no interest in finding a bride. I have little to offer one in any case." The rueful snort indicated that his low status was a source of relief rather than disappointment. "In any case, I enjoy my freedom."

Bain gave him a conspiratorial wink. "So, you are here to spy on the rest of us, then."

Kort sketched him a mocking bow. "At your service, milord. What will you offer me for such services?"

"My undying gratitude, sir, as I have no coin to spread about."

"A fine bargain. I pledge my service to you. At least until a better offer comes."

Their joint laughter brought several heads up as they wended their way to the tables where the maids had kept ale and wine flowing and platters of food replenished. Their host spared no expense.

In a loud voice, with his two companions egging him on, one young lordling jeered, "Please, share the jest, gentlemen. What do you find so amusing?"

The hall went silent as many heads swivelled in their direction.

Kort, perhaps emboldened by having already been into his cups, swept a goblet from the nearest table and waved it high. "A true gentleman never betrays his source. Some things must remain secret."

Bain, knowing he would have had nothing clever to say, decided he owed Kort a debt of gratitude. He also suspected the show had been a feint and that Kort was not nearly as tipsy as he let on. He made himself a promise to court this friendship. It could prove very useful.

Bain forced a laugh as he drew Kort's attention to the food tables. "Time to fortify ourselves."

To his great relief the three lads made no attempt to press the confrontation and no one else took it up. Making sure they would not be overheard he leaned towards Kort. "You saved my back there. Thank you, friend."

Kort just grinned and reached for a platter.

Bain spent the rest of the day introducing himself to the other guests, trying his best to decipher which lords and heirs resented him, which ones were indifferent, and which ones accepted him – more or less. Speaking to them also helped solidify their names and where they came from in his memory. The ones with marriageable sisters seemed less inclined to look on him with favour.

He met up with Kort again for the evening banquet and managed to spirit him away after the meal to debrief on what he had learned and to get Kort's opinion of his conclusions.

Kort seemed pleased to be consulted. Bain began to suspect that Kort's lack of interest in looking for a bride might have nothing at all to do with being the third son. He paid scant notice to any of the ladies. The young men seemed to draw more of his attention, though he was circumspect about it and avoided those who had obvious designs on the ladies present. Bain told himself to take care not to become the object of Kort's affections. *No, Kort knows I am not that way inclined. He knows I desire Phaera. And I must make certain I do not acquire the wrong reputation.*

Bain had managed to put Phaera out of mind until now, but as he headed to the barracks to seek out his bed, Kort called after him, "Will you be at weapons practice tomorrow afternoon? 'Tis a good way to attract some attention from the ladies – if you have any skill, that is."

"Yes, I will be there. My skill may surprise you." Bain grinned at his friend's back as Kort turned and strode off in another direction with a backward wave. *To a different kind of tryst?* Bain wondered if the other men suspected Kort was a lover of men? He, himself, had no hatred for such men, as his mother had taught him that he had nothing to fear from them. Other men, however, were not so accepting. Men like Kort often led a double life, either living in the shadows trying to avoid notice, or compensating by striving to outdo other men. *I must be vigilant.*

The thought of meeting Phaera in the morning brought his focus back with force. *Phaera! She invited me back.* With a satisfied sigh he lay down, wrapped his blanket around his exhausted frame and fell instantly asleep.

No matter how he tried to get her attention the crow circled away from him each time he moved in the direction of her eye.

This bird stood out from all the others, with inky feathers that gleamed with a blue light all their own. And she had the most unusual eyes, cornflower blue.

He'd never seen a crow with eyes that colour. They mesmerized him. Somehow he had to get her attention.

But the crow turned away in seeming disdain every time he approached her. No matter how shiny his offering, or how tasty the morsels he lay before her, she refused to meet his eyes. Instead, she resolutely kept her back to him, moving in the opposite direction each time.

All the while she pecked at grains and stones around her, ignoring the shiny bits and offerings he had left for her. It seemed as though she did not even see them, though she stepped neatly between them without touching them. She knew they were there.

Bain woke in a sweat, so bound in his blanket that he had to struggle to disentangle himself. The realization of where he was brought him back to the present with a jolt. Reality hit him like a bolt of lightning. *She has no interest in me. She only wants to know about my mother, to learn if I have any healing knowledge she can use. She called me "bastard", remember? Whatever made me think I had a chance with her? I have only five more days before I must return home.*

CHAPTER FIVE

I WILL NOT WED

Yet, as he lay back down to salvage what he could of the night, the stubborn hope remained that he might be mistaken. Sleep eluded him and when the first glimmers of light told him dawn approached he rose silently, grabbed his boots, and tip-toed to the exit. *Will she welcome me this time?*

He made a quick pass through the kitchens where he managed to scavenge a cold turkey leg. By the time he reached Phaera's apothecary he had gnawed it down and tossed the bone to a prowling dog. The doors already stood open and he spotted Phaera inside taking a jar down from a shelf.

Not wishing to presume, he waited in her doorway. "Good morning."

"I suppose it is, as no one stood waiting before I arrived." She did not even turn her head to acknowledge him.

Bain entered. "May I be of assistance?"

"I doubt it."

Bain felt foolish standing there so he entered and approached the table where Phaera had set the jar. Beside it stood a bowl filled with lanolin and an empty jar. "If you measure that lanolin and," he bent to sniff the powder in the first jar, "balsam into that mortar I am sure I can mix it properly for the balm you need."

She turned her head and with a quick raise of her eyebrows, reached for the mortar and pestle, measured the ingredients into it, added some mint powder, "for the scent" and handed them to him. Reaching under the table she retrieved two more of the small jars and said, "Fill these as well".

They did not speak while he mixed and filled the jars. Bain felt that waiting for more instructions would make him look weak. Remembering that his mother always covered the open jars, he took the initiative to work as Phaera's partner and not her student. "What do you cover these with?" It worked. She answered him.

"There are cloths and string under the table by your knees."

Though she seemed to take no notice of him Bain caught her sideways glances. He allowed himself a moment of pride that he had not lost his skill as he tied the cloth covers on with fingers deft from long practice.

Since it appeared Phaera had no intention of initiating conversation, merely handing him various potions and jars to fill, Bain took a silent breath for courage before breaking the silence. "I did not see you at the banquet last evening."

"No. I have no interest in them."

"Perhaps the question is impertinent, but may I ask why?"

"Yes, it is impertinent. I did not attend because I have no need to find a husband. I will not wed."

"I would think that hard to avoid, as the only daughter of a powerful lord."

"My Lord Father has sworn to me that he will not force me to wed against my will. So I will not."

"Is there nothing that might induce you to change your mind?"

She whirled on him, eyes blazing, causing him to take a half step backward. "Can you imagine that I would ever consent to give up my freedom to do this work to become the pretty puppet of a fop who sees me only as an ornament or a brood mare?" She turned back to her work but Bain could see that her hands shook and her back was rigid with emotion. "Leave that to the vacuous maids who care only for gowns and jewels, who have accepted that they have no minds of their own."

Bain stopped his work and turned his back to the table, leaning on it slightly as he studied her, thinking about what she had revealed. Knowing he had nothing to lose he decided to challenge her.

"It need not be that way. Indeed, I know that there are lords who show their wives great respect, perhaps even consult with them. My father speaks highly of Lady Flor." When her only response was an angry shake of her head he continued. " I have not been at court long but from what I have observed Lady Flor commands a great deal of respect and has a good deal of authority within the castle – and all that without producing an heir."

At that moment a man arrived, chalk-faced, gripping his left forearm. Blood dripped from between his clenched fingers. "My Lady…"

Bain was closest to the door. He reached the man first, supporting him to the stool Phaera pulled out. "What happened?"

Phaera shot him a glare as she got between them and took the man's arm to examine it.

The man faced Phaera as he answered. "I were butchering the old sow, the one that be past breeding. She be heavy. She rolled and the knife slipped."

By this time Phaera had ripped the sleeve from the man's shirt. Bain could see that the wound was deep and bled freely. *The bleeding will make it clean.* Anticipating Phaera's need he handed her a strip of clean cloth from the pile in the basket behind them. She barely glanced at him as she took it and tied it above the wound, slowing the bleeding to a trickle.

"Here … spirits to clean the wound." Bain reached the flask in her direction.

"You clean it. I will get my needle and thread." Phaera pulled her travel basket out from under the table. "Then fetch clean water."

The man gave a yelp of pain as the alcohol poured into the gash.

Bain moved aside as Phaera pulled up another stool and began to stich the wound. He admired the skill with which she pressed the edges of the muscles back into place before making tidy stiches to close the wound. *It will heal well if he avoids using it until it is ready.*

Instead of taking the bowl and cloths from him Phaera rose from the stool leaving it to him to bandage the arm as a young man approached, limping in pain.

Apparently Phaera thought him competent enough to leave Bain to finish and turn her attention to her next patient. Bain allowed himself a small smile. "There." Bain tied a sling and placed the man's arm in it. "I am afraid someone else will have to finish butchering that sow. You must not use this arm for a week. And we will need to look at it before you do. If the pain gets worse, or you feel heat through the bandages, return to have it looked at immediately. If you allow it to fester you could lose the arm."

The man's eyes grew round with fear. "Nay, I canna lose it."

"Then do as I said and it will heal clean."

The man's head bobbed up and down vigorously.

Phaera had taken a moment to inspect Bain's handiwork. "Yes, it will heal. But you must do as Lord Bain instructed. And it may not return to full strength for some time."

The man flashed Bain a startled look. "L..lord Bain?

Phaera had already turned her attention to the other lad.

Bain gave a derisive chuckle as he helped his patient up. "Not yet. One day." *Well, at least I am not "the bastard" any more.* As he helped the man to the door he repeated, "Rest that arm. Understood?"

"I will ... Milord." With a quick backward look over his shoulder the man tottered off.

Over the next hours Bain acted as Pheara's assistant. They spoke little to each other but Bain was able to anticipate what she needed and she accepted his efforts with little comment.

Bain heard his stomach growl, letting him know it was time for the midday meal. "Milady, I must take my leave as I am expected at weapons practice. May I have your leave to return tomorrow?"

Phaera started but quickly collected herself. She turned her back to him, as though returning to her earlier work. With a tone that struck Bain as too casual, she replied, "As you wish".

Is that because she does not wish to admit she enjoyed this morning? The glow of that thought died at the realization that he would be leaving for home four mornings hence. Certainly not enough time to change the mind of a woman so determined not to be snared into marriage.

As he approached the castle he spied Kort coming from the opposite direction, in animated conversation with a young man dressed in bright colours, who leaned his head just a little too close and smiled just a little too shyly at Kort.

It confirmed Bain's suspicions that Kort preferred to share his bed with men. That would make life more difficult for him. While some people who found out would either avoid or ignore him, other men could use it as an excuse to beat him or abase him. The rest, including most women, would do nothing in his defense. Homosexuality, while not illegal, was seen as an aberration, one which created suspicion and fear.

As soon as the two noticed him they moved apart abruptly, the young man leaving off to Kort's left, toward the central square lined by shops.

Kort, a worried crease between his brows, waited for Bain to catch up with him.

Bain decided to put Kort at ease. Feigning a conspiratorial air he said, "A pretty lad." When Kort blushed deep red, confirming that Bain had been correct, he added, "Your secret is safe with me," He flashed Kort a reassuring grin, "as long as you agree that my desire for Phaera remains between the two of us."

Relief flooded Kort's face. "Of course, your secret remains between us."

"Good." He lowered his voice to just above a whisper. "I was with her this morning."

Kort's head shot up and his brows nearly met his hairline. "What?"

Pleased that he had caught Kort by surprise, Bain added, "Yes, at her apothecary - and she invited me back."

Kort shook his head in mock disbelief. "Well, congratulations, my friend. That is a major coup."

They each took a platter from the pile at the end of the laden table and began to load it.

At the other end, as they grabbed a mug of ale, Bain suggested they take their meal to the courtyard, thus avoiding the hostility of those who did not accept him.

Kort shook his head. "No, we are already seen as too friendly. You do not want to be seen spending too much time alone with me. You have enough strikes against you already." He looked around the hall and jerked his head toward a table with a few spaces left open on the bench. "There, let us join them. Perhaps some talk of weapons will send the correct message."

The men at that table, while not openly hostile toward Bain earlier, had also not made any friendly overtures when he had introduced himself at the first banquet.

Bain's shoulders dropped a bit. "You are right, of course. Let us gird our loins for battle, then."

Kort grinned approval and headed toward the empty seats. "Gentlemen. Tis a fine day, is it not? Will you be at the practice field later? My friend here is anxious to demonstrate his skills to the ladies."

As the men at the table reluctantly widened the space for the pair one growled something unintelligible under his breath. The only word Bain could make out was "bastard".

One man sitting across, however, took a different tack. "So, will you join us at weapons practice?" He met the eyes of his two companions, who grinned encouragement. Then he made a show of placing his forearms on the table and leaning across toward Bain, the implied challenge unmistakable. "I am eager to see if you have skill."

Bain chose not to take the bait, treating the challenge as matter-of-fact. "Indeed I will. Perhaps we can spar together. My sword arm could use some exercise."

The man slammed his palm onto the table with a look of triumph. "Indeed. I look forward to testing you."

The guffaws from the others told Bain they expected him to be easily bested. His challenger must have an envied reputation for his swordsmanship. *I must be on my mettle. Am I ready for this?* He inclined his head to his challenger. "I welcome the challenge ... Garent of Werth is it not?"

Later, as they made their way to the practice grounds, Bain asked Kort, "Will you be joining the sparring?"

Kort barked a laugh, holding up his hands in mock surrender. "No, my friend, I go to watch."

Bain noticed that Kort's hands had no callouses on them. *OF course. Why did I not notice that before? I must take greater care in my observations.* "Ah, I imagine the sights will be so much the better for the warm weather."

"Indeed, indeed." Bain met Kort's infectious grin with one of his own.

CHAPTER SIX

WEAPONS PRACTICE

Phaera's rounds took her past the sparring grounds. She did not admit to herself that another way would have served as well as this one. She found herself scanning the field for a certain young man. She spotted Bain paired against Garent of Werth. Remembering that Garent had a reputation of some note with the sword, Phaera cringed a little inside. While the practice blades were dull they could still land some serious blows and the resulting bruises could be deep and painful. The sparring occasionally resulted in broken bones. She wondered if today's exercise would end in such, and she would have to treat him.

As she approached the rail to take a longer look she spied Kort watching as well. His expression confirmed her suspicions. Kort would not vie for her attentions, nor those of any other maid. She kept an eye on Bain as she closed the short distance between herself and Kort. A glance sideways told her that Kort watched the same pair that had her interest. "How fares your friend, Master Kort?"

Kort stuttered in surprise. "My friend, Milady?"

"Am I mistaken, then? Have I not seen you in conversation with Bain of Marston?"

"Er, yes, we have spoken, Milady. He is new to court. I have provided him with some of the information he sought."

"Good." Phaera once again watched Bain. "How fares he on the field?"

"He acquits himself very well, Milady. They have sparred for some time, now, and Bain still stands. Garent is not having the easy win he expected."

No sooner had the words left his mouth than a clever feint caught Bain off-guard and the following blow had him on the ground. The match was over with Garent the victor. Bain rose and offered Garent his hand in congratulation.

Garent had apparently not expected this. For a fleeting moment his face registered surprise, but he recovered and accepted Bain's hand.

Phaera smiled. "Garent's gesture will raise Bain's status among the others. I am pleased to see that from him."

"Indeed, Milady. Bain deserves it."

Phaera turned to go, then halted mid-step. "Master Kort, what sort of man is this Bain of Marston?"

Kort raised his eyebrows. "Milady?"

"What sort of man is he, or do you not know him well enough?"

Kort seemed to be searching for words. "We have broken bread together, Milady. As little as I know him I find him honest, direct, and thoughtful. Tis a pity the others do not recognize his merits. Perhaps today's games will begin to change that."

Phaera decided to be blunt. She needed to know, though she did not know why it was important. "You are not lovers, then?"

Kort went white. "N-no, Milady. Er, we are becoming acquainted, that is all."

"And does he know your – inclination?" When Kort did not reply immediately she added, "I do not condemn you Kort, nor will I reveal what I know. I am a healer. I do not share the hatred others have for your kind."

A look of profound relief spread across Kort's face. "Thank you, Milady. Yes, Bain knows – and, like you, does not condemn me for it."

Phaera sent him a warning glare. "Then, if you are friend to him, tell Bain to beware his reputation if he wishes to find a bride." She turned and walked away without waiting to see Kort's reaction. "I must be back to my work." She pushed away the tiny sense of relief, not acknowledging to herself that she cared that Bain was not a lover of men, or that he had done well against Garent. Nor did she admit being relieved that Bain did not reject Kort but treated him with respect. She left the fact that Bain had risen in her estimation determinedly unexamined.

As she neared the first home on her rounds a soldier approached her from the opposite direction signaling that he wished to speak to her. She stopped and waited for him, annoyed at the interruption. Messengers usually meant something would take her away from her work. She stood still and tried to compose herself so that her annoyance would not show. After all, it was not his fault.

"Milady." The soldier gave her a short bow before continuing. "Lord Danza requests your presence."

"Can it not wait until I have finished my work?"

The young man's discomfiture told her that her attempt at composure had failed. "I ... he did not say, Milady."

She allowed herself an inward sigh and softened her tone. "Of course not. Tell him I will be there presently. But there is one woman I must tend to first." Her father knew how important her work was to her but it did not hurt to remind him of that by not rushing to his summons.

The messenger looked about to protest, but seemed to think the better of it. With another short bow he replied, "As you wish,

Milady," turned on his heel and strode back from whence he had come.

Phaera resumed walking to the home of the woman she had mentioned. She had lanced a painful abscess on the woman's foot the day before. She needed to make sure it had begun to heal and that the woman was staying off it.

After looking in on the woman and seeing she did not need to lance the wound again, Phaera made her way to the castle.

As was the plan with most fiefs the castle stood in the centre of the city protected by a thick stone wall. The city itself added a layer of protection as enemies would need to cross through the populace to reach it. The shops, dwellings, and places of work close to the centre thinned out toward the outskirts. Another wall surrounded the city as well, but, over time, as the population grew, dwellings and places of business had grown up outside the walls. Beyond those, stood the scattered crofts of farmers. There they grew the crops and raised the animals that fed the city: orchards, grains, sheep, fowl, and some cattle. Hunting and foraging supplied the remainder of their food.

Phaera knew where she would find her father. He was a creature of habit. At this time of day he would be in his private chamber mulling over what he had learned from that morning's briefings with his advisors and the information he had gleaned from the visitors to his audience chamber. He was a man given to caution, one who made decisions only after careful thought. It was a trait that had earned him considerable respect, both from his own people and from the other lords and their councils.

As she expected, when she was admitted to his chamber she found him sitting at his table, a platter of food to his left along with a mug of ale, scrolls spread open in front of him. When he looked up to see her, the usual broad smile was missing. In its place a worried crease drew his brows together. But, as was his custom, he rose from his chair and rounded the table to envelop her in a bear hug. "Ah, Phaera. Please sit and eat." He indicated the chair opposite him and gestured to the laden platter.

Phaera could not help but smile. Her father had developed a slight paunch. His fondness for eating was no longer offset by sessions in weapons practice. Seeing the food reminded her that she had eaten nothing since early morning. She almost reached for the smaller platter her father tried to hand her but shook her head. The frown on her father's face worried her enough that she found she did not want to sit, let alone eat, until she found out what was on his mind. She felt too restless to relax. His summons had come at an unusual time as well. What was amiss?

"Thank you, Papa. Perhaps later. What is it you wish to see me about?"

She watched her father's frown deepen and he looked away, increasing her concern. Something serious and important was bothering him – so unlike their usual easy visits. "Papa?"

Her father gave a heavy sigh and raised his eyes to meet hers. "Phaera, several years ago I made you a promise. You know that I do not take my oaths lightly – not to you, nor to anyone else." He paused as if waiting for a response. When Phaera gave none, now too worried to speak, he stood up and began to pace.

A knot began to form in the pit of Phaera's stomach. What could possibly have made her father so agitated ... and so hesitant to speak freely. He had often discussed matters of court and politics with her. She knew he respected her insights and opinions. So why did he hesitate now? And what was this talk of broken promises? The chamber, usually so welcoming, suddenly felt cold. She drew in a deep breath. "Papa, what is this promise that you fear you cannot keep? And what has occurred to put you in this position?" She could think of only one thing that could bring about such a change. "Is there threat of war?"

Her father turned to face her, his expression both grave and proud at the same time. "My child, you are wise beyond your years or your sex."

That made her bristle. The frisson of anger also loosened her mind and her tongue. "Father, you know that my sex has nothing to do with it, and you know that I am a woman grown. What is this news that makes you forget it? Stop beating about."

For a fleeting instant Phaera got a glimpse of the father she knew and loved. He barked a short, wry laugh, the familiar twinkle in his eyes. No one else would dare to speak to him thus. Nor would she, except in their private times together. But she did not even have time to return his smile before he became serious once more.

"Ah, daughter of my heart. Perhaps it is my sorrow that makes me forget." He hesitated again. "You are partly correct when you speak of war. We have lived in peace with our neighbours for many years, now. Perhaps that led me to believe it would never change – not during my lifetime, at least. And we do not have news that enemies are planning to attack us or our allies – not yet."

"What do you mean, not yet? Please Papa, speak plainly. And what has this to do with a promise?"

"As you know, Belthorn has a new lord. Mathune rules since his father's recent death. His father, while not friendly to us, nevertheless always adhered to our agreements on trade and borders. But Mathune is not his father. He is young, ambitious and a hothead." He looked at Phaera, waiting.

"Yes, I know him. He is arrogant and too full of himself. I like him not at all."

"Just so." He looked at the two empty chairs. "Phaera, please sit." He made to sit in his own chair but stopped when she made no move to join him.

"No, I cannot sit. I cannot make pretense at ease when you are so clearly not."

Lord Danza nodded acquiescence and resumed his stance facing her. "This morning two of my best spies, one in Belthorn and one in Exalon, informed me that Mathune is fomenting unrest in Exalon. They tell me he plans to invade Exalon and annex it to Belthorn. As you know, Exalon's lord Dern is old and in poor health. His son, Erstine, has a reputation for debauchery and womanizing and shows no interest in his duties. That makes Exalon an easy target for Mathune. The people of Exalon begin to fear for their futures."

Exalon lay on their eastern order and provided a buffer between themselves, here in Kinterron, and Belthorn. If Belthorn invaded and annexed Exalon it would put their eastern border at risk. Phaera was beginning understand why her father was so worried.

"I can see how this may bring our other alliances into question. We will need to re-affirm them and strengthen them. But what has this to do with me, or with a promise?"

Lord Danza studied his hands for a moment, and then reached for a small scroll on his table.

"Phaera, I made you a promise that I would never force you to wed. Now, I must break that oath." He held out the scrap to her but did not relinquish it right away. "These three fiefs are the ones we must rely on if our borders are threatened. Each of them has an heir who has not yet chosen a bride." He let her take it from him as he continued. "You must choose one of them and agree to wed him." He reached up and pinched the bridge of his nose, squeezing his eyes shut as he did so, shoulders sagging.

Phaera did not even look at the names. "What! You cannot. You swore ... my work! You agreed I am not a pawn to be bartered away. I will not..."

Lord Danza sank heavily into his chair, face shadowed behind his hand, elbow on the table. When he raised his head and met her gaze, his expression had become stern and determined. "Phaera, we have spoken many times of duty. I did not choose my position. This cloak is not one I wear easily. But I am bound by duty to our people – yes, our people – yours, too. And that duty overrides sentiment. My personal wishes must not prevent me from doing what is necessary to safeguard our citizens."

"And I have a duty to those I heal. You swore that was enough." Even as Phaera spoke she knew, from the lump of dread growing in her stomach, that the argument was a hollow one. This new duty was greater. The position of her birth took personal choice away. Her father had long ago made her understand that she could not enjoy the freedoms taken for granted by those who had no power over others.

Lord Danza's countenance softened but she could tell he did not waver in his decision. "If I could take that promise back, if I had not made it, how would that change things, now? I made it in good faith, never thinking I would be forced to break it." He spread his hands in a silent plea. "I hope you will understand and that you will forgive me. But I must stand by what I have just told you." He nodded to the still unopened scroll crushed in Phaera's hand. "Please, read the names. They have been chosen with care. They know nothing of this. Only you and I do and I it will remain between us alone – at least for now."

Phaera whirled toward the door, then back again, jabbing a finger in her father's direction. "You have betrayed me!" With the unopened scroll still clutched in her fist she yanked the door open and rushed from the chamber, slamming it behind her, seeing, but not registering the astonished look from the guard. She did not slow down until she reached the sanctuary of her apothecary. With a last burst of rage she slammed and barred its heavy door… and found herself standing alone in total darkness with nowhere to run. When she became aware of the scroll still clenched in one hand she hurled it from herself as if it were a venomous snake.

Something broke in her, then, and with a shudder, she sank to the floor. "Mamaaaa…" The moaning plea ended with strangled sobs and a great convulsive shudder that wracked her entire body. She hugged her knees to control the shaking and whispered, "I don't want to die... Mama, please don't die." But the darkness stole her plea and flung it unheeded into the silent darkness.

Phaera had shut that memory away, but now, faced with a similar fate, she and Mama became one in her mind. She relived the horror of that day, the day Mama died giving birth to Phaera's still born brother. Every detail returned as fresh as if it were happening now. She lived again the moment when her father had led her to her mother's bed. Her dead brother lay swaddled and tenderly placed in the crook of Mama's arm.

Mama barely breathed. But she reached out a weak hand and wrapped Phaera's small one in it. "My precious girl." Phaera had to lean close to hear, her cheek almost touching Mama's. "I have no wish to leave you. But your brother will be all alone. He needs me. I am called to go with him." Mama coughed weakly. Her last words to Phaera were, "Be strong my precious one. I love you". Her last sighing breath caressed Phaera's cheek and she lay still.

Phaera waited for the next breath that did not come. "Mama?" No response. Louder as Phaeara drew back to see Mama's face, "Mama...?

Her father tried to take her gently by the shoulders but Phaera jerked away to stand in shock by the bed. "Mamaaaa, noooooo..."

SHE HAD KEPT HER FEAR LOCKED AWAY IN SOME CRAMPED RECESS deep in her mind, never to be acknowledged. Now, that lock had been sundered.

Phaera rocked back and forth, continuing to weep, whispering, "Mama," over and over until she had no more tears left. Slowly some semblance of calm returned and she could bring her thoughts to the present. Even then, she whispered them aloud, as though Mama was with her and could hear her.

"Must I die, like you, Mama? Is this my duty, my destiny?" When she received no response she fell back into silence. *Is this why I became a healer ... so I could save other women when I could not help Mama? Is this why I fear marriage so, why I extracted that promise from Papa?* The realization that she had never admitted this possibility allowed some clarity to enter her mind. *I never knew. I never told Papa. He doesn't understand. Will it make a difference if I tell him? ... No. It changes nothing. He will tell me I will be fine, that I will not die, that duty is more important than one life when many could be endangered. I cannot tell him. He will think me weak. Mama said I must be strong.*

Another wave of panic swept over her. Hugging her knees again she rocked back and forth until it subsided. Finally, stiff from remaining so cramped and small, she unfolded herself and rose to her feet. There she stood, inert, unable to think what her next move should be. Somehow her trembling hand found the candle in the wall and lit it, hardly having the strength to hold it upright. She turned slowly in a circle, taking in her familiar sanctuary as the flame chased the shadows and revealed the details of table, jars, mortars, and pestles. A measure of calm returned. She made her way to the door and pulled back the heavy bar with effort. She cracked the door open and was met by total darkness outside. *Have I been here that long?* An answering rumble from her stomach confirmed that it had, indeed, been that long.

Seeing that no one waited outside, or walked the path back to the castle, she opened the door the rest of the way, blew out the candle, replaced it in its sconce, walked out, and closed the door again behind her. She kept to the familiar path that led to her private entrance and her chamber so no one would see her or could accost her, or notice that she had been weeping.

Once in her chamber, having eluded her ladies, she fell, exhausted, onto her bed and wept silently again until sleep overtook her.

She still had not read the scroll.

CHAPTER SEVEN

BAIN MAKES A VOW

*A*fter weapons practice Bain washed up and strolled around the castle wall, only mildly surprised to find himself standing at the door to Phaera's apothecary. *She draws me as a moth to flame, even when I am not aware of it.*

What did surprise him was that the young lad who ran up to the door ahead of him found it closed from the inside. He turned to Bain. "Sir, my mother sent me to find my Lady. She is usually here, or if she has gone to help someone she leaves the door open so we know to wait for her return."

Bain shrugged. "I am as surprised as you. Are you in urgent need of assistance?"

"I do not think it urgent. My sister fell out of the apple tree and her ankle is painfully swollen. Mamma fears it is broken, but I do not. Jess can stand on it some. Mamma frets too much."

"Perhaps you are correct but it is best to be certain. Show me where you live and I will look at your sister's ankle."

The lad's eyes narrowed. "You, sir? But you are a man."

Bain laughed. "Indeed I am, but I am also a trained soldier and we must know somewhat about caring for battle wounds." *He will accept that better than telling him I am healer trained.*

"Oh, pardon sir. Our home is this way." He turned back the way he had come, looking over his shoulder once to see if Bain followed.

"I am Bain, of Marston. What is your name, young man?"

The lad turned back and waited for Bain to come alongside. "P..pardon sir. I am Larn."

As they resumed their walk side by side Bain spotted a young girl sitting on a fallen piece of log outside the door of a hut. Her face was tear-streaked and she clutched her left ankle.

A woman came out into the doorway and, seeing Larn, called out, "There you are. And who is this? Where be Milady?" She raised a hand as if to cuff Larn's head.

Before she could do so Bain raised his in greeting. "Madam, I am come in her place. Lady Phaera was not at her apothecary. Let me take a look at our daughter's ankle."

"And what know you of broken bones?" She gave a derisive sniff, set her hands on her hips, and glared at Bain.

"Mamma, he is a soldier and they know how to care for battle wounds."

Bain sent the mother his most reassuring smile. "Indeed, missus. Your son has the right of it." Without waiting for permission he knelt in front of the girl and reached for her leg. "Larn tells me you fell from a tree."

Out of the corner of his eye he saw the mother move to intercept him, and then step back again. She still hovered close behind his shoulder, arms crossed.

Bain ignored her. "So, lass, how is it you were climbing trees instead of helping your mother?" He sent the girl a conspiratorial wink. When she relaxed with a small smile he turned his attention back to the ankle. "I see that it is swollen, but Larn tells me you can stand on it. Will you show me?"

When he held out his hand to the girl she took it with a shy smile, showing a dimple in one cheek. "Yes, but it hurts."

Bain nodded. "I can see that it does. Now let me see you take a few steps." He let go her hand and moved his arm out of the way. When the girl hesitated he gestured for her to go ahead. She gingerly placed her weight on the foot, wincing, and took a short, limping step – more of a hop.

"Good, now two more steps." When she complied Bain turned to her mother. "Madam, I do not think it broken. Do you have any clean rags I may tear into strips. I will bind the ankle. She must keep it bound for three days, then unbind it at night but keep it bound during the day for another three days."

The mother gave a curt nod, disappeared into the hut and came back with some rags of dubious cleanliness. Bain took them without comment, tore them into strips, and set about binding the ankle. "Watch, missus, so you can do it again." When he finished he patted the girl's knee. "There. You must stay off it as much as possible for today and tomorrow. No running for a week. No more tree climbing until it is better."

He rose to face the mother.

She stood there, arms still crossed. "I have nought to pay ye."

"I need nothing. I am glad to be of assistance." He touched his forefinger to his brow in salute and strode back in the direction of the castle. The complaining from his stomach told him not to waste time or he would miss the evening banquet.

He looked for Kort as he entered the hall but did not see him so he grabbed a platter and, remembering his purpose in coming here, found an empty space at a table filled with young men he had not yet spoken with. "Gentlemen, I am Bain of Marston." He recognized one man from weapons practice. Nodding to him he said, "I saw you sparring this afternoon. You acquitted yourself well, sir."

The young man straightened his shoulders and sat taller. "Next gathering I will best Garent, mark me."

His companion snorted. "Next gathering Garent will be even better, too. No one bests him." He turned his attention to Bain and stretched out a hand. "I am Galton, of Krellin. I saw you there as well. You made Garent fight for his victory."

Bain took the proffered hand and shook it warmly. "Ah, our ally to the north. I thank you, sir." *Being tested by Garent was a piece of luck. I have risen in the estimation of some.* The rest of the meal was spent dissecting the skills of the other young lords amid lewd comments about how that would attract the attention of certain ladies.

When Bain headed back to the barracks with the sense he had made some progress with his reputation he spied Kort. Kort kept to the shadows of a narrow alley and gestured for Bain to join him. Sensing that this meeting needed to be unnoticed, he kept silent until he and Kort were well alone. "Is ought amiss?"

Kort made a wry face. "You would do well to take more account of general opinion, my friend. I have taken to heart milady's warning that my taint must not sully your reputation. We must not too oft be seen together."

When Bain made to protest Kort forestalled him with a gesture. "Nay, my friend. It is not so dire. But Lady Phaera did indeed tell me you 'must beware your reputation if you are to find a bride', and she has the right of it."

Before Bain had a chance to question him further Kort continued. "There is news I think you will do well to hear. Changes are afoot. You know of Mathune of Belthorn, do you not – the arrogant one who accosted you at table?"

Bain nodded but said nothing.

"I hear things that others do not." Kort put his finger to the side of his nose. "I have friends in strange places, you see." He barked a short laugh. "It appears young Mathune has plans that may spell chaos for the rest of us."

Bain slunk further into the alley, to Kort's other side, looking about to make sure they were alone. "What do you mean 'plans' and what has that to do with me?"

Kort explained the same news Lord Danza had given Phaera.

Mathune was gathering forces to overthrow Exalon, and annex it. "He makes a show of befriending Erstine of Exalon, all the while plotting to take his fief from him. Erstine is a sot and a fool. The people of Exalon are ready to revolt against Erstine, though they fear what will become of Exalon under Mathune as well."

Bain said nothing for several moments. "Kort, if this is so we must all look to our allies. I fear this may upset old allegiances."

Kort nodded. "Just so, my friend. And your position is not a secure one." He cleared his throat, "Being a bastard and all." He looked sideways at Bain and when Bain took no offense he added, "So you see why it is even more important to safeguard your reputation as a man."

Bain barely heard him. He leaned his back against the wall, deep in thought.

After some silence Kort repeated, "So you see, do you not, that it is even more important - that you must not be seen to be too friendly with a lover of men?"

Kort's worried tone shook Bain out of his reverie. "I do see. I also see that there will be even more pressure to find a bride to strengthen alliances. Kort, I thank you for this information and will be grateful for any more you can glean." He stood straight and faced Kort. "You know there is only one woman I desire. I cannot, in good conscience, wed another." He ran his fingers roughly through his hair. "As you know, Kinterron borders Marston. We are allies already and must remain so. A union between Phaera and myself would make both our fiefs stronger."

Kort sighed. "Ah, my friend, I fear you set yourself up for heartache ... and political chaos as well."

"But you see, do you not, that it makes sense?"

"Indeed. I do, but the lady will not."

"Then I must find a way to make her agree."

Kort shook his head and rolled his eyes.

Bain changed the subject. "Kort, you must visit me in Marston.

I have need, not only of a friend, but of information. It is much to ask, but I must. May I rely on you?"

Kort brightened, grinning. "I do love a good intrigue. This could prove most entertaining." He stuck out his hand. "Shall we shake on it?"

Bain could not help but smile, though he did not share Kort's glee. This was much more than an adventure. He took the outstretched hand and gripped it firmly. "I will, my friend. But have a care. This is not child's play."

"Do not fear. I have learned how to hide in plain sight. It is a skill my kind develop early." With a broad wink he added, "Oh, and if I can help your cause with a certain frosty lady know that I am your man." With that he turned on his heel and strode down the alley whistling a merry tune just loud enough that Bain thought he recognized it.

Bain watched him go, and with a bemused shake of his head, made his way to the barracks to seek out his bed. Sleep, he knew, would not come easily. Too much had transpired today and in three days he would have to return home to Marston. He must make contact with Phaera again. And he vowed to show her he had more to offer than the hand of a bastard.

CHAPTER EIGHT

PHAERA HEARS A CHALLENGE

Once the angry tears subsided the stillness of her beloved apothecary had the effect of clearing Phaera's mind. In that comforting darkness she found again that core of determination she had relied on through the struggles of learning her calling, and of convincing her father that he could not force her to wed a man of his choosing.

The memory of how she had come to be a healer calmed her, so that she could once again think clearly. Though it did nothing to convince her she had no say over her destiny. She faced a duty, to be sure. But it need not be the one her father had laid before her.

AFTER HER MOTHER DIED IN CHILDBIRTH LORD DANZA HAD indulged his adventurous and curious daughter with far more freedom than her rank should have allowed. Not only did they discuss history and politics over many pleasant dinners together, so that she had a keen understanding of those subjects, but Phaera had been given free rein to roam the city unaccompanied once she had completed her lessons. She had been able to convince him that everyone would recognize her and no one would ever harm her. He had come to realize that Phaera had a way of slipping from sight, so attempts to guard her were doomed to failure in any case.

At ten years old, two years after the death of her mother, she had come upon a commotion in the street and wormed her way to the front of the gathering crowd to see what drew their attention. A wagon loaded with potatoes on their way to market had fallen over and pinned the merchant underneath. As she approached she saw men lift the wagon and two more drag the man out from underneath. The man's leg bled profusely. Someone had shouted, "Fetch the healer - fast!" No sooner had he spoken than the crowd parted to admit a woman carrying a large basket.

The woman rushed to the injured man and put pressure on the leg above where it bled. She shouted over her shoulder, "I need someone to keep the pressure on this."

The images made Phaera smile. She still did not know how she had found the audacity to jump forward and kneel beside the woman. "Where shall I press?" The woman had not even looked up to see who had come to her aid, merely taken both Phaera's hands, placed them on the leg above the bleed and said, "Here, press as hard as you can. If you do not, this man will surely die."

It had taken some badgering to get Mergana to accept her as an apprentice, and even more to convince her father to allow it. He had relented once he realized his willful daughter would do as she pleased with or without his permission. She kept regaling him with her adventures to demonstrate that fact. Her enthusiastic tales, at their dinners together, of what she had learned, wore him down. She had simply acted as though she already had permission. Phaera still felt some guilt over deceiving Mergana into thinking she had her father's consent before she actually did.

The memories soothed Phaera. She had to admit that her duty lay with her people first, and that her father had no choice but to cement an alliance through having her wed, but she was determined that the choice of husband must be hers. She could not become a broodmare to any man whose name she suspected her father had written on that scrap. She refused to even look at it. And surely she had a few days before he would require her decision. And that is what it would be... her choice.

As she calmed, and her resolution cemented itself in her mind, her natural curiosity got the better of her. She lit a lamp and searched for the crumpled scroll under the table. With shaking hands she smoothed it out and held it to the light. One name shocked her. There, at the head of the list, she read, "Bain of Marston". *The bastard? Her father actually considered him a suitable candidate for her hand?* She sat back down on the stool, not bothering to read the other two names on the list. *I suppose Marston is our biggest and most important ally.* The more she thought about it the more she saw where the decision to include Bain had come from. Next to Kinterron, Marston was the largest and most powerful fief of the seven included in their loose alliance, and they shared a large boundary. The other, outlying fiefs did not bear serious consideration. Lord Danza had always respected Lord Makin. Belthorn also shared a partial border with both Marston and Kinterron, but Belthorn was the actual problem. *Lord Makin is still hale and could rule yet many years before Bain must. Is Papa counting on that? And Papa must be aware that his mother is a healer....*

When Phaera emerged from the apothecary, darkness had fallen. She drew in a deep breath of the crisp, evening air, squared her shoulders and took the narrow path that would allow her to enter the castle and reach her chamber unseen. Her two ladies would be in the adjoining one, as she had trained them. They knew better than to wait up for her. Often they would sneak off of an evening to spy on the court from the balconies. Phaera suspected one had a suitor but had not seen fit to question the girl about it. There was nothing conventional about this arrangement but it suited Phaera to keep it that way. It gave her the privacy she desired and offered more freedom to her maids. She strongly suspected the two young women felt the same way.

The next morning Bain arrived at the apothecary just as Phaera opened the doors.

She made a dismissive gesture. "I have no need of assistance today, nor am I in the mood for company."

"Then I shall not remain long, milady, but I ask your indulgence for a few moments." Bain took a deep breath and pressed ahead. "Sleep eluded me last night. As you know, the gathering comes to an end and I must return home to Marston in two days."

"That is none of my concern."

"Perhaps. But as I lay awake I gave our conversations a great deal of thought. You made it plain that you have no desire to wed, suggesting that such a union would curtail your freedom to continue with your work, and that you do not wish to submit to any man for the purpose of supplying him with an heir. Am I correct?"

Phaera, uncomfortable with the direction of Bain's questions, turned away and made a show of organizing her shelf of bottled ointments, though they all stood in a straight line with their label facing forward. "And why does this concern you?"

"I have become privy to certain information that may have a bearing on that. Also, I have some opinions on it."

Phaera whirled on him, hoping the shadows hid the angry tears that threatened to spill over her eyelids. "Do you imagine I care one whit for your opinions?"

Bain acknowledged that with a solemn nod. "Perhaps not. But I think I have some understanding of your position. Hear me out."

Phaera turned away again. "You give me little choice." But she found herself listening more carefully.

"I will not be long … And that is the crux of what I have to say

– choice – or rather the lack of it. You see, I too, have lived a life of choice until recent events took that from me. As the bastard son of a peasant healer-woman, my future was not determined by fate. I had several options as to what occupation I would pursue. While none would make me wealthy, I was content. Then, two years ago, without warning, Lord Makin plucked me from my mother's home and trained me to my current duty."

Phaera did not turn back to look at Bain, but this strange turn piqued her interest enough that her hands stilled. No rebuttal came to mind.

Bain continued. "Do not imagine that I welcomed my new status, that the wealth and power of it lured me, or that I did not feel the immensity of the burden thrust upon me. No. Henceforth my life will be driven by duty – the duty to safeguard my people, to govern them with justice and what wisdom I can muster, to ally with those who will make it more likely that unrest, even war, can be prevented. If I am to meet the challenges before me then almost all choice has been taken from me. My life is now driven solely be duty. Or rather, any choices I make will be determined by duty."

When Phaera did not respond he asked, "Do you understand?"

"I am listening."

"You resist the fate that your accident of birth has placed upon you. I understand that. But what I present to you is that your father, mine, myself, all those who hold the fates of others in their hands, also have few choices. When one is responsible for the future of many, duty must take precedence over desire. I did not choose to be heir to Marston. And I, too, will be required to find a bride and produce an heir so that stability may be preserved for my people. We are not so different in this."

Still Phaera did not turn to him, shaken by the truth of what he said. *He sounds just like Papa.*

After a moment's silence Bain said, "I thank you for listening … and I have more that may bear on how you receive what I have told you. News has come to me, from a trusted source, that there is unrest in Exalon and Belthorn. Since Lord Dern of Exalon is in poor health it seems that it will not be long before Erstine inherits. I have no doubt that you are fully aware that he will not be an effective ruler. Lord Mathune, recently come to power in Belthorn since his father's death, is ambitious and, I think, devious. My source tells me that he is rallying support and that he plans to overthrow Exalon and annex it to Belthorn. That will place the balance of power in jeopardy and threaten the alliances on which we rely for peace."

Now, Phaera did turn to face him, surprised. "You know of this? How? I only learned of it yesterday."

Bain raised his eyebrows. "You are aware of it already?"

Disdain crept into Phaera's voice. "My sex does not deprive me of intellect. I am aware of events that may affect the balance of power. My father has his informants. And I am well versed in politics and strategy."

"I do not doubt it, milady, but this news is so recent."

Phaera could see she had caught Bain off balance. But the flash of surprise passed quickly.

"Now, Milady, as you have made it plain that you wish to work alone I will take my leave of you. I have spoken what I intended, if only to let you know that I have sympathy for your position, and to suggest that mine makes me different from other men. I am not indifferent to your plight as it is not so different from my own." He gave Phaera a low bow, and left…

CHAPTER NINE

PHAERA MAKES A PLAN

He stopped short of suggesting we ought to wed. Why? And I must give him his due. It took courage to be so direct with me. Phaera had slept little for two nights. Bain's speech had added to the turmoil her father had begun. *Does he know of my dilemma? Surely not. Papa would never let that slip before we come to an agreement.*

She rose before dawn and, after forcing down some bread and honey, followed by a small wedge of cheese and some sage tea, donned the same gown she had worn to the first banquet.

This was the day all the guests would gather at the gate on horseback, dressed in their finest, and ride out in procession to return to their respective home fiefs.

The tradition provided a final grand spectacle to mark the end of each gathering. The people lined the square to watch them ride out. Two chairs, elaborately carved with the Kinterron coat of arms on their backs, stood on a platform just inside to the left of the gate where Phaera would sit beside Lord Danza on the one normally reserved for the lord's lady. A few other dignitaries would also have chairs under the canopy to watch their guests leave. Every guest would be dressed in their finest - the young lords in court attire, and the men charged with keeping them safe, in dress uniform.

Each party wore its colours and had its family crest embroidered on the blankets that draped their horses' rumps. Banners fluttered from poles attached to saddles, held proudly in place by the riders. When the gate opened a trumpet fanfare would accompany their departure.

Phaera's ladies wove pearls into her hair and arranged it high on her head, accenting her long neck. More pearls hung from her earlobes and around her neck. A heavy sapphire pendant at the bottom of the double strand rested just above the edge of her neckline, where it accented the hint of breasts below. The sash around her waist also had pearls embroidered into it with gold thread.

Phaera frowned at her reflection in the polished silver mirror. Usually she did not even bother to check her appearance. Today she studied herself without knowing why and made an adjustment to her sash. Her admirers had often told her how much pearls accented her raven hair and translucent skin. She had to admit they were right. But she wished even one of them would see the mind behind the decorations. She sighed as she turned to leave. *At least Papa will be pleased today – a proper ornament for the dais as the guests all prance and preen before going back where they belong. I suppose I can take some comfort from that.*

On the dais as the procession began Phaera found herself searching for Bain in the crowd and spotted him, surrounded by his men. He rode a proud roan stallion that tossed its head, eager to be off. She admired the control Bain had over his mount, the ease with which he sat him. This was also the first time she had seen him in court attire. The dress tunic of deep green, embroidered with the coat of arms of Marston, and the matching cloak, set off his deep russet hair, tied into a neat club at the nape of his neck. There was nothing of the bastard in his bearing. He sat, tall and proud, answering his men with a nod here, a few words there.

So... his men show him the respect due an heir to a fief. They have accepted him. Phaera had to admit that Bain cut a handsome figure.

A glance to her left caught her father watching her, following the direction of her gaze. She abruptly sat straighter, tossed her head and stared in the other direction, feigning disinterest. They had not spoken since her father's declaration. Nor was she ready to do so now.

Bain's group was second last to exit the gate. As he passed the dais he turned and bowed from the saddle, first to her father, then, a sad smile sketching his lips, another directly to her before sitting straight and signaling his men to ride out.

As soon as the procession had gone Phaera rose and, without a backward glance, strode to her chamber. She needed to take off the heavy jewelry that seemed to mock her. Its weight mirrored her dark mood. But donning her comfortable work shift did nothing to allay the burden on her mind.

By midday she reached a decision of sorts. She flung open the door to her father's chamber, unannounced, and stood, feet planted and arms akimbo, in front of the same table where he had announced she must wed.

It disturbed her somewhat that he did not seem surprised to see her.

Lord Danza indicated the vacant chair beside her with a calm sweep of his hand. "Phaera, how good to see you. Please sit down." When she made no move to take the proffered seat he simply relaxed into his and waited for her to speak first.

"We need to talk."

The calm raise of one eyebrow told Phaera her father had expected something of the sort.

He said nothing more; merely clasped his hands loosely together and placed them in his lap. It made Phaera want to stamp her feet and shout at him. This familiar response when her father expected her to say or do something outrageous put her off balance. *How dare you not take me seriously.* She hid her hands behind her skirt so that he would not see her clenched fists and fought for self-control. An image of Bain, as he had made his speech to her, the dignity with which he had spoken, showed her what she needed to do. She unclenched her fists, relaxed her shoulders and lowered herself into the chair beside her, taking time to gather her thoughts.

"We are at an impasse. You wish me to marry – contrary to your oath to me – and I do not."

"Go on."

"We both know there is only one name on your list that I would even remotely consider."

"I assume you mean Bain of Marston. I expect you understand my reasoning."

The matter-of-fact way he said it confirmed Phaera's deductions. *I will not fall in line so easily.* "Yet, I will not be forced."

Silence.

When she could bear the silence no longer Phaera said, "It could be very awkward if I refused publicly. I have no desire to cause you such embarrassment so I hope we can come to an agreement."

She watched a ripple of anger cross her father's face, gone so quickly she almost missed it, before he answered, once more in control.

"I am gratified to hear it."

He leaned forward, forearms in front of him on the table, hands still loosely clasped. "Perhaps it will be wise of me to hear you out before I come to the conclusion that I have been too indulgent in not impressing upon you your first duty, which is to our people. Think carefully before you speak."

That stung. She had come with the intention of holding the upper hand. But her father had neatly taken that from her.

Before she could think of a response Lord Danza softened slightly. "I assume you came here with something to say – a proposal perhaps?"

"I need to know more before I agree to consider a betrothal to Bain. My reputation is at stake. Do you forget that he is a bastard, undesirable by most standards – or that I can have any man I choose?"

"Phaera, such immodesty is unbecoming."

Phaera bristled at the rebuke. "So honesty is now immodesty? Is that what we have come to?"

Lord Danza studied her a moment before giving his head a slow, sad shake. Without acknowledging her challenge he went back to their original conversation.

"And what is it you need," Lord Danza went on, "that will help you with your decision?"

Phaera leaned toward him, placing her hands flat on the desk.

"Time. I need time to let my patients know I will be leaving. And I must know more about Bain, to see how he acts - as heir to Marston, as a man, a leader. Three short conversations are not enough to tell me if I can tolerate him – if I can ..." She lowered her head to hide the blush she felt rising in her cheeks. "I need to know more about him, about Marston, about how he is with his men, at court ... and more about his mother. How does the court treat her?" Her voice cracked as she added, "And how can I give up my life's work? It is too much to contemplate. I need time to prepare myself...to grieve." She buried her face in her hands.

"Indeed. And the losses will not be yours alone, but mine, too, and that of the people you serve so faithfully. I cannot say how much I will miss you." He unclasped his arms and opened them on the desk, toward her. "I, too, have been thinking. It is yet early spring. We have a little time still – though the decision must be public before winter makes travel difficult. Perhaps a state visit to Marston, you and I, would help. You can become reacquainted with the area, the court, with Bain - possibly even his mother, before a formal decision is announced." He brightened somewhat, adding, "I have seen that Bain has eyes only for you. You may find him more attractive than you expect."

"Do not distract me with romantic nonsense. I care nothing for his 'eyes'."

Lord Makin's eyes crinkled as he smiled at her. "You may be surprised by what such things can achieve. You must at least allow for the possibility."

"And if I refuse to wed him?"

Lord Danza sighed. "You know, according to the law, I *can* force you ... You also know that I cannot bear to send you into any union with a man you despise."

The admission surprised Phaera, though she knew in her heart he was correct. Relieved by his confession she took a moment before responding.

"Then I will travel with you to Marston. Bain's mother is a healer. My hope is that she will become my friend, that I will find someone who will understand my ... will understand me."

"My hope is that Bain will become that person."

Phaera had no answer for that. She knew he was right. Yet she could not bring herself to consider how that might happen. "Lord Makin will conclude that we are already considering a match."

"Then I must make him understand that nothing is decided. I also need a promise from you."

Phaera's head shot up, a prickle of warning creeping up her spine. "What sort of promise?"

"That you will behave in a manner that befits your position and your duty to our hosts. With me you are free to speak your mind. There you must remain circumspect. Show them the respect they are due. Do I have your word?"

"I will do my best not to embarrass you ... and I must have some time privately with Bain's mother."

"I will make the request. More I cannot do."

"How soon must we leave?"

"I will show you the scroll tomorrow before I send it. I think we must allow them two weeks to prepare. You will not be able to avoid some public banquets and such." He sent her a warning glance. "I think five days there will suffice. Else they will surely assume a match is already decided."

Phaera gave a resigned nod, rose, and made to leave. "I will prepare myself."

As she opened the door she heard, "Please join me at dinner tonight, daughter of my heart."

The softness in his voice made her throat catch. Without turning back, so he would not see the tears that threatened to spill, she said, "I will Papa."

CHAPTER TEN

BAIN'S QUANDARY

"Father, I cannot, in good conscience, wed a woman who has no feelings for me, who has no wish to wed. Nor can I lie with a woman who does not wish it. Lady Phaera has my heart but if she is pressed to wed me against her will she will hate me. She has shown nothing but disdain for me – and for marriage."

Lord Makin remained firm. "Time often changes such feelings. She will come to see that you deserve her respect. And she will understand that it is best for her people and the alliance."

"Even if that should happen, it is not enough."

"It must be enough."

Bain shook his head. "I will not put her in such a position. If she will not have me willingly, then I shall endeavor to find another who will."

Lord Makin remained impassive. "Perhaps. You have some time yet – though it cannot wait much longer. Do not try my patience too far."

"Besides, she has a bad temper."

Lord Makin's laugh followed him out the door.

The conversation had taken place in his father's private chamber on Bain's return from the Gathering.

He had a similar one with his mother, Nurias, the next day. She listened with care, eliciting details he had left out with his father.

The scent of herbs hanging from the rafters, the humble hearth, that even in this warm weather was kept lit, lent a comforting warmth to the familiar cabin. It soothed some of the tension out of his body.

Nurias put an arm around Bain's shoulders. "Duty can be a painful burden. Your father and I were very much in love when you were conceived. But we were young and soon he was called to his duty - as are you, now. And, in time, he too found another to whom he could give his heart."

"But you did not."

"I had offers. But I had you. I had my work ... and I was never again so foolish." She gave his shoulder a squeeze before dropping her arm. "But you have no child, no union with her. You will get over her and accept another."

"Was one of them the millwright?"

Bain watched a wistful smile cross his mother's face. "Yes, he was a good man. But he could not give us the life we needed. He needed a mother for his sons and I needed to continue my work. He found another."

Ten days later the scroll arrived from Kinterron with the request for a formal visit. When Lord Makin showed it to him Bain was incredulous. "This must be due to pressure from Lord Danza. She would never agree otherwise. It changes nothing." *Does it? Surely not.* He shook the thought away along with a frisson of excitement and hope.

Lord Makin's voice was stern. "Do not discount fortune. We both know you are the logical choice for her. And you must have a bride."

Bain bit his lip to suppress a retort. *I will not wed her against her will, no matter it be strategic.* Instead he schooled himself to calm. "We shall see." *Or not.* It took Bain a while to understand why he felt so angry. *Her hand is being forced, as is mine.* His mother's words echoed in his mind. *"Duty can be a painful burden."* He saddled his horse and rode out to the countryside where he gave his mount his head and galloped full speed across the grasslands to clear his mind.

"Whoa, friend, what sends you off at such a pace?"

Bain looked up, startled, and recognized Kort riding toward him. "What brings you to Marston?"

Kort made a mock face. "What? Did you not invite me when we spoke in Kinterron? I have news."

That brought Bain to the present. He managed a smile. "Of course. I am happy to see you. But what brings you here at this time? What is this news I need to hear?"

"The grapevine tells me you expect a certain visitor soon."

Bain grew grave again. "So I am informed, though I dare not set hope on it."

"Why not? Surely this bodes well?"

"Strategically, perhaps, but I need more than that."

Kort eyed him sideways a while as they walked their horses together, reins slack. Finally he ventured, "And what is it you 'need', my friend?"

"If, and that is not given, the visit is to suggest a betrothal, I will not accept unless she is truly willing. A union with one who resents it is not one I wish to enter, no matter my feelings for the lady."

"Ah, I see." They walked slowly in silence for a time. "Perhaps I can offer some assistance in that regard."

"I doubt it."

"Did you know she wishes to meet your mother?"

Bain swivelled his head to meet Kort's eyes, which crinkled with mirth. "No, that was not in the message Lord Danza sent. How is it you know so much?"

Kort grinned. "I suspected as much. That would give too much away. But I have it from a good source that she insists on it." He gave a sly wink. "Why do you think she has made such a request?"

Bain shrugged it off. "I suspect she wishes to learn from her, to add to her healing knowledge."

"Hmmm, perhaps, but there is also the possibility she wishes to learn more about you, no?"

"Doubtful. Even if she does it will only be to see if she can tolerate me."

Kort laughed again. "Such pessimism. But the request suggested a possibility to me – a way you might gain her trust."

"I fail to see a connection."

"Think, my friend. What does she love most?"

Bain stopped is horse and waited for Kort to do the same. "Her work – her healing work."

"Yes! Correct the first time." When Bain did not respond he added, "Think. Who else in the land has the understanding and wish to see her able to continue with that work? Who can make this possible? And what rewards might that man reap?"

Bain let that sink in. He stood for several moments in silent thought, wondering if it would be possible, and if he could somehow make it a reality. It certainly might gain her respect, if not admiration, possibly even love. Then he gave himself a mental shake and shrugged again as he faced Kort. "Kort, I appreciate what you are suggesting, but it is not possible. If she becomes my Lady she will have too many duties at court. She will not have time to do any healing work ... and once she has a child she will have even less." When Kort looked about to protest he added, "And my father will never agree to such an unusual arrangement. It is bad enough that his heir is a bastard. To have that bastard wed a woman who chooses such a vocation over her court duties would destroy any respect I may have gained – and may also see my father lose his."

"So you refuse to woo her in a way she will appreciate?"

Bain made a cutting gesture with his free hand, and shouted, "I refuse to entertain wishes that cannot be! I have a duty. I must do mine, even if she will not. If she cannot then I must find a bride who can. – No, enough, Kort. You speak dreams, not possibilities. Leave it be."

Now it was Kort who shrugged. They climbed back onto their horses and resumed their ride back to the castle. As they approached it Bain said, "Forgive my harsh words, my friend. Will you stay a few days?"

"Of course. No apology necessary. I know how close to your heart this is." After a short silence he ventured, "But think on it, Bain. Do not dismiss this so easily."

Bain only shook his head, his expression pained.

CHAPTER ELEVEN

TO MARSTON

Six days later Phaera gave brief instructions to her maids about which gowns to pack and left the rest of the decisions to them. Knowing that she would be required to take at least one maid with her she chose the one she suspected of having a lover. She had no wish to dismiss her in shame for the possible results of her dalliance. This journey would, at least, delay the inevitable. Both maids showed disappointment in that decision, though for obviously different reasons.

When she examined the packed trunks she added one of her work shifts. *For when I meet Bain's mother. So ... I am ready, Papa.* She chose her most comfortable riding gown for the journey that would begin after breaking fast the next morning.

Phaera drank in all she could of the scenery on their journey, fearing she would soon have to leave her beloved Kinterron for good. June was the perfect month for travel, burgeoning with new life, the greens still bright and fresh and the newly sown fields just showing the first tips of growth and the promised harvest. Most orchards had passed their bloom, but here and there, cherry trees still showed a blush of pink.

The forest's trees had achieved their full leaf and provided shade during the hot midday. Wild flowers, white, yellow, and lavender, dotted the forest floor. It rained only one day and night, but they found welcome shelter in a village they passed. Phaera noticed the next morning that the land looked even brighter and fresher than before.

The journey took six days, as they travelled in state and slowly enough that the people would be able to see as they processed by. The party managed to find shelter in village inns for all but one night. In each village children ran to greet the travellers and direct them to the inn. In two of the villages men approached his head guards asking for an audience. The first wanted Lord Danza to settle a dispute over who owned a calf that had been born. The cow had drifted onto a neighbour's field to give birth and that neighbor insisted that the resulting calf belonged to him. Lord Danza told the man to give the calf back in exchange for three chickens. Both were satisfied. The other dispute was over an inheritance after a woman's second husband died. Both her son and her husband's son lay claim to the land. In that instance Lord Danza ruled that, as the woman's son was the elder, and the land had first belonged to the son's father he had the right of inheritance. The other son, while not happy, accepted the decree, knowing that it was correct.

The one night spent on the trail in tents was the most enjoyable for Phaera, though her maid complained she missed a warm bed and cooked meal. Phaera preferred it to the fuss made over them by the village people, honoured to be visited by their lord and wanting to make a good impression. She crept unseen out of her tent to drink in the night sky and breathe the perfumed, earthy air. It was the only time during the journey she felt truly at peace. Though she had travelled with her father before, this was the first time she managed to be completely alone- no ladies, no guards, just quiet punctuated by the occasional melancholy hoot of an owl.

Her father seemed to be enjoying the journey as well. They

spoke little, but the silence was a comfortable one. Even the men with them seemed affected and were unusually quiet. *Why have I never noticed all this before? Did I always resist these visits so much that I missed the beauty along the way? What else have I been unwilling to see?*

As Marston shared a long border with Kinterron they had no alien territory to cross. They encountered only one band of travelling trader families, with whom they shared a midday meal. Though the guards kept a careful watch, they met no threats to their safety.

Late morning on the sixth day they reached the stele, the stone obelisk that marked the border of Marston. The land opened up more here, the trees thinned and gave way to grassland. Phaera saw sheep and cattle grazing, kept together by well trained dogs that seemed to know which animals belonged to which shepherd, in spite of no visible boundaries. In the distance she spotted two shepherds' huts. When she waved at a shepherd he returned her greeting with enthusiasm, as though not surprised to see visitors.

They had not entered far into Marston when an honour guard rode up to greet them and escort them to the castle. Phaera's peace was over. From now on she would be expected to act like the "Lady" she was. She caught her father's warning glance, though he said nothing.

Phaera did not see Bain in the group that came to escort them to the castle. *Did I really expect him to be here?* She brushed aside the hint of disappointment and concentrated on the scenery. The road here was broad and well-travelled. Marston city, and the castle at its centre, stood a normal day's ride from the border with Kinterron, making this last leg of the journey easy – no more rivers to cross, no more narrow forest trails. In fact, Phaera saw only a few small copses of trees. This terrain was quite different from the more rugged and hilly countryside of Kinterron. She could understand why the city had been set here. With little natural protection available the wide view of the countryside would give ample warning should an enemy choose to attack. The only barrier to approaching the city lay in the river that seemed to arc around its walls, creating a partial natural moat. She recalled from her studies that Marston was the only fief to have a double wall built around the city and an additional one around the castle at its centre as well. She remembered, too, that it had withstood a long siege once because of the natural spring at its centre that offered a clean supply of water even when the people could not exit to draw water from the river.

They reached the outer wall by early afternoon. This time Phaera paid more attention to the layout of the city than the last time she had been here. It pleased her to see that the outer and inner walls both looked in excellent repair and were well-guarded.

They collected an entourage of curious children as they processed through the city. The fact that they could follow unsupervised boded well for general safety. The city appeared well run with few beggars or ruffians in the streets. *Just like at home. And so different from Exalon or Belthorn. It seems Lord Makin respects his people and has earned their respect in return.*

As soon as they entered the castle itself maids and porters hurried to show them to their chambers and see to their needs before dinner. The tea, a mix of several herbs that she recognized but had not seen blended in that way before, refreshed her as she and prepared for dinner. *I must inquire after it so I can make it at home.*

When told that the first formal banquet would wait until the next day Phaera was relieved. The reprieve allowed her to enjoy a bath in the large copper tub without the need to fuss over gowns and the dressing of her hair. *I will wear my pale blue gown and only the gold earrings. Riya can put my hair up into a simple knot. That must be enough, Father. Let them see that I am not a preening Dandybird.* She allowed Riya to hold the silvered mirror and nodded, satisfied.

"Milady, are you certain you will not add the gold chain around your neck?"

"No, Riya. This is enough." Seeing her maid's disappointment she added, "They will soon see that it is I who decide and that it is no reflection on your skills."

Riya bobbed her head, eyes lowered. "Yes, milady."

CHAPTER TWELVE

MARSTON

*P*haera endured two days of being on public display, dressed, banqueted, and introduced to all and sundry of any importance. She tried to make the most of it by leaning all she could about Lord Makin, Lady Flor and, of course, Bain. The fief of Marston was slightly smaller than Kinterron and somewhat less wealthy. This was reflected in the degree of opulence with which she and her father were hosted. Phaera approved of the calm manner in which both lady Flor and Lord Makin interacted with their subjects, from the highest rank to the lowest. It lent an air of respect and efficiency akin to that in Kinterron under her own father.

Do I imagine it or have they deliberately held back? Is this how things always are for important visitors or did Bain tell them I do not appreciate being feted? While she could see that all protocols were properly seen to, in keeping with their status, she got the impression that somethings were deliberately understated. If that was on her behalf she appreciated the gesture, but could not be sure if she had judged correctly. *I hope it is not on our behalf. If this is normal that is so much the better.*

Both nights, at the banquets, her father was seated directly across from Lord Makin, at a side, with no one at the actual end of the table, as was proper due to their equal status. To Phaera's relief, she had been seated next to Lady Flor and not near Bain. Bain sat at the opposite end of the table – a place of honour, to be sure, but away from her. She had expected he might be seated beside her, which would give the court the impression that a match was imminent. That they seemed to have intentionally avoided this impression eased some of the tension and expectation Phaera felt. She found Lady Flor gracious and actually began to enjoy conversing with her. Lady Flor seemed genuinely interested in Phaera, and drew her out about her healing work. Neither Bain, nor his mother, were mentioned until the end of the second night.

It was Lady Flor who brought up Bain's mother. She did it so naturally that Phaera's estimation of her rose considerably. "Since you have so much in common might I suggest that you visit with Nurias. Perhaps tomorrow will be a good time. A ride in the country may please you as well. The weather looks to be fair tomorrow." Lady Flor smiled as she added, "And it will no doubt be a welcome break from this." She indicated the long table filled with guests with a sweep of one hand, before leaning toward Phaera conspiratorially so the others would not hear. "I find this somewhat tiring. I find I need some quiet or a good ride outdoors in between my duties as hostess."

Relief flooded Phaera, along with gratitude for Lady Flor's insight. "Thank you, Milady, I would like that very much. I had hoped such an opportunity would arise. I expect I will benefit from … Nurias, is it? … from her knowledge. She has been a healer much longer than I."

Lady Flor nodded her understanding with a genuine smile. "Good, that is settled then."

"Thank you, Milady. I shall look forward to it."

A sudden thought struck Phaera, robbing her of the glow she had begun to feel. *Will they send Bain to take me there? I want to be alone with Nurias.* But that was a question she knew she must not ask. It would either be seen as improper or could leave the impression that she wished to see more of Bain.

In spite of her fatigue Phaera slept little that night. Her mind raced with conflicting thoughts about the day to come. On the positive side she would finally meet Bain's mother, the one thing she wanted from this journey. *Will she be willing to share her knowledge with me? Will she respect me? Will Bain get in the way? Does she know I am under pressure to accept Bain? Does he want that? Oh, I hope Bain stays away.*

Since her arrival she had had little contact with Bain. It had given her the opportunity to observe him from a distance, in his court environment; how he acted there, and how the members of the court responded to his presence. What she saw left a good impression, both of Lord Makin's court, of Bain – and indeed of Lord Makin and Lady Flor. In spite of having had only two years at court learning the duties of a future lord, Bain showed no vanity, put on no airs. He seemed at ease in his new role. Others showed no resentment to his presence or his authority. *It seems there is much of his father about him. It bodes well for the future of Marston.*

However, the lack of contact or conversation between them also left Phaera uneasy. She had expected Bain to make more effort to engage her. *Is he avoiding me? Has he been warned not to approach me directly? Has he lost interest?* Her mixed feelings left her unsettled. Her efforts to convince herself she did not care met with only limited success.

The next morning Riya protested when Phaera chose her working shift. "But Milady, ought you not to wear your riding gown?"

"No, I am a healer going to meet another healer."

"But you are a Lady. Surely you wish to make a good impression. The people must see you as a member of court, not as a peasant."

"Enough, Riya. Do I not wear this garb when I work at home? This is how I wish to be known." Irritated, she spat out, "You forget your place."

Riya paled at the rebuke but said nothing.

Phaera felt her staring at her back as she left the chamber. She did feel a pang of guilt, as she was not in the habit of speaking to her ladies that way, but was too stubborn and too stressed to soften her comment. She still did not know who would accompany her on her ride. And she had to admit, finally, that she would not only be speaking about healing with Nurias. The subject of Bain would most certainly come up and Phaera had no plan as to how she would handle that. *And if Bain is present?* It did not bear thinking about. The whole day would be for naught.

Her worst fears looked about to be realized when Bain approached her after breaking the fast.

"Lady Phaera, I must apologize for being unable to introduce you to my mother today. I will be hunting with Lord Danza and my Lord Father. Lord Danza expressed an interest in seeing more of our countryside. Lady Flor has arranged for an escort and has decided to accompany you. I hope your day is a pleasant one. I trust you and my mother will have much to talk about. I look forward to dining with you again tomorrow evening. Lady Flor has informed me that dinner will be simpler tonight as she expects you will be too fatigued for a full banquet."

Relief robbed her of speech for a moment. She collected herself with effort. "Thank you, yes, a quiet dinner will be more to my liking." *And I am so glad you will not be with me today. Thank you, Papa for suggesting the diversion for Bain.*

She watched a strange expression cross Bain's face, then vanish with the return of inscrutability. Was it anger, disappointment, understanding, hurt? It was too fleeting for her to interpret.

Lady Flor set a leisurely pace as she took the time to draw Phaera's attention to points of interest along the way.

"Our fief must appear unusual to you. Since our lands are

more fertile and less rugged we are able to grow more crops. See how evenly the maize grows over there. And to the left we have orchards of apples, pears, and plums." Lady Flor beamed proudly at Phaera. "We do a strong trade with Kinterron for these, in return for iron and copper from your mines. Both our lands are richer for the long peace we have enjoyed and the trade that comes from it."

Is she aware that peace may be in jeopardy? "Indeed. We have been strong allies as well."

Lady Flor's brow furrowed and she grew serious. "I hope we may remain so, especially in light of recent rumours of instability in Exalon and Belthorn. I am old enough to remember less peaceful times."

So, she knows – or at least has some information. I need not pretend ignorance. That knowledge pleased Phaera. It meant Lord Makin also discussed politics with his wife. "I am aware of unrest in Belthorn and Exalon that may affect the alliances we rely on. Lord Dern is in poor health and his son Erstine has shown no interest in the duties of lordship."

Lady Flor's eyebrows rose. "How much do you know of that situation?"

"Lady Flor, may we be frank with each other?"

"That would please me."

"Good. My Lord Father has educated me in history and politics and discusses events with me. I have it on good authority that Lord Mathune is gathering support in both Belthorn and Exalon. When Lord Dern dies we expect Mathune will attack Exalon and annex it to Belthorn without much resistance. Mathune is a ruthless and ambitious man with no respect for the people. With his father recently dead there is no one to hold him back."

"We have the same information. If Mathune is successful he will be in a strong position to upset current alliances further. It is one reason our alliance must remain strong."

They had no time to continue their conversation as Nurias'

cottage had come into view. Their guard escort, which had maintained a respectful distance as they rode, halted and the front guards turned to face them. "We have arrived, milady. What are your wishes?"

The four guards who had ridden behind them came forward to assist them from their mounts.

"You may hobble the horses and repair to the shade of those trees. We will be here for some time. I will call you when we know our plans for the night." The ride had taken half the day and they were not expected back at the castle until late.

Lady Flor turned to Phaera. "Come, let me introduce you to Nurias. I think you will like each other."

Nurias stood waiting just outside her door and dipped a small curtsey as they approached.

It was well that Lady Flor had the situation in hand as Phaera suddenly had nothing to say. Before her stood the woman she had wanted so much to meet, but about whom she knew so little. Now that they finally stood face to face Phaera's tongue seemed cleaved to the roof of her mouth.

As Lady Flor greeted Nurias, Phaera took advantage of the momentary reprieve to collect herself and take stock of Bain's mother. She was tall for a woman, and in spite of her age and years of hard work, she still stood straight and strong. She bore an air of deep calm, not in the least nervous about the situation. Phaera got the impression that this was Nurias' realm, in a sense, and that she had unquestionable control here. Her simple shift, belted at the waist with a cord of scarlet, denoting her status as healer, skimmed a spare body topped by wide shoulders.

As lady Flor stepped aside to introduce Phaera, Nurias took one hand in both of hers and looked deeply into her eyes. "So, this is the woman who has troubled my son so." The warm tone and kind smile belied her words. "Please, come into my home and be welcome."

Piqued, Phaera found her tongue. "Madam, I am honoured."

A braid of iron grey hair hung down Nurias' back, wisps escaping around her hairline, their reflection in the midday sun creating a halo effect around her face, which disappeared as she stepped back into the shadow and gestured that they should enter.

"I have some sun tea, made with mint, that I think you will find refreshing after your ride."

They had spent just enough time in small talk to drink their tea when Lady Flor said, "Nurias, may I offer some tea to my men? I'll have another cup, myself, too, and enjoy that bench in the sun so that you and Phaera may speak in private together. I am sure you have many things to say to each other."

Phaera's jaw almost dropped at the easy familiarity and willingness to wait alone outside. It elevated Lady Flor even more in her estimation.

In another moment Phaera and Nurias faced each other across the short wooden table, alone in the cool dimness of the cabin. Phaera, although accustomed to taking control, still found herself unable to find the right words that would convey all she wanted to say.

Nurias seemed to understand and made it easy by asking, a small twinkle in her eye, "Do you detect anything other than mint in my tea?"

That small challenge let Phaera enter an area where she was familiar. "Oh, yes, I taste chamomile as well, though it is mild. Did you suspect I might be anxious in meeting you?" She decided to be daring. "Or is this a test?"

Nurias laughed, a warm, easy sound that put Phaera at ease. "Perhaps a little of both."

"And have I passed?" Phaera was able to smile for the first time since arriving.

"Not so fast." Nurias sent Phaera a conspiratorial wink. "I see you came dressed for work. Let us see what sort of healer you are." She rose and beckoned Phaera to follow her. "Let me show you my apothecary so we may share our knowledge."

The two women spent a pleasant hour smelling this or that jar, identifying various herbs and their remedial uses until loud voices could be heard outside the hollowed-out earthen mound behind her cottage that Nurias used as her apothecary.

Nurias hurried to the door with Phaera close on her heels.

Two guards held a struggling young man. As soon as he spotted them he shouted, "Ashin says you must come quickly. The birth is not going well."

Nurias gave him a sharp nod, disappeared into the apothecary and reappeared with a large woven grass basket over her arm. As if it were the most expected thing in the world she nodded to Phaera. "Come, we have work to do," and strode after the anxious young man. As she passed the shade tree she announced to Lady Flor, "I am called to a birth. You may follow if you wish but keep your distance when we arrive … or wait here. The cottage is at your disposal. I will see that our guest comes to no harm."

Lady Flor nodded understanding and said, "We will wait." She turned to one guard and ordered, "Go with them and see to Lady Phaera. We will remain in the cottage and await you here."

On the way Nurias explained to Phaera that the young man's wife was in labour with their first child, that she was very young, and that Nurias had sent her apprentice Ashin to attend, as she knew Lady Flor and Phaera would expect to meet her today. "Ashin has attended many births with me. She is well trained so I fear something unexpected has happened."

Loud wails greeted them as they approached. The young man gave Nurias a terrified look which she seemed not to see, though Phaera had not missed it. When the guard made as if to follow them into the hut Phaera waved him back. "You cannot enter. This is women's work. Wait outside."

The guard backed off looking relieved.

Ashin, her hands red with blood, pressed the shoulders of a young woman back into a cot as she let out another loud wail. At a glance of recognition over her shoulder she said, "The cord is around the neck. If I let the babe come this mother will bleed to death from tearing the placenta loose and the babe will die from loss of air. I have prevented the babe coming out but cannot loosen the cord."

Nurias took over, barking orders to Phaera and Ashin. As Ashin held the woman down and did her best to prevent another contraction from forcing the babe out, Phaera held her thighs open. At the end of the next contraction Nurias slid her hand into the woman's womb and, before the next spasm began managed to slip the cord over the babe's head and remove her hand again. The babe's body slipped through, and with another push, the head was born. The baby was blue and limp.

Nurias put her ear trumpet to the tiny chest. "The heart still beats." With a single smooth motion of her finger she cleared the babe's mouth and placed her own over the tiny one, blowing in a small breath and releasing. After three more such breaths the tiny chest heaved and it took its first breath. Amid loud cries its skin turned bright pink and its tiny arms and legs flailed in the cool air. Nurias took only a moment to hold the babe up for the new mother to see. "You have a son." She handed the child to Ashin and turned her attention back to the mother. She displayed none of the concern to the young mother that Phaera felt on seeing how much blood lay underneath her. "You have done well, my dear. Now we must see that we look after you. Ashin has your son well in hand."

That brought a wan smile from the new mother. While Phaera took cloths from the bowl next to her and wiped the woman's brow, murmuring soothing words about how well she had done, Nurias examined the afterbirth that had slipped out. Finding it intact she turned her attention to the mother's womb, kneading and massaging it from the outside. Phaera knew how crucial this was for slowing the bleeding. If the woman continued to lose more blood she would be beyond saving.

Darkness had fallen before Nurias and Phaera left the hut to return to Nurias' cabin. Ashin stayed behind to continue her care of mother and babe.

The guard lifted them both onto the back of his horse and walked it back. After a few moments of silence Phaera offered, "The babe seems well, but I still fear for his mother. She has lost too much blood."

"I cannot promise she will recover but I will send bone broth and beef tea tomorrow to give her strength. I am hopeful." She squeezed the arm she had around Phaera's waist a little. "I was glad for your presence today. You are indeed a healer and needed no direction from me. I am honoured to know you, young Phaera."

Phaera glowed with not only the praise, but with the familiar address. Nurias saw her as a fellow healer, not a court lady. Tears pricked behind her eyes as she pressed the arm closer against her in gratitude.

When they reached Nurias' cabin one of the other three guards had remained outside, waiting.

Nurias took charge. "I have blankets for you all and will show you where you may bed down in the stable. It is not used in summer and the straw is clean. You will be comfortable there. I have a kettle of stew on and one of you may come back for it once you have settled. There is not room in the cottage for us all to sit together."

Phaera admired the efficient way Nurias handled the arrangements. It took hardly any time at all before she, Lady Flor and herself sat at the table eating the rich stew, dark bread, and drinking hot spearmint tea.

When they had eaten Nurias made up a narrow cot for Phaera to sleep on and invited Lady Flor to climb into the loft where Bain's bed had been. She would have more privacy there. As Phaera drifted into an exhausted sleep a thought occurred to her. *We have not even mentioned Bain since I first arrived.*

CHAPTER THIRTEEN

CRISIS

They woke at dawn and, after a quick meal of bread, hard cheese, and raspberry leaf tea, Phaera helped prepare the bone broth Nurias planned to take to the new mother. She had just put the cork into the top of the second jug when they heard the thunder of several horses galloping in the direction of the cabin. Before either of them had the chance reach the door to see what had caused the din it flew open and their guard stood limned in the morning light, sword in hand, ready to defend them.

"Stay inside," he ordered, and turned to face whatever approached. He lowered his sword when he recognized the guards that galloped toward him, and sheathed it by the time they reached the cottage.

The lead guard shouted, "Milady, you must return to the castle immediately. Hurry."

Nurias pushed their guard aside and stepped into the sunshine, Phaera close behind. Lady Flor stayed in the doorway right behind Phaera.

The Guard acknowledged Nurias. "You are summoned as well."

"What is amiss?" Phaera stepped out from behind Nurias and let her gaze scan the dozen guards. Her eye fell on the one man not in uniform. "Kort, what do you here?"

"Come, Milady, on my horse and I will explain on the way."

When both women hesitated the leader shouted, "*Now*".

Phaera and Nurias exchanged glances and Phaera ran back into the cabin, emerging with the two jugs of bone broth. She thrust them into the hands of the guard who had escorted them. "Take these to Ashin and the new mother. Take your horse. Then follow us to the castle."

"But my duty…"

"Your duty is to do as you are ordered. Now go." There must have been more authority in Phaera's tone than she actually possessed in this strange land because the soldier jerked upright and, jugs in hand, went to his horse without further protest.

Nurias sent Phaera a grateful look as she mounted her own mare, ready to follow. Phaera hurried to where Kort sat his horse, motioning away the guard who tried to intercept her with a brusque wave of her hand, and allowed Kort to hoist her up in front of him. "So we may speak without shouting," he explained in her ear. Phaera understood that to mean "so that they could speak without being overheard" and nodded. She told the guard to lead her own horse back. The guards formed a circle around them. They kept a fast pace back to the castle but not before Nurias managed to ask, "Bain…?"

Kort answered before a guard could. "He is well but there is grave news." Then they were taken out of earshot from each other, the horses eating up the distance that had made such a pleasant ride the morning before.

Phaera turned her head to look at Kort. "Tell me all … now."

"I raced back from Belthorn as soon as I could to inform Bain and Lords Makin and Danza. Dern is dead. Poison is suspected. Dern's son Erskine is also dead, an accident they say, but I know Mathune had him assassinated. There was … a witness. Mathune has taken over Exalon and now controls both Belthorn and Exalon. His success makes him bold and now he threatens to invade Marston. He must not succeed or Kinterron will have enemies on three sides.

Phaera had noticed that when Kort mentioned a witness his voice had taken on a strange, dead tone. He knew more than he was telling. "What are you leaving out, Kort. Tell me. I must know." She turned her head back again so she could see Kort's face. When Kort blanched and shook his head to protest she said, "I am not asking Kort. That is an order. Tell me all – now, before we reach the castle. I must know."

When Kort shook his head again, a stricken look on his face, Phaera hardened herself not to give in. "Now, Kort – every detail." She glanced around to make sure the other men kept enough distance so they would not be overheard. "Quickly. We have not much time."

Kort's voice cracked and his hands shook as he held the reins. "Mathune is no ordinary man, Milady. While I take my pleasure with other men, he finds pleasure only in cruelty. He is a monster. He has not a shred of humanity in him."

When Kort hesitated Phaera nudged him in the ribs. "Now, Kort. We are only minutes away from the castle."

"I travel to gather information for Bain."

"You are a spy?"

"In a manner of speaking. Men with my nature learn how to stay in the shadows and hear things others may not."

"Go on."

"Two days ago…" Kort's voice broke and he took a shuddering breath. "Milady, it is too terrible for your ears."

Phaera growled through gritted teeth. "Now Kort, I see the castle ahead."

"I was at an inn where I have a … friend." When Phaera nodded understanding Kort swallowed and continued. "Mathune came in, crowing that he was now lord of both Belthorn and

Exalon and wanted to celebrate. I had just gone to fetch another draft of ale and so was hidden from Mathune's view." Now tears flowed freely. "Milady, it could have been me."

Phaera fought the urge to comfort Kort, lest she not hear the rest. "But it was not you. Speak."

"Mathune had two of his men hold down my friend while he castrated him." A sob escaped Kort. "Then Mathune sodomized him, as he filled his hands with the blood and smeared in on my friends face, laughing all the while my friend screamed in agony. When he finished he strutted about the inn crowing, "That this is what happens to unnatural freaks."

Phaera watched a look of sheer horror cross Kort's face as he stopped speaking. "There is more, Kort. I must have it." She glanced ahead and saw that they were close enough that she could make out the castle gate. "Hurry."

"He held up my friend's scrotum, then threw it on the floor and ground it under the heel of his boot…and…"

"And?"

He said, "This is how I will bring that arrogant wench to heel. She will lick my boots. She is mine. She will not scorn me again."

There could be no doubt who Mathune had meant by the "wench".

"Oh, Milady, forgive me. I did not want you to hear this."

Phaera went numb. They had just reached the gate and waited for the guards to open it.

"Milady…?" Kort's voice reached her through a fog. She pulled herself together with all the strength she could muster. "Thank you, Kort. You have done well." The words sounded hollow and distant to her own ears but she saw a small nod from Kort before he hung his head and wept openly. She did not notice when she was helped down from the horse and led into the castle. Her ears buzzed and her skin prickled. She heard nothing and saw nothing.

Two guards guided her into the private audience chamber and left, closing the door behind them after admitting Nurias.

CHAPTER FOURTEEN

A DECISION

*I*t was Nurias who took Phaera gently by her arms and led her across the chamber to Lord Danza's side. While against protocol in such audiences, he accepted Phaera's hand from Nurias and pulled her into a long, firm embrace.

The silence in the chamber remained unbroken for some time as Lord Makin, Bain, and Nurias stood aside and waited. While the room had comfortable chairs in it no one sat. The very air felt pregnant with doom and pain.

Lord Danza stroked Phaera's hair and rocked her slightly. After several minutes tears began to slip down Phaera's cheeks and she managed to look up at her father.

"I made Kort tell me all. Such horror…"

"All?"

Phaera nodded. "Even Mathune's threat against me." She accepted the handkerchief her father offered, and dried her eyes before stepping back, once more in control though clearly still stricken.

The only one who looked puzzled was Nurias. Lord Makin filled her in, leaving out the scene Kort had described to Phaera, but including the declaration that Phaera would be Mathune's.

Bain's chest went tight when he saw Phaera's face and knew she must have extracted the full details from Kort. *So like her not to shy away from it, no matter how terrible.* It had been hard for him not to step forward when she entered the room and try to comfort her. He was grateful to his mother, and even more to Lord Danza, that they had broken protocol and done what he could not. The sight of her looking so wounded, without the mantle of strength she always wore, melted all the anger and doubt he had about being able to care for her. He clenched his fists behind his back and forced himself to remain silent. *I must not shame her. She must not think I see her as weak.* He did not see her as weak at all, but knew that was how she would take it if he tried to offer words of comfort.

He pulled his attention back to Lord Makin who began to speak.

"Friends, we are now at war. There is no other way to see it. Mathune must be stopped, however that can be done." He looked at Lord Danza. "That makes our alliance more important than ever. It must remain unassailable."

"Indeed." Lord Danza spoke now. "The threat to the safety of both our lands is real and immediate. And you and I are agreed on what must be done."

Lord Makin turned and faced Bain, and Nurias who stood a step behind him. "My son, there is no place for pride in what must be done."

Then Lord Danza turned to Phaera and stood formally facing her. "My daughter, you, too, must let go of pride and do what must be done."

The speech must have been rehearsed and agreed upon by the two lords, they were so similar.

Lord Makin continued. "Even before our hands were forced Lord Danza and I agreed that a match between our children would be a good one. Politically yes, but also personally. We had hoped that you would come to the same conclusion without pressure or the threat of war. There is no longer time to wait for that." He turned again to Bain. "My son, will you accept that this marriage must take place, and that it must happen immediately?"

Bain looked at Phaera but could not read her expression. *I swear, my love, that I will strive to make you content.* Aloud, turning back to his father, he said, "I do my Lord, and I swear to do all I can to give Lady Phaera the life she deserves."

Lord Makin gave him a curt, satisfied nod and stepped back.

Now Lord Danza stood in front of Phaera. "Daughter of my heart."

The endearment was most irregular in such formal circumstances but Bain was pleased to hear it, and to see the softness in Lord Danza's eyes as he faced Phaera. *Is he pleading with her or offering comfort? No, he has taken her hand. It must be comfort – or grief.* He paid close attention as Lord Danza continued.

"My ability to protect you and to allow you the freedom that has made you so happy has ended. I know you see it as well." Bain could hear the anguish in his voice as he went on.

"Daughter of my heart, Phaera, will you accept that this marriage is your duty? Will you agree to marry Lord Bain, trusting that I believe this to be a good match and that it is the best way I can think of to keep you safe?"

Bain thought he saw tears threaten Phaera again, but she took a deep breath and drew herself to her full height, straight and proud. *How magnificent she is, even in this. Such courage.*

With only a slight quaver in her voice Phaera answered, "I will my lord, and will do what is necessary to strengthen the safety and future of our peoples."

Lord Danza sent her a grateful smile. "I never doubted it."

To Bain's surprise his father reached into a small leather sac tied to his belt, pulled out a ring he had not seen before and handed it to him. "My father presented this to my mother at their betrothal. I would have wished this might be done in a more joyful way. I trust you know what to do."

Bain looked at the jewel in his hand. The gold work was intricate without being too ornate. *A stone of many colours, from the Great Conflagration – the traditional symbol for unity.* "Thank you, Father."

Bain looked across at Phaera. *Does she agree merely out of duty? I cannot read her. She is still so pale.* He took the three steps that brought him in front of her and knelt on one knee. "Lady Phaera, *lady of my heart, though I dare not speak it,* will you accept this token of our troth and wear it as a symbol of that pledge?"

"Lord Bain, I accept this token and will wear it in honour of that pledge." Phaera lifted her hand to Bain and allowed him to place the ring on her third finger and then touch it to his lips. "Please rise, my lord."

Her voice is strong. May I be worthy of her. Bain rose, made a deep bow to Phaera, and stepped back to his place in front of Nurias, who, he could not help but notice, looked proud and pleased.

Lord Danza stepped forward and shook his hand. "Congratulations, Lord Bain."

Lord Makin stepped over to Phaera and bowed over her hand, brushing his lips to her fingers. "Congratulations, Lady Phaera."

Lord Makin went to the door of the chamber and opened it. Lady Flor waited there in the hall holding Phaera's blue gown. Beside her stood an official, dressed in his robes of office. "Please, come in, Lady Flor." He nodded to the priest. "I will call for you when we are ready."

Lady Flor moved confidently to the rear of the chamber, where she pulled back a heavy drapery to reveal a small door. "Please, Phaera and Nurias, come in."

Nurias took Phaera gently by the elbow and led her into the hidden chamber, closing the door behind them.

Lord Makin opened the outer door again and spoke to the guard who stood there. "Please locate Kort and have him attend us here. I believe you will find him in the kitchens, where I have ordered him to wait. He must make haste."

Bain raised his eyebrows in question at this father.

"I am aware of young Kort's role as your informant, Bain – and I approve. Now we need him again."

"You trust him, then, my lord?" Bain's mouth went dry as he as spoke the words.

"You trust him. And he has shown his loyalty. That is enough. We need him."

A knock on the door stopped further discussion. Lord Makin opened it to admit Kort, still looking pale and shaken.

"How may I serve you, my lords."

Lord Danza reached out to shake his hand. "We owe you a great debt, Master Kort – one I hope one day to be able to repay." He hesitated before continuing. "But first we require your services again. May we rely on you?"

"You may. I have prepared myself, my lord. I expected it when you had me remain. What would you have me do?"

"Are you loyal only to Bain or will you swear allegiance to myself as well?"

"You have my oath, Lord Danza. I will do whatever I must to bring this demon to justice."

"Good." Lord Danza looked at Lord Makin, then at Bain and back to Kort. "We three are all agreed that we must ally closely together to protect our lands and our peoples."

Lord Makin spoke up. "We need as much information about the actions and intentions of Mathune as possible so that we may set our defenses in place and plan our strategies."

"I understand, my lords."

Bain broke in. "My friend, you have seen such horror. I would that you might take some rest. But our need is too great. Can you do this? Have you the strength?" *Do they understand how deeply Kort suffers from the loss of his lover?*

Kort seemed to understand the concern behind the question, as his rigid stance softened and he managed a weak smile for

Bain. "I will not seek revenge until we have defeated this monster. I know the danger in carelessness driven by rage. And I know I will be useless dead.'" He brought himself to attention, faced the two elder men and bowed. "Command me, my lords."

"You must leave immediately. We need two things." Lord Danza spoke first. "You must let as many as possible know, without leaving your identity exposed more than necessary, that the Lady Phaera has wed Lord Bain and that she now resides with him in Marston."

Kort met Bain's eyes and gave him a broad smile, almost his old self. "Then my efforts have not been in vain. Congratulations, Lord Bain."

Bain could not help but return the smile. "It would not have been possible without you, my friend. I will be forever grateful."

Lord Makin raised an eyebrow in question but did not pursue it, turning back to Kort. "Your second order is to find out as much as you can about the plans and actions of Mathune and his followers. I fear he may already have spies and assassins travelling throughout the lands. You have provided us with much needed news but we need more – much more."

Lord Danza now spoke. "I return to Kinterron at dawn tomorrow. I leave it you as to how you will get information to both Lord Makin and myself. Recruit whomever you trust."

So, he means he will accept Kort's circle of friends as informants. That bodes well.

Lord Makin gave a grave nod. "But we need to keep your identities as safe as possible. Messages must not be written down lest they be intercepted. They must be spoken only."

Kort had gained some colour during the audience. Now he bowed deeply to each man in turn, ending with Bain. "I am sworn to your service and am ready to leave."

Lord Makin went to open the door. As Kort made to exit Bain called after him, "Be safe my friend, be safe."

Kort turned and waved over his shoulder, a small, hesitant smile sketching his lips. Then he was gone and the door closed behind him.

CHAPTER FIFTEEN

A MARRIAGE

Lady Flor placed the gown on a chair next to a small table at one side of the antechamber, upon which stood thee mugs. On the other side, near the wall, stood a small brazier on which a large pot of tea stood keeping hot.

Lady Flor turned to Phaera taking both her hands in hers. "My dear, I can only imagine how overwhelming all this must be." She let go one hand and drew Phaera to a vacant chair, pressing her into it. "I believe we may take time for a calming tea before we prepare you for the marriage ceremony." She indicated the gown with one hand. "Bain has told me how much he admired you in that gown. I thought it more fitting to the occasion than your healer shift."

She hesitated a moment, as though not sure what to say. But she nodded, as if to herself. "Phaera, as you know I have no son of my own. It is a life-long regret. But when Lord Makin legitimized Bain and brought him here to train him as his heir I have come to see what an honorable and intelligent man he is. I have grown fond of him. While I cannot be his mother," she turned to smile at Nurias, then back to Phaera, "I hope you understand that I wish the best for him – and for you. You may rely on me to do what I can to see to the success of this union."

Nurias handed Phaera the mug of steaming tea she had poured as Lady Flor spoke. "We have all been dealt a shock." She poured two more mugs and handed one to Lady Flor before lowering herself into a vacant chair, setting the mug back on the table as she did so. She reached over to pat Phaera's hand. Taking it and rubbing it between her own two she said, "You are cold. Drink your tea and let me prepare a plate of bread and cheese for you."

"Already done, Nurias. Here." Lady Flor handed Nurias a small pewter plate. Nurias broke off a piece of bread and small bit of cheese and lifted it to Phaera's mouth. "Here, child. I know you think you cannot swallow it but you will be surprised. And it will help. I promise."

Still numb, Phaera accepted the mothering from the two women in silence. Once she had finished both the small repast and her tea she found she did indeed feel better.

Lady Flor rose, shook out the gown and held it up. "Come, we have dallied long enough. We will help you dress."

Phaera rose obediently. Once she was dressed the two women stood back to admire her.

"Bain is a fortunate man, do you not agree, Nurias?"

"I do, Lady Flor, and we are both fortunate as well. This will prove a happy match. I feel it. And Phaera, I know that this is what Bain has wished from the beginning. He loves you."

Lady Flor grew serious. "My dear, this is not the wedding we all envisioned, to be sure. Would that this could be a more celebratory occasion, and that you had been more prepared."

Phaera found her voice. "I care nothing for ceremony. I am ready. And I am grateful to you both."

Lady Flor went to the door and knocked. It was opened by Lord Makin. He looked Phaera up and down in appreciation. "I have never seen a more beautiful bride. Come."

Phaera heard a sound across the chamber and saw Lord Danza

open the outer door where the official stood waiting. Behind him stood a scribe holding a formal looking scroll, a quill pen, and an inkwell.

Lady Flor went to stand beside Lord Makin. Nurias led Phaera to stand beside Bain, who waited between each lord, and helped her turn to stand beside Bain. Then she took her place on Lord Danza's other side as he indicated she should. It was the place her mother would have taken. Phaera appreciated the honour this gesture represented for Nurias.

While she stood and listened, as duty expected her to, much of what the official droned did not register. It was just another ceremony, another lecture about duty, another repetition of the tale of the Great Conflagration, the Long Darkness and the Renewal. The only point at which she paid close attention was when Bain took her hands, looked into her eyes, and repeated his vows. His face held so many emotions she could not read them all; pride, eagerness, anxiety – even concern for her, she thought. She kept her voice strong as she repeated her side of the vows. *Strange. I feel more at peace now than I have in many months. Is this what I have wanted? Have I been fooling myself? Or is it only relief that the decision is out of my hands?*

She paid more attention, however when it came time for all to sign the scroll, first Bain, then herself, both lords, Lady Flor - even Nurias added her mark as official witness. This was repeated three times. One scroll would remain in safekeeping at the castle, one with the official and the third would go with Lord Danza to Kinterron. Thus, if one or even two documents were destroyed there would still be another to witness the union. No one would be able to deny it.

When the official and scribe had gone, and the group found themselves alone together again, the air seemed lighter, as though a heavy cloud had been lifted. Lord Makin and Lord Danza shook hands with Bain and clapped him on the back in congratulation. Lady Flor and Nurias embraced him. Phaera, in her turn, was embraced warmly by all four elders. They shared a glass of mead from a bottle and glasses that appeared from behind a chair in a corner.

Soon, however, Nurias announced that she must leave as she wished to attend the new mother and see how she fared.

"I will send guards with you, Nurias." Lord Makin interrupted her. "I no longer believe it is safe for you to travel on your own. You are now not merely an unknown healer and we find ourselves in dangerous times. If you were to be captured it would compromise our ability to oppose Mathune effectively."

Nurias looked about to protest, then, seeing the concern on Bain's face, relented. "Very well, though they may not enter my cabin or apothecary and must keep a distance when I approach those who need my care." She sighed deeply. "I do hope this business is over quickly as I do not relish a future in which I cannot move about freely to do my work."

As soon as she had gone Lord Danza announced, "I fear I must leave by first light. I must see to my men." He embraced Phaera once more. "I will see you, daughter of my heart, before I ride out. I cannot tell you how proud you have made me today. Or how much I shall miss you. But you will be safer here and that gives me some comfort." He examined her face. "You must try to get some rest, ere you fall down from fatigue."

Bain, standing at Phaera's side assured him, "I will see to it, Lord Danza. You have left her in good hands."

"I do not doubt it. I know of none better."

CHAPTER SIXTEEN

IT IS DONE

*L*ady Flor took charge of Phaera as soon as Lord Danza left, whisking her to her chamber for some rest before the evening's banquet, only a few hours away. "Bain, your lady must have some rest. You may claim her tonight."

Bain nodded his understanding. "We have our whole lives, Milady."

Addressing Phaera she said, "My dear, I regret that this banquet must serve as a celebration of your union. Else I would have excused you from attending."

"I understand, Milady."

Lady Flor waved the maid Riya away. "I will attend to Lady Phaera." She soon had the gown off, replaced by a night shift, and pressed Phaera onto the bed, pulling the blanket over her. "Try to rest now. I will return to wake you in time to dress." With that she placed a light kiss onto Phaera's cheek and slipped out of the chamber.

Though the day was still young, exhaustion must have robbed her of any strength Phaera had left. She fell almost immediately into to a deep sleep and knew nothing more until she felt a gentle shaking of her shoulder and opened her eyes to a smiling Lady Flor.

"Good. I feared you would not sleep." She drew the blanket off Phaera and helped her up. "Will you wear this gown again or is there another you prefer?"

As Phaera lifted her shift over her head she replied, "It is the best one I brought. As you know, I am not fond of pageantry, so this one will be fine." With one arm already into her gown she gestured with her free hand. "You will find some jewelry in the case on the table beside my hair brush."

"Good, if you will permit me I can assist you with your hair."

"I would be grateful, Milady. Riya is skilled but at this time your company is more welcome."

"Then I shall not leave your side until we enter the hall." Lady Flor gave her a reassuring squeeze around her shoulders.

A short time later Bain and Phaera were seated side by side at the far end of the long table, across from Lady Flor and Lord Makin. As Lady Flor had seated her she had bent and whispered in Phaera's ear. "Be strong. I cannot stay here with you," before joining Lord Makin.

Bain, already seated, patted her leg secretly under the table and gave her an encouraging smile. She wasn't sure how she felt about the familiarity. Neither of them said much during the banquet, both doing their best to nod, smile, and accept congratulations. When they had eaten, and the musicians began to play dance music, Phaera let Bain lead her onto the floor for the obligatory dance, to the cheers of all present. It was hard for her to treat the traditional bawdy remarks and sexual jibes with good humour. *Must I endure that, yet, ere this night is over? Will they demand stained sheets in the morning? If so they may be disappointed. I have ridden across my mount, instead of side-saddle, too often.* She went cold at the next thought. *Will he believe I am a maid? Can I convince him?*

But Bain surprised her. When they were finally led into their marriage chamber, and left alone in their night shifts, he pulled a small blade from his boot and drew it across his palm, drawing blood. Pulling back the top blanket he smeared the blood in the middle of the bottom sheet.

"You have endured too much this day, my love. This is not the time to expect even more from you. I can wait."

Phaera felt her knees grow weak with relief and gratitude. Before she realized it, Bain's arm was around her waist, steadying her. He helped her onto the bed and lay down beside her, watching her face.

It was more than she could bear. Overwhelmed with the events of the day, and now this unexpected kindness, the dam opened and silent tears streamed down her cheeks, into her hair, and onto the pillow.

Bain tenderly lifted her head to put his arm under it and drew her to him until her head rested on his chest under his chin. Once settled he stroked her hair and repeatedly kissed the top of her head until she slept. They were still in that position when light crept through the window and woke her.

She only realized where she was when she heard the beating of Bain's heart under her ear. When she tried to rise the weight of his arm, slack and heavy, told her he still slept. Taking care not to wake him she slid out from under his arm and raised herself up enough to study him in sleep.

You are a strange man. Would any other have done what you did for me last night? Was it because he was a healer's son? Yet, at court, he acted very much a lord's son. When Bain gave a deep sigh and found a more comfortable position she could not help but admire the ripple of his shoulder muscles. A tuft of curls sprouted between the opening in the neck of his nightshirt. Gingerly, Phaera reached out and touched one, then turned her attention to the sleeping face. *Will war remove the peace I see?*

A distant rumble she recognized as the sound of many horses

jolted her out of her musings. *Papa! You promised not to leave without saying goodbye!* She flew to the window, reaching it just as a knock came to the door. By the time she turned around to answer it Bain had sprung out of bed, instantly awake, and had his breeches half-way on. He reached the door first.

Riya stood there, eyes lowered, a dressing robe over her arm. She held it up, still averting her eyes. "Here Milady. Lord Danza waits in the next chamber."

Relief flooded Phaera as she grabbed the robe and pulled it on, tying the sash as she hurried next door. "Papa. I feared you had gone." She ran into his waiting embrace.

"Did I not promise?" The words, though chiding, sounded more like a caress. They stood like that for a few short moments before he took her shoulders and made her face him. "I must away. I can delay no longer."

"Those horses I saw out the window. I feared you were with them."

"A decoy. We sent a troop ahead and I will follow with another."

That was when Phaera noticed the tunic he wore. "Oh, you wear the colours of Marston."

"Yes, another ruse. The troop that left wears both colours." He took both Phaera's hands in his. "We are at war. I must reach Kinterron safely and see to our people and our land. Pray that this conflict is over quickly and that we may all return to peace."

The words fell on Phaera like a cold wind. "Be safe, Papa."

"And you, daughter of my heart." He drew her close again, then, just as abruptly released her. "Bain is a good man, as is Lord Makin." He looked like he wanted to say more but did not. Instead he squared his shoulders. "I must go. Know that I am proud of you." He strode to the door, opened it, and marched down the hall and away. At the last second before turning out of sight he turned and called back, "Be well, both of you."

That was when Phaera realized Bain had come to stand behind her.

"We will see him again." The worry in the smile Bain gave her belied his faith in his words. In a firmer voice he said, "Come, let us dress and break our fast. Then I have something to show you."

CHAPTER SEVENTEEN

A SURPRISE

As Bain led her outside, flanked just out of earshot by four guards, he said, "My lord father is preparing troops. It is likely I will be sent out with them very soon, perhaps as soon as tomorrow." When they reached an old section of stone wall he pulled out a large iron key and pulled back some ivy to reveal a heavy wooden door.

Once inside Bain took an old torch off the wall and lit it, then told the guards, "Remain here, we may be some time." Once inside he closed the door firmly behind him. "There, now we are alone and can speak freely."

Bain moved along one wall and lit two more torches, in sconces there, before turning to Phaera and spreading his hands wide to take in the space. "Will this suit, do you think? It was Kort's idea, really, to find a place. I told him he was mad but..." When Phaera looked around without saying anything he explained. "It was used for storage, hence the bags and barrels against the walls. But those can be removed and a table and shelves put in. The torches will be replaced with proper lamps. I know my mother would be pleased to help you stock it and set it up."

"What?... How?..."

"It was Lady Flor who showed this to me when I mentioned Kort's idea to her. She did not think it so mad as I imagined. She told me that she is still able to carry on many of the duties of the court and castle, as she has been, and that she would be happy to spare you time to establish as a healer here." When Phaera finally turned, astonished, to face him he opened his hands out in apology, "I had hoped to woo you with this. Circumstances intervened."

He cleared his throat. "But I cannot promise this will be yet. We have not approached my lord father. It will require his approval, though with Lady Flor's support I think he will be persuaded." The thought struck him that the changes of the last days might make it less safe for Phaera to act as healer. *I won't mention it yet. Let her hope this is possible.*

Phaera looked at him, eyes wide. "I do not know what to say. This... this is wonderful ... you ... can this be ...?"

Bain thought he saw a glitter of tears threaten to spill from Phaera's eyes but they did not fall. "I hope so. Perhaps not immediately..."

To his great surprise Phaera suddenly wrapped her arms around his chest and hugged him fiercely. She lifted her face to him. "Thank you ... oh, thank you."

His mouth was on hers and he found himself pressing her against a sack of grain. When she showed no resistance his desire became almost unbearable. He lifted his head to look at her face, then withdrew abruptly, taking her hand and lifting her back to standing. "No!" His voice was hoarse. "This is wrong. This is not how it must be."

When Phaera looked confused he shook his head. "I am not a rutting stag. You deserve better." He clenched his fists to stop them from trembling. "I will wait." He looked away and took a few deep breaths to regain his composure.

They spent some time planning how to turn the huge storage chamber into a working apothecary, then returned to the castle.

Lady Flor met them as they arrived. "I have gained you this one day as a reprieve." She smiled broadly at Bain. "Your father has agreed to suspend your duties until tomorrow, due to your newlywed status."

"But we need to prepare."

"Indeed, but he has already sent orders to gather provisions and troops and says he can spare you this one day." She turned to Phaera. "I told him it is the least he can do. He concurred."

Bain met her eyes, a look of understanding passing between them. *By this time tomorrow I will likely be on my way to the border.* When he looked at Phaera he could tell she had the same thought.

CHAPTER EIGHTEEN

NIGHT

After a meeting with Lord Makin and his advisors Bain confirmed to Phaera that he would, indeed, leave with a cadre of soldiers in the morning.

"I will be leading a band to the left border and Father another, larger one to the right side. A unit has already set out ahead this morning on Father's route and scouts and informers have been dispatched. " Bain looked worried. "We have sent a messenger ahead to Kinterron with our plans – two actually – using separate routes in case one is intercepted. It is hoped we can coordinate with him to protect our borders. Messengers have also been sent to Krellin, Parth, and Neck asking for support. But, as they do not share borders with Belthorn or Exalon they will not feel the urgency we do. Even if they send troops their arrivals will be delayed. This will be our fight, at least for now."

"Mathune must be stopped. We have no choice. He will not hold back as long as he thinks he can win."

"Indeed. And Mathune has declared you to be the prize he seeks. I doubt our marriage will prevent him." Bain took both of Phaera's hands in his. Phaera thought she felt a tremor in them before he squeezed harder. "I will protect you with my life."

"I know it. But it is more important to protect our people. You must take care - to return, to rule. Do not let sentiment sway you from your duty." As an afterthought she added, "And I will do the same." She withdrew one hand to touch his cheek. "Now, husband, we must to dinner so Lord Makin can tell the people we are at war." The smile he bestowed on her at the word 'husband' made the deliberate choice worthwhile. *It is all I have to add strength to this fight.* "And I swear not to do anything that will put me in danger. I will not ride out alone or go anywhere unescorted."

"Good."

The dinner was a sombre affair. While many had not heard of Mathune's actions the few who had added their words of support to the plans, which included how many soldiers would remain to guard the castle.

When the speeches ended and Bain was no longer needed he reached under the table, put a hand on Phaera's thigh, and leaned in to murmur, "We are no longer needed. Let us retire." As she followed him to their chamber he reached back to draw her beside him. "We have only this night. I wish to spend it alone with you."

Phaera felt a prickle go up her spine. *Of course I will give him what he wants. But is it what I want, too?* Apprehension turned to relief when Bain did not reach for her the moment the door closed. Instead he strode to the table and poured two goblets of wine from the flagon waiting there and handed her one.

"To a long and prosperous future. To success in the campaign." Bain took a breath then gave her a look full of hope and intent. "And to a happy and fruitful union."

"May it be so." Phaera lifted her goblet to his, gave him what she hoped was a confident smile, and took a sip. She noticed that Bain did not drink his down either. Instead he set his back on the table, and seeing that she drank no more, gently took hers and set it down as well. There could be no doubt as to his intent when he reached for her and drew her into his embrace.

So this is it... She did not have time to finish the thought. His lips were on hers and his arms drew her tight, his desire pressing against her gown.

"My love." His voice was hoarse in her ear as he reached to untie the sash at her waist, then gently pull the ribbon from her braid and run his fingers through her hair until it cascaded down her back. Then he pushed himself away from her, tugged his tunic off over his head and dropped in on the floor.

The sight of his muscled torso brought back the image of him at sparring practice. *Only short weeks ago? What is that scar on his shoulder?*

His voice brought her back.

"I would see you entire, my love. Will you permit me to remove your gown?"

Permit? It is his right. The gesture gave Phaera a lump in her throat. Unable to speak she gave a small nod and held her arms up so Bain could lift the gown over her head. He dropped it beside his tunic and with feather touches stroked her shoulders before drawing her into a tender embrace.

The contact of her skin against his sent a strange feeling deep into her womb, a heat, a pain even, and she trembled with the force of it.

Bain must have misread the reaction because he loosened his arms enough to look into her eyes, though he did not release her. "I will be gentle my love."

Still speechless Phaera nodded her head and wrapped her arms around him, placed her cheek against his chest and heard the mad thumping of his heart. When she found her voice she said, "I am not afraid." Then she pulled back just enough that she could see the scar on his shoulder. Running a finger along it she asked, "How did you come by this?"

He chuckled. "Nothing brave or noble I fear. A fall, head first, off a horse. I landed in a creek and my shoulder hit a branch stuck between some rocks."

Her hands searched and found another scar, lower down. She felt him shiver. "And this?"

"Weapons practice."

She barely heard the whisper. He had lifted her up and laid her on the bed where he began to kiss her everywhere, beginning with the hollow under her ear, then the one in her throat, his touch so light she almost had to beg him to stop. Instead she closed her eyes and felt that deep ache rise.

When a tiny moan escaped her he kissed her mouth again, rose and removed his breeches before sitting beside her and resuming his explorations with lips, tongue, and fingers. When he finally opened her knees and lay between her thighs, she found her hips rising of their own accord to take him in as she clutched him close. The heat inside her burst and spread over her entire body just as he spasmed, shuddered, and went still, arms still holding her tight.

When he left her and rolled off before pulling her to lie on top of him, she felt a languid peace unlike anything she had experienced before. They lay like that for some time, he stroking her hair and back, kissing the top of her head, she exploring his chest, fingering the moles and small scars as she found there. Neither spoke.

When she was able to think again she found she could not remember parts of what had happened. But the sense of peace persisted. The last thought, before she fell asleep, still lying on top of Bain, was, *"Is this love?"*

CHAPTER NINETEEN

FAREWELL

*P*haera still slept peacefully beside Bain as the first light of dawn woke him. He slid off the bed and dressed silently. Then, knowing she'd never forgive him if he left without saying goodbye, he sat on the bed and gave her shoulder a gentle shake. At first she only squirmed and with a soft moan settled back down. But at the second shake her eyes flew open and she sat up, instantly aware and awake.

"Is it time already?"

"Yes, my love. Will you break fast with me and see me off? We meet in the small dining chamber with Father and Lady Flor."

Bain didn't even have time to finish the request. Phaera was up and pulling her gown on. He admired her lithe body and the smooth movement with which she slid her healer gown over her head before he handed her the sash. She slipped bare feet into slippers, tied her hair into an untidy knot, and stood ready. When he gave her a smile she quipped, "It is good enough for a healer; it must be good enough for a family repast."

Bain chuckled. "And so it must. Come." He tucked her hand in his and drew her out the door into the corridor, stopping briefly for a deep kiss. "What will you do while I am away?"

"I will clean out my new apothecary and begin to set it up."

Bain raised one eyebrow. "Without Father's approval?"

"Lady Flor approves. I will not begin to attend to anyone until you have returned safely. But I need to work or I shall go mad. Lord Makin's permission will come when he sees I am determined."

"Hmmm. I hope so. He is not *your* father." Bain stopped and turned Phaera to face him. "Promise me one thing." When she said nothing he added, "Tell me you will not go foraging for plants and herbs until this war is won and we have returned. I cannot fight well if I must worry for your safety."

Phaera gave him a steady look, then a slow nod. "I understand. And what of your mother? She may also be a target."

"She will not stay at the castle. But we have stationed four guards to protect her at all times. She tried to forbid that but Lord Makin insists."

"Good."

A guard opened the door to the dining chamber to admit them. Before proceeding to her chair she looked at Bain and added. "I do hope she will visit often, as I doubt I shall have the freedom to go to her."

His response was a questioning tilt of the head, one eyebrow raised. "My hope is that she does not dismiss her guards or slip away from them. No one knows the countryside better than she."

The meal was a hurried, simple affair; porridge, cheese, fresh bread, butter and honey, boiled eggs, and sage tea. No one spoke of war; indeed no one said much of anything at all. Lord Makin looked grim, Lady Flor worried.

As soon as they had eaten Lord Makin rose. "Come, Bain, it is time. The first troops have already gone. We join the second unit. When we reach the gate you will split off to the east with half the men to join the fifty that have already gone that way."

He turned to the women. "Ladies, your horses have been

saddled and your guards wait with them. You may ride with us to the gates but no further and must return immediately."

Bain glanced back at Phaera as he followed Lord Makin out. She looked pale but strong. Lady Flor hid her concern less well. He thought he saw her bottom lip tremble before she stilled it between her teeth.

At the gates the four dismounted for their last farewells. When Bain embraced Phaera she hugged him back fiercely. As he let her go she grabbed his arm and said, low so that only he could hear, "Come back to me, my love. Come back to me whole."

Bain's heart swelled with joy. *She loves me. Oh fortune be praised.* But to Phaera all he said was, "I swear it, my love."

The men leapt back onto their mounts. Lord Makin turned to address the troops. "Brave men of Marston. We go to fight an evil. But we will return victorious. We will quell that evil and we will return to peace and to our families. Are you ready to fight for them?"

A roar set up from the men, along with thumping of chests and clanking of swords against shields. Bain could not still a wave of pride and excitement. *May I become such a leader as he. I will make you proud, Father. I swear it.*

With an imperious raise of his hand Lord Makin turned to lead the men out of the gate. Bain hurried to come astride. They exited the gate side by side.

Bain managed one quick glance backward to catch sight of Phaera and raised a hand when he spotted her standing straight and tall beside her horse. When she returned the gesture his last thought, before turning his attention back to his father was, *be safe, my love.*

An hour's ride brought them to the dividing point. Lord Makin turned to Bain. "My son, you know what must be done."

"I will not fail you, my lord."

"If our allies stand behind us this will be a short conflict. But not all will return whole or alive. I need you here as my heir. Do not act the coward – but also, do not act in haste. Your life is more valuable than the rest. Do not forget this."

Bain had heard the admonishment before and, while a part of him wanted to lead and to be the first in danger, he understood the importance of his survival, both to his father and to his people. "I will remember what you have taught me. You may rely on it." *Is that pride I see in his eyes?*

"Lord Bain, lead your men away. May success be with you." Lord Makin gave Bain the traditional salute, fist to heart, and waited.

After returning the salute Bain turned to face the men assigned to him. He lifted his arm in the air fist clenched. "Men, follow me," turned and rode away, not looking back. The men galloped after him in a cloud of dust that soon blocked any view of his father or the men that rode in the other direction. *I will be worthy.*

Bain pressed hard and by midday he and his men caught up to the troop that had gone ahead. Their captain immediately handed over command to Bain.

"Any news, Captain?"

"Nothing, Lord Bain. All is quiet. We will reach the border by dusk. May I suggest we set camp there? The scouts have not returned." He cleared his throat. "Perhaps it would be best to wait for their reports before proceeding."

"I agree, Captain." He met the man's gaze and added, "Captain Reynce, you are a man of training and experience. Never hold back on suggesting strategy to me. While I may not always agree I will welcome your opinions and will consider them."

The captain looked relieved. "I will remember that, Lord Bain."

"Good. Our goal is to win this war. Pride must never interfere."

A short time later a figure slipped from between the trees to their left, arm upraised in salute. The captain raised his arm in reply. "That is Durn, one of the scouts."

Bain nodded and halted his horse, waiting for the man to approach. "What news?"

"Ah, Lord Bain. You have made good time." He saluted before answering. "All is quiet to the north-east. The local citizens say they have seen no strangers and I have seen nothing out of the ordinary."

"Good. Ride with us until we set camp and have eaten. We will await news from the south before sending you with new orders."

The scout saluted and stepped back, making way for Bain to pass. The captain, who had waited behind Bain to hear the scout's report, came alongside.

"Let us hope Merkel also has no news. We can hope that Mathune's men have not reached this far yet."

"Agreed. But I will not assume so even if we receive no news. If his reputation is correct he is devious. I have no doubt he has men who manage not to attract attention."

The captain nodded. "Indeed."

By the time the second scout returned camp had been set and stew kettles bubbled over fires. This scout also had nothing to report. Weary men sat on blankets or a fallen log to the side of the clearing, the only exceptions being the six men the captain had set on watch. These stood looking outward scanning the trees for movement.

A scuffle and muffled voices caught Bain's attention. He turned toward the sound to see two of the guards holding a man by the arms between them and propelling him forward to stand before him.

"This man was found skulking through the forest." The soldier gave his prisoner a hard shake but did not let go of the arm he held.

The prisoner looked terrified. Bain could see that he had not lived rough. His tunic was of fine cloth and his boots had not seen hard use. His hands had no callouses. The man looked like he would be more at home in an inn drinking wine, or dancing at court, than travelling alone in the forest.

"Have you anything to say, sir?"

The man nodded vigorously before stammering, "I carry a message from Kort."

Bain turned to the man still holding the prisoner, the other having let go but still ready to grab him should he try to run. "Let him go. He is here to speak to me." Bain looked around until he located the captain and caught his eye.

At a jerk of Bain's head the captain set down his bowl of stew and hurried over. The prisoner still stood, shaking visibly, the two soldiers only a step away, ready to seize him. "Leave us. I am in no danger." The soldiers backed off, looking dubious.

Bain turned his attention back to the prisoner. "What is your name?"

"Ferrin, my lord."

"Welcome Ferrin. You have news?"

"I do."

"Captain, have one of the men bring our guest food and drink. We will meet in my tent." He turned back to Ferrin. "Come. We will not be overheard there."

Bain's tent had been set up to one side a short way apart from the rest. The corral with the horses stood between his tent and the forest guarded by two of the men on watch.

"So, Ferrin, what is the message from Kort?"

The three men sat huddled on the floor of Bain's tent.

Ferrin had stopped shaking but still looked nervous and had difficulty controlling his stammer. "I come from Thoren in Kinterron. Kort…" he looked at Bain. When Bain nodded recognition Ferrin continued. "He met with myself and two others at an inn and informed us of your need." When Bain nodded again he said. "We are all sworn to your service."

"Thank you. Please go on."

Ferrin hesitated, sending a sideways glance in the captain's direction. When both men remained silent he took a deep breath. "I overheard three men sitting at a corner table. They spoke quietly but I have excellent hearing ... they said ... Mathune has sent spies to Marston. They knew Lord Danza and Lady Phaera had journeyed there." He stopped and a small smile played over his lips. "I do not think they knew of your marriage, Lord Bain. I congratulate you."

When Bain's only response was a nod he went on, suddenly serious and frightened again. "They said Mathune would have her before the passing of a fortnight. They laughed over Mathune boasting that 'the healer would need a healer' ... Forgive me Lord Bain."

Bain felt as though an icy wind passed over him. "How many men? Do you know?"

"They did not say."

"Spies ... so not obvious. Did they say anything about what route they would take?"

"Nothing, Lord Bain. This is all I know."

"How long since you overheard this?"

"Evening before yesterday. I came immediately to bring the news."

"You have done well." Bain knew the man was exhausted and ought to rest. But Phaera and Lady Flor, possibly even his mother, were in danger. "Ferrin, are you able to go on to Marston castle? The commander there must be informed immediately. I hope we are not already too late."

Ferrin hesitated only a moment, then seemed to swell as he drew himself up. "I am sworn to your need, Lord Bain. Command me."

Bain almost smiled at the gesture. *He is so unprepared. Yet he is willing. I must use him.* Aloud he said, "I am in your debt, Ferrin. Go to the castle and inform Captain Raskir, the commander of the guard. He knows that Kort is in our service and will admit you and hear you. Or Lady Flor or Lady Phaera, whomever you see first." He thought a moment. "I have another idea. Nurias is a healer in the village south of the castle. Go by that route. If you find Nurias first you must tell her also. Your presence will be less suspect speaking to her than trying to approach the castle. Nurias knows about Kort and your band as well. If you see her first she will know the best strategy for informing the castle."

"Your mother, Lord Bain?"

"Yes, and fearless. But do not forsake your own safety for speed. It is imperative that you deliver the message. Do not be found out."

Bain stood and Reynce and Ferrin followed him out of the tent. "Come. I will have food sent with you."

"Thank you, Lord Bain. I will not rest until I have informed them."

"Good man." Bain shook Ferrin's hand. "Most important – do not get caught. Capture will render you worse than useless."

Ferrin slung his pack, now bulging with food, over his shoulder and slipped between the trees into the darkness.

Bain watched him disappear. *Good luck. May fate be with you – and all of us.* The knot in his gut tightened. *I promised to keep you safe, my love. But here I am, helpless.*

CHAPTER TWENTY

IN MARSTON

No one spoke on the way back to the castle. Phaera was left alone with her thoughts. A look at Lady Flor's sombre expression told her that lady's thoughts mirrored her own - worry about the safety of their peoples, their husbands, their futures.

Phaera had lived in peace all of her short life, a peace that had enabled her unprecedented freedom. Now, it seemed, she would be stuck in the castle with little to do. Lady Flor would still manage the household, leaving Phaera at loose ends. *Must I go mad? I need my work.* A sideways glance at Lady Flor, withdrawn and pale, warned her that this would not be a good time to bring the issue up.

Though she could see everyone going about their usual business, clearing tables, carrying clean linens into bedchambers, and getting directions from their betters, a pall hung over the castle. The usual cheerful chatter was missing, as were the smiles and shouted orders in the halls. *I need to find something useful to do - now.* The aromas coming up from the kitchens drew her in that direction. Memories of finding friendly companionship in the kitchens of Kinterron as a child, where Cook had shown her how to bake bread, among other skills, lured her in the direction of those comforting pastimes. *Lady Flor may not approve.* Noticing that Lady Flor seemed unaware of her presence Phaera hung back until she could slip down to the kitchens unseen. The mood in the kitchens was not much better but the preparation of food had a soothing element. Phaera felt it as soon as she entered.

"Milady?"

The head cook's look of surprise brought the tiniest bit of amusement to Phaera. She held her hands out, palms up. "Velna, these hands need work. Tell me what I can do."

Velna shook her head as she began a stammered protest, but Phaera cut her off.

"Velna, you know I am a healer. I am accustomed to work. I know how to use my hands. Please, there must be something I can do that will help." To her left, on one of the long trestle tables, she spotted a bowl of bread dough ready to be kneaded. She walked decisively over, gesturing toward it as she did so. "This looks like it needs some attention."

"I..I was about to send Myra to knead it, Milady."

"Then send Myra to some other necessary task." Phaera had reached the table and, without looking for approval, gave the dough a few satisfying punches, where it deflated with a few high-pitched squeaks. She looked over to smile at Velna, "I am not new to this." She turned her attention back to the yeasty dough, grabbed a handful of flour to dust the table, dumped the dough out onto the surface, and began the rhythmic punching, pushing and turning that would bring a smooth spring to it. A sideways glance at Velna revealed that woman gaping in surprise. Phaera ignored her and kept on with her kneading. Velna left.

About ten minutes later Phaera rolled her dough into a smooth springy ball and placed it back in the waiting wooden bowl, spread a damp linen cover over it and set it aside to rise again. She spotted Velna at the other end of the kitchen, her back to Phaera, directing some scullery maids.

A survey of the table Phaera had worked on brought a mortar and pestle into view, surrounded by fresh herbs at the far end. *Mmmmm, these will be for the mutton stew.* With deft hands, she soon had the herbs ground into an aromatic paste. A sense of someone coming to stand behind her shoulder made Phaera turn to see Velna, wearing a look of both surprise and approval.

"Well, Milady, it seems you do know your way around a kitchen. Thank you for your assistance." She lifted the linen off the bowl and peeked at the dough. "And I see you have done this before." She poked a finger into the dough where it left a springy dimple and turned to smile at Phaera, though with a lingering uncertainty.

Phaera's answering grin seemed to remove the last hesitation from Velna's face. Phaera knew she had won a friend.

"Yes, I feel much more at home in a kitchen or an apothecary than dancing in a fine gown at court. You will see more of me here."

"If it pleases you, Milady, you are welcome at any time."

"Good. Now put me to work. What do you need?" Phaera gestured to another group cutting meats and loading platters. "I can wield a knife, too."

By morning's end Phaera's spirits had lifted enough to join Lady Flor and their ladies for a simple meal of greens and herbs from the gardens, wild mushrooms cooked in lard, sliced roast venison, cheese, bread, and butter, all helped down with either sage tea or ale.

Lady Flor eyed her. "I missed you this morning. Where have you been? Surely you did not leave the castle?"

Phaera laughed at the veiled admonishment. "No, Milady. I needed to be busy and useful, so I worked in the kitchen. That platter of meat was cut with these very hands." Lady Flor's relieved smile amused her. "However, kitchen work will not satisfy me for long. We must discuss how I may begin setting up my apothecary. While I hope it does not happen, I want to be prepared for any injured men returning from the field. They will deserve the best care we can give. Nurias already has her hands full."

Lady Flor studied her hands before finally raising her head to face Phaera. "Yes, I understand your need and your desire to help. I have no wish to thwart you, Phaera, but we must proceed with the greatest caution. Let me make some inquiries as to how you may be protected. It may take a little time. Can you promise you will bide with me until this can be sorted?"

"How little time, Milady? I will wait, to be sure, but I need to begin as soon as possible."

"Give me two days and we will speak again."

"Thank you. I will satisfy myself with kitchen work until then." Phaera paused, thinking. "Or, in the meantime, perhaps I can gather some supplies from within the castle, such as herbs from the kitchen gardens, and begin to prepare them there, as well as bandages and other remedies. That is if Velna can spare me a closet or corner."

Lady Flor brightened. "An excellent idea."

Phaera had no idea what preparations Lady Flor had in mind but knew enough to let her have the two days. She worked in the kitchen again next morning before approaching Velma. "Do you think you can find me a small space where I can gather supplies and create some remedies and potions?"

Velma thought for a moment then led Phaera behind a wall at the far end of the kitchen where a narrow stair led up to the gardens. Under the stair was a small closet with a door that could be locked. When Phaera entered it her nose told her it had once held herbs and spices, though those now graced shelves on the walls of the kitchen itself. On one wall, and under each step, narrow shelves had been built, now covered with a thick layer of dust.

"If this will suit, Milady, I will have it cleaned for you."

Phaera clapped her hands in delight. "Yes, this is exactly what I need. The only thing missing is a table to work on, but I will use a corner of one in the kitchen as there is not space for one here." She gave Velna a conspiratorial grin. "And I shall clean it personally. It will allow me to organize the space in my mind."

Velma tried to protest but Phaera waved her off with a firm gesture.

By the time Phaera and Lady Flor were to meet to discuss the outside apothecary again, the small closet was filled with everything she could glean and prepare from items available within the castle and its gardens. It was a start but a far cry from what she needed. Before meeting with Lady Flor she stood to survey her paltry stores, wondering what arguments would convince the lady to support her quest to open and supply the one Bain had shown her. Certainly a show of temper, or pressure, would not work. Under the current circumstances she was not sure even her father would agree. With a deep sigh she closed and locked the door and sought out Lady Flor. Her only available strategy was logic and logic often lacked the power to convince when emotions ran high.

The discussion began much as Phaera expected, that is to say, not well.

"My dear Phaera. I understand how important this is to you, and I would like nothing more than to see you have your way. But, as you, yourself, know, keeping you safe must take precedence. We have both sworn to see to it. I have spoken with the head of the guards left behind, and he refuses to even consider it. He says it is impossible to ensure your safety if you leave the walls of the castle."

"But the back entrance is almost at the wall of the castle. Only a few steps from safety."

Lady Flor shook her head in exasperation. "That is a few steps too many. It takes time to unlock and open a door."

Phaera knew she was right. She remained silent for a moment, thinking. "Milady, there may soon be soldiers and others coming in with injuries who need my help. If I cannot do it from that apothecary we must find a way to do it within the castle."

"If that were possible I would help in any way I can." Lady Flor's shoulders relaxed slightly.

"It may be." Phaera leaned closer to Lady Flor. "If we can find a larger space within the castle … it need not be well appointed. All I need is space for shelves, a table long enough for a man, two chairs, access to water…"

Lady Flor looked cautious but did not immediately protest. "I suspect that is not all is it?"

"No, that may be the easy part. I need supplies, herbs, roots and such that can only be gathered outside the castle walls, some quite a distance away." When Lady Flor's hands began to flutter in protest Phaera took them in her own. "I know I cannot gather them myself. But if I were to make a list and someone were to deliver that to Nurias…"

Lady Flor sat straight, removing her hands from Phaera's grasp. "I fear that would put her in greater danger, and take time away from her own work."

"Should that not be Nurias' decision? I believe she would want to do it, in case something happened to her. Then there would still be somewhere and someone people can go to for help."

Lady Flor regarded her silently for a long time. Then she rose heavily. "Make your list. I will try to find a space for you. If Captain Raskir can spare a man to deliver your request, and Nurias agrees to the plan, some part of it may be possible." Part way to the door she turned back to face Phaera. "But you must swear that you will, on no account, leave the safety of the castle." When Phaera hesitated, she added, "I must have your oath on this or I will do nothing."

"Very well. You have my oath. And Lady Flor, I do appreciate how difficult all of this is for you, with Lord Makin absent. I swear I will not endanger the castle – or myself."

With a small nod, and a look of relief, Lady Flor left.

And now I will explore the castle in earnest to find a suitable space.

CHAPTER TWENTY-ONE

THE DREAM

*T*hough the rest of the night remained uneventful, Bain tossed for most of it, thoughts of Phaera in the hands of Mathune or his cronies preventing sleep. Yet, toward morning he fell into a restless slumber.

PHAERA, RUNNING THIS WAY AND THAT. NO MATTER WHICH WAY SHE turned another enemy soldier appeared to grab at her and block her flight, sneering and mocking. Bain reached for her but his hands turned to mist before his eyes. He tried to shout, but he had no voice. His legs seemed planted deep in the earth and could not move. Run, Phaera, run!! But his scream was only a strangled breath. The further Phaera ran the more crazed, wild men chased her until he was sure she could never escape.

BAIN WOKE IN A SWEAT, HEART POUNDING, ARMS FLAILING. "No!" This shout brought him back to the present. He was in his tent.

Phaera and the enemies were not here. As he sat up to shake the dream off he heard a soft call outside his tent.

"Lord Bain, is all well?"

"Yes." He crawled to the tent flap and lifted it to see a concerned face peering in. "I am fine – a dream, that is all. Go back to sleep."

The young guard smiled. "I am on watch Milord." He gestured to the sky. "Dawn is breaking. Soon we will all be up."

Bain looked to where the man had indicated. The first light of morning made it barely possible to see beyond the fires. The sun did not yet show above the trees but the sky was lighter there.

"Ah, no sense in going back to my blankets, then."

"No, Milord. The cooks have already stoked the fires and are stirring the porridge. Tea will be ready. Shall I fetch some tea for you?"

Bain unfolded his body as he emerged from the small tent. "Thank you, no. I am up and will fetch it myself. I take it there is nothing to report?"

"Nothing."

"Good, you may resume your post." He walked to the cookfire and was handed a mug of chicory root brew. The hot, bitter liquid sent the last vestiges of lethargy from his limbs. Cup in hand, he strolled about the camp, greeting his men as they woke, giving each a nod or word of encouragement, just as he had seen his father do. By the time he completed his rounds and returned to the fire the porridge was ready. He was handed the first bowl, a large, yellow spoonful of butter melting on top. He took the bowl, a second cup of the strong, wakeful tea, and found a log to sit on. He could still watch the men, and they him. Though the log lay at the edge of the forest, several paces from the others, he believed he still had enough space at his back that he would not be taken by surprise. *It is good to sit alone.*

He had swallowed the last of the porridge and tea, and risen to return the bowl to the cook, when he spied one of the sentinels waving frantically in his direction, sword drawn.

"Lord Bain, on your left!" The man pointed. Bain only had time to drop the bowl and draw his sword from the scabbard at his waist as two men set upon him. *How did I not hear them?*

He managed to knock one sword away with his own, putting his assailant off balance, and whirled to meet the other, but not before feeling a searing pain slice into his upper left arm. That pain put him into automatic fighting mode, a result of thorough training. By the time his own soldier joined him in the fray, followed by two others, he had spun in an arc, sword sweeping upwards through his opponent's belly and across his chest. That man fell with a scream. Bain pivoted, looking for the second assailant, only to find the man lying inert on the ground, a sword through his chest. His three protectors looked at him with what must be a similar expression to his own.

Realizing the danger was past his men wiped and sheathed their swords before rushing to examine Bain's arm, where bright blood dripped freely from his sleeve.

Bain had forgotten the injury but now the pain returned as the red haze of battle left him. He held up his other hand to forestall the men. "I will live." He pointed the tip of his sword at the man he had felled. "That one yet lives. See that he remains alive until I question him. We must learn what he knows."

The troop's medic had appeared, opening his pack on the run.

Bain waved him to the injured man. "Keep him alive and able to talk. I will bandage my own arm." He sliced off his sleeve with the dagger from his boot so he could examine his wound. "This needs stitching." He met the medic's eyes. "I have what I need in my tent. I will return as soon as I have tended to this. Have *him* ready for questioning when I return."

He strode to his tent, leaving the medic staring after him, open mouthed.

One of the youngest soldiers followed him. Bain looked at the man. "How are you at needlework? This is an awkward place to reach to do it myself."

"Milord, the medic…"

"The medic is busy." By this time Bain had found his own healers' pouch and opened it, extracting needle, fine thread, and the herbs for a poultice to prevent festering, which he mixed with some water to make a paste. He threaded the needle and held it out to the soldier. "Hold that." He took a bottle of spirits and poured some into his wound, trying unsuccessfully to hide a grimace of pain. Then he took back the needle. "Here, I will show you how by doing the bottom stitches. Then you must finish as I cannot reach well enough to finish the top."

The man watched closely, his expression anxious, as Bain made the first three stiches.

"There, you see how it is done. Finish it. Be sure to hold the edges of the wound together and use as many stitches as will fit. If they are too far apart they will not hold well … and the scar will be much bigger." He handed the man his needle.

The soldier's hands shook, and he looked a little green, but he took the needle and began stitching.

Bain watched and coached him on how to make his stitches look neater. "I am a vain man, sir. You must do a pretty job." A reassuring chuckle wiped the sudden, fearful look from his man's face.

"It is finished, Milord." The man let the thread slip from the needle.

"Good, now cut off the loose end. I will place this poultice over it and then you can help me get the bandage in place."

As soon as it was finished Bain tore off his bloody tunic and pulled on a fresh one. He gave the soldier a clap on an arm, smiled and said, "That was well done. Come, it is time to question our enemy before he dies."

On their return they found the injured prisoner propped against a tree. The medic had managed to staunch and bandage much of the bleeding but it was clear the man would not live long. Such wounds never heal.

The dead man lay where he had fallen.

Bain had a strong aversion to torture. It went against his training as a healer with his mother. Now that he had calmed down, and knew he would recover, he dreaded what he might have to do to get the man to talk. One look at the hate-filled glare on the prisoner's face told him it would not be easy. The man surely knew he was dying, and that even if he did not succumb to his wounds he could not be left alive.

Captain Reynce had arrived and now eyed Bain with a questioning look. "He has refused to tell us even his name, Milord."

"Then it is good you are here, Captain. He *will* talk, one way or another." Bain swallowed hard and faced the prisoner. "You have a choice. Answer all our questions, fully and honestly…" When he saw the defiant smirk the prisoner gave him he added, "Do not concern yourself with lies. I am trained to recognize falsehoods." Bain lowered himself to a squat, eyes level with those of the prisoner. Indicating his own arm, he smiled. "You see you have failed. Your fellow is dead while I am well and my arm will recover fully. You, of course, will die. But you may choose how you will die. If I am satisfied that you have told us all you know, you will receive the coup de grace and be put out of your misery. I would prefer that choice but…" Bain watched the man's eyes flicker to Captain Reynce and back again. Bain let the unspoken threat sink in.

"Of course, if you do not cooperate death could be long coming, and very, very painful." Bain reached over and removed the bandage. He shook his head and tsked in mock sympathy. "That will surely fester. Dying from a gut wound … well I am sure you know what to expect …" Leaving the bandage loose he rose to his full height and barked, "Your name?"

When he received no response his gut clenched. *I am not made for this. How will I get through it without making a fool of myself and losing the respect of my men?*

The captain interrupted him with a touch on his arm. "Lord Bain, a word if you please." He moved out of earshot of the group with Bain in his wake. On the way he gave the prisoner's leg a sharp kick, jolting him into a cry of pain.

Keeping his voice low, and sending many meaningful looks toward the prisoner, he said, "Keep your voice low. Nod even if you disagree with what I say, and look at him the way I do. It will unnerve him further."

Bain nodded and did as instructed but said nothing, wondering what the captain had in mind.

"Lord Bain, I think everyone knows that this is the first time you have interrogated an enemy. This is only my third time, so I understand that it is difficult. But we both know that this is a test you must pass."

Bain nodded along with the captain as both sent glares toward the prisoner, who missed none of them. "Thank you Captain. I am grateful for any guidance you can give me." He kept his voice level but his gut churned with fear and loathing for what he knew he had to do.

The captain nodded. "You have made an excellent beginning, Milord. It was a good gambit."

"How do you suggest we proceed, Captain?"

"You *will* need to hurt him. Ask me to assist you, to hold him. I will see to it that he cries out whenever you hurt him. I will cause the most pain, but you must be seen as the one in charge. And it will help if it seems you are the one causing his pain."

"Captain, I..."

"My Lord, it is a common strategy, to do this as a pair. I understand. I do not find satisfaction in it either. And I will see to it you get what you need, both from the prisoner and in the eyes of the men. The first time *should* be difficult. If it were too easy I would doubt your ability as a leader."

"Thank you, Captain. I will follow your lead."

"Good, but do not make it obvious." Captain Reynce gave him

a grim smile and turned back in the direction of the wounded man. "You first, Lord Bain."

With a curt nod and another glare at the prisoner Bain strode back to take his place, the Captain right behind.

Bain gave another sharp kick at the prisoner's boot. "Your name?" When all he got was a pained grunt he said, "I see you have made your choice. So be it. You may change your mind at any time. There is no one to carry your failure to Mathune, no one to see your shame." He gave the boot another kick, harder this time. "Is this what you truly want?" When there was no response Bain shrugged and, without taking his eyes off the prisoner said, "Captain, this man will need some persuasion. Sit behind him so he will not be able to try to move away… and there is no need to be gentle."

"Yes, Lord Bain."

Captain Reynce moved the man roughly aside, then crouched on his haunches behind him, one knee in the man's back, partly to prop him up, but also to allow for maximum pain should he use the knee to inflict it. The man screamed and let out a string of curses.

Bain schooled his face to remain impassive and regarded the man's wound casually. "Ah, I see the bleeding has resumed." He squatted to take a closer look. "No, I do not think it will end things too soon. I will leave it open. Do you agree, Captain?"

"I think he will last long enough to tell us what we need to know."

Bain caught the captain's quick look of approval. *You would not approve if you knew I am about to lose my porridge.*

To Bain's great relief it took only ten minutes before the man begged for mercy. Between screams of pain and sobs of shame as the captain thrust in his knee and jerked his shoulders back every time Bain jabbed him or kicked him, he told them all he knew. When it was done Bain turned to the young soldier who had run to his aid and stitched his wound. "I would know your name, sir."

"Jessin, Lord Bain."

"Jessin, you have done well today. I give you the honour of delivering the coup de grace. You have earned it."

Jessin began to gape but closed his mouth immediately. "Th… thank you My Lord." The look on his face was a mix of fear, reluctance, and pride.

"Now, Jessin. Do not leave him in agony any longer. Use your dagger and slit his throat. It is his wish and he will feel little. It will be over instantly."

Jessin gave a nervous nod, pulled out his dagger and obeyed, shutting his eyes as the knife went through.

"Well done, Jessin. I know it is not easy to kill a man who cannot fight back." He clapped the young man on the shoulder. "And now I know I can count on you to keep your head in battle."

Bain strode toward his tent, beckoning the captain to follow. *I am a coward. I ought to have delivered the cut. Now poor Jessin will bear the burden of my cowardice.*

Captain Reynce followed him into his tent. "That was well done, Lord Bain".

Bain shook his head as he sank to the ground. "No, Captain, it was not." He dropped his head into his hands. "Poor Jessin."

"It was a good lesson."

"The final blow ought to have been mine. You need not flatter me."

Captain Reynce remained silent for a time. "Lord Bain, I do not think the men will see it that way. And Jessin will be a hero."

Bain just shook his head, his face still in his hands. "It was *my* duty."

The captain picked up the flask of spirits from the small stand, shook it to determine it still had liquid in it, and thrust it toward Bain. "Drink, milord. It will clear your mind."

Bain took the flask without looking up, tipped it to his mouth and emptied it, ending with a fit of coughing.

The captain waited a few moments before speaking in a low

tone. "Milord, there will be other opportunities. For now, the men need to hear from you. You cannot remain here. You must speak to them. They rely on you for strong leadership."

Bain barked a harsh laugh. "Leadership…"

"Yes, Lord Bain. It will not wait." He rose as if to exit the tent, and waited in an expectant stance, one hand toward the tent flap as if to hold it open for Bain.

Bain rose with a groan. "You are correct, of course. I thank you."

"I am here to serve, milord." The captain opened the flap and followed Bain out.

CHAPTER TWENTY-TWO

FERRIN

*P*haera was still exploring all the unused spaces in the castle looking for one that would suit her need when angry voices and sounds of a scuffle caught her attention.

The hall at this end of the castle led to a small dungeon and ended in a door to the outside, so prisoners need not be paraded in front of the inhabitants or servants. The door had a strong lock which could only be opened from either side with a heavy, ancient, key. Since this part of the castle was rarely used it was lit with rush torches set into sconces high in the wall. Curious, Phaera lit the one nearest the door with her candle and looked about for where the key might be kept. She did not see any spot that could hide it.

Hearing a key grind in the lock from the outside sent a frisson of fear down her spine. She backed into an opening, out of sight and in shadow, and blew out her candle. One hand went to the dagger she kept in a pocket under the folds of her dun healer's gown, and drew it out, ready.

The door opened inward and three men stood limned in the glare of daylight behind them. Phaera recognized two as castle guards but the one held between them was unfamiliar. The man was bedraggled, and looked about to faint from exhaustion. His clothes, though covered in the dust and grime of travel, looked to be of good quality cloth and well made. The soles of his shoes flapped, ready to fall off altogether. They had not been made for hard use, the leather being soft and fine.

Phaera could see that the man could no longer keep himself upright, but he seemed determined to say something. His voice was hoarse and cracked as he protested but she made out a few words.

"Must speak ... Lady Phaera ... Lord Bain ... message ... spies ... danger..."

As he spoke the guards manhandled him past Phaera's hiding place and opened the door to the first cell, dropping him in with a rough shove that ended in a pained "umph" from the prisoner.

As the guards locked the cell and turned to leave one said, "You will speak to the captain of the guard when he sees fit." Shaking his head he sent a derisive snarl to his partner. "Speak to Lady Phaera, indeed."

When they got to the door his partner looked at the torch. "How did that get lit?"

The first one shrugged. "No matter. Leave some light for the prisoner so he can see his future."

The carelessness and callous attitude of the guard made Phaera fume, but she held still until she heard the key grate in the lock again, and the pair trudge away. Once she could no longer hear them she slipped out of her hiding place, relit her candle from the still burning torch and took it toward the cell door. On the way she spotted the niche in the wall where the keys to the cells hung on a nail. The location of the outdoor key remained a mystery. *Perhaps that is just as well. The temptation to use it might be more than I could manage.*

As she peered into the cell she could hear the prisoner mumbling and groaning. She thought she could make out the words, "failed ... too late ... forgive me, Lord Bain..." and quiet weeping. Her first impulse was to speak to him and question him, but her healer role took over and she could see he would not last long if he did not get water. He lay face down, and had not seen her candle flame, so she took a moment to look for a source of water. Every dungeon must have one as prisoners needed it to survive. She walked in the other direction from the door, lighting another torch as she passed it. When she approached the far end she heard the trickling of water. She had almost dismissed it as a leak and turned away from it when the candle flame glistened on liquid too large to be a mere leak. On closer inspection she saw that a spout had been carved into the rock wall directing a tiny stream of water into a clay urn underneath, from which it overflowed and disappeared into a crack in the floor. To one side stood a small stool covered in a thick layer of dust. On it, barely visible through the dust, was a chipped clay cup.

Phaera picked up the cup, returned to the spout and sniffed the stream. *Some sulpher.* She placed one finger in the stream and held it to her lips. *Not the best I have tasted but it appears safe.* She rubbed the dust from the cup, cleaned it as best she could with her fingers, and filled it to the brim, taking it to the niche with the keys. Certain the man was too weak to present a danger she unlocked the cell and knelt in the stale rushes beside the prisoner. He had gone quiet but when she touched his shoulder he started and let out a long groan.

"Sir, I have water." She set the cup down and placed an arm under the man's shoulder, turned him and helped him lift his head and shoulders, then picked up the cup and held it to his lips.

He drank greedily until he had emptied it. "More…"

"Let that settle for a few moments or you will not hold it down." Phaera lowered him back to the floor. "I am Lady Phaera. I heard them bringing you in. You mentioned my name and Lord Bain." She watched for the man's reactions…

His eyes had been closed as she put him down, but now they flew open. "You? … You are Lady Phaera?"

"I am. Who are you?" She brought the candle closer to her face so he could see her, then set it down again. "Who sent you and why have you come?"

The prisoner struggled to sit upright, a slow smile of astonishment spreading over his face. "My Lady?... Fate be praised, I am not too late." He stared at her as if to reassure himself.

"I see you have travelled hard, sir, risking your own health and safety. Tell me who you are and why you have come." She held up the cup. "Then I will fetch you more water."

He barely glanced at it, continuing to stare at her as though entranced. "Lady Phaera…"

Phaera grew impatient. "Sir, your name."

"It is Ferrin, Milady."

"Good. Who sent you?"

The man looked confused. "Kort … that is … Lord Bain … that is … I have a message."

When he looked about to fall over, shaking with the effort to remain upright, Phaera gently guided him back down. When he shook his head in protest she said, "Ferrin, you are in no condition to be concerned about protocol. You have heard of my dislike for it, I am sure. Rest here and I will bring another cup of water before you give me Lord Bain's message."

With a grateful look Ferrin let his eyes close his shoulders relax as she rose with the cup.

When Phaera returned she found Ferrin asleep, snoring softly, his face relaxed and a small smile playing about the corners of his lips. *Kort's man. So loyal. You do not deserve the aversion men have for you. I shall see you are rewarded for this service.* Knowing that there was no immediate urgency to hearing him out, as they would not likely be interrupted for some time, she let him sleep while she examined him more closely. He had clearly never seen hard labour. His hands were soft, with a few blisters from holding onto his pack, which lay beside him where the guards had thrown it.

She removed his shoes and winced at the broken, oozing blisters there. *I will tend those as soon as I move you to better quarters.* His tattered clothing hung loose over muscles that had grown too thin. She watched the peaceful rise and fall of his chest for a moment before pulling his pack toward her and looking inside. *And empty water flask. Dried salted meat which he was too weak to chew, with no water to get it down...* She set the pack aside with a sympathetic shake of her head. *Poor man. I must wake him and hear his story before the guards bring the captain.* With great reluctance she placed her arm once more under his shoulder and shook him gently.

Ferrin woke with a start, wild eyed. Then, on seeing Phaera, he calmed and helped her as much as he could. With her help he downed the second cup. "I thank you, Milady."

"Are you strong enough to give me your message and tell me what happened?"

"Yes, thank you, Milady."

"Take your time and leave nothing out. Here, let me help you to the wall so you will have some support."

With some grunting and effort Ferrin soon leaned against the stone wall, legs long in front of him, breathing hard.

"Rest a moment, Ferrin. I have nothing to eat but I can bring more water."

Ferrin gave her a grateful nod so she went for a third cup. When he had drunk that one he looked slightly stronger.

"First my message, Milady, as it is most important."

Phaera said nothing, only nodded her understanding.

A frightened look came over Ferrin's face. "Mathune ... He has sent spies here. He means to capture you ..."

Though the news was not unexpected, it still sent a shiver down her spine. "Thank you, Ferrin. I will inform the others. Your news does not surprise me. How long have you known of this?"

"Four days. I ... sought out Lord Bain. Kort sent me. I found him at the border. Lord Bain said I must inform you at once – or

Lady Flor, or Nurias – or the Captain of the guard. But those two guards would not believe me."

"Do you know how many?"

"I am not certain but I believe there are at least four ... and they mean to infiltrate the castle. They may be familiar to the court and be thought of as allies. I fear they may be here already. Please, Milady, you must all be careful."

"Did you meet or hear of Nurias?"

"No, Milady. I passed close by her dwelling but as I needed to remain hidden I could not inquire after her. And I needed to inform you as quickly as I could."

"I assure you, that has not gone unnoticed. Your bravery and loyalty will be rewarded." Phaera rose from the floor, where she had been kneeling facing him. "Ferrin, in order that we do not arouse suspicion among the guards, lest they come back before I am able to, I must lock you in again. I am going to make arrangements to move you to more deserving quarters. You will not remain here long."

"Thank you, Milady. I understand."

"Let me help you back to where they left you. Rest until I return. I will come soon with help." Phaera snuffed the second torch, left the first smouldering its last, and hurried in search of the captain of the guard. *What is his name? Oh, yes, Raskir, Captain Raskir. Lord Makin said the captain knows of Kort's men and will treat them as allies.*

Along the way through the castle she came upon a worried Lady Flor. "You have been gone so long. Where did you go?"

"Come with me and I will tell you as we walk. There is not time to stop. We must speak with Captain Raskir." As they strode side by side Phaera explained what had happened.

"Spies? Here already?"

"Likely, yes." They exited the castle, flanked by four guards who joined them at the door, and headed for the practice yard where they knew the remaining guards not on duty would be sparring under the tutelage of the good Captain Raskir.

He spotted them as they approached and hurried over. When they had told him what they had learned he said, "That is bad news indeed. I know of the prisoner and have sent the two guards back to fetch him to me here in the guardhouse. Wait." He looked around until he chose two of the better swordsmen and beckoned them over. "Two others have been sent to retrieve a prisoner here from the first cell in the dungeon. Find them quickly. Tell them my orders are to treat the prisoner as a guest and to show him every respect as they help him here. He is an ally, not an enemy."

With a quick salute the two jogged off.

"Captain, the other two were very rough with Ferrin. I do hope they do not harm him further."

The captain only looked at where the two men had gone, then beckoned Phaera and Lady Flor. "Come, I have been ordered to keep you both fully informed." He ushered them into the guard room, indicated two stools, closed the door, and sat on the third stool facing them.

Lady Flor half rose. "Perhaps I should go and have a chamber prepared for our guest."

The captain shook his head. "No Milady. Lord Makin insisted you be fully apprised. I think it prudent to remain and hear what Ferrin has to say, and what steps I decide to take to find these spies and see that you come to no harm."

Lady Flor resumed her seat, her expression leaving no doubt that she had no wish to remain.

CHAPTER TWENTY-THREE

BELTHORN BORDER

Bain walked among the men. They had set up camp at the border where Marsten met both Kinterron and Belthorn. The day had been without incident. Bain grew impatient as he surveyed their fires and tents, knowing that they could go no further without reports from the scouts. He needed more information about Mathune's whereabouts and what he and his men were doing. He also chafed at not being able to return to protect Phaera and the others at Marston Castle. Inactivity did not sit well with him.

A scout from Kinterron arrived with a message from Lord Danza. "Lord Bain, we have troops on the border further west and have set up camp there. Have you messages to take back to Lord Danza?"

A messenger from Lord Makin also showed up to say they had set up camp to the east. That meant four units, two from Marsten and two from Kinterron were stationed at strategic points, two on the Kinterron border and two on that of Marston.

Bain called the scouts together with Captain Reynce, around the small fire in front of his tent. It sat somewhat apart from the rest, providing some privacy but still well guarded. "As yet, we have received no word of reinforcements coming from our more northern allies. Scouts have been sent with that request. As none of them border on either Bethorn or Kinterron it is possible that they will wait to see if it is necessary."

Bain turned to the two scouts. "Where is Mathune and has he shown his hand in any way? Tell us both what you know and what you suspect."

Before the two could speak a skirmish broke out at the edge of the forest, from the direction of Kinterron. Two guards led a man roughly to the edge of the light from the fire. One asked, "May we approach, Milord?"

"Come."

"Lord Bain, this man claims to have a message for you. We have disarmed him." The soldier, a sneer on his face, held up a short, ornate dagger.

Bain met Captain Reynce's eyes and received a small nod indicating he understood. "You may leave the dagger with me. Let the man be seated and bring food and ale for him. He is an ally."

The man gave Bain a grateful look as he sank to the ground next to the scouts. "Thank you, milord."

"You are welcome here. Tell us your name, sir, and the news you bring." *I will not mention Kort. Reynce is aware. Best to keep that secret from the scouts.*

A soldier arrived with a bowl of stew and a large mug of ale, which, with a nod from the captain, he handed to the newcomer and hurried away.

"I am Kelthin, Milord, and come by way of Belthorn, near the border with Exalon. Mathune is amassing troops and making for that border."

Bain nodded. "We have that area well protected."

"But it is suspected that he uses this as a ruse, to draw help away from Exalon. He has imprisoned Erstine, son of Lord Dern. Lord Dern is dead, some say with help, as I suspect you are aware. With Erstine imprisoned in his castle Mathune is running amok in Exalon. There is no one to oppose him. He systematically, with his loyal cronies, hunts Erstine's friends and any men of influence who had been loyal to Lord Dern. It is done in secret, under cover of darkness. In the mornings the people find the bodies, some mutilated, women and girls raped, children stabbed or throats cut. It is slaughter, Milord." Kelthin paused and hung his head with a shudder. "Others he kills … in the most cruel ways." The stew remained in the spoon untouched. He glanced at it. With another shudder he shook his head and set it aside.

Bain leaned toward him, picked up the cup of ale and placed it in the man's hand. "Drink, Kelthin. You have need of it."

Kelthin raised horror filled eyes to Bain, took the cup as though in a daze, squeezed his eyes shut and gulped half of it down. When he met Bain's gaze once more he whispered, "Such horror, Milord, such horror."

"I understand. You need not say more about that. What else can you tell us? What do they say is Mathune's aim in this?"

"The people of Exalon live in terror. More and more, they turn informant against their neighbours and friends. All of Exalon is in chaos. They warn that Mathune will publicly execute Erstine and take his place. He uses the promise of a return to order to prevent any rebellion against his coup."

Captain Reynce broke in. "This looks like a purge to gain total control of a fief that has been in disarray for some time. The people desire order. That promise may well induce them to submit. What have you heard of incursions into Kinterron or Marston? You say there are troops at the border of Marston that appear not to threaten ours yet."

"I have nothing more on the troops sent to the border at Marston, sir. But I believe the real threat is from Exalon." Kelthin turned back to Bain. "I have no specific information, Milord, but based on the activities in Exalon I fear there may already be many spies in both Kinterron and Marston. Mathune brags …"

"Go on."

"He brags that he will have Lady Phaera at any cost. That he cares not what he must do to get her, even if it means killing anyone in his way." The man shot Bain a fearful glance but said no more.

Bain clenched his fists tight, hoping his panic did not show on his face. "There is more you are not saying. I must hear it."

"Forgive me, Lord Bain. I cannot."

Phaera! Bain scrubbed his face roughly with both hands. "No matter, I have heard enough." *If Ferrin was correct, it has already begun. And I can do nothing about it. I hope he reached Phaera to tell her.* He took a deep breath. "This is not new to me, Kelthin. I received earlier information that he has sent spies to Marston and with just that purpose. I thank you for your service."

He looked at the two scouts. "What have you to add?"

They both shook their heads. One said, "This concurs with what we have learned, Lord Bain. We, too, believe the troops at the borders are a smoke screen. Mathune has no honour. His actions make it clear he will not obey the rules of conflict."

Bain turned to Reynce. "Captain, we have much to discuss. See that these men are well looked after for the night and meet me in my tent."

The captain rose along with Bain, and with a short bow, left to signal a soldier to carry out Bain's orders.

Bain stood rigid in the centre of his tent, his hair brushing the oiled canvas, and clenched his fists, filled with rage and with fear for Phaera. Even so, he could not prevent the deep shudder that overtook him. *Mathune must be stopped, whatever the cost.*

He turned his head when the tent flap opened to admit Captain Reynce and gestured for him to sit. Then he sat as well, facing the captain.

"I have ordered strong mead to be brought, Milord. We need fortification."

You mean I need it. Aloud he said, "Thank you, Captain." He took advantage of the pause until the drink arrived to gather his wits.

When they each had taken their first swallow Bain met the captain's gaze. "Captain, we cannot sit here waiting for the enemy to attack. While our original strategy was to carry on into Bethorn and engage Mathune's troops this new information makes me think that needs to change."

"I agree Lord Bain. Have you a plan in mind?"

"Captain Reynce, I am a proud man, but not so proud that I cannot admit when I have less knowledge and experience than you. My desire is to rush back home to protect those in the castle, though I am painfully aware that is not possible. Another is to find Mathune personally and kill him like the cur he is – again, not possible or wise. But one thing is clear to me. We, too, must abandon the rules of conflict. We must fight him on his terms or we will lose. My thought is that we must enter Exalon, where Mathune is engaging in his campaign of deception and cruelty. And we must hunt him and his followers down with the same stealth he uses. We must also steal back into Kinterron and Marston, where I suspect he, himself has gone to capture Phaera or kill Lords Makin and Danza. But I admit I question whether my instinct is borne from rage or reason. And reason must prevail if we are to succeed."

Bain took in the thoughtful nod from the captain. "So Captain, as you have the greater experience in both training and strategy I ask for your advice. Be frank. I will listen and consider. Then we can discuss together before agreeing to a plan."

"Lord Bain, you have asked me to be frank and I take you at your word." He paused a moment, as if trying to find the right words. "Milord, you are young and new to leadership. Yet, in my opinion, you have already demonstrated qualities I look for in a leader. You must not underrate yourself. Eventually self-doubt will interfere with your judgement and your men will see it. That must not happen, especially now, when we fight an enemy with no honour, one who ignores the rules of conflict. Whatever plan we make, you must show confidence in it. It is wise to have doubts within oneself. Overconfidence leads to costly mistakes. But your men must not see those doubts." He looked at Bain and waited.

"I thank you Captain, and I will keep that in mind. However, we need a plan and I need your help in devising it."

"That is what I am here for. I will help you, but the men must see it as your plan. And I agree with your assessment. The rules of engagement will not win this war."

"I understand. Thank you."

Darkness fell long before they emerged from the tent. When the men spotted them they all gathered by the central fire.

Bain scanned his troops wondering how his unusual plan would strike them, whether it would cause them to doubt his leadership. He glanced over his right shoulder and received an encouraging nod from Reynce.

"Men, some of you have already heard. For those of you who may have heard but misunderstood you all need to know that we face an unusual enemy, one who fights by stealth, one who uses pain, fear, and cruelty to achieve his goals. His aim is not, as one would normally expect, to annex another fief, or to rule more people, and amass more wealth in doing so. Mathune's aim is to create such chaos that friend cannot be distinguished from foe, that even father cannot trust son, nor husband wife. He does not engage us face to face, but acts under cover of darkness, and slips away leaving the dead to be discovered with the dawn. The strategies of war that we have been trained in are useless in the face of such an enemy."

Bain took in the rapt faces of the men, many with frowns of confusion, others curious, striving to follow what he said.

"Men, listen closely, for what I tell you will be far from what you expect." He scanned the men again before continuing. "At dawn you must all have broken your fast, have packed, and be ready to depart. The cooks will give you rations for several days each. They will distribute these along with your morning porridge." Bain paused to let that sink in.

"We will not depart together. By full light you will have received your orders from Captain Reynce and myself. You will be split into pairs. Each pair will be given separate orders as to where to go, what to look for, and what to do. You will be sent in many directions. You will be given tactics in how to seek out the enemy, how to engage him, how to gather information, and when and how that information will go to those who need it. You will wear civilian clothes and leave your uniforms behind."

As Bain watched the men glance at each other in confusion, he added, "That is all you need know for the moment. Get what sleep you can. This will be the last night we will spend together until this war is won. And it *will* be won. We will defeat the enemy at his own game. Dismissed."

Bain turned on his heel and strode back to his tent, Reynce alongside.

The Captain chuckled softly. "I doubt there will be much sleep had tonight. No uniforms? That alone will make them uneasy."

"Indeed, Captain, indeed. I hope their thoughts will prepare them for more of the unusual as they receive their individual instructions."

When they reached Bain's tent he turned to the captain and clapped him on the arm. "Sir, you, too, are in need of rest. I will not need you for the rest of the night."

The captain rewarded him with a broad smile. "As you wish, Milord ... and well played." He saluted smartly, turned, and strode away.

Bain watched as the darkness swallowed him. *If you could see me as I do. Am I an imposter?*

CHAPTER TWENTY-FOUR

TREASON

*F*errin recovered quickly with rest, good food, and Phaera's care. By the third day he told Phaera that he wanted to be useful and needed to get his strength back.

"Good", Phaera said, "Perhaps you can wander the castle and see if anyone seems to look oddly at you, or you may overhear something that might indicate if we have already been infiltrated. Any small thing would be helpful."

"Gladly, Milady."

"And, tomorrow, if you feel well enough, I will send you to seek out Nurias. She has most certainly eluded her guards. I am concerned for her welfare and also have an important message for her." Phaera had one of Ferrin's feet in her hands and applied salve to the healing blisters. "I think we can do without bandages today but we must find you more suitable shoes if you are to prevent more of these". She pointed at the biggest sore. "And other clothing if you are to travel without arousing suspicion."

Phaera called to a maid passing by in the corridor. "Mira."

Mira backed up and stood in the doorway. "Yes, Milady?"

This man needs new clothing. Find a warm tunic, vest, breeches…" Phaera eyed Ferrin. "…in dun and green, I think. Also two pair of soft stockings and serviceable shoes. They must all be of good quality but not new." She waved Mira on and turned her attention back to Ferrin. "We shall see how walking with stockings and shoes works today. If I see no further injury you leave tomorrow to find Nurias. Walk as much as you can today without re-injuring your feet."

"You are most kind, Milady. I am eager to be of service."

"And so you shall, though I wish it were not necessary. You must join us at dinner tonight. I will send someone for you."

"You honour me, Milady."

"You have earned that and much more, Ferrin."

By the time Phaera had seen to all his wounds Mira returned with the clothing.

"Thank you, Mira." Phaera took the bundle, gave it a short, critical glance, nodded, and placed it on the bed. "These will do nicely." Last, she examined the shoes and held them against the soles of Ferrin's feet. "Yes, these will accommodate the extra stockings." She looked up at Mira with an approving smile. "Thank you, Mira. You may go."

Mira dipped a small curtsy and left.

"So, you are free to explore, but stay inside the castle. I look forward to seeing you at dinner." She smirked before adding, "The green suits you, I think." Not waiting for a response she turned and left.

I dare not send a scroll with him lest it fall into the wrong hands. Now that I have found a space in the dungeons, and an outside door, I need supplies to fill it.

On her way to her newfound apothecary chamber she commandeered two men who looked less occupied than they ought to be. "You there. I need assistance with preparing an apothecary." To the one on the left she said, "Find me a table long enough for a man to lie on. If you cannot find one then find some planks and make one. I will be in the cell furthest from the door." As the startled man hesitated she added, "I will also need planks to make shelves to attach to the walls, and braces with which to attach them."

When the man still hesitated she barked, "Tell me your name."

"Dunth, Milady."

"Dunth, you have a job to do. Go."

"Yes, Milady." Dunth gave a short bow and hurried away.

I like him not. It seemed as if he did not know me at first. I must have Captain Raskir check him out.

She faced the other man. "And who are you?"

"I am Kennitt, Milady."

"Kennitt, tell me what you know of Dunth."

"He is newly hired, Milady. We are assigned to making small repairs and searching out vermin."

"Where did he come from?"

"I am sorry, Milady, I do not know. He has been here only two days."

"I see." *Yes, he must be watched.* "Well, Kennitt, you will be assisting me today with cleaning that cell and putting up shelves. Water is not plentiful there, so I have already had three large crocks brought. You will fill them at the source and bring them to me."

By this time Phaera had reached the cell, Kennitt following close behind. She took one torch, already lit, from the wall and lit two more, then took one into the cell and lit two tallow lamps she had already brought the day before. Lastly she lit a torch in a sconce on the far wall. "There are the crocks. Take one and follow me. I will show you where to get water." She set the original torch back in its sconce before striding to where the water trickled out of the spout in the wall. "This will take some time. I go in search of a broom and rags. Use the first crock to fill the bucket in the cell."

She watched as Kennitt placed the lip of the crock under the spout, where he had to hold it on a slant to get it to fit.

Phaera watched for a moment and sighed. "This will take too much time. I must find a better way."

"Indeed, Milady. Perhaps someone can be assigned to see to it the crocks are kept full."

"Yes, I will see to that. I daresay you will not be finished before I return." She strode away to find her supplies. *I will need two stools and a cot ... and many jars and bottles. I can get those and a mortar and pestle from the kitchen.* She smiled to herself. *Velna is eager to help, and curious as to what I have found. I will invite her to bring supplies from the kitchens so she has an excuse to see the space.* A low chuckle escaped her. *No doubt she will be shocked and think it most inadequate.*

Along the way back to the kitchens, seeing the extra guards who had been posted throughout the castle after Ferrin's arrival reminded her to be more careful. *Captain Raskir has not been informed of the location of my new apothecary. A guard ought to be there as well.* She motioned to a guard in plain clothes whom she recognized. "Sorkin, I have a message for Captain Raskir. Please tell him we need at least one guard posted by the cells as I have claimed one for my apothecary. Also, there appears to be a new man working with Kennitt, one Dunth. I need to know where he is from and how he came here. I do not trust him." She gestured with one hand in the direction of the barracks. "Quickly. He will wish to act immediately on it."

"Right away, Milady." Sorkin strode off, stopping only long enough to indicate to the next guard to cover for him.

Velna greeted Phaera with a broad smile. "Milady, it is good to see you here again."

The warm greeting lifted Phaera's spirits and allowed her to forget her suspicions for a moment. She sniffed the air. "What is that delicious aroma? Honey cakes with currants?"

Velna laughed. "You have a good nose Milady." She turned, hurrying to fetch one from the long table where they sat cooling. "Here you are, Milady. Still warm."

"Ah, you know the way to my heart," Phaera laughed as she

took a big bite, making Velna beam. Out of the corner of her eye she spotted the guard posted near the door, trying unsuccessfully to remain serious, while each maid whose duties gave her an excuse to come near him, flirted openly. The playful scene and the guard's obvious discomfort almost made her laugh aloud.

Velna followed her gaze and gave an exaggerated sigh. "I shall have to scold them again, though it does no good."

"I daresay the young man enjoys the attention. But it distracts him. Perhaps I will say something before I leave." She turned back to Velna. "But that is not why I have come. I have information for you and require your assistance if you are able."

"Anything, Milady."

"I have found a more suitable apothecary ... in the dungeons." *Aha, that got your attention.* "Once it is prepared the things under the stair will be moved there. But I need to gather many more supplies. I hope to have sources for the herbs and remedies I need from outside the castle. To that end I will need many small jars and bottles, even some larger ones, and most importantly a serviceable mortar and pestle. Perhaps two, a small wooden one and a large stone one. I cannot take those that you need here, but perhaps you know of some that are not in use."

"You may rely on me, Milady. But the dungeons? Surely there is a more hospitable space that will suffice?"

"I am afraid not. It is close to an outside door and a source of water, albeit a disappointing one."

By this time Phaera had finished the honey cake. Velna reached out to snag another one but Phaera shook her head. "One is more than enough, Velna. Thank you." She looked around the kitchen. "Where may I find a spare broom and several rags for cleaning? The cell has not been used for some time and is filthy."

Velna sent her a shocked look. "Surely you will not clean it all yourself?"

Phaera laughed. "Not this time. I already have two men assigned to the heavy work. When they have finished I will request some women for the rest of it, at least until it is ready for me to start filling the shelves. That is when I shall send everyone away and enjoy some privacy." Velna's relieved look made her smile to herself.

Her good humour fled when she reached the dungeons and heard angry voices from her new apothecary. She drew out her small dagger and held it hidden between the folds of her split riding skirt, her choice of dress when not at court, tucked the front flap that covered the split into the cord at her waist and crept silently forward. When she came close enough to peer into the cell she spotted Kennitt, his hands trussed behind him, seated on the floor against one wall. Dunth, his back to her, had a torch in one hand and pointed a sword in Kennitt's direction with the other.

"Silence, or I will gut you."

Kennitt pulled his feet back as Dunth thrust the sword threateningly in his direction. Then Dunth turned his attention back to the torch and began to thrust the burning end into the stale rushes on the floor. When the damp reeds did not immediately catch fire he growled his impatience.

Let me remember my lessons, Papa. Phaera eased into the light to catch Kennitt's attention and held a finger to her lips. He gave a frightened nod.

Dunth must have seen some movement in the shadows because he whirled toward Phaera with his sword at the ready.

Knowing that her dagger would be no match for the sword Phaera feigned a jump backward. When Dunth lunged wildly and nearly lost his balance, she ducked under his arm into the cell next to Kennitt. *Kennitt, you are no fighter, but I need your help.*

When Dunth again lunged at her with a wide swing Phaera was ready. She jumped back as far as she could, just out of reach of the sword. "You need me alive, Dunth. Mathune will not be pleased to see his prize injured or dead." She still kept her dagger hidden.

That seemed to take Dunth by surprise. He hesitated before lunging again, this time feinting to deliberately miss her.

Kennitt had been watching closely but Dunth took no notice of him, having eyes only for Phaera. As Dunth took another step forward for a lunge, Kennitt stuck out a free leg between Dunth's two. He swung it hard into the back leg. Dunth lost his balance and almost fell but managed to regain his footing. The effort took his attention off Phaera for a split second.

Phaera leapt forward, and slashed at Dunth's neck, the only part of him within reach, cutting him but not deeply.

Dunth snarled an obscenity as he wheeled back at Phaera. His sword swung wide and wild. This time he did fall.

He certainly is no trained soldier. Phaera was ready. She backed out of its reach, leapt onto Dunth's back to make sure he completed the fall and plunged her dagger between his ribs. In the next instant, she jumped up and stomped hard on the wrist above the hand that held the sword, sending it clattering away. With one smooth motion Phaera pulled out her dagger and swapped it into her left hand. She leapt to grab the sword before Dunth could reach it with his uninjured hand. She settled the sword into her fighting hand with another smooth motion. Without hesitating, as Dunth made a mad reach for her, she swung the heavy sword down hard on his fighting arm, severing it above the wrist.

Dunth now writhed in pain and fury, bleeding profusely from both the arm and his back.

If I am to question him I must slow the bleeding or he will die in minutes.`

As if Dunth understood, he stopped writhing and lay still, grabbing the severed arm above the cut to slow the bleeding. He said nothing but his eyes begged for mercy.

Phaera reached behind Kennitt to cut his bonds with her dagger, keeping the sword at the ready. "Tie his feet and knees." Kennitt hurried to obey. "Now find two guards. This man needs to be questioned. Hurry."

"But, Milady, I cannot leave you."

Phaera did not look at him but barked a short laugh. "I am safe enough, Kennitt. He will not harm me. Go."

As Kennitt ran off she set the sword behind her out of Dunth's reach, tore a strip from her gown and used it for a tourniquet on the arm. Then she rolled Dunth over with one foot, face down, and applied pressure to the wound in his back. *I doubt he will survive. But he must live long enough for questioning.*

Kennitt returned with two soldiers. "Here we are, Milady. And word has been sent to Captain Raskir."

"Good work, Kennitt." She turned to the two soldiers and jerked her head to the other wall. "See that plank there? Bring it. Place the prisoner on it to carry him to the barracks. He must remain face down and I must keep pressure on the wound or he will bleed to death before we can question him."

Their efforts were to no avail. Dunth took his last breath moments after they reached the barracks. Raskir hurried to meet them.

Phaera clenched her fists by her sides as she let out a long curse. "No! Filthy scum. No!" She sank to the ground, her legs no longer able to hold her, the battle rage no longer sustaining her.

"Mead," Raskir barked at one of the men before kneeling beside Phaera. "Milady, you are suffering from shock." He reached for the cup his man handed him. "Drink this. It will revive you."

Phaera took the cup and gulped it down in one draft. Then her whole body began to shake. From somewhere, someone wrapped a blanket around her shoulders.

Raskir still knelt beside her. "You are safe, Milady. You are safe. It is over."

As Phaera's shaking slowed he said, "Let me help you up into the guardhouse. You can collect yourself there."

Phaera brushed him off with one raised hand, remaining as she was on the ground. "I failed. I had him and I failed."

"No, Milady, no one could have done better. You are

unharmed. The enemy is captured and dead. No one could have done more."

But I killed a man. I am a healer, and I killed without hesitation.

When Phaera finally stilled she met Raskir's gaze. "See that Kennitt is rewarded. He saved me." When Raskir nodded she added, "I am weary. Please escort me back into the castle." When a soldier attempted to support her under an arm she shook it off, once more in control of herself. "I can walk." She took several steps, each one more sure than the last, then addressed Raskir over her shoulder. "Captain, I leave it to you to inform Lady Flor."

"It shall be done, Milady. Rest."

CHAPTER TWENTY-FIVE

CLOSE ENCOUNTER

Bain addressed the young man beside him. "Jessin, you will accompany me. Your courage in delivering the coup de grace to our prisoner shows me you are a man of loyalty and courage, just the man I want by my side."

The memory of that day still haunted Bain. He knew he ought to have given the mercy cut himself. Daily, he questioned his ability to rule and to lead. He was torn between his early training at the side of his mother, saving lives, and his current duties which might require him to take lives without a thought. He knew the other men would not think twice about killing an enemy in combat. Did his turmoil make him weak?

Jessin's eyes widened at the words, followed by a proud squaring of his shoulders. "Thank you, Milord. I am honoured."

They spoke little that first day in Exalon. The people who ventured into the streets, mostly men who had no choice but to open their shops, to tend their work, and to find the food for their families, did not meet their eyes. At one cottage a mother hustled a small child who had wandered into the street back inside. No children laughed or played. No women came out to the shops.

The silence left an eerie pall over the scene, leaving Bain in no mood to break it. He suspected Jessin felt the same.

Bain spotted a large, dark stain on a wider, cobbled street, still slightly shiny, unmistakably dried blood. As they passed it he jerked his head toward it to catch Jessin's attention. Keeping his voice low he said, "They have taken the body away. No doubt we shall see more such." He stole a sideways glance at Jessin, whose pale face and pained expression confirmed that the young man shared his horror. Like him, Jessin's hand hovered near his sword, as if expecting to be confronted at any instant.

Bain kept mostly to the alleys and lesser used pathways. "We are two men together, both armed. That alone may draw attention. We must remain as inconspicuous as possible." Bain had explained this to all his troops. Now the warning felt almost unnecessary. It seemed everyone here did their best to remain as invisible as possible.

Yet, nowhere did they see men in the livery of Belthorn, or indeed, Exalon. When they entered a narrow alley where they would not be overheard Bain turned to Jessin. "Either Mathune's men have gone, which I doubt, or he has ordered them not to wear their uniforms, just as we were informed."

"It will make it more difficult to detect them, Milord."

"Indeed. Keep your ears open to any conversation you can pick up. And watch the people. If they appear to specifically avoid anyone they will be the ones to watch."

"Understood."

A scream pierced the air just as the pair reached the end of the alley. Jessin drew his sword and made to rush out but Bain grabbed his arm, holding him back. When Jessin looked at him in surprise Bain held the forefinger of his free hand to his lips, shaking his head. He waived Jessin to stand behind him. He crept to the exit, his back tight against the wall, and peeked out. Two men disappeared at a run into the next alley. On the street a woman knelt over a body, keening with grief.

Bain turned to Jessin. "I must help this woman if I can. If she is approached by both of us she may run. I need to question her. Only show yourself if I am in clear danger or signal that it is safe to do so."

At Jessin's reluctant nod Bain added, "If something happens to me I need you to remain out of sight so you can bring the news to Captain Reynce." He peered into the street again. Seeing no one coming to the woman's aid, or alternately, returning to attack her, he slipped out and came to squat beside her, though the woman seemed not to notice.

"My good woman, what has happened here? Who has done this?"

At the sound of Bain's voice she jerked as though struck and scuttled to the far side of the body she had been cradling. She looked about to run away but at seeing Bain kneel on the other side she hesitated. She crouched, watching Bain wide-eyed, hunched and rigid, ready to flee.

"I have no wish to harm you. Please, let me help you take this man to a safe place."

The woman gave a wild shake of her head and choked out, "He is dead."

"Yes, I am sorry. But he needs to be removed from the street. Do you know him? Do you wish that he be taken somewhere where he may be treated with some dignity?"

Bain watched a little of the tension seep from the woman, though she remained wary.

"My husband."

"I am sorry. Do you wish to take him home?" Bain looked around, noting that the disturbance had not brought anyone outdoors. The street was still bare.

"You endanger yourself, sir."

"No matter. I am trained to protect myself."

By now the woman had risen to her feet and stood waiting, as if undecided.

Bain rose as well. "Wait a moment. I will return to help you take your husband home but I must do one thing first." Bain slipped back to the waiting Jessin.

"I will take this woman's husband's body to their dwelling. Follow me but remain unseen if possible. Only come to my aid if I am accosted. When darkness falls I will step outside and light a pipe. That will be the signal that it is safe to approach. I hope this woman has information, perhaps even food and a dry place to lay our heads tonight."

"Understood, Milord. Be safe... but, you do not smoke. Do you have a pipe?"

"No, you will give me yours." Bain held out a waiting hand. He returned Jessin's low chuckle of amusement.

Bain looked out to see the woman about to leave, shoulders sagging, head down. Making sure no one else had arrived he strode out toward her, and called to her, his voice low. "I am back. I will help you now."

She turned half-way back, looked over her shoulder and waited.

Bain knelt by the body and lifted it into his arms as though cradling a child. The man was not tall and surprisingly light. *Lack of food, no doubt.* As he neared the wife he murmured, "Lead the way. I am right behind you. Anyone who sees us will think I am a friend."

The woman hurried ahead in silence until they reached a poor cottage not far away. She entered without looking back, leaving the door open. A young girl rushed toward her then stopped midway and froze. As Bain entered the dwelling she backed away into a dark corner.

The women indicated a blanket she spread on the floor.

As Bain bent to lay the body down he heard a choked sob behind him. "Papa?"

The woman, still silent, drew her daughter into her arms, squeezed her tight, then pressed her back to stand behind her.

Bain lifted a corner of the blanket and covered the dead man's face before standing to face the pair.

"Is this the work of Mathune's men?" At the stiff nod of affirmation he asked, more gently, "Can you tell me what happened?"

The woman began to shake and looked about to crumple to the floor. Bain grabbed one of two stools and set it behind her, helping her lower herself onto it. The child fled back into the shadows.

Bain pulled out his flask from the pouch at his waist, uncorked it and held it to the woman's lips until she took a swallow.

Returning it to his pouch he retrieved the only other stool and sat to face the woman. "Why was your husband slain? Why did they choose him?" Then he caught himself. "Forgive me. I forget myself. Please, what is your name?"

The spirits had calmed the woman a little and she shook less violently. "Mag, sir."

Bain could hardly hear her. "Thank you, Mag. I saw two men leaving. I heard nothing before that, and so believe this was a planned attack. Those men knew you and your husband would be there at that time. They wanted you to see."

When the woman remained silent and wrung her hands into her apron Bain made an effort to soften his tone. "Madam, I am not from Exalon but I know there is treachery about. I know that Lord Mathune is behind it and have come here to help. But I need information."

When Mag lifted her head and met his eyes Bain tried again. "Why was your husband there?"

Mag began, hesitantly at first, then all in a torrent. "We were told to meet a friend. We were promised oats, a few eggs, and cabbages. They said it would be too much for one person to fetch and I must come, too." A great sob emerged before Mag was able to continue in a long wail. "But it was all a lie! They attacked from behind. One grabbed me and made me watch." Her face contorted with the horror. "The other called Girn a traitor. He cut his throat and threw him to the ground. Then they ran."

Bain drew out his flask again and offered Mag another swallow. "Mag, I know it is difficult for you to speak of this. Think a moment and try to remember who your Girn has spoken with in the last few days. Who would think him an enemy and wish to see him dead?"

Mag shook her head in confusion. "Girn is a common man, sir. He fixes things. We are poor and often those he fixes for can only pay in eggs or vegetables. He is not important."

By this time the young girl had sidled up to her mother. Mag wrapped an arm around her daughter and drew her face into her shoulder where the child began to sob quietly.

Realizing that Mag needed some time, and that both needed comfort, Bain stopped questioning. He scanned the hovel for food. Seeing only a small cauldron of thin, cold porridge hanging on the hook in the hearth he reached into the pack he had dropped inside the door and pulled out his rations of dried meat, beans, and journey bread. Under those he discovered a chunk of hard cheese.

He bent over the cauldron and sniffed. "Mag, this porridge smells good but I have some things to add to it. I will rekindle the fire and stir in this meat. In an hour we'll have a fine meal with my bread and cheese." Without waiting for an answer he poked the fire to uncover the banked embers and added three solid sticks of wood from the pile beside the hearth. When they caught flame he swung the cauldron over it. He cut his meat into small pieces and stirred them in with the wooden spoon hanging on a thong on its peg in the wall.

He took only a surreptitious glance at Mag, pleased to see her eyes less fearful and her posture less rigid. Then he found three wooden bowls and placed them on the table. With his knife he hacked the dry cheese and bread into chewable chunks and divided them beside the bowls.

That done he turned to Mag. "Madam, where are your cups and spoons? I see your kettle there. Where may I find water? That stew may need more and I have some sage that will make a nice hot tea."

The simple, homely gestures seemed to rouse Mag to her duties as hostess. She stood up slowly, disentangling herself from her daughter, and reached for the kettle. "Here, I will fetch water."

Bain handed it to her, grateful that he would not need to expose his presence outside.

By the time they had all eaten, and sat warming their hands on chipped mugs of tea, Mag had revealed that Girn's last "fixing" had been for a stranger staying at the inn. When the stranger had refused to pay him Girn had protested, and called out for the magistrate. He had returned home angry and empty-handed.

By now darkness outside had dimmed the hovel so that only enough glow from the fire remained for them to move about without bumping into things. Bain drew out Jessin's pipe, stuck a small piece of kindling with which to light it into the embers, and nodded to Mag. "I have a friend who travels with me. I told him to remain hidden. He also will not harm you. May I invite him inside?"

At Mag's timid nod of assent he opened the door and stepped outside, limned from the back by the remaining glow in the hearth.

From around the corner Jessin emerged into the deserted street and silently followed Bain back in.

Mag handed him a bowl of the porridge stew and gestured at him to take a stool at the table.

CHAPTER TWENTY-SIX

PHAERA'S DECISION

When Phaera's monthly bleeding began, a few days late, her initial reaction was of profound relief. To her surprise she also felt a fleeting sadness before reason prevailed. *I cannot have a child now. I am not ready to die. I need to establish my healing work.* What struck her even more was how much less urgent that felt. The fear of childbirth was still terrifying but now she also felt an indefinable sense of missing something. *What is wrong with me? Am I going soft? Am I losing my good sense? Stop this nonsense. There will be time for it later - much later. Besides, it is not safe now. This war must end first. Mathune must be destroyed and peace re-established.*

She dismissed the pang of regret and gave it no further thought. Instead she searched the small chest of remedies she always kept with her whenever she travelled. She began to feel anxious when what she sought did not immediately come to hand. That ebbed in a rush of relief when she spotted the tiny, familiar sac under a number of other items. Soon she had the herb steeping on the brazier in her chamber. *Bain will not be happy but I must make him understand. I am not ready. I will convince him.*

As the hot, bitter brew warmed her she knew she had made the best decision. There would be many years to give Bain the heir he needed. She knew the tea was not foolproof. Some women still conceived even when drinking it daily, but it reduced the chances of quickening. It was better than nothing.

The bigger worry was whether she could obtain more of the herb. Being cloistered in the castle prevented her from hunting for it or even asking Nurias for help. *Would she even help me? Or would she see it as treason? It is a well- kept secret among healers. Is it even lawful here as it is in Kinterron? Even there it is seen as suspect.*

Phaera retrieved the sac from where she had placed it on the fireplace mantle and peered inside. *Enough for a month, perhaps. I must procure more.*

A knock on the door brought her out of her reflections. "Enter."

Mira opened the door, a troubled look on her face. "Lady Flor requests that you meet her in the small dining chamber off her apartment. She says to tell you Captain Raskir is already present."

"Thank you Mira." Phaera put the sac back into the small chest and placed it on the mantle beside the cup. Then she took a small key from the chain at her waist and carefully locked the chest.

Phaera caught Mira's puzzled frown as she left the room. *She cannot suspect what I am doing.* She strode to the meeting wondering, with a pang of concern, what could make it so urgent and private. When she walked through the door held open for her by the guard she stopped short. "Kort!"

"Milady. It warms me to see you well."

Phaera took in Kort's emaciated state and the pain etched on his face. She sat in the chair next to him and seized his hand in both of hers. When Kort winced she quickly loosened her grip but did not let go. "But you are not well, my friend." A closer look showed her swollen knuckles and cracked, reddened skin. "When we are finished here I will tend to your pain. You may tell me more about that in private."

"I have no wish to speak of myself when so many have suffered more."

"Yet, you shall. I insist."

Kort rewarded her with a wan smile.

Raskir cleared his throat.

Phaera let go Kort's hand, giving Raskir a nod of confirmation.

"We have business to discuss," Raskir began. "Kort has not relayed all of his news to me, asking that he need only tell it once to all of us together." Raskir turned to Kort. "You have our attention, sir."

Kort took a big gulp from the goblet of wine in front of him, his hands shaking. "You have spies in the castle – at least one, likely more."

Raskir interrupted him. "Yes we have discovered one already. Or rather Lady Phaera did. He is dead."

A look of profound relief swept over Kort. "That is well. But there may be more, both inside and outside the castle. I am glad to see you both so well guarded." He met the eyes of Phaera and Lady Flor in turn.

He shifted in his chair with a wince of pain. "I have sent out men and they have spread into both Exalon and Belthorn. Several have already given their lives." He ran a hand over his eyes, heaving a great sigh. "Others have brought information. I have already told you the first. Mathune appears to have left Belthorn. Some say he is in Exalon but no one knows for certain. Knowing his need for revenge on you, Lady Phaera, I beg you to take extra care. Some rumours have him already here, in Marsten."

Phaera felt a chill down her spine and could not prevent a visible shudder.

"In both Belthorn and especially in Exalon he has men in plain dress killing, stealing, and raping at will. No one is spared. There is no one to stop them. Freaks, like the crippled, slow-witted and ... my kind ... have been targeted. Many have died under torture. Exalon is under a state of siege. Women and children huddle in their dwellings. Men are accosted and killed in the streets for no reason we can know. Mathune's thugs demand that people inform on their families and friends. Those who refuse do not make it home. They are left in the streets as warnings, to be discovered. These things are also happening more and more in Belthorn."

Kort turned to Raskir. "Captain, Mathune does not conduct warfare in the traditional ways. He sends no troops to fight other troops. He cannot be bested on the battlefield. There is no battlefield as we know it. He fights by stealth and deception."

Raskir looked grim but kept silent.

After Kort had answered more questions and filled in more details Phaera declared, "We have much to think about. But there is nothing to be done that cannot wait until after dinner. Kort, here, needs my attention. I suggest we all meet here again over dinner to discuss plans."

Lady Flor, who had not spoken, rose hurriedly. "Yes, I shall have the meal served in here." Her face lost a little of the pallor it had taken on during the Kort's tale. "I think this is all we can comprehend for now."

Raskir rose as well. "Agreed, Milady."

Phaera reached out to support Kort, who failed to hide his pain, in spite of a visible effort, as he tried to lever himself out of his chair.

"Come. You will have some relief before we meet tonight, I promise." She debated with herself whether to take him to her chamber, which was closer, or her new apothecary where she had more supplies, minimal as they still were. "Are you able to walk with me a way?"

"Of course, Milady." His gasp as he had risen from the chair betrayed the brave tone but he managed to remain upright and put one foot ahead of the other.

"Lean on me, then." To argue with him would have embarrassed him.

"Milady..."

"Do not try to speak yet. You need your strength until we get to my apothecary. I will tend to you first. Then we will speak." She looked back to make sure her two guards followed behind. Somehow they were more welcome than before.

A low moan of agreement was Kort's only response.

Their progress was slow but Kort did not ask for rest and Phaera left him his pride. Once inside she helped him sink into one of her two chairs, placing one cushion under him and another behind his back. Though she could have helped him lie on the table she decided against it. He would feel freer to speak if they were face to face, even though the table might offer more comfort. He had earned that bit of dignity.

"Rest, Kort, while I brew a tea to help with your pain. Take time to collect your thoughts." Phaera looked out the barred window in the door to make sure the guards were alert, then closed the shutter she had had installed there for privacy. As she waited for the water to boil on the brazier that was kept hot during the daytime, she took the candle she kept lit at all times from its sconce in the wall and used it to light her two lamps. The new light banished the shadows and eased some of her tension. A look at Kort, head lolling to his chest, told her he had fallen asleep. *Good, I can use the time to prepare some dressings and heat more water to clean his wounds and examine them.* A sudden thought made her halt. *Have they castrated him? Might that be what causes him such pain?* She shook the thought away just as quickly. Had that happened he would not be alive now.

As soon as she had arranged her supplies she set the other chair opposite Kort, sat facing him, and began to examine him with mostly her eyes, only gently lifting edges of clothing away to check for bruises or other injuries. It became clear that he had lived rough and eaten far too little. His skin, between the bruises, was loose and dry, with little muscle underneath. She suspected his elbows and knees would be as swollen as his hands, and just as painful. Had he lived on no more than water?

She rose, drew back the shutter, and spoke quietly to one of the guards. "Find someone to fetch bone broth from the kitchen. And soft bread and honey."

"Yes, Milady."

She listened to his footsteps echo until he reached the end of the hall, then low voices, and his returning footsteps. *Why do I feel afraid? Nothing has changed here.* But it had. She knew it deep inside. No one was safe anymore. *Are you safe, Bain? Papa?* Would Kort know anything about them?

Kort let out a loud snore, which seemed to waken him, then groaned as he tried to lift his head. Phaera took the cup of willow bark tea over. She held it to his lips with one hand as she supported his head with her other. "Drink this. It will relieve some of the pain. I have bone broth coming."

Kort grimaced at the bitterness of the tea in spite of the liberal amount of honey Phaera had stirred into it, but drank it all. Just as he finished Phaera heard female steps approaching. "That will be your broth." She set down the cup and took out her key to open the door. She sniffed the contents of the bowl as she took it from the maid. "Thank you. You may go"

She sniffed the broth again. *I must be becoming spooked.* It smelled fine but she dipped the end of her forefinger into it and licked off a drop. Finding no signs of poison she took it to Kort. "Here, this will help you get back some strength." When Kort tried to take the cup from her she placed her hands over his to steady them. He drank it eagerly.

Phaera set the empty cup down, broke some bites from the soft, fresh, bread, removed the crust, and dipped it into the honey before feeding it to him. After several moments she could already see Kort's colour improve and his eyes showed more life.

"Thank you, Milady."

"Kort, it looks like you have not eaten well in some time. Your body is covered with bruises and your joints are swollen. A few more days and I fear you would have been beyond my ministrations. Can you tell me what has happened to bring you to such a state? These bruises are not from blows."

Kort met her eyes, not making any attempt to hide the sorrow there. "I have had to flee the company of others, Milady. I have hidden in the forest. Only a very few trusted friends knew how to find me. They brought some food when they could but …" A single tear slipped over his left lid and made a slow track down his cheek. "So many of them dead, Milady. Mathune and his men hunt us like animals. Most who still live have gone into the forests as I had to do. We are not trained to know what is safe to eat. Some die from starvation, others from poisoned plants."

Phaera took his hands in hers, taking care not to squeeze too hard. "Oh, my dear friend. This is horror. But you are safe here. I am glad you have returned alive and I am able to see to your recovery."

"Milady, there is rumour. I cannot confirm it. But I have heard that Lord Bain has discovered Mathune's tactics and ordered his men to pair off without uniforms and infiltrate Exalon in secret. At the last word he is still safe."

"Kort, have you heard if anyone has been able to reach Lords Makin and Danza with this news? If they remain in armed formations, as they were, it gives the advantage to Mathune. He expects us to follow the rules of war while he does not."

"I cannot say for certain, Milady. Some of my band have tried to get word to them. I do not know if they succeeded. I will set out tomorrow again to get through with that information. That is my next mission."

"You will do nothing of the kind. I will not allow you to leave until you have your strength back."

Kort smiled his gratitude but shook his head. "There is no time, Milady. I must."

"No, we will find another way. You have served us beyond

duty. And if you leave before you are well you will never reach your destination. When we meet at dinner with Raskir we will find another way." She rose to stand beside Kort's chair so she could help him up. "Now, let us return and find you a chamber with a soft bed where you may sleep for a short while."

Kort made no protest.

CHAPTER TWENTY-SEVEN

THE INN

Mag had welcomed Bain and Jessin's protective presence for the night but knew little more than what she had already told Bain the evening before. He did glean from her where in the city he would most likely find some of Mathune's men. Rumour had it that they favoured two of the largest inns.

"I think his men have likely taken over these inns entirely," Mag said they are close together. We will seek them out there."

Jessin looked dubious. "But Milord, that might be a trap. Even if it is not, surely we will be discovered and killed. You are Lord Makin's heir. You must not risk your life so readily."

"That is so, Jessin, but," Bain jerked his head slightly to the right and behind him, "do you not see those two men in conversation in front of that shop?"

"Yes."

"And those shadows receding into that alley?"

Jessin looked puzzled. "Yes, but..."

"Do not look closer, but all four are our men. That you did not recognize them shows how well they have kept hidden. I have spotted them, and others, now and then. They search for Mathune, yes, but also keep track of our movements."

Jessin's eyes widened. "I ought to have recognized them, too, Milord."

Bain chuckled. "No, Jessin. Two of them are scouts, trained to hide in plain sight. The other two are seasoned soldiers - under orders to stay hidden where possible. You are well trained in weapons but these tactics take years to master."

In spite of the reassurance Jessin looked unhappy. "Are there more we have not seen, Milord?"

"I have not seen more but I suspect Reynce is not far. While I gave orders to disperse I am certain he has higher orders from Lord Makin that I am to be protected at all costs. I do not doubt he is nearby."

Jessin looked relieved and seemed about to speak, then change his mind. After walking in silence for several minutes he ventured, "I must be more observant."

The idea that he needed such protection rankled Bain but he knew better than to think it unwise. *I must live to produce an heir.* He pushed a worry about Phaera aside as they approached the street where the first inn stood, and slowed his pace. "We will enter as mercenaries wishing to join Mathune. They will not question our swords, then. We will say we have heard of his power and know he is the man to back." When Jessin gave him a startled look he added, "You are my man. Follow my lead and do not speak unless necessary. You will call me Krell. Do not forget that – Krell."

"Krell." Jessin rolled it over his tongue a few times, then squared his shoulders and met Bain's eyes. "I will not forget." His voice had taken a new resolve.

Bain strode to the door of the inn with Jessin close behind, pulled it open and boomed, "Is this where two good men may offer their services to Lord Mathune?" He remained limned squarely in the doorway, one hand on the hilt of his sword, the other on his hip, and waited. The inn fell silent. All eyes turned in their direction.

Bain gave them a moment. Without taking a step into the inn he swept his left hand toward the men at the tables. "What, have I the wrong inn? Come, who is in charge here? If you have no need of us I shall find another who does."

A man sitting with his back to the far wall rose with deliberate slowness, leaned forward and placed his palms flat on the table in front of him. "We have no need of more men." His eyes bore into Bain.

Bain make a quick decision. He gave a mocking laugh. "Ah, then you must be unaware that Makin has troops all over Exalon." He watched the men exchange glances before turning back to the one who had spoken.

"You lie." It was a clear challenge.

Bain laughed again. "And you, sir, cannot afford to take that chance." He did not give the man time to respond. "I know Mathune has this land under control … for now. My man and I wish to see that it remains so." He gave a loud chuckle. "And we like what we see here." He grabbed his crotch and thrust his hips forward, catching the eye of a man with a frightened looking young girl on his lap.

A low rumble of laughter ensued but stopped abruptly when the leader slammed a palm loudly onto the table.

"So, do we talk?" Bain planted his feet further apart and thrust his chest forward.

The man at the table had not moved. Now he rose to his full height and folded his arms across his chest, still glowering, eyes narrowed. "Who are you and where are you from?"

Bain took a step into the inn making room for Jessin to edge in behind him. He trusted, without checking, that the men they had seen outside were close at hand and observing. "I am Krell. This is Jessin. We claim no land. We follow fortune." He swept his free hand over the men again with a wide grin. "And fortune has led us here." He took another step into the room, allowing for Jessin to stand beside his shoulder. "And how may I address you, sir?" Bain knew he had to let the man understand that he accepted his leadership. He lifted his hand from his sword and placed his hands on his hips, though he remained alert and ready.

"Call me Freskus - Captain Freskus." A cunning look came over the man's face. "So, you like 'em young?" He indicated the man with the girl on his lap. "Take her. Show us how much you enjoy her." With a sly leer he added, "Gunt, give the wench to our new recruit."

Gunt scowled but shoved the girl off his lap in Bain's direction. Bain caught her forearm with one hand and, in the same motion, swung her behind him and out the open doorway. His sword was in his hand before the motion had finished, as was Jessin's.

As he had hoped the sight of the girl careening out the door with a scream brought four men into the inn, swords drawn.

In the short melee that followed Bain became aware of Reynce fighting back to back with him, though he had no time to wonder how Reynce had managed to position himself so well. When the shouting and clashing of swords ended five of the enemy lay dead or dying. Ten others cowered in the corners. "Freskus" lay pinned on the floor, a sword at his throat, until one of Bain's men trussed him up.

Bain looked at a body at his feet and at his bloody sword and realized he had cut the man down - his first kill. Before that could register he noticed two of his own men on the ground. One dead. The other - *no – not Jessin!*

From what sounded like far away he heard Reynce. "It is over Milord. We are safe."

It did not fully register. He knelt by Jessin and heard a groan. *Alive.* The relief was fleeting. A short examination showed him the young man was mortally wounded.

Jessin opened his eyes and smiled as he saw Bain. "Safe, Milord..."

"Yes my friend, we are safe. We have prevailed."

"Am I ... will I ...?" Jessin gave a weak cough and bloody foam bubbled over his lips.

From behind Bain felt a hand on his shoulder and recognized Reynce.

Jessin coughed again. "Milord ...?"

Bain grasped the young man's hand in both of his, brought it to his own chest, and shook his head slowly, fighting back the tears that threatened to spill.

Jessin did not take his eyes form Bain's face but a look of anguish came into them.

Bain felt a squeeze from the hand on his shoulder and sensed Reynce standing and backing up. He was alone with Jessin. What could he say?

"Jessin, my brave and loyal man. You have saved my life this day. You fought nobly. I shall not soon forget your sacrifice."

Jessin's voice grew fainter. "Mamma...? ...please..."

"I will tell her of your bravery. She shall have your sword from my own hand. You have my word."

When Jessin coughed again the blood on his lips was brighter. Bain could see he was near the end. He bent down and put an arm under Jessin's shoulders. He drew him up, until the young man's head rested on his chest, and cradled him.

Jessin's breathing became shallower. Bain held him until, with a last bubbling cough, he went limp in his arms. Bain laid him gently back down. He took out his own handkerchief, tenderly wiped the blood from Jessin's face, and smoothed back the damp hair from his forehead. He remained kneeling beside the body until Reynce once more placed a gentle hand on his shoulder.

With a great effort Bain rose and faced his remaining men. "You have fought well today. We have prevailed. I am grateful to you all." He turned to Reynce. "Captain will you see to the prisoners? I will question them after I have dealt with Freskus." To his remaining three men he said, "See that the building is secure – all doors barred and windows shuttered. We remain here tonight." He scanned the room and spotted movement behind a far table. "You. Come out."

"P-please ... mercy." A scrawny girl of about twelve, crept into sight.

Bain noted the bruised face and the blood on her skirts. "Child you have nothing to fear from me – or my men."

The girl stood hugging herself, shaking.

"Are you acquainted with the kitchen here?"

She gave a timid nod.

"We all require food. What can you feed us?"

When the girl merely shook more and wrung her hands he went to her, took her gently by an elbow and said, "Show me. I will not harm you."

The girl led him wordlessly into the kitchen and watched him examine the meagre stores there.

"Do you know where the others are ... the innkeeper, the cook? Can you find them?"

The girl hesitated at first then gave a small nod.

"Ask them to return. We will protect you all from Mathune's men."

After a long moment the girl gave a quick nod and hurried toward the back.

One of his men approached Bain as he returned to the main room. "The inn is as secure as we can make it, Milord. Captain Reynce has placed the prisoners upstairs in an empty room where they are guarded."

"Good. Relieve Reynce upstairs."

Bain and Reynce met in another of the inn's rooms.

"So you knew we had not left you unguarded?" Reynce raised an eyebrow.

"I did. I depended on it."

"Your skills grow, Milord, as does your leadership."

"Yet I doubt myself. I was not born to lead."

"May I speak frankly, Milord?"

"I expect nothing less, Captain."

"I have not risen to this rank because I never doubted. Quite the contrary. It is my opinion that a man who never doubts is a man who makes decisions rashly. A man who never doubts is one who loses sight of the final goal, one who sees only one path and remains blind to other possibilities." Reynce met Bain's eyes squarely. "I see much of your father in you."

Bain began to shake his head in disagreement but Reynce cut him off.

"Weakness comes only when an action needs to be taken and doubt interferes with it. I have not seen that in you today." Reynce gave Bain a long look before continuing. "And a good leader cares for his men. Your compassion for Jessin will be remembered. It will earn you greater loyalty."

"Thank you, Captain." Bain sighed and squared his shoulders, knowing that he did not feel the resolve he attempted to show. "Now we have prisoners to question."

"Yes. They were mostly poorly trained and poorly armed. I suspect not all were Mathune's willing followers."

Reynce agreed with Bain's assessment that seven of the eleven prisoners had likely been forced into service. They protested they had either not fought in the melee or had backed off as soon as they saw that Bain had the upper hand. Some had already lost family members to Mathune's thugs. Others were there under threat that harm would come to their wives or children if they did not obey.

"Let them go to spread the tale of what we have done here, and find a more secure cell for those four."

Reynce agreed. "Perhaps it will give the people hope - and it may draw Mathune to us when he hears."

The only exception was the one who called himself Captain

Freskus. They had interrogated him in front of all the others. His show of bravado crumbled almost as soon as he believed he would be tortured. From him they learned that Mathune was, indeed, in Exalon, though he did not know where, as he moved about daily.

"Then we will make him come to us." Bain motioned one of his men. "Find a rope suitable for hanging."

Together Bain and Reynce placed the noose around Freskus's neck and held him, struggling and begging for his life, in front an open upper window facing the street. The noise soon brought a small audience outside. Bain looked at Reynce, who nodded. It took both of them to shove the pleading man feet first over the sill. His scream was shut off by a sudden, strangled silence.

Bain stuck his head out of the window and addressed the watchers. With a gesture to the still twitching man dangling below he declared, "This is what awaits those who follow Mathune."

To his guard he said, "Take these prisoners to the cellar." The four who had come from Belthorn under Mathune's orders were taken together to a storage cellar that had a lock. One soldier was posted as guard, as there was no other way out.

When only he and Reynce remained he sank onto a stool and buried his face in his hands.

Reynce remained silent a moment, then closed the door and sat on the bed. "It had to be done. And the day it becomes easy will be the day you are no longer fit to rule."

Bain did not respond.

CHAPTER TWENTY-EIGHT

SEEKING NURIAS

"Milady, I feel useless. I am well enough to return to my work. I gave Lord Bain my word." Kort's voice betrayed his frustration as he and Phaera broke fast together in a corner of the main dining hall. Phaera had met him there at his request. At this late hour all the others had eaten and gone. The last maid clearing tables respectfully avoided approaching theirs.

"I understand your desire to return to service. I have been giving thought to that. You are not yet recovered enough to travel as you did before. However I do have a mission for you here in Marston – something that I cannot undertake as I am confined to the castle."

"And what is it, Milady?"

"I have heard nothing from Nurias since Lord Bain left. If, as you say, there are enemies in Marston, she will also be a target. Find her and convince her to come to the castle. Neither will be easy. Her work takes her from her home and she is loath to leave those who rely on her. And, with spies and enemies about she will take care to keep her locations as secret as possible, though not so secret that those who need her cannot find her." Phaera paused, reluctant to say aloud what she was thinking. "Since we have had no news of her it is also possible she has already been taken or … killed. We - no I - need to know."

"I will leave immediately, Milady."

"Good." Phaera handed him two scrolls. "Give this one to Velna, the cook, she will put together travel food for you – enough to last a good while. And this one is for Nurias. It is a request for any herbs and remedies she can spare to add to my supplies."

Kort stood up, squaring his shoulders. "You may rely on me, Milady."

"I know I can. But do not take undue risk. Nurias knows almost everyone near her home. If she needs to hide there are many who will assist her. Take care who you speak to. Trust no one."

"I understand."

They left the dining hall together. Kort had already turned toward the kitchen when Phaera's voice halted him.

"And Kort…"

He stopped and looked back, noticing the concern on Phaera's face. "Yes, Milady?"

"If she has been taken or killed we need to know. It is paramount that you return, with or without Nurias."

"I will not fail you."

After receiving his pack of food, warm clothing, new footwear, and some of Phaera's willow bark powder with instructions on how to make the tea for himself, Kort went to the stables. There he received an unremarkable horse, a worn saddle, and saddlebags filled with assorted goods. To anyone watching he would be just another travelling peddler.

Nurias's cottage could usually be reached within a half-day's ride but Kort took a less direct route. A peddler would not be in a hurry. The slower pace allowed him to keep his eyes open. If people avoided him or entered their homes when he approached he would know that something made them fearful. He took care not to approach anyone until he neared where Nurias lived.

Dusk had already fallen before Kort spotted a youth chopping wood outside a mean cottage showing signs of neglect. He did not need to exaggerate his fatigue and knew his thinness would add credence to his ruse.

"Young man, I seek the healer hereabout. Do you know where I may find her? I have heard there is a fine one in this region."

The youth lowered his axe and studied Kort for a long moment. "You are a stranger here. Why do you seek a healer?"

The suspicion in the youth's voice warned Kort to take extra care. He lifted a sleeve up to one elbow and held his arm out. "I am in pain with these joints and have no remedy left. My travels do not allow me to seek help often."

The youth came close and examined the swollen fingers and scrawny arm, finally nodding. "Perhaps Nurias can help." He seemed to hesitate, as if he had said too much, then made up his mind. "I do not know where she is but ask the lady at the cottage over that hill, the one with flowers beside the door. She gave birth only days ago and may know more."

"Thank you, young man."

The lad gave him a curt nod. Kort sensed the long stare at his back before he heard the lad return to chopping wood.

By the time Kort rounded the hill and found the cottage full night had fallen. A male voice answered his knock but the door remained closed. "Who goes there?"

"A traveller in need of a healer."

Kort waited while a muted conversation took place behind the door. Finally, it opened part way. A heavy-set man stood there holding a long kitchen knife. Kort waited in front of his horse, one hand loosely holding the reins, the other away from his body, to show he was not armed.

"Please. I have come a long way in search of the healer called

Nurias. I am told she is the only one who may help me. I am cold and in much pain. If she is not here I beg shelter for the night for myself and my horse. I have food I can share with you and your family."

A woman's face peaked out from behind the man's shoulder. "Kennat, let the man in. I cannot think he will harm poor peasants. He looks near death." She pressed her husband's knife arm down, nudged him out of her way, and opened the door wide. "Come in, sir, and welcome. Kennat will see to your horse."

Kennat still looked wary but he stepped outside and took the reins from Kort's hand. "There is good grass out back. I will hobble him there. We have no grain for him."

"I am most grateful, sir. And to you, missus." Kort reached into one pannier before Kennat could lead his horse away. He pulled out a corked crock and a flask before stepping into the warmth of the cottage. "I did think I would find shelter sooner but there is no inn nearby and the homes are far apart. I feared I would spend the night in the open again. A warm fire will greatly ease my pain." He took out the wide cork and held the open crock toward the woman. "Only a poor stew of beans and pork fat but I am happy to share it with you."

A small face peered out of the shadows, followed by the rest of a girl of about six years old holding a sleeping infant. "That smells good, Mamma."

"Yes. Now put Rorin down and get out bowls and spoons for all of us. We have a guest."

As the girl turned to obey, Kennat re-entered the cottage, closed the door firmly behind him, and barred it with a stout pole, an unusual precaution. The hearth provided the only light.

Kennat pulled a stool directly in front of Kort, sat on it, and studied him for a while with narrowed eyes. His knife lay within easy reach on the table. "Who are you and why are you here? I checked your panniers. You are no peddler."

Kort took care not to move quickly. "Do you read, sir?"

As Kennat shook his head is wife spoke up. "I read - a little."

"May I retrieve something from my pack?"

At Kennat's slow nod Kort pulled out the scroll intended for Nurias. "This is for Nurias – written in Lady Phaera's own hand. I seek Nurias with a message from Lady Phaera, and to give this to her. Nurias and I have met and she will remember me." Kort handed the scroll to the woman.

She studied it, her mouth puzzling out the words in silence. Then she handed it to Kennat. "Tis a list of healing plants, I think."

Kennat opened the scroll in a pretense of reading it, then handed it back to Kort. "What is the message?"

"That is for Nurias' ears only."

"Hmph."

"Do you know where I may find her?"

After studying Kort again Kennat seemed to make up his mind. His shoulders relaxed. "She moves about. You, a stranger, will not find her. The people protect her."

Kort felt a huge relief at Kennat's declaration. "I am most happy she is safe, then. But, as you see, I must find her to deliver Lady Phaera's message and to return with the supplies on that list. Can you help me?"

Kennat exchanged glances with his wife. "Perhaps ... Mirin?"

Mirin went to the back of the cottage where baby Rorin lay and brought him to show Kort. "See, our son was born but three days ago. Nurias was the midwife. She promised to return in four days to see that he and I are well. We expect her tomorrow, or, if she is needed elsewhere, the day after."

Kennat broke in. "You will remain here until then. I will not endanger her, or another, by telling you more."

Kort could not believe his good luck. "I am most grateful to you both."

In the morning Kort shared his remaining journey food, knowing he would not need to keep travelling in search of Nurias. "Honey cake - from the kitchens of the castle." His grin widened when he saw the delight on Mirin's face and her daughter's eagerness as she scrambled over to look.

Nurias arrived well after dark. When Kort relayed Phaera's request to come to the castle she shook her head. "Nay, I need to continue my work. I am not needed at the castle." She took the list Phaera had sent. "I have many of these things but cannot collect the rest. I will send what I can spare with you."

"Nurias, Lady Phaera says it is urgent that you come with me to the castle."

Nurias only smiled. "I am safer and more useful here. And here I can keep my ears open. If I hear anything important I will see that the information reaches the castle." She began to divide her remedies and pack them into Kort's travel sac. "Take these to her. They are all I can spare. Tell her I am well. She will understand that I cannot leave my charges. Explain that the people here keep me safer than I would be at the castle." She handed the half-full pouch to Kort before turning to Mirin.

"Now, Mirin, this man has need of a strengthening tea. Do you have boiling water?" She grabbed a cup and dropped a powder into it. She took the steaming kettle Mirin held out to her, poured, stirred, and handed it to Kort. "Drink this. I added more to the sac. Phaera will know what to do with it. It is better than mere willow bark."

Kort did as he was told. He left, alone, at daybreak feeling more rested and stronger. While Nurias did not accompany him, he deemed his mission a success.

CHAPTER TWENTY-NINE

THE BAIT

"It is a risky strategy, Milord." Reynce eyed Bain.

"Yes, it is. Though I think you will agree that to do nothing only delays the inevitable. Mathune will hear of events here if he has not already. And we cannot defend this position long in any case. We have not the men."

Reynce gave a reluctant nod. "It is the best plan, though I do not like that it places you directly in more danger. Yet, if it draws Mathune, it may give us the opportunity we need to defeat him and end this bloody conflict."

"Good. Please accompany me while I inform the men." Bain stood and tugged his tunic straight. "It is unfortunate I do not have a uniform."

"Indeed. But the men know who you are."

"Yes, but perhaps the people here do not."

Reynce insisted that two soldiers open the door and stand guard, swords drawn. He also preceded Bain out, and stepped aside, ready to defend him.

Bain followed close behind and halted a step outside the doorway, feet planted firmly apart, tall and proud. The morning sun shone fully on him. Its glow, he knew, added to the impression of power. They waited, saying and doing nothing, until their presence drew the curious. When a small crowd had gathered close enough to hear him Bain took a step forward and swept one arm toward them.

"Good people. You have seen how we defeated your enemies in this inn. You have welcomed some of your men back home." Bain pointed to the body of Freskus, still hanging out the window. "Here is their leader who has met his just end."

As he spoke more people had come to listen. Bain paused a moment while his audience exchanged glances and low comments.

"Good people..." Bain's voice took on a timbre that carried easily over those listening. "I am Bain, heir to lord Makin of Marston. Know that I, and all those who follow me here in Exalon, have come to defeat Mathune. We will restore peace and justice to your land. Let it be known that Bain of Marston awaits the coward Mathune, if he has the courage to face me."

Bain stood still again and let the looks and murmurs of the small crowd roll over him as his words sank in.

"We welcome any who wish to support us in our common aim. We cannot supply you with weapons. But it will take more than armed combat to defeat him. Mathune will have men – men on horseback. We have a plan to take that advantage from him - with your help. There are ways you can assist that do not require swords, or weapons training. Are you ready to take back what has been stolen from you?"

Bain knew he had struck the right cord when he saw nods and people began to speak and gesticulate between themselves. He waited a few moments before his final statement.

"Any man wishing to join our fight, come to the stables behind this inn at dusk." Then he turned on his heel and strode back into the inn, Reynce at his back. The guards followed and closed the door.

"The people will come, Milord. We must prepare quickly.

Mathune, I suspect, will not be able to resist your challenge. But we must not underestimate his cunning."

"He will want the opportunity to kill me himself. He will want to gloat." Bain faced Reynce. "And he will bring men with him – on horseback." The full import of what he had just done made Bain begin to doubt the wisdom of his decision. "Will we be prepared? Will our men arrive?"

"You may count on it, Milord. As soon as the news spreads, and your presence is no longer secret, they will come."

Bain acknowledged that with a curt bob of his head.

"We are at a distinct disadvantage. Having to leave behind our horses to keep our presence hidden in Exalon means we must unhorse them if we are to fight hand-to-hand." Reynce looked concerned.

"First we must take the other inn." Bain turned to a guard. "Gather the men, armed and ready. There is no time to waste."

"Yes, Milord." The guard turned on his heel with a quick salute and a grin, and let himself out.

Bain caught Reynce's eye. "A little too eager for action, I think."

"They did not come here to sit idle."

"Hmm. I too, am eager to act. Waiting does not sit well."

"The other inn, the Horsehead, awaits." One corner of Reynce's mouth twitched in the hint of a smile. "But you must remain here under guard."

"You know I cannot. " Bain met the taunt directly. "I will not be left behind ... though I am not so reckless as to attack without back-up. How soon can we expect our men?"

"I expected as much, though I advise against it." Reynce looked resigned. "Men are watching already I am certain. As soon as I nail this glove outside the door they will show themselves."

Bain reddened, and he faced Reynce with fists clenched at his sides. "I did expect to be well guarded but you had no right to withhold that information from me. Do not keep me in the dark again."

"I apologize, Milord. It will not happen again. I ought to have known by now you would not act rashly."

Bain's only acknowledgement was a tight-lipped nod. "Put out the glove. I need to see how many men we have."

Within the hour nineteen had joined them. Bain wasted no time. He chose three. "You will remain behind to guard this inn. There are prisoners in the cellar. "You," he pointed to one of the youngest, "relieve that guard there and tell him to join us."

Reynce stood silent behind Bain's shoulder as he inspected the remaining men, insuring they were armed and ready.

"Men, we now take the Horsehead. I want our enemies kept alive for questioning. Let no one leave the inn. As we know from what happened here there will be men who are not there by choice. I want to spare them as much as possible."

Bain saw a few surprised looks and raised eyebrows, mostly from those who had not been present when this inn had been seized. "Those we spare will become allies."

"Lord Bain is correct." Reynce stepped forward. "But do not forget your first duty. Lord Bain must not be harmed."

"Captain Reynce will lead the charge." Bain nodded to Reynce. "After you, Captain."

Bain and his men followed Reynce for the short walk to the Horsehead.

"You three, block any escape." Reynce indicated the front door to the first man and sent the other two to find and block any other exits. "Ready?" When Bain nodded Reynce threw open the door and the troop burst in.

The inn had only four of Mathune's men in it. The remaining men and three women were locals who had been "conscripted" to protect their families.

The melee was short. The "conscriptees" made themselves scarce if they could, or turned against the four who held them. When it was over one of Mathune's men lay dead at the feet of a woman who had taken revenge with a knife. She had stabbed him repeatedly. It took some persuasion to convince her to stand down.

When her rage waned the woman explained that both she and her daughter had been raped by him. "It was for my daughter, you see. He had to die." She began to shake violently, then crumpled onto a stool. "She was only ten years old." The woman pulled herself back to her feet, stumbled to the far corner and returned cradling a limp body in her arms, tears streaming down her face. "She died of it. He killed my baby. And then left her there like a rag. They laughed at me and would not let me go to her." The woman sank onto a bench and rocked back and forth, cradling her daughter's body, able at last, to mourn.

"I understand, Missus. You did right. He deserved to die – and at your hand. And I will see that you are able to give her a proper burial soon."

Then he turned to Reynce. "Now, Captain, let us question this lot."

The "conscriptees" were quick to relay more tales of abuse and horror before Bain released them to their families. They learned that when Mathune's head man here heard Bain had taken the other inn he had sent three of his men to seek out and inform Mathune.

Bain indicated the three of Mathune's men who remained, turned and chose three of his own to guard them. "Take these pieces of filth and have them join the prisoners at the Crow and Hawk."

Later, alone with Reynce, Bain said, "Had he not sent those men away they might have been able to attempt a fight."

"Yes, and I do not doubt Mathune heard the news even before these men could reach him. I suspect he will not keep us waiting long."

Bain clenched his fists. "We must be ready."

"Many more of our men will come to our side."

"Mathune is mine."

"Milord, may I speak freely?" Reynce faced Bain, eyebrows raised.

"I expect no less. Speak."

"Milord, I urge restraint. Mathune must be seen to be brought to justice. The people will wish to believe they participate in bringing him low. A quick death will deprive them of that."

Bain bit back an angry retort, spun on his heel and strode to the door. "We have prisoners to interrogate. You two, come with us."

Reynce stayed close behind him as Bain marched back to The Crow and Hawk. Neither spoke.

That evening, as they sat together at the corner table at the inn, Bain broke his silence.

"Captain, I must thank you for your guidance and your candor. You are correct about Mathune. If possible, he must have a public execution. I must not let my hatred cloud my actions."

Reynce looked relieved. "Becoming a leader does not happen overnight, Milord." He took a long swig of what served for ale at the inn before adding, "You are well on the way already. Your lord father will find he has made a good choice."

They both sat in a more comfortable silence for a while before Bain spoke again, avoiding Reynce's eyes by studying his hands, worried that Reynce would not approve, or would disagree. "I hope I do not forget that I am also my mother's son."

Reyne gave a low chuckle. "I think you need not have fear of that, Milord ... and what she taught you will also stand you in good stead. I have already seen evidence of that."

After another long pause Bain ventured, "Do you think the castle is secure?" *Are you safe, my love? Do you already carry my heir? Will I be welcomed back?* He swept that last thought aside with a rough wipe of his hands across his face.

"We left it well guarded, Milord."

"Hmmmm."

CHAPTER THIRTY

BATTLE

The Crow and Hawk became a makeshift barracks, crowded with soldiers, many of whom had to sleep in the stables in order to remain nearby. By next morning they were sixty-seven strong and eager for action.

About thirty men and older boys from the town had come at dusk to join them with knives, pitchforks, and whatever they could find to hand. Bain sent three lads under 12 back to their mothers. "Who will look after your families if your fathers die? I applaud your courage but you are needed at home."

The few horses in the stable had been taken out and corralled, leaving the entire space for the men. Even so, they stood shoulder to shoulder as they listened to the plan, soldier next to local man, the armed beside those with only rage or courage to strengthen their resolve.

When Bain began to speak, all eyes turned to him, rapt, determined. Their silence added weight to their resolve.

"Mathune and his men will be on horseback. If they remain so we will be massacred as we have no horses with us." Bain met the eyes of several of the local men. "They must be unhorsed – before we engage them with our swords."

The silence grew uneasy.

"Not all of you will survive. You are not soldiers. I cannot ask you to give your lives in this fight."

One man in the crowd shouted, "I am ready to die. I will not bow to them."

"If we do not we will remain slaves to them."

"Aye, they will rape our wives."

"Kill our children."

"We must be free again."

Bain let the swell of response grow before holding his hand up for silence. "Your courage and resolve does you proud. Here is what you must do." He reached behind him, took an unlit torch from Reynce, and held it high. "These will be your weapons. Horses fear fire. Try to stay out of sight until they are almost upon us. We, some of my men and I, will stand waiting in sight, swords drawn as though we expect to meet them hand to hand."

Bain gave them a moment to understand. "When Mathune and his men approach light these torches such that they flame high and wild. Then run at the horse's heads. Make them rear. Make Mathune's men fight to remain seated. As soon as this happens my men will race to join you in the melee and engage those that have been unseated, or try to topple those remaining. Your work will be to continue to create as much chaos as possible. Burn the horses and the men if needed. Do whatever you can to get them off their mounts. Spook the horses. If you manage knives in your other hand, slash out at whatever you can reach, horse or man. But, more important, keep the flames in the faces of the horses. Keep them milling and rearing. Do not let the soldiers regain control of them."

His own men had already been informed of the plan and now began to slap the shoulders of the local men to encourage them. Bain watched as the local men were drawn in, as their confidence and enthusiasm grew.

After several moments Bain again raised the torch and held it high. "One more thing. The horses, once their riders have fallen, will need to be taken out of the way so my men can engage the enemy directly. If you see a horse without a rider, do whatever it takes to get it out of the way. The man who takes a horse out of the way is not a coward. He is doing what is needed to allow my men to fight. It is of the utmost importance." Bain paused to make sure they understood. "Do not forget this."

All the men were told where to wait. A scout had arrived earlier and informed Bain where Mathune had been located so they knew which route he would travel into the town, there being only two.

The plan was put into motion. Bain sent the inn's servant women home and left the inn empty with doors barred and lamps on, to look like it was occupied in case they had misjudged what Mathune would do. By dawn everyone was in place, ready. Ten more of Bain's men arrived overnight and were sent out again to take up posts along the route where they expected Mathune. Each one had two others with him, ready to feign an ambush and distract Mathune and his men. The men with the torches hovered close by, ready to run out with flames alight as soon as these soldiers shouted the order.

Bain arranged his remaining men, swords drawn and ready, twenty on either side of the road, the remaining thirty-eight across it. He hoped that the last several of his original troop had received the call and would still arrive to add their swords to the fight.

Mathune did not keep them waiting long. By midmorning Bain could hear the distant rumble of horse's hooves. Moments later he heard a woman's scream, followed by a sudden silence. He knew she had been cut down. The realization made him shudder and clench his free fist. He took a deep breath and said, just loud enough for most of his men to hear, "Steady, men. He wants us to lose discipline. He knows we are here, waiting." *I hope he does not know the rest of the plan.*

Even as he waited, Bain spotted three more of his men. They caught his eye, then faded back into the shadows. He glanced at Reynce, who nodded that he, too, had seen them.

"There will be more."

Reynce had insisted that Bain stand behind the others in the ranks. "The men know what to do. My work is to fight at your side. We do not want them to lose focus thinking you are at risk."

"I have seen Mathune at practice. You and I are the only ones skilled enough to match him."

"He will seek you out."

"Let him. He is mine."

"Steady, Milord. Remember your resolve."

Bain had not answered. Even now, he doubted that he could hold back. Every time he saw himself with his sword poised for the killing thrust he saw Phaera's face and watched himself plunging the blade into Mathune's heart.

"Steady Milord."

Reynce's quiet voice brought him back to the present.

The sound of the horses' hooves stilled. Just over the low rise the flutter of a banner announced Mathune's arrival, though he did not ride into sight. Instead, a lone man took the last steps ahead on foot until he had a clear view of Bain's men. There, with a mocking salute, the man turned and strode back toward Mathune.

This time Reynce made sure most of the men heard when he repeated Bain's, "Steady men."

Mathune's hated voice rang out as he crested the low rise into view. "What, no horses?" This was followed by a derisive laugh.

When there was no response Mathune gave his order. "Forward, men."

Bain's men waited until the horses were in plain sight.

As soon as Mathune saw Bain's waiting troops he shouted, "Slaughter them all. But Bain is mine," and surged toward them.

At the same instant Bain heard the signal from his own men in behind, then the whoops of those who had been hidden as they raced toward the horses, torches flaming, weapons drawn.

His troop surged forward into the melee. Horses screamed. Men fell from saddles or had to forget about their swords as they fought to retain their mounts. Whenever one man dropped his torch, or was cut down with it, another picked it up, continuing to harass the horses. Some were trampled before the horses could escape the flames.

Bain watched it as though from above, moving without seeming to guide his limbs. He hacked two men to death, each moment taking him closer to Mathune. When he whirled to meet the next opponent he spotted Reynce engaged with two of Mathune's men, no longer able to stay by his side.

Now, only two horses remained within the battle, only one of those with a rider. An injured man, torch still in hand, was about to be trampled when he threw himself on his back, under the horse and thrust his torch into the beast's genitals. The horse kicked back with an anguished scream, threw off his rider and fell on top of the man underneath. A soldier caught the rider with his sword as he fell, killing him.

Bain saw dead and wounded litter the street, not able to tell which side they were on. The soldier he had been fighting lay dead at his feet.

He heard a crow of triumph and whirled to his right, barely deflecting a sword. At the same instant he recognized the man who wielded it. Mathune.

"I have you, whelp."

They exchanged blow and parry, feint and thrust, an even match. With each move, Mathune taunted Bain.

"Bastard." Thrust. Clash.

"Coward."

Bain saved his breath until Mathune threw the taunt that cost him his self-control.

"I have your little whore." Clash.

Bain barely deflected the thrust.

"I shall break her to my will."

Feint, parry, slash, whirl.

"She shall bear my bastards." Parry. Thrust. Clash.

"Chained." Feint. Thrust. "In my dungeon."

With a roar of rage Bain swung hard with no thought to his own safety. The blow caught Mathune's wrist. It severed his right hand, the sword still in it. It clattered to the ground. Mathune fell back with a cry, a look of astonishment on his face.

Bain raised his sword to its full height, preparing for the killing blow.

"Lord Bain!"

Reynce's warning barely penetrated through Bain's fury.

Again he heard the firm voice. "Enough!" By now Reynce stood at his shoulder.

Bain saw Mathune let go of his bleeding arm and reach for the dagger still sheathed at his waist. Blood pumped in spurts from the sheared wrist. With a wild scream he lunged at Bain with the dagger. Reynce kicked it away before it could reach him and knocked Mathune to the ground, who once more grabbed his wrist to slow the bleeding.

Bain stood with one boot on Mathune's chest, sword still ready.

Reynce faced Bain, eyes full of warning. "It is over. We have won."

Under Reynce's penetrating gaze Bain's rage ebbed. He steadied. He breathed deeply again.

Reynce repeated, "It is done, Milord. It is done."

Bain lowered his sword, the motion seemed to take too long, the sword weighed too much, until the tip rested on a cobblestone.

Reynce raised his voice enough that all could hear, but clearly speaking to him alone. "What would you have us do with this prisoner?"

Bain understood. Reynce was telling him to take charge. He wanted the people to see that.

Bain broke from Reynce's gaze and made himself look at Mathune. "Have his arm bound to stop the bleeding and throw him in the cellar with the others. Let them see what his boasts have come to."

Reynce gave the order.

Bain looked over the street, littered with men, some dead, some wounded, some his, some Mathune's, some local. The moans of the wounded brought him back to his duty.

A few of his soldiers stood guard over what remained of Mathune's men, those with no or minor injuries. "Bind them to those trees." He indicated three small trees to the side of the road. He gestured to the two men tending to the wounded. "Have our wounded brought inside where they can be attended."

Finally, he looked at the nine remaining wounded – the enemy - lying untreated. "You," Bain pointed to three of his men, "have them brought to the stables and tend their wounds there. Set guard. They will be dealt with later."

Bain saw that some locals, both men and women, with grim but proud faces, held knives, one a pitchfork, another a cudgel. All were bloodied. They had joined the fight. Now others gathered to join them, mostly women and children, searching for fathers and husbands. Bain listened to the cries of joy when some were reunited, wails of grief from others who had lost their loved one.

One man stepped forward and accosted Bain.

"What will ye do with that lot?" He spat in the direction of the prisoners. "We demand justice."

Bain squared his shoulders. "You shall have it." He paused only a moment before adding, "But it shall be done by law."

The man looked about to argue, but backed off when Reynce stepped to Bain's side. "There will be no more bloodshed today. You will see justice served."

Aside to Bain he said, "Milord, may I see to a more secure place to hold these prisoners?"

"I leave them to you, Reynce. I must see to our wounded."

Bain trudged into the inn, limbs heavy as logs, but with his mind clear and focused. Inside he found twelve wounded men lying on makeshift pallets receiving attention from the uninjured and two women who had returned. Three had critical wounds. Two of these had already lost consciousness and would clearly never awaken.

The men with lesser wounds had already been bound and tended to. Bain noticed that one of the returned serving women had offered them all ale.

He knelt beside the soldier who was still conscious. The young man had a gut wound. Bain knew that meant a lingering, and very painful, certain death. His own gut clenched at the prospect.

The soldier met his eyes, his expression both knowing and filled with anger. He grabbed Bain's forearm and spat, "Make him pay, Milord."

"He will. You have my oath on it."

"How long…?"

Bain understood the man referred to his own state. "Days at most." Bain swallowed and took a deep breath. "It is Bennick, is it not?"

"Yes."

"Bennick, your courage and actions today have helped us capture Mathune, thus ending his reign of terror. Our people will be able to return to peace. They will once again raise their families in safety. Your sacrifice will not be forgotten."

Bain swallowed again, gathering the courage to say what knew he must. "Bennick, you have earned a choice. I think you know your death will be slow and filled with pain and, in the end, delirium. We will tend you as long as you wish it and do our best to lessen your pain … but, if you choose it, you have earned the coup de grace. You will linger no longer than you wish to."

When Bennick looked as though he wished to speak Bain stopped him. "Do not answer immediately. Think about any messages you have for those back home, what you wish to say to your friends here, and lastly, how you wish to die." Bain took Bennick's hand, which had fallen back to the pallet, and squeezed it tight. "When you have decided, I swear, your wishes will be honoured."

Bennick's face lost its fear. Bain felt him squeeze back. "Thank you, Milord." He heaved a sigh that turned into a moan. "Have we laudanum, Milord?"

"Only a little – but it is yours."

Bain took a tiny vial out of the pouch he still carried at his waist and opened it. He lifted Bennick's head, let a few drops of the sticky liquid fall between his lips, and waited for him to swallow. "I have enough to do this twice more." He lay the young man's head back down. "Rest now."

Bain stayed beside Bennick, keeping one hand on his arm in comfort, until he saw his body begin to relax and his breathing become steadier.

Reynce had come in but not until after Bain had offered Bennick the choice. Bain watched him assess Bennick and shake his head in concern.

"Captain, where are the rest of our men, those not injured or tending these here?"

"They have found rest in the stables. I have kept them at the opposite end from our prisoners. The local horses are still in the paddock. I have also sent men to gather the horses that are still loose. Those that we can we will care for. Those that are past tending will be slaughtered." Reynce hesitated. "May I suggest, Milord, that we find a few men who can slaughter the animals and divide the meat among the people. They have been short of meat. It would be a shame to waste it."

"Yes, of course." Bain beckoned to the serving woman. "Are you able to find others to assist you? There are good men in the stables who need food and ale. And I need two men who know how to butcher. You will all have meat tonight."

The woman bobbed a quick curtsey. "I will see to it Milord." She set down her jug and hurried out.

Bain turned to Reynce. "Come, Captain. I see that things are well under control here. Let us consult in private."

Reynce closed the door behind them and came to sit on the cot, wiping his hand roughly across his face, leaving the only stool for Bain.

Bain allowed himself a few deep breaths before speaking. *I wonder if I look as bad as he does. I am weary to my bones. No matter. Neither of us will find rest yet.* He raised his gaze to meet Reynce's, who said nothing, eyes full of questions.

"Captain, you have seen that Bennick cannot live." At Reynce's slow, pained nod Bain hastened to continue. "I have given him the choice of the coup de grace. If he chooses it I will deliver it personally. He has earned that honour."

Reynce's expression changed to relief. "I am pleased to hear it." After studying Bain for a long moment he said, "Lord Bain, you have been tested and proven yourself a true leader. I am no longer your mentor. I am honoured to serve you."

Bain thought Reynce's words over. *He is correct. I no longer rely on him for my decisions.* "Thank you Captain. Yet, I hope I may still rely on your frank counsel."

"Always, Milord. It will be my privilege."

"We must decide how to proceed. Mathune's actions have harmed the peoples of Exalon and Belthorn most. But Kinterron and Marston have also been affected. All must be shown that justice is served."

"Indeed. A tall order."

"I am of the opinion that this decision must be delayed until Lords Makin and Danza meet us here, and that we must not remove any prisoners from Exalon until they have arrived and been consulted."

"A sound strategy, Milord."

Was that a hint of a smile or did Bain imagine it? "But the people are hungry for revenge. I fear they will not be willing to wait until the law can run its course." Before Reynce could respond he continued. "I am also aware that capturing Mathune is not the end of this conflict. If stability and justice are to be restored all his men must be found and purged from these lands. Both Exalon and Belthorn will need new rulers."

Reynce leaned forward and when he spoke he could hear the approval in his voice. "I agree these people do not wish to wait. But it is you who have won this victory. That gives your voice a large measure of authority. I believe they will not challenge you overmuch."

"So you think I can persuade them to await Lords Makin and Danza."

"I do, but we will need to move our prisoners to a more secure location – though not far, lest the people see it as a betrayal. As you ordered, I have located a small warehouse around the corner that will be easy to defend and has a storage chamber that can be locked and guarded."

"Excellent. We will move our prisoners there and set guards both inside and outside."

Reynce paused. "To your other concern. While we do have Mathune, the castles of neither Exalon nor Belthorn have been taken or surrendered. Whoever become the new rulers there will need to be approved by the remaining lords and will need to swear oaths of non-aggression."

"I had not realized the needs for such oaths. It seems I still have things to learn."

Reynce acknowledged that with a wry smile. "I expect, as it was you who captured Mathune, the other lords will respect your counsel on this. You may wish to give it some thought while we await Lords Makin and Danza."

"I see. My training continues, Captain Reynce. I am once more in your debt." Bain returned Reynce's smile with a rueful shake of his head. *But will they listen to a bastard? Are the others ready to accept me? Am I ready to take this on?* With a deep sigh he turned his attention back to the present.

"Now, Captain, will you see to rehousing our prisoners? Is there a separate chamber for Mathune? Or is he well enough to be thrown in with the rest?"

"Perhaps it will be best to keep him here, where we can guard him more closely, lest someone take revenge – even one of his own."

"Leave him in the cellar here, then, but with double guard."

"As you wish."

They rose as one, Reynce opening and holding the door for Bain.

"I will check on Bennick." As Bain entered the main room of the inn he spotted the serving woman and beckoned her over. "Selia, our wounded men need laudanum but we are running out. Are you able to find someone who has more? Is there a healer about who will come to our aid?"

The woman looked dubious. "Our healer was murdered and her apprentice escaped. We have not seen her since. I will see if I can find her, Milord."

"Do your best. It is likely she has heard of our victory and may be found."

"There are two more women here, now, Milord. The men have been fed."

"Thank you. And if any more women are willing to help here we will be grateful. We have many more men to feed than before, here as well as in the stables, including the prisoners." Bain fished in his pouch and drew out two coins. "This one is for the laudanum if you can find some, and this one for your services. The others will be paid as well."

Her eyes grew wide. "Thank you, Milord. I shall do my best." She hurried off.

CHAPTER THIRTY-ONE

NO NEWS

"It was all she could spare, Milady. She sends her regrets."

Phaera looked at the meager pouch Kort had brought back and sighed. "I expected as much. Nor did I truly think she would come at my request. I well understand how important her work is."

Kort looked worried. "It would help if we had more news. Have there been no messengers?"

"No, and I do not know what to make of that. It could mean our scouts have been intercepted or it could mean there is nothing new to tell. Both are reasons for concern."

"I could leave again – to see what I can find out."

"No, Kort. If you have not met anyone with news in your efforts to bring Nurias I expect there is none nearby to be had. I do not like it. It is too quiet."

"Then how may I serve you, Milady?"

Phaera had already considered this while she waited for Kort's return. "I do have a mission for you. I trust you will not think it beneath your station."

Kort's expression was a combination of hurt and rebuke. "No service to you or Lord Bain is beneath my station, Milady."

"Forgive me." She sighed. *Am I losing my balance? Is this confinement to the castle costing me my trust of friends? And the common people I love?* Aloud, she said, "This war has made us all suspicious. We look over our shoulders constantly. And now, we even begin to question loyal friends. It must stop."

"I take no offense, Milady. What is it you would have me do?"

Phaera grasped his hand and squeezed it with a relieved smile. "Healer work."

Kort's eyes widened. "Milady?"

Phaera let go his hand to retrieve the pouch of remedies he had brought and look inside. "This will not help me much. I need more supplies ... but I cannot go out seeking and collecting them." She looked up at Kort with a mischievous twinkle. "You can."

Kort's jaw dropped before closing again.

Phaera waited, hands on hips, eyes crinkling.

"But I am not trained, Milady. I may bring the wrong plant – or ... and I do not know where to find what you need."

"All that is true, Kort. Even I am new to this part of the land and do not know the location of many of the plants and roots I need. But I will teach you what I can. And though you will make mistakes, I will have you collect things in such a way that I will be able to tell." Phaera gave a teasing laugh. "Perhaps you will become so interested you will apprentice to become a healer."

Kort's initial look of shock faded into incredulity and then curiosity. "Why not? I am already not considered a man by many ... and why can a man not be a healer?"

"Why, indeed? Though I expect women in childbirth might object. There would be some limits to what a man might do." Phaera set down the pouch from Nurias again and beckoned Kort to follow. "Come, your lessons begin." She turned and headed toward the dungeons and her makeshift apothecary. "Fortunately you read well."

Phaera stopped a maid they passed in the hall. "Fayni, please fetch ten small scrolls and bring them to my apothecary. Oh, and ink and plume as well."

"Yes, Milady." With a quick dip the maid hurried off.

Phaera spent the next days with Kort, making painstaking illustrations of plants and roots, explaining and writing down how to recognize their environments, where and how they grew; some in the open, others at the foot of trees, under rotting logs or on tree trunks. Some grew in shade. Others needed sun. She taught him how to harvest what she needed without killing the source so it would continue to grow. She showed him how to save each item in a way she could recognize to make sure it was correct. "Keep everything in a separate sac. If they do not belong together combining them could create a poisonous result." She explained which items could be allowed to dry, and which must be closed up in jars to retain their juices.

At the end of the third day Phaera looked at her table - items, scrolls, sacs, and jars neatly arranged. Two empty panniers waited at the foot of the table, ready to receive it all with plenty of space left for what Kort might collect.

"You are ready. Pack these up and name each one again as you place it in. Tomorrow you will be on your way. I have already let the stablemaster know you will need a sturdy, but unremarkable horse."

"The one I rode last time suited me well, Milady. It knows me now, so might be a good choice." Kort laughed. "With the exception of how my backside feels riding him I almost regard him as a friend."

Phaera laughed with him. "Ah, I had not thought of that." She thought a moment. "But will you be recognized on that mount?"

"I doubt it, as no one seemed to take note of me last time."

"Very well, I will send word to the stablemaster."

Phaera saw him off at the castle doors after breaking their fast in the dining hall. "You will not find everything I seek. Even so I want you back here in ten days with what you have. Having some things in short order is better than taking too long to find them all. Besides, I want to know you are safe."

"Ten days then, Milady. And perhaps there will be news to share as well."

"I hope so. Farewell." Phaera stood in the open door and watched Kort as he strode out of sight toward the stables. *Farewell, my friend. Stay safe.* A wave of loneliness kept Phaera standing there, her two constant guards just outside, to each side of the door. When she heard one clear his throat she ignored him. She looked at the small patch of sunlight that had found its way over the wall and now brightened a few cobblestones outside the door. With one long step she stood in it, closed her eyes and lifted her face up, drinking in the meager warmth from its morning rays. She ignored the urgent steps of the guards as they came to stand so close they almost touched her. *When will I, no when will all of us be able, once again, to walk freely in the sunshine? When will I gather my own remedies? When will we all be safe again? ... Bain, are you safe?*

She was still enjoying the sun on her face when a commotion from the direction of the stables made her open her eyes. A man ran toward her chased by a guard.

At that same instant the guards at her sides each grabbed an elbow and forearm, lifted her off the ground, and lifted her backwards through the open doors before setting her back on her feet. One let her go and rushed to close and bar the doors. Phaera had only a second to glimpse the man being tackled by the guard before her sight was cut off. As soon as the bar slid across the second guard let her go. Then they both faced her with expressions that said they expected a reprimand.

Phaera had no such intention. The men had done no more than their duty, though it had annoyed her.

"Thank you," was all she could manage.

Before they could reply she turned to signal another man

standing guard half-way down the main hall and strode toward him, leaving her two with no option but to follow.

"Matten, find Captain Raskir. Have him report to me in Lady Flor's private dining chamber. Something has happened outside the stables. There was shouting. I need to know what it was about."

Phaera saw the confirming nods from her guards at Matten's raised eyebrows before he gave a short bow. "Right away, Milady."

I must remind Raskir that the men need to heed me. I am not Lady Flor.

When the guard was out of earshot she said to the other, "You may escort me to the meeting chamber. Then find and ask Lady Flor to join us. Do not embellish what you saw. Things seemed to be well in hand so there is no need to worry her. Then find a maid to bring food and drink. I will have sage tea."

As Matten turned to obey, brows furrowed and lips set in a concerned frown, Phaera called after him. "Matten, if Captain Raskir is unable to attend right away have him send someone with news."

"As you wish, Milady."

The man's relieved look told her she had been correct in realizing Captain Raskir might not take well to such a direct order from her. But Lady Flor had not the temperament for authority and Phaera needed to be completely informed and included. She had never acquiesced to expected roles at court and was not about to begin now. Let them chafe if they liked.

Captain Raskir sent Matten back quickly with word that he would meet with them after he had dealt with the incident.

"Did he say what had happened?"

Matten looked decidedly uncomfortable. "No, Milady. I saw guards holding a prisoner and the captain came out only long enough to receive your request."

"Then we shall await him. You may go back to your post."

Matten gave a short bow, turned and strode back to his position down the hall.

Phaera took a deep breath to control her frustration before facing Lady Flor who had just been admitted. "It appears our good Captain has the situation well in hand." With another sigh she added, "It is frustrating to be confined here."

"Yes, but surely you now see that it is necessary."

"Perhaps, but I need not like it."

A worried nod was lady Flor's only response. She sat rigid in her chair, face pinched, hands between her knees.

A rap at the door announced the maid with the food and drink. As soon as she left, Phaera looked at Lady Flor. "Wine for you, Milady? Or shall I have mead brought?"

"Wine will be sufficient."

As Phaera poured she said, "We are safe, Milady. The guards are doing their work well, as you see. And I am confident that this war will soon be won and we can return to normal."

"I am worried about Lord Makin ... and Lord Bain."

"As am I, Milady. Forgive me. I do not intend to belittle your concern. I share it, I assure you."

Lady Flor answered with a wan smile as she accepted the wine. "I miss my lord husband."

Phaera hesitated, not sure what she ought to say. She did worry for Bain, and she missed her home and father. But did she also miss Bain? "I hope they return to us safely, and my lord father as well. I also worry for Nurias's safety."

For Lady Flor's sake Phaera changed the conversation to more day-to-day topics as they waited.

The wine and the conversation seemed to relax her a little, though when the knock announcing Raskir's arrival came she jumped as if burned.

"Captain, thank you for joining us." Phaera indicated a chair and poured him wine. "What can you tell us?"

"We have a prisoner, Milady. His orders from Mathune were

to get into the castle and unlock the rear door, the one by the dungeon ... and your apothecary ... from the inside so others could enter. The goal was to kidnap you and to kill Lady Flor." When he saw Lady Flor flinch he stopped.

"Milady, I know this is distressing to hear but I assure you, you are safe inside. We have seen to it that no one new works in the castle or has entrance to it."

Lady Flor drew herself up straight. "Of course, Captain. I do not doubt it."

Raskir nodded before addressing Phaera again. "As you saw, the prisoner was apprehended outside the castle and is now held in the barracks prison. We will interrogate him again tomorrow but I fear he has not much more to tell. I have increased the guard again on the outer wall and tripled it at the back." He gave Lady Flor a reassuring smile. "Milady, there is no need for concern, as you see."

Phaera, impatient to know more asked, "If he was to open the doors at the back that means there are others nearby."

"Yes, I expect so, though I am completely confident they will not get in. The man was drunk and seemed not to know how he was to inform the others the door had been unlocked. Perhaps they saw no need to be told but will go there directly. He said all he had to do was to unlock it from the inside." Raskir shook his head in frustration. "Perhaps he will recall more details tomorrow, when he has sobered, though I doubt it." Raskir shook his head. "If this is Mathune's best this war will be won in short order."

"I am concerned that no scouts or messengers have brought news for over a week."

"As am I, Milady, as am I. I know Kort brought no new information. I saw he has gone again?"

"Yes, I sent him out this morning ... to gather both news and remedies. As you know he brought no news other than to say he had located Nurias, she is safe, and she refused to come here."

Raskir nodded. "If there is nothing more, will you excuse me, ladies, so that I can return to my duties?"

"Of course, Captain. "Lady Flor rose to open the door. "Please let us know as soon as you hear anything."

"Always, Milady."

CHAPTER THIRTY-TWO

AFTERMATH

*I*t took a week for Lord Makin to arrive with a third of his men, and another day for Lord Danza. Bain had also dispatched messengers to Marston castle to let them know of Mathune's capture. *Though you are not yet safe from his men, my love. Do not risk leaving the castle.*

During the wait for the two lords Bain took it upon himself, as the best qualified, to act as healer to the injured. While he could have left tending Mathune's wrist to someone else, with only instructions, Reynce had emphasized the importance of keeping him alive and well enough to stand trial.

Reynce is right, of course. And am I not a healer? But THIS man? I want him to suffer, to die in agony, to pay for some of the suffering he has wreaked on others. No, not others. I want him to suffer for the fear and pain he has caused Phaera and Kort.

When Bain had hesitated Reynce had given him a hard, long look before saying, "He will goad you."

"So I will provide him a quick death?" Bain scoffed, not bothering to hide his disdain. "No, Captain, *that* he will not have."

Reynce held his gaze, his face stern. "Or to make you suffer."

Another hard look. "You cannot send another. You have too much to lose in the eyes of your men."

"So now they want a healer and not a soldier?"

When Reynce merely looked at him, expressionless, Bain realized Reynce had not deserved the sneer. He gave himself a mental shake, ashamed. "Forgive me, Reynce. You are correct, as usual."

Reynce relaxed and ducked his head in acknowledgement. "Perhaps you can use an assistant."

Bain felt cold resolve wash over him. "No, Captain, I do this alone." He ignored Reynce's furrowed brow and strode out of the chamber.

Mathune had been moved to a more secure cell away from the other prisoners and from the attention of the locals. The truce Bain had achieved might be broken at any time and they could take no chances. They now kept him in a root cellar with no windows and only one door, heavily guarded and barred. They had allowed him only a pallet and a wooden cup and plate, lest he use them to harm himself or as a weapon. The door admitted no light but they denied him a lamp or torch for fear, like crockery, he might use it to attempt an escape or to harm himself.

Bain took a lamp down into the cellar and saluted the two guards as he approached. "Let me in and keep the door closed behind me. This light will suffice. I will knock three times when I am ready to come out."

The guard closest to the side which swung open hurried to obey while the second came to stand behind him, alert, hand ready on his sword hilt.

Bain entered holding the lamp in front of him and found Mathune on his pallet.

Mathune blinked in the sudden light and pulled himself to sitting as the door closed behind Bain.

"You." His eyes narrowed as his lips took on a defiant snarl.

Bain watched him struggle to his feet. *He is weak. I must not let him die.* He did not have long to wait, though, for the first taunt.

He watched Mathune's face twist in hate and derision. "A boy to do a woman's work?"

"I am here to see that you live to stand trial."

Bain set the lamp to one side and opened his sac of remedies and supplies, keeping one eye on Mathune.

Mathune tried a futile lunge for the lamp but Bain, ready, tripped him so that he fell hard knocking his severed wrist. This elicited a feral scream before he scrambled back to his feet. He faced Bain, eyes glittering, his rage lending new strength to his hate. Spittle spewed from a mouth that seemed unable to find words.

Bain used the opportunity to do what he came for. "Give me your wrist." He held out his left hand, a small knife in the other with which to cut off the soiled bandage.

When Mathune spotted the glint of metal he swung his good arm at it in an attempt to take it from Bain. The swing was wild and weak. Bain grabbed the arm by the wrist, twisted it behind Mathune's back and forced him to his knees. *He is much weaker than I expected.* With his free hand he held the knife to Mathune's throat, pushed him onto his stomach and straddled him between his knees, the good arm pinned underneath him.

With his prisoner now immobilized Bain grabbed the injured arm and cut off the bandages. Mathune, finding it difficult to breathe under Bain's weight, gave up struggling. Bain pulled the lamp close to examine the arm. A dark line had made its way halfway up the inner forearm. *This may be causing the fever and weakness. I need to stop it or he will be dead in two days.* He made a poultice of herbs that would draw the festering away and wrapped it around the wound, followed by fresh bandages. Once finished, he pulled Mathune's head back to feel his forehead. It was slick with grease and, as he had expected, fevered.

Without getting off Mathune Bain poured some cold willow bark tea into the wooden cup in the cell. Then he rose and lifted Mathune to his feet with his free hand.

Mathune drew two deep breaths before his face creased into a sneer. "I will tear it off, bastard."

"No, you will not, or you would have already." Before Mathune could reply he added, "But to be certain I will tie you up such that you cannot." He grabbed a handful of hair and forced the cup to Mathune's lips. "But first you will drink this." When Mathune spat the first mouthful at Bain's face he once more pushed him to the floor, seated against the wall, pressed a knee into his chest, and grabbed his nose. Soon, choking and sputtering, Mathune was forced to swallow the healing draft.

Bain hauled him back to his feet, leaving the cup on the floor. To one side he spotted the plate, empty. *No he will not harm himself. He wants to live.* Bain thought about making good his threat to tie the good hand behind his back but decided against it. *He needs to eat and I will not have a man feeding him, exposing him to his vitriol.*

On the way back to the inn he thought about how weak Mathune had been. *I expected more from him.* More would likely come when Mathune's fever died – if it did. *Do I pity him? Surely not.*

Bain returned that evening to administer a second dose of the tea. Mathune tried to refuse it again, but when Bain threatened to force him he took the cup and downed it in one defiant draft. Bain again took notice of the empty plate and a wet spot in the corner where Mathune had relieved himself. *He eats and drinks. Good. He will survive.*

"So your whore spreads her legs for a nursemaid." The taunt fell on Bain's back as he knocked the code for the door. "What do you think she does for a real man?"

Bain clenched his free fist and fought the urge swing back and knock Mathune's teeth out. The door opened and, lamp in hand, Bain stepped out of temptation. *He will do better when the fever breaks. As must I.*

When Bain returned the next morning the fever had broken. He made Mathune drink a last draft of the bitter tea before removing the bandages and poultice and examining the arm. He had decided he would not speak to Mathune at all. *If I do not say the first word I cannot utter a second.*

Mathune did not fight him on the bandages after the first day. He did keep up a steady stream of invective and taunts, testing Bain's resolve.

Bain clenched his teeth and forced himself not to hear. The litany receded to mere noise. He concentrated on his work. *The poison is receding. Tomorrow I may not need the poultice, only bandages.* He finished and picked up the lamp, turning to leave.

The thump of Mathune's fist on Bain's back made him whirl back, knocking Mathune to the floor with one violent swing of his free arm. He lost his grip on the lamp, which fell to the floor with a clatter and went out. He heard no sound from Mathune. *Did he hit his head? Have I killed him?* He felt his way to the door and gave the code. When the light spilled in he looked for Mathune. The man sat on his pallet, eyes glittering, and cackled with glee.

He knows what I was thinking. Bain gritted his teeth, gathered up the shattered pieces of the lamp and left, seething at being caught out.

Reynce saw him enter the inn and approached him looking concerned. "Is all well, Milord?"

Bain's fury ebbed. He managed a smile. "Well, enough, Captain. We will both live."

Reynce acknowledged Bain's sarcastic chuckle with a relieved half smile. "I am glad to hear it."

MAKIN, DANZA, THEIR TWO CAPTAINS, BAIN, AND REYNCE convened in the dining hall of the Horsehead, as the other inn was still serving as infirmary and barracks. Soldiers stood guard all around the building, both to keep them safe and to insure privacy.

Lord Danza began. "Let me be the first to commend you, Lord Bain and Captain Reynce, on capturing Mathune. Your strategy was brilliant."

Lord Makin nodded, a proud, but controlled smile on his face. "I concur."

"Thank you, Milords." Bain and Reynce responded in unison, eliciting a chuckle from the others.

Bain addressed the two lords. "Captain Reynce and I have discussed options at some length. We are fully aware that there are still many of Mathune's followers who may not have heard of his defeat and capture. They must also be apprehended and dealt with. Here is what we propose. We think that the people who have suffered directly at their hands need the opportunity to accuse each of these men personally, to name the crimes committed against them individually." Bain made his case. "If the people are informed, before the actual trials, that they will be allowed to step forward, that they may voice their accusations before all, before we pronounce sentence – which in some cases will be death - we believe they will be satisfied and allow us to remove Mathune for trial."

After much discussion, and with some reluctance, it was agreed that each fief would have those enemies they captured locally stand trial immediately before the people there. Sentencing would be carried out publicly, on the spot. Both lords had already dispatched men to seek out and bring prisoners to the closest village if they were too far from the central city. Scouts would bring the orders to carry out the trials locally, to be overseen by the local magistrates.

Lord Danza addressed the final decision to be made. "Lord Makin I am satisfied that Mathune be brought to trial in Marston. Since my daughter has become Lord Bain's wife and now resides there, and since she has been a particular target of Mathune's, I will not insist he be tried in Kinterron. I will attend his trial in Marston, if that is agreeable to you."

"It is, and I thank you." Lord Makin agreed, before turning to Bain. "Are you agreed as well, Lord Bain?"

Bain was pleased to be asked formally for his opinion. It signified full acceptance into the consultation as one who had earned his place there. He gave a short bow from his seat. "I am, Milord."

Only Mathune and his two head captains would be taken to Marston to face trial in that city, transported in separate wagons, closed in with wooden sides so they could not be seen. They would travel under heavy guard to deter locals from trying to take them.

Later, finally alone with him, Lord Makin spoke to Bain. "My son, I am pleased with what you have accomplished, and what you are becoming."

"Thank you, Milord. But none of it would be possible without Captain Reynce's counsel."

Lord Makin chuckled. "And that is another reason you have made me proud. You know when to listen, even when you outstrip your advisor in rank."

Bain did not know how to answer. Instead he changed the subject. "Mathune will need to be gagged while we transport him. He must not have an opportunity to taunt the populace into action."

"Indeed."

The two sat in a new-found ease together as they watched the sun descend behind the stables.

Bain could not sleep that night. He tossed on his cot in the chamber he shared with Reynce, his mind a jumble of thoughts. *I am not the same man I was. Who am I now? Father is proud of me. But what of Mamma? Will you approve of what I have become? Indeed, what have I become? And Phaera. I ache to see you again. But I am not the man you wed. Am I? Will you welcome the man I am now? Will I need to woo you again? I have killed. But I am still the son of a healer. How could I kill? Yet, it was easy. I did not even hesitate when the moment came. What does this make me? Oh, Phaera. I need you to be proud of me, too. Have I changed too much? Or is this the man I have been all along? Is this who I want to be? But who is that? Who am I?*

These thoughts raced around his head, with no answers. With the first rosy light of dawn, still sleepless, he rolled out of bed. He dressed and went into the enclosed courtyard to cool off and try to clear his head. He nodded at the guards posted there. *"Even here I cannot be alone. Will I ever find peace again?*

CHAPTER THIRTY-THREE

IT IS OVER

When the missive from Bain arrived for Phaera it filled her with emotions she found both vexing and confusing. She had hurried to her private chamber to read it and now sat in her favourite cushioned chair eyeing her bed – the bed she would again share with Bain.

She unrolled the leather scroll and reread the message.

My dearest Love:
I hope you are still safe, as I have had no word.
Victory. We have Mathune and several of his henchmen. In a few days we will be on our way home. We bring Mathune as a prisoner to stand trial in Marston.
Dearest, the danger is not over. Mathune has men scattered throughout the lands. They are being apprehended but it will take some time before we are all safe again. Remain in the castle, under guard, until I return or word comes that it is safe to leave. How I long to see you again, to hold you, and to resume our life together.
Please stay safe, my love. Heed my warning.

Bain

CERTAINLY PHAERA WAS ELATED AT THE NEWS OF MATHUNE'S capture. The war was over, mostly. The good side had won the day. And Bain was safe, as well as both their fathers. But Bain ordered - yes ordered - her to remain in the castle, even so. Though she understood his reasons, the idea that her confinement would not end yet made her want to ... no Bain was right. Of course he was.

She knew he would have said more if he had had time. A messenger could have been sent with this scroll, almost certainly had been, along with several deemed more important, and all in haste. Those had undoubtedly been taken to Captain Raskir first. News of Mathune's capture was too important to delay. Yet Bain had taken the time to pen her personally and to send it. Perhaps Bain had even made the messenger wait until he had written this.

Did she want him to say more? Was she disappointed he had not? What would she have wanted him to say? Phaera chided herself. No, those were the notions of a romantic girl; they were beneath her.

She read it again and once more eyed her bed. Resume their life? Did she want that? What of the heir he expected from her? She was not ready. She had so much she wanted to do first. What of her apothecary, the one in the outer building? What of her healing vocation? And she was drinking the tea that would, she hoped, prevent quickening. If he knew that what would he say? Would he insist she stop? Would she obey if he did? No... she would not tell him. This was her decision alone. Or was it? Was she being honest with herself?

She threw the scroll on the bed in a pique, then as quickly admonished herself. By the time the knock came to her door she had herself in hand again and could answer calmly.

"Enter."

Phaera expected Mira but one of her guards opened the door

and halted in the opening. "Milady, your presence is requested in Lady Flor's private meeting room."

"Thank you." Phaera rose to follow him. *So, a message, no doubt, and too important to send Mira.* "Who else will be there?"

"Captain Raskir, Milady, and a messenger."

"I hope he brings good news." Phaera looked for a reaction from the guard that might indicate he had already heard but detected none.

"Indeed, Milady." He knocked on the door of the meeting room. On hearing, "enter," he opened the door and admitted Phaera, remaining outside as he closed it again.

Captain Raskir was pouring himself a cup of ale as Phaera looked around. Lady Flor sat with her hands folded in her lap in an unsuccessful attempt to look calm and patient. A messenger sat in the second empty chair, a cup of ale in his hand. *Good, Lady Flor offered him a chair. He looks about to fall over from fatigue. And they have not begun without me. Raskir is learning.* She took the remaining chair and nodded to Raskir that she was ready.

"Mellin, here, says he had orders that we must all receive his news together." Raskir inclined his head to the messenger. "Mellin, please proceed."

Mellin straightened, a broad smile spreading across his face. "Lady Flor, Lady Phaera, Captain, I have splendid news. Mathune has been defeated and captured and is even now on the way here to stand trial."

Lady Flor's hand went to her mouth, stifling a cry, as Mellin continued. Captain Raskir relaxed visibly but stayed calm and alert.

Phaera let the man speak as though she had not already been informed. The others need not know of her letter or its contents.

"Both Lords Makin and Danza, as well as Lord Bain, are unharmed." He bowed his head at Lady Flor. "They will be home as soon as they can, but travel with prisoners so it may take some time."

Lady Flor had placed her hands between her knees and after taking a deep breath, regained her composure. "Thank you, Mellin. That is most wonderful news."

Raskir brought Mellin's attention back. "There is more, I think."

Mellin looked a little embarrassed. "Yes, Captain. I am to inform you that not all of Mathune's men, or his spies, have been found. You are among the first to hear this news and others will not yet know of Mathune's defeat. Our enemies will continue to fight, to infiltrate, and to attempt to carry out Mathune's orders until they are apprehended. I have orders to tell you that all precautions must remain in place until the trials are over, until all our enemies know the truth and have either been brought to trial or withdrawn in hopes they will not be found out." He faced Phaera. "Lord Makin regrets that this must be so."

Phaera pressed her lips together to hold back her pique at being singled out. Mellin had not said the comment was directed at her but she knew it was, and by the look on his face, and on those of the others, they all knew it, too. *Do they still take me for a fool who must be treated as a child? If they expect an outburst from me they shall not have one.*

She took a breath, taking care to modulate her voice when she answered. "That is wise. We must remain under protection until we are confident that all reasonable (she put the emphasis on 'reasonable') danger is passed. Thank you for bringing us this news so promptly." She faced Raskir, asserting some authority. "I assume we want this news to be spread, that we want our enemies to learn of their defeat." Was that approval she saw in his eyes? Was he beginning to respect her according to her due?

"I agree, Milady. I shall have messengers sent out immediately."

Phaera looked back at Mellin. "Have you been given an estimation of how long before we may expect our lords' return?" Phaera turned to Lady Flor. "We will want to welcome them home and celebrate their victory." *I know that side of my duties, too.*

Lady Flor brightened, looking both relieved and grateful. "Yes, indeed."

Mellin gave a slow shake of his head. "I cannot say with any certainty, Milady, but was told it will be at least a fortnight and perhaps twice that. There may be trials of enemies apprehended along the way, and, as I am sure you understand, travelling with prisoners will slow them down."

"Is that all, Mellin?" Raskir resumed control.

"Yes, Captain."

"Thank you. You may leave us. There will be food and a bed for you at the barracks."

"Thank you, Captain."

Mellin rose, bowed sharply, and left.

Raskir leaned forward, hands flat on the table as if to push back his chair. "Lady Flor, Lady Phaera, this is tremendous news. If you have nothing further to discuss I must see that it is sent out."

Lady Flor shook her head. "No Captain. Lady Phaera and I will see that the castle is informed."

With a relieved nod Raskir rose from his chair and left.

Lady Flor burst into tears. "Safe, all safe ... and Mathune captured."

Phaera put an arm around her shoulders, murmuring, "Yes, all safe. Such good news. Such a relief for us all." She poured wine into the still empty cup sitting in front of Lady Flor and put it in her hand, then poured for herself. "Here, a toast to victory."

Lady Flor raised her head and with a brave attempt at a smile lifted her cup. "To victory."

When Phaera was certain Lady Flor had regained some composure she stood up and declared, "Milady, we must share the good news. We have celebrations to prepare."

Lady Flor rose with an expression of delight mixed with appreciation. "Yes. Let us spread this wonderful news."

As they left the room together Phaera said, "May I suggest

sending extra wine and ale to the barracks so that the men may celebrate as well?"

"An excellent suggestion."

Phaera allowed herself an inner congratulation. Lady Flor was once more in possession of herself and doing what she loved. She would not be embarrassed. *Patience. My turn will come.* But patience chafed.

The news soon had the castle in a buzz of high spirits. Smiles wreathed every face. Everyone went about their duties with a renewed sense of purpose and satisfaction.

Everyone except Phaera, though she did her best not to show it. When she was finally able to return to her chamber for the night, and to send her maid away, she sank back into her chair. The bed seemed less welcoming than before, though she was weary to the bone. Her eye fell on the little, locked chest on the mantle. She had forgotten, amid all the excitement, to drink her medicinal tea. If she did not drink it daily it would be less effective. The small chest beckoned. Yes, she must not forget.

The ritual of making and drinking the herbal tea comforted her enough that she was able, at last, to roll into bed and sleep.

CHAPTER THIRTY-FOUR

TRIALS AND CHANGE

*A*s they wended their way to Marston, Bain became concerned about the accusations of the people toward those captured and put on trial. This was not the road to peace he had anticipated. He watched families torn apart by betrayal and hate, even those whose actions had been minor. It pained him to see neighbours and friends turn on those they had trusted and loved. Too many of the accusations were minor, involving actions that under peaceful times would have been dealt with in local courts with far more leniency. This was not what he had looked for.

Watching angry people make accusations too petty for crimes of war also brought his lessons in history to mind, both what was taught from the ancient lore about how the earth had almost been destroyed by such conflicts, and his own peoples' history in more recent times.

At the end of the second day he requested a private consultation with Lords Makin and Danza.

"My son," Lord Makin began, "You are troubled. What is it?"

"Our ancient lore serves as a warning to us that we must never repeat the errors of the past and allow our world to be destroyed again."

Both lords leaned in. Bain had their attention. He began his carefully prepared speech.

"Our own histories have shown us that whenever a war comes to an end we do not return automatically to how things were before the conflict."

"That is so. It takes time for wounds to heal, for trust to be re-established."

Lord Danza's voice was neutral but Bain could detect the hesitation, the underlying questioning. He would have to present his case carefully.

"We have presided over seven trials already. Other fiefs face similar ones. I see a pattern that disturbs me, one I believe will make returning to peace and trust more difficult and prolonged."

Lord Makin looked cautious, his tone letting Bain know that he trod on dangerous ground. "We already break with tradition in allowing the people to face and accuse their enemies – your suggestion as I recall. Are you now saying this was an error?"

Bain shook his head. "I do not believe so, Milord. Please hear me out."

When both men regarded him with carefully controlled neutral expressions Bain took a deep breath. He had not expected this to be easy but it was proving even more of a test than he thought.

"What I see during the trials makes me concerned for the future of our peace. The most important element of our healing is the re-establishment of acceptance, trust, and cordial relations. Many of those now accused have been exposed by former friends, neighbours, even family. Many of the charges are for offenses that in times of peace would be handled by local magistrates or even mediated between the parties themselves."

Bain could see both lords listening with less resistance, now. "Milords, I begin to question whether some of these accusations ought to be dealt with as actual crimes of war. Some are merely the result of old jealousies, or minor disagreements that have been made to appear as though caused by the war. Others are the result of fear for families and property. Some, mere greed. I now see that making the lesser of these accusations public actually causes greater distrust rather than leading to a sense of justice."

"So you do say your suggestion was misplaced." Lord Danza's tone was challenging.

"I do not, Milord. But I do think we ought to modify how it is carried out." Bain faced two stony expressions. "I think we ought to hear the accusations in private first, so that we may bring only those we deem to have truly committed a crime of war to public trial. We can re-direct the lesser accusations back to their local magistrates. I would also warn those magistrates not to allow their judgements to be swayed beyond what they would have decided prior to the war. We need to return to peace, not inflame hate."

The silence felt interminable. Finally Lord Danza turned to Lord Makin. He said nothing, merely searched his face.

Bain sensed that his father now faced a test. He had named Bain his heir, aware that he had not been raised as such. Bain came with a past that could conflict with the training he would otherwise have received. He could only imagine that his father might now question that choice.

Lord Makin came to a decision. "Give us examples of which of the last two days' trials you deem not related to the war."

Once again both pairs of eyes focused on Bain, giving nothing away.

"Certainly the rape of the young woman and the burning of the baker's home were acts of war and as such are exempt from what I refer to. They were carried out as a direct result of the conflict, and by followers of Mathune. Those accusers saw real justice when sentence was carried out. But what of the woman who accused her neighbor of screaming false accusations of theft?

What of the man who blamed his daughter's pregnancy on deceit, when it appears it would have happened in any case? The girl was duped, it is true, but this had little to do with the war."

Bain gained confidence as he listed each one. "What of the sheep that was stolen and slaughtered on orders of Mathune's men so they would have meat at the inn? What would have happened had the thief refused? Have we not seen cases where people committed offenses because they felt they had no choice, that they were protecting their families? Indeed, did we not send many of these men home to their families when we took the inns? Are we truly administering justice when we condemn and sentence them as though their offenses are far more serious than they really are?"

After further consultation Lords Makin and Danza concurred with much of what Bain presented. He was relieved when they agreed to send out messengers to the other regions with orders to refer all accusations, except those that had created serious injury or loss and were deemed directly the result of the war, back to their local magistrates. The number of trials diminished and progress home sped up as a result.

Keeping Mathune and his henchmen alive, safe, and secure was a greater challenge. Even with a circle of guards around the closed wagons, enraged citizens tried to intervene.

Angry men and women pelted the wagons with stones, shouting invectives. The men guarding the wagons wore full fighting uniforms, including leather breastplates and hardened leather helmets. Yet that did not protect all of them.

Bain watched as one poorly aimed missile hit a guard in the neck, just above his breastplate. He rushed over to tend to him, as he bled heavily. While he did need stitches, which Bain took care of personally, the wound was not deep enough to be dangerous. "You may rest the remainder of the day, but I expect you back in uniform tomorrow."

"Thank you, Milord, but I am ready to return to duty."

"I know you are but the day is nearly over and the others are more than able to handle it." He clapped the man on the arm. "Enjoy the rest."

The broad smile he received told Bain that the guard was relieved. "I will, Milord."

When the pelting and shouting continued as they moved on, with another guard taking a cut to his arm, Lord Makin halted the troop. "Arrest them. They cannot be allowed to take matters into their own hands. We must return to law and order."

Bain admired his father's command of the unusual situation when he addressed the offenders at their unexpected trial.

"The war is over. We return to a state of law. Breaking that law will not be tolerated." Lord Makin stood on the bed of one of the wagons that had been commandeered as a makeshift stage for the trials. "You, Rossik, are the one who hit my man Derst in the neck. And you, Fanten, hit another in the arm." Lord Makin turned to the small crowd that had been following them. "I will not tolerate my men or my prisoners being put in danger to satisfy your anger." He gestured to the two accused. "These men will receive five lashes each. And others who are caught with stones in their hands, whether they throw them or not, will be subject to the same. You are all warned."

The subdued group watched the sentences being carried out, though Bain noted that the lashes were not dealt with full strength – no doubt at the order of Lord Makin who had spoken with the man in charge of carrying out the order.

Only one watcher protested. The others hung their heads, knowing that this was just. The protester, too, was soon silent.

When it became known they would be flogged the people backed off. Bain heard some grumbles. Yet, underneath, Bain sensed relief. *People want predictability, security. They see it returning now.*

Kort met the party two days travel into the border of Marston.

Bain recognized him from a distance. "Milord, there is Kort. I will ride to meet him."

At Lord Makin's nod he turned his mount away, one hand high in greeting. Both men jumped off their horses at the same time, striding forward to meet in a great hug.

Bain took Kort by the shoulders and pushed him to arms' length, grinning ear to ear. Kort's expression matched his own.

"My friend, it is good to see you whole." Bain slapped Kort on an upper arm. "What brings you here? Have you news?"

Kort laughed, shaking his head. "No news, Milord. All is well. But your lady sends me with a request." He spread his hands in mock resignation, still grinning.

"Hah, why does this not surprise me?"

They each took their horses' bridles and began to walk toward the others, who had kept their slow progress forward.

"Lady Phaera says she is aware that you have prisoners who will need to be kept in the castle dungeon."

"Of course she is." Bain let out a wry chuckle. "She will never be a typical court lady."

"What you may not know is that she has set up a temporary apothecary there."

Bain's eyebrows rose slightly. "No, but I might have expected as much. At least it means she remained within the castle."

It was Kort's turn to chuckle. "Indeed, though she has chafed mightily at the confinement."

"So what is her request?"

"She says it will not work to have prisoners in the same area as those who seek her services. She requests, now that Marston once again appears secure, to be permitted to move the apothecary to the location you found for her." He eyed Bain sideways. "I do not know where that is but ..."

Bain grew serious as they neared the others. "Is it truly safe again? Are you confident that all dissenters and spies have been apprehended or have gone?"

"Captain Raskir believes so, but he wishes to wait until you have actually returned before lifting the order to remain in the castle." Kort cleared his throat. "As you may imagine, this did not please Lady Phaera."

Bain nodded. "And you, Kort, what is your opinion? You have the lay of the land."

"I believe we are safe, Milord, but also think it wise to keep some precautions in place, especially around Lady Phaera." He looked up at Bain, his expression one of slight embarrassment. "Lady Phaera has asked me if I might wish to apprentice as a healer." He indicated the panniers his horse carried. "She has sent me foraging for supplies, as she cannot."

Surprised, Bain stopped and faced Kort. He studied him a moment, then smiled. "Trust Phaera to think of something so unconventional. And I see it interests you, too." He walked a few steps on before adding, "I can predict benefits from this. Women may not wish you to help them in some cases but certainly there will be those in the barracks who will welcome such services – those that can abide another man other than a field surgeon tending them."

Kort looked doubtful. "Even if they see a lover of men? That will spread if even one man in the barracks discovers it."

"Hmmm, that may be a problem. It will not remain secret."

"Be that as it may, I have a suggestion, Milord."

"Yes?"

"While I make my decision I will return to help Lady Phaera with the move to the new apothecary. You know I would give my life for her."

Bain nodded.

"And Raskir can still post two guards with her at all times until you and Lord Makin deem it safe for her to venture alone again. I will pose as her assistant for the time being."

Bain gave Kort a searching look before turning once again toward the group, which had by now added some distance between them, and resuming their walk. "The decision is not mine. I will speak with Lord Makin and present the request."

They remounted and closed the rest of the gap in silence.

CHAPTER THIRTY-FIVE

MOVING

*P*haera wasted no time when she received the scroll telling her she could move her apothecary to the large out-building Bain had shown her. It rankled that two guards still hovered over her protectively and that Raskir had still posted two men at the back entrance to the dungeon, where she would cross in and out of the castle, as well as the new apothecary. But Kort's cheerful company and able assistance replaced her lingering anger with elation and hope. They had spent almost the entire first day clearing the stone storage building, having bags and barrels, long abandoned there, removed, and sweeping and scrubbing the floor and walls. Whitewash would follow.

Kort looked over at her and broke into a laugh. "Milady, I think the scullery maids are cleaner and better groomed."

Phaera struck a pose and quipped back. "If you see one that looks worse I have not achieved my goal."

It felt so liberating to be in Kort's company. He was the only friend who, when they were alone together, dropped his courtly deference and did not censor his speech. With the doors closed the two guards outside could not overhear. How long had it been since she had felt so free? She thought back and realized it had not happened since she left Kinterron ... over three months ago.

She stretched her back, still holding the corn broom in one hand. A huge apron covered almost all of the plain riding gown she usually wore when she plied her healing.

Her hair was wound with a linen cloth that looked dustier than the floor she had just swept. From it hung several cobwebs, one of which dangled to the tip of her nose. She sneezed and swiped at the offending filament with the back of one grimy hand, leaving a smear across her nose and cheek.

"Well, my friend, my stomach tells me it must be time to stop for today and prepare for dinner."

Kort gave her an appraising look. "I fear that will take longer than usual, Milady."

Phaera made a face at him. "You look no better. Perhaps the guards will not recognize us and ban us from the castle."

"I think you would like that." Kort grinned over his shoulder as he drew the heavy door open and stepped aside to let Phaera precede him out. As soon as the guards posted outside could hear the doors open Phaera saw Kort drop his light demeanor and assume his court deference. She also took on her other self. Inwardly she still laughed. *Two sorry drudges pretending at airs.*

A small chuckle escaped her, which Kort noticed. When he caught her eye she gave him a tiny wink the guards could not see. She almost laughed aloud when Kort quickly glanced away, pinching his lips together to prevent himself from betraying his mirth.

Phaera beckoned the first maid she saw as they entered the main castle. "We will both need tubs and hot water for baths immediately."

The maid tried to hide her distaste at their appearance before hastening to obey, but the look was not lost on Phaera. Her chin rose slightly in defiance but she said nothing and avoided looking at Kort in case they both succumbed to unseemly glee.

It took three more days of hard work before Phaera was content with the state of her new apothecary. It looked larger than she had thought, now that it had been cleared. It had been so dirty when they began that she had not noticed the two windows, covered by shutters that had not been opened in years. When she opened them they let in some light and a cross breeze. They had no glass in them, so would need to be kept closed in inclement weather until that lack could be remedied. At the far end a huge hearth stretched across nearly the entire width. It would supply not only warmth and some light, but provide the fire she needed to boil water and prepare those balms and medicaments that required cooking.

Phaera commandeered a trestle table long enough for a large man to lie on with room left over at one end for some bandages or medications. She had another smaller one placed in front of the hearth to use for preparing her supplies. To one side, against the right wall stood a cot, clean folded linens on top of it. On the left, all along that wall, hung several shelves, shallow ones at the top and broader ones within easy reach underneath. Most of these still stood empty but Phaera knew they could soon be filled with all manner of herbs, balms, tinctures, and powders.

Tomorrow Velna will see that I have all the bowls, jars, and corks I need. Phaera almost hugged herself in anticipation.

The clean, white walls now held six new sconces for oil lamps and six more for candles, each backed by reflectors to increase the light. Two standing oil lamps stood at one end of each table. The space would be filled with light even with the shutters closed. Three comfortable chairs sat along the wall next to the cot.

"You have done it, Milady."

"No, Kort, we have done it." She turned to face him. "I have not asked you for an answer to my offer to take you on as my apprentice. Have you decided?"

"I have. It will be an honour." Kort looked troubled then he cleared. "I know I will face resistance but that will be no more than I already see from those that know me for what I am. I have had a taste of what it is to do important work. I have no wish to go back to my former life."

Phaera acknowledged that with an understanding nod. "That is so. But as my apprentice you will also have a measure of protection."

Kort flashed her grateful smile and changed the subject. He swept his hand around the room, eyes alert with anticipation. "Soon this will be filled – with all your new supplies and then with those who come for your help."

"I hope so. I wonder when I will be free to go gathering. And how soon we will see Nurias. I look forward to her advice." She sighed. "My court duties will take me away from this more than I would like. That will slow your studies as well. If Nurias agrees would you also take instruction from her?"

"Of course … if she is agreeable."

"Good. I will speak with her."

Phaera took one last, satisfied look around, straightened and headed for the door. Kort anticipated her and reached it ahead of her to open it.

As they walked the short distance to the entrance to the dungeon and into the castle side by side Phaera mused, "I wonder how much longer it will take our men to return?"

"Not long, now, I think."

After a short silence Kort looked at Phaera with and expression that suggested he was not sure he ought to speak.

"What?"

Kort kept his voice low and avoided meeting her eyes. "He truly loves you as you are. You are not merely a prize." He glanced at her and looked quickly away again at the ground.

A guard stepped forward to open the castle door.

Phaera sighed. "I know."

The guards escorted Phaera to her chamber as Kort turned off toward his own.

As she bathed and prepared for dinner she wondered, not for the first, or last, time, what her life would be after Bain's return. How much freedom would she have to work? What would be expected of her at court when things returned to normal.

Yes, she did believe he loved her, but what would that really mean for her life? And would he stop loving her if she insisted on waiting to have his heir, if she insisted on having her healing work? Bain was not her father, whom she could always sway a little too easily. What pressure would come from Lord Makin? Would Nurias understand and support her? Or would she side with Bain if he insisted he wanted an heir as soon as possible.

How free would she be to gather her plants and medications? What would Bain think when he saw her drinking her anti-quickening tea? And how would she feel if that tea failed and she fell pregnant? The terror hit her again. She doubled over and clenched her hands over her abdomen. *I am not ready to die. I need more time.* Would she be able, and indeed allowed, to continue her healing work once she conceived or after the child was born?

She made herself straighten and raised her chin.

One thing she was sure of. If she survived childbirth she would not simply hand her babe to a wet nurse. She would not abandon her child to a stranger in order to do her healing work. The babe would have to come with her. She knew Nurias had kept Bain with her as a child. It must be possible. *If she survived. If… I must have time before I conceive. I will not give up all I have worked for so soon.* But a still voice in her mind whispered, "You may die". She shook it off with effort.

She also wondered how the war might have changed Bain. Would he still feel the same toward her? And would she still want him? Had she ever, really? Was that one night merely her body betraying her true wishes?

No answers to any of her musings presented themselves. She knew Bain's arrival was imminent, likely a matter of days. She slept fitfully, with dreams of dying in childbirth, alone, and of a furious Bain shouting at her when she told him she needed to work.

CHAPTER THIRTY-SIX

HOME

There it was, the hill topped by the familiar horizon that signaled home. Bain felt his heart speed up with anticipation. *And Phaera.* He looked to his left, where the two lords rode beside him and grinned at them.

"We will reach the castle by afternoon."

Lord Makin's return grin almost matched his own. "Yes, in time for dinner."

"And a bath." Bain gave an exaggerated shrug, as if he itched all over which brought a laugh from both lords.

"I think our ladies will insist on it."

Lord Danza agreed. "A bath and clean clothes will be most welcome, perhaps even more than good food."

Bain heard the chatter of the men rise behind him. When he turned to salute them and shouted, "We are home, men!" they pumped their fists in the air and cheered.

I am the heir, now, not the questionable bastard. The realization filled him with a deep satisfaction, and no small measure of pride. *I have earned this.* He sat straighter in the saddle, head high, shoulders back, all fatigue forgotten.

Yet, that pride was tempered by conflicting emotions, most of which circled around Phaera. *I have changed. I am a warrior now, as well as the healer's son. I have taken life. She will expect as much, surely. Will it turn her away from me when we have just begun? I know she will be pleased with the permission to set up her new apothecary. Will that be enough?* How pleased would she be to see him again? Would she still see the same man she saw when he met her? He knew he wasn't – yet he was. And how would she feel when she conceived? He had no doubt that would happen soon. *Surely she would not refuse me.* She had seemed agreeable the night he had first made love to her. Would she respond the same way again? She was strong-willed. It was one of the traits that attracted him to her. But what if that kept him out of her bed? He could order her to submit but she would hate him if he did. In any case that was out of the question. He had always known he would have her willing or not at all. *She will wish to continue with her work, even after she conceives and our child is born. Will she choose her work over our child? Surely not. But how much will her work take her away from her court duties? And from me?* Would they quarrel over that? *Oh, Love, please let us not quarrel.* His chest contracted at the thought.

Bain was brought out of his reverie by the approach of Captain Raskir leading an honour guard of ten men to welcome them home and escort them to the castle, which was now coming into view. Raskir halted in front of Lord Makin and saluted. "My lord. Welcome home. Congratulations on your victory."

"Thank you Captain. It is good to be home."

Behind the honour guard rode another ten soldiers. "My lord, may these men remove the prisoners to the dungeon? Your men will be weary."

"Indeed, Captain. Have them do so."

Once the prisoners had been removed the honour guard took their places and the entire party made its way to the gates of the castle. Cheers met them as soon as they came into sight. The people lined the road waving and shouting. They thronged through the gates after them. For a moment Bain wondered that

Lord Makin did not have Raskir prevent this. While people were normally free to come and go the war had made it necessary to check all that entered and left.

Bain looked at the jubilation of the crowd and understood that his father had taken a calculated risk. The people needed to celebrate. He noted with approval that Raskir had placed many extra guards within the area, at strategic points, and that they were alert. A line of soldiers also stood at attention several feet in front of the door to the castle itself. Behind them…

Phaera stood next to Lady Flor, erect, dressed in the sapphire gown he had so admired that first night he saw her. Instead of the pearls she favoured, she wore a heavy necklace of the multi-coloured jewels of fire created by the ancient cataclysm. Its many colours flashed in the late afternoon sun, lending her an aura of magic. Her raven hair had been left loose to flow down her back. Where the light breeze lifted it he thought he saw reflections of those jewels in it. The sight took his breath away. This was not the headstrong young woman he had left. No, this was a woman of power, regal and proud. His chest swelled with pride and awe … and some doubt. *And what do you see when you look at me, my love?*

The two lords and Bain dismounted and strode ahead, halting in front of the waiting women. The line of guards parted and the honour guard joined them as Bain and the two lords reached it. Then it closed again behind them.

Lady Flor rushed forward to her husband, decorum forgotten. He grinned and enveloped her in a long, deep embrace. "It is good to see you again. I have missed you."

Lord Danza had stepped back and stood watching his daughter, a mixture of pride and concern in his face.

Bain waited, his heart twisting in agony. Phaera did not move but stood as if rooted to the stone under her feet.

Then, as if shaken out of a spell, she met his eyes and stepped forward to greet him. He took her hands in his, afraid to embrace her.

She looked up at him and smiled. The sun rose in her face and in his heart.

"Welcome home, Milord. I am so glad you are safe."

Bain wrapped her in his arms, feeling her yield into him. The world faded.

From what seemed like far away the chatter around him brought him back. He heard the words "bath" and "banquet", amid others. The spell broke.

He held Phaera's hand as they followed the others into the castle and heard the doors thud closed behind them, shutting out the din of the people outside. Inside, however, the entry hall was also lined with the castle household, who took up the cheering, echoing the joy and excitement of those they had shut out.

They stood there a few moments, allowing their people time to voice their delight. Then Lady Flor let go of Lord Makin's arm and stepped forward, clapping her hands for attention, her face still suffused with joy.

"Thank you all. But our lords are tired and hungry."

The servants melted away, with many backward glances, the women tittering amongst themselves as they went.

Lady Flor once more had command of the castle. She called to a maid. "Kenna, escort Lord Danza to his chamber and see that he has all he needs to bathe and rest until the banquet."

"Yes, Milady." Kenna bobbed a curtsey and turned to gesture him. "Please follow me, Lord Danza."

Lady Flor turned to take Lord Makin's arm again. "And we," she said, beaming at Phaera, "will look after our husbands' needs personally".

Bain had not let go of Phaera's hand. Now he looked at her, one eyebrow raised in question.

She returned his smile. "Your bath awaits, Milord."

Bain's heart rose at the warmth in her voice.

When Phaera opened the door two maids were already pouring buckets of steaming water into a gleaming, copper tub.

As soon as the maids spotted them they straightened, bobbed curtsies and hurried out, empty buckets in hand. Phaera had let go Bain's hand and stood to one side as he surveyed the familiar room. Next to the steaming tub someone had set a small table within reach. On it stood scented soap, a comb, a pitcher, a ewer of wine, and a plate of fresh, light bread, butter, honey, and slices of fowl. In another bowl he spotted dried apple slices, raisins and nuts. His mouth watered.

When he began to reach for the meat Phaera stopped him with a playful slap at his hand. "In the tub first. Look at your hands."

He laughed. *Now I am home.* She took his travel clothes as he stripped and tossed them into the basket beside the table. As he lowered himself into the tub she took the basket and set it outside the door.

CHAPTER THIRTY-SEVEN

THROUGH PHAERA'S EYES

When a soldier had come during their morning meal to announce to Lady Flor that the men would arrive that afternoon the castle had erupted in a frenzy of preparation. Phaera had done her best not to let her misgivings show as she assisted Lady Flor in organizing the banquet and making sure that Lord Makin, Lord Danza, and Bain would have everything they could wish for. The copper bath tubs were readied in their chambers, with scented soaps and oils to hand. The best wine was brought up from the cellars and placed within reach. The great hall was hung with pennants and bunting. The best goblets and platters were set on long trestle tables brought into the great hall for the occasion. A dais was raised at one end upon which the head table stood, decorated with tapestries embroidered with the coats of arms of both Marston and Kinterron.

In spite of all the bustle, Phaera could not shake her anxiety.

Lady Flor remarked on her distraction. "My dear, what is it? What prevents you from sharing the joy we all feel?"

Phaera admonished herself silently. "My Lady, I do share your joy. We are safe once more and our men return to us unharmed." She thought quickly. "Perhaps it is that I am still a new bride and nervous." Well, that was true, as far as it went. She was relieved when Lady Flory sent her a knowing smile and said nothing more.

When a messenger had let them know that the party would arrive in a couple of hours Phaera and Lady Flor had made a last inspection round together. Satisfied that all was in order Lady Flor had turned to Phaera.

"It is time for us to adorn ourselves. We must look our best. Come with me. I have something for you that I hope you will wear."

Curious, Phaera had followed Lady Flor into her private chamber. Lady Flor chose a small key from among those hanging on the chain about her waist and unlocked a beautiful, small chest, ornately carved and enameled in a floral pattern. From the chest she took a heavy necklace made from the multi-coloured stones taken from the mines left by the cataclysm.

"This is for you. I have waited for the right occasion to present it to you. It would please me to see you wear it today, as a symbol of your status."

Phaera was speechless for a moment. The necklace was an exceptional example of those special jewels, stunningly carved, strung with gold and silver wires wrought into fine interwoven patterns. She understood what an honour this gift was, that it meant that all must respect her as the future Lady of Marston. *Well, I certainly cannot wear my pearls now, can I?*

"My Lady, you honour me too much. I have never seen such a fine necklace. I will be proud to stand beside you today with it around my neck."

Lady Flor had studied her for a moment, as if questioning the readiness of her acceptance, then gave a satisfied nod. "Good. Then let us prepare ourselves."

Phaera had wondered at Lady Flor's reaction as she left to bathe and dress for the banquet. Had she thought Phaera might refuse? How could she? It would have been a serious breach of etiquette. What did that say about Phaera's reputation at the castle, with Lady Flor, and others? She promised herself she must take more care not to appear too defiant and independent. The people here had not yet grown to love her as those of Kinterron had.

Phaera chose the blue gown that she knew Bain admired. Its deep hue would also set off the new necklace. Once Mira finished dressing her hair she sent the maid away and stood before the polished silver mirror.

Mira had trembled with awe at the sight of the necklace and seemed afraid to handle it. In any case, Phaera had wanted to put it on herself. She had never truly liked these heavy gems. They were too ostentatious for her tastes. But, today, she knew, they would make a statement, both to the people and to Lord Makin and Bain. With a deep breath she lifted the heavy chain from the small table in front of her and held it around her neck, still hesitating to fasten it. It glittered with every small movement she made, reflecting all the colours of the rainbow, scattering beams of tinted light onto the walls. Her reflection, holding the jewels to her throat, seemed that of a stranger.

AT A LIGHT KNOCK ON HER DOOR AND HER MAID, MIRA, SAYING, "IT is time Milady", she had fastened the necklace and called, "Enter. I am ready."

Mira halted abruptly upon seeing Phaera, eyes wide, and took in a deep inhalation of awe. "Oh, Milady, how beautiful."

"Thank you, Mira. Lady Flor is most generous." She stepped forward, smiling. "Shall we go?"

Lady Flor waited at the end of the hall, resplendent in her own jewels of state. Her hands fluttered in front of her until she clasped them together. "Come. They will be here soon. We must be ready."

Phaera stepped in beside her, the beating of her heart echoing Lady Flor's hands.

Liveried attendants opened the castle doors and stood at attention as they stepped out into the afternoon sunshine. Outside, ten guards took their places beside and behind them, dress tunics cleaned and brushed, boots polished, hair, those who wore it long, clubbed at the napes of their necks, shoulders proudly back. All along the walkway stood more guards, all in uniform dress tunics. Phaera noted with pleasure that the two guards closest to her wore the colours of Kinterron, a nod to both herself and the arrival of her father Lord Danza. They had not long to wait. The first things they spotted, rising up behind the low hill past the gates, were the pennants of both fiefs flying high and proud above the front horses. A trumpet sounded their arrival and all heads craned to see.

Phaera felt her pulse beating faster. Beside her, Lady Flor clenched her hands tightly together, her whole body visibly thrumming with anticipation. *She welcomes home a beloved husband. Who do I welcome?*

She spotted Bain immediately between the two lords. This was not the untried young man who had ridden off to war. No, this Bain sat proud, self-assured, larger somehow than she remembered. He was covered in the dust of the journey. His uniform was worn and dirty, the coat of arms on his tunic barely discernable. Yet, they sat on him as regally as the finest dress uniform might – no, better. He needed no adornment. His expression, the proud lift of his chin, the way he sat his horse, this was a man who knew himself, who had earned the posture he carried. Phaera stood rooted to the spot, unable to tear her gaze away.

She saw Bain search her face, watched a flicker of emotion crease his brow, then disappear as quickly as it had come.

The three lords slid from their mounts, handing the reins to the waiting stablemen, and stepped forward. The guards closed in behind them, leaving the three to stand inside a circle, facing the two women.

When Lady Flor rushed forward to embrace her husband Phaera barely noticed. A roar of cheering woke her from her trance. She shook herself and stepped forward to meet Bain, hands outstretched for him to grasp and smiled into his eyes as she said, "Welcome home, Milord. I am so glad you are safe." Her full heart told her she meant it. She let herself be drawn closer and relaxed into Bain's embrace.

They followed the two lords and Lady Flor into the castle amid tumultuous cheering. Phaera noted Bain's possessive grip on her hand. The din barely lessened upon the closing of the castle doors behind them as the servants inside set up their own cheers. It was as if the last shreds of darkness surrendered to sunshine. Every voice and every countenance reflected joy and light.

Phaera looked up at Bain to see him beaming. She had to admit to herself that she, too, had caught the mood. How could she not?

When Lady Flor sent the servants about their duties Phaera met Bain's eyes. "Your bath awaits, Milord."

Phaera saw Bain reach for a slice of meat waiting on the table beside the tub. She gave his hand a playful swat.

"In the tub first. Look at your hands."

Bain's earthy laugh eased more of her tension. As he stripped she took his dirty clothes and tossed them into a basket and outside the door. By the time she turned back he had lowered himself into the tub. A contented sigh escaped his lips and his eyes closed so that she could watch him unseen. The red, puckered scar on his upper arm took her by surprise, a sharp reminder that he was not the same man she had bade goodbye.

Phaera hesitated, not knowing what to do next, worried that any action might be seen as an invitation, one she was not yet ready to make.

When Bain opened his eyes he seemed to catch her uncertainty. His light tone reassured her somewhat. "My love, if you can help wash my hair I will be clean sooner."

Instead of reaching for her he handed her the soap. "I know you have done this many times for others in your work."

Phaera let out the breath she did not know she had been holding as she accepted the soap. This was not an invitation – yet. She decided to act in kind and treat the procedures with the same light tone. With her free hand she took a slice of meat and held it to his lips. He took it with a teasing grin, eyes twinkling.

She turned away quickly, feeling a blush rising, and covered her embarrassment by filling the pitcher next to them with water from the tub.

"Bend your head forward."

They shared a laugh when he said, "You wish to drown me already?"

"Perhaps later. Now close your eyes. Here comes the soap."

Bain scrubbed his own body, asking only that she feed him as he did so, "Or the water will grow cold."

That reassured Phaera further. She let the last vestiges of tension seep away. "Just remember I will not be your servant tomorrow."

He winked at her, and with mock seriousness, said, "Assuredly, Milady."

Throughout, Phaera took pains to avoid looking below his waist. She wanted these moments to remain light and companionable. When he rose out of the tub she handed him the drying cloth, still averting her eyes.

As he wrapped it around his middle she looked at her gown. With an exaggerated gesture she scolded, "Look what you have done to my gown. It is ruined. Now I shall have to find another for the banquet." The laugh they shared was free and easy.

Bain kept his back to her as he dressed, for which Phaera was grateful. *He understands. Or is he as shy as I am?*

Once dressed Bain turned to face her, tall and regal in his official regalia.

So handsome. I am the envy of all the young women. No one can deny what a fine figure he presents ... but I prefer the other man, the one who is at ease in less formal attire.

Phaera felt another blush rising as his eyes travelled her body from head to toe, finally meeting hers with a knowing nod as he took in the wet gown. "Yes, this will never do. You will need a clean gown. A shame, as this one is my favourite."

His eyes held her captive. She could not look away.

He reached for her. "Now may I finally kiss you, my love?"

His kiss was long and tender. Phaera felt herself melting into him, losing herself.

It was Bain who broke the spell, gently pushing her to arms' length again. One hand left her shoulder and slid to the jewels still around her neck, his voice rough with emotion. "I shall never forget the vision that greeted me home." His hand moved to her chin and lifted it so she could meet his eyes. "Never. But the woman I love wears pearls and often a simple riding gown as she works."

Phaera's emotions tumbled over one another, leaving her speechless. All she could do was beam at him as she fought the tears pricking behind her eyes.

She felt a loss when he let her go.

His expression betrayed the same thought. "I must leave you to dress, now. Our people await."

Overcome with a sudden shyness, she could only nod before turning and walking to her adjoining chamber. Once there she sank onto her favourite chair. *How can I not love this man – this wonder who knows my spirit, who sees into me, from whom I can hide nothing? I am lost.*

A light knock brought her to the present.

Phaera took herself in hand and regained her composure. "Come."

Mira entered. "I understand you have need of me, Milady."

Back in control, Phaera stood and strode to her wardrobe. "I shall need another gown for the banquet. This one is quite unsuitable, now."

"I think the green will set off the jewels just as beautifully, Milady."

Phaera fingered the gown in question, finally taking it with her and standing in front of the mirror, holding it below the necklace. Mira was right. The rich green did complement the jewels. She would have preferred to switch to her pearls to please Bain but in the end she sighed and left the necklace on. It would please the others, especially Lady Flor. The pearls could wait. Bain would understand. *Why does it matter that he understands?* The question remained unanswered as she allowed Mira to help her dress.

CHAPTER THIRTY-EIGHT

BANQUET

*P*haera studied Bain again, attired in his dress uniform, and gave him a mockingly formal curtsey of approval. "You do present a fine specimen."

His eyes said more than his words, his tone anything but mocking. "You, my love, take my breath away."

Phaera felt a small shiver of delight run down her spine. *Stop that. You care nothing for beauty.* This time, though, she knew she was fooling herself. "Are you ready?"

Bain held out his arm for her to take his elbow.

Well, this is a solemn occasion. I suppose I can behave. She gave him her most winning smile as she placed her hand delicately in the crook of his elbow. *Come to think of it, this is our first formal occasion together. Our wedding certainly does not qualify. Thank goodness I did not have to undergo that particular torture.* A secret smile played on her lips. When Bain raised his eyebrows in question she gave him a minute shake of her head and mouthed, "later", then looked straight ahead again.

Lord Makin, Lady Flor and Lord Danza waited to one side of the entrance into the great hall. They would all process together.

To Phaera's delight Nurias stood waiting with them. She looked rested, bathed, and wore a gown of soft, sage linen, cinched with a woven sash of many colours, simple but somehow appropriate for her. Around her neck hung a single jewel like her own on a fine gold chain. Her hair hung in a thick braid down her back, just as she usually wore it. It was the first time Phaera had seen her in anything but her drab healing gowns. She could see, now, what had attracted Lord Makin to her. Even at this age she was a handsome woman.

When Nurias spotted the pair her face glowed with pride and joy. She did not come forward but held out her hands to them as they approached, taking one from each of them as they came close enough.

"I am so happy to see both again at last."

They did not have time to respond as a blast from ten trumpets split the air, announcing their arrival. Lord Makin and Lady Flor led in, then Lord Danza followed by Bain and Phaera. Nurias fell in behind them as they entered and were shown to their seats, Nurias at the end, to Phaera's right, then Bain, Lady Flor, Lord Makin, and at the other end, Lord Danza.

Banners and pennants hung from the rafters in between the huge chandeliers bright with twenty candles each, which lit up the tapestries lining the walls. The entire great hall blazed with light and colour.

The hall had remained silent as they took their places, everyone standing at rapt attention behind their benches, facing the dais. *They must have been prepared.* Phaera had never seen anything like this. The solemnity of it awed her in a way no other occasion ever had. For the first time she understood the importance of, and was grateful for, the efforts she had taken to look her best. This occasion called for it. The people deserved it.

A soon as the party sat down a great cheer rose up, repeated three times in unison.

"ALL HAIL, ALL HAIL, ALL HAIL."

Another trumpet blast filled the air and died down before the guests took their seats.

The remainder of the evening became a blur of feasting, music, speeches, and drink. Phaera took pains to limit how much wine she drank and was pleased to see that Bain did as well. Nor did the others on the dais show any signs of inebriation.

When Lord Makin indicated it was time for them to leave Phaera was pleasantly surprised. It was not as late as she had anticipated.

He stood for attention, goblet raised. "Good people, we have had little rest these past days. It is time for us to take our leave of you. I thank you all for sharing this occasion with us. The servants have been instructed to keep food, wine, and music coming for as long as you wish. You have all earned this celebration. Make merry." He held his goblet high then took a last swig from it before setting it down.

That brought another swell of cheering, though this one had no order to it.

Outside the hall they wished each other a good night and went to their separate quarters.

Once in their chambers Bain made it obvious why he had remained sober.

"My love, I have dreamed of this since the moment we parted." He pulled her into a tender embrace, freed one hand and began to take down her hair.

Phaera, while in no way inebriated, had drunk just enough wine to relax. Soon they lay beside each other on the sheepskin in front of the hearth, the small fire there the only light. The shadows made by the flames sent enchanted shadows dancing over their skin.

Phaera was pleased that Bain seemed in no hurry. He explored every inch of her, played with her hair, and planted feather-light kisses wherever a shadow danced on a different part. Phaera soon found herself returning the playful gestures. She noticed his scar again when she stroked his arm and looked more closely to examine it, frowning at the rough, puckered ridge.

"This was not stitched by a woman, that is certain."

Bain laughed. "My battle wound. No, the medic was busy with another so I instructed a young soldier. It has healed. No matter."

"I did not know you were wounded."

"Tis nothing." He followed with a suggestive wink. "But if it concerns you perhaps you can kiss it better."

Phaera made a show of doing just that, then shook her head in mock dismay. "I fear I have no magic, my love."

He rolled her over with a laugh, his body half across hers and held her gaze. "Oh, but you do ... most irresistible magic."

As does he. Those eyes ... my love, how can I resist ...

Their first joining bloomed in a heat of passion. The second was slow and enchanted, allowing no thoughts of fear or pain to interfere. They were alone, in a cocoon of peace that would not be broken. They lay together afterward, complete and languid. Only when the fire died to embers, bringing a light chill, did Bain rise, lift her, and place her on his bed. He slipped in beside her where she snuggled close and rested her head on his shoulder, the blankets covering their twined bodies.

They woke in that same position with rays of sunlight on their pillow and in their eyes, and made love again before rising.

It was only as they dressed that Phaera remembered she had not drunk her tea the night before.

CHAPTER THIRTY-NINE

TRIAL

The morning after the banquet Lord Makin convened a hasty meeting with Lord Danza, Bain, Captain Reynce, Captain Raskir, and his four other top advisors.

"May I suggest we invite Phaera to be present?"

Bain's suggestion met with a round of raised eyebrows and quick shakes of most heads.

"This is a matter of state, Son."

Bain almost protested but decided the better of it. *She need not be exposed to such matters. What if she has already conceived? This would be too stressful in that condition.* He could not help but smile at the memory of their love-making. In spite of their fatigue and the lateness of the hour she had responded without hesitation to his advances. Phaera had looked so beautiful when she woke, her face still rosy, suffused with sleep, hair tumbled across the pillow. She had looked into his eyes then. Without either saying a word, they had made love again. *No, Father is correct. This is no place for her.*

"Mathune has gone completely mad." Lord Makin's brow furrowed. "I am concerned about what he will say, in his ravings, about Lady Phaera – and whether it will affect her reputation. I fear some will have doubts. Such speech has a habit of growing, once heard."

Lord Danza nodded. "And he rales in his madness about not being affected by death, even that he will return more powerful. Some people are superstitious and may see their misfortunes as signs of his revenge."

"Yes, this is one of those times when I would prefer the public not be present." Lord Makin sighed.

Raskir looked surprised. "Surely we cannot consider that. This trial must be public, as must Mathune's execution."

Nods followed around the table.

Raskir settled back into his chair looking uncomfortable about his outburst.

Lord Makin gave a rueful shake of his head. "Indeed, Captain. Though I wish it were not so. I also regret that it will be necessary for Lady Phaera and Lady Flor to witness both the trial and the execution. We cannot ignore protocol on such an important occasion. The people would see it as weakness – or even disapproval."

"My daughter will not be pleased with that, but I understand. If she objects let me speak with her."

Bain tried to keep his voice level. "That is my concern, now, Lord Danza."

Bain held his gaze a moment before Lord Danza gave him a small nod.

"As you wish, Lord Bain." He seemed to be hiding a smile behind one hand, though Bain could not be certain.

Lord Makin brought them back to the matter at hand. "We must bring Mathune out for the people to see. And custom dictates that he be allowed to say something in his defense but we must be ready. As soon as he begins to rant we must gag him."

Bain was relieved when all were in agreement.

"I think he ought to be beheaded." Reynce was the first to suggest the method of execution.

Raskir nodded agreement but Lord Makin shook his head. "It

has been so long since anyone has witnessed a public beheading. It is a brutal and bloody death. While I do not doubt that Mathune deserves such, my concern is for our ladies. Nurias will join us as well, I am certain. She and Lady Phaera are both healers. Lady Flor has a tender nature. As a mercy to them I suggest hanging." When this was followed by an uncomfortable silence he added, "We have lived in peace for many years, now. Public executions have been very rare. I would avoid encouraging a lust for revenge. The more peacefully we can accomplish what must be done the better."

The room fell silent. Bain could see the struggle on each man's face as he warred with himself. *And what do I want? What is best?* He cleared his throat for attention.

"Gentlemen, there is no doubt that Mathune deserves beheading. I also understand the argument for hanging. Our first duty is to our people. They must view the sentence as just. On the other hand, as Lord Makin has pointed out, most have never witnessed an execution of any kind. I believe that hanging will be enough of a shock. If there are those who protest we may say that losing his life is all the same to him, no matter the method."

Lord Danza shot him a pointed question. "Is this the healer or the heir speaking?"

"I speak as a leader who wishes our people to desire peace over vengeance, Milord. Our duty is to remove the threat to our peace and safety, not to provide a spectacle for the bloodthirsty."

Lord Makin gave him a long look, then a slow approving nod. "Good. It is settled then. Mathune shall hang."

OVERNIGHT A DAIS HAD BEEN ERECTED IN THE MARKET SQUARE, A canopy over it to shield the lords and ladies from the sun, which could still be bright even at this early stage of autumn. Across from it they had built a platform where the trial and execution would take place. On one side of it stood a scaffold, at the other the block and axe for beheading. The sentence would not be declared until the end of the trial.

They all went out to examine the preparations. No one spoke.

After a few moments Bain said, "May I suggest that the block and axe be removed. It will prevent a cry for beheading."

Lord Makin turned to Captain Raskir. "Have your men remove them, Captain."

"Right away, Milord."

Bain saw that the square had already begun to fill with onlookers. Some had brought children, which made him shudder in disgust. *Have we learned nothing from the cataclysm, from this war?* But he knew he had no authority to send them away.

Around the perimeter food vendors had set up shop, no doubt hoping for a brisk trade. Bain could not blame them, though it lent a carnival air to the event that would detract from its solemnity. Here and there he spotted individuals he thought he remembered following the prison caravan home. He wondered if Phaera would recognize some arrivals from Kinterron, come to witness on behalf of that region. How would they see the choice to hang instead of behead? Would they see justice being carried out?

With the inspection complete and last minute orders given the men returned to the castle to join the women for a light meal.

Bain could not read the expression on Phaera's face as Lord Makin explained the proceedings. She had taken on a blank look, which he took to be a fight for composure. It revealed nothing about how she felt, both about the need for her to be there or about the decision to hang Mathune. He had been such a personal threat to her. Did she want to see him beheaded? Or did she abhor the very idea of watching a man hang?

"I am sorry, my love, that you will have to witness this."

"It is necessary," was her only response, her face remaining a mask that gave nothing away. When he grasped her hand under the table it was ice cold. Nor did she return his clasp.

There was no time to speak with her alone. As soon as their meal finished Lord Makin gave the signal to Raskir that it was time to assemble. They all rose in silence and followed him out to the dais where they were shown to their respective chairs.

Bain looked at Nurias and saw her study Phaera with a concerned expression as well.

By now the square was packed with spectators, some sitting on the cobbled stone of the courtyard, the rest standing around the perimetre. The rise and fall of conversation reminded him of the annual Harvest Festival, though at that time the people would have been milling about rather than sitting in one place. *No, it is not the same. There is no joy in this.* The hubbub had almost gone silent when the party ascended the dais. Then it resumed, but with a different, more watchful, expectant tone.

When Raskir and Reynce took their places facing the dais, one at each end of the gallows platform, the crowd hushed. At a nod from Lord Makin both men marched off in the direction of the dungeons. Bain noted that four more guards had taken up posts at the back of the platform and that the hangman stood ready to one side of the gallows, feet planted apart, black hood in his hands.

When Reynce and Raskir reappeared with Mathune held between them a murmur passed over the crowd and people pointed them out to friends and children.

Bain saw Phaera shudder and look down at her hands, which she held tightly clenched in her lap. Nurias, on his other side looked almost as stressed. Lady Flor had gone dead white and kept her hands secured between her knees. Lord Makin took worried glances at her but Bain knew he could do nothing to help her, not even take her hand. *It would be seen as weakness. Why must we watch this? He needs to die. That is certain. Why can we not have the trial and pronounce sentencing without having the hanging public? What good purpose can it serve? Perhaps this is something I can change when I am Lord.*

The head magistrate took the platform. The guards turned

Mathune so they stood face-to-face in the center. At a nod from Lord Makin the magistrate listed Mathune's offenses and the evidence against him. He had clearly been trained for this as he hada voice that carried over the crowd.

Mathune had stumbled up with his head down, but as he listened to the charges his head rose, his shoulders straightened, and Bain could see both pride and rage come over him. He tried unsuccessfully to shake off the guards holding him but his stance made it plain he had no regrets.

At the end of the litany the magistrate asked the formal question. "Mathune of Belthorn, have you anything to say to these charges?"

"*LORD* Mathune! You have no right to accuse me." He began to shake, and managed to get one arm free long enough to raise an accusing finger at Phaera. Spittle foamed at his lips and he struggled to get words out of his mouth. "She….she…witch…whore… need to purify…"

Lord Makin did not give the signal to gag him. Bain approved. Mathune's speech was unintelligible and incoherent so there was no need. The people would see no power in it. They would see nothing amiss.

After allowing Mathune to rave for several minutes, leaving no doubt as to both his guilt and his madness, the magistrate signaled to the guards to pull him back. Mathune continued to sputter but the magistrates ringing declaration drowned him out as he pronounced sentence.

"Mathune of Belthorn you have been found guilty of the crimes charged. The penalty is death by hanging, to be carried out forthwith." He turned to salute Lord Makin. "May we proceed, Milord?"

"Proceed."

The rapt crowd heard that single word. The only other sounds were Mathune's strangled squeals of protest as the executioner pulled the hood over his head, tied his arms behind his back, and placed the noose around his neck. He was lifted onto the tall block and held in place while the noose was tightened. The executioner looked at Lord Makin. On receiving the signal to proceed he kicked the block from under Mathune's feet.

Bain stared in morbid fascination as he watched Mathune jerk and twist. A dark stain spread across the poor dun breeches that were his only garment.

Only then did the crowd erupt into cheering. The sound sickened Bain and shook him out of his trance. A look across the dais showed Lady Flor covering her face. Phaera's was white as alabaster, seeming sculpted from that stone. She stared straight ahead, eyes wide and expressionless. Nurias looked ashen as well, and he watched a single tear track down the crease beside her nose.

The two lords watched, grim but unflinching, until the last twitches ceased. Lord Makin turned to Lord Danza and the two rose as one to stand at the centre front of the dais.

Lord Makin took a deep breath before declaring, "It is finished. Justice has been served. Let all our peoples return to peace."

Lord Danza saluted him. "Let it be so."

Lord Makin gave a signal to the executioner. "Cut him down and bury him outside the city in an unmarked grave. Let him be remembered only as a lesson to those who would flout the laws of the lands and pervert them to their own purposes."

With that the two lords turned their backs on the crowd. They approached the women to lead them from the dais. Lord Danza escorted Nurias.

Bain offered Phaera his arm. She rose and took it as though in a trance. At the thud of the castle doors closing behind them she jerked as though struck.

CHAPTER FORTY

CLASH

"You have betrayed me!"

Bain stormed out of her chamber. The crash of the door slamming shut behind him drowned out the last of her, "No, I have not...", and left her staring mutely at the space Bain had just occupied.

Stunned, she whispered to herself, again, "No I have not."

The ten days since Bain's return had gone so smoothly. Phaera was finally beginning to relax into her married status. Her feelings for Bain had settled, leaving her content in the knowledge that he loved her, that he would not discourage her from her healing work, that she had time ... and that she did love him as well.

The niggling doubt she had suppressed about what Bain's reaction would be when he discovered her tea drinking habit resurfaced. Had she betrayed him? The answer remained unclear. While she had not hidden the habit from him, neither had she brought it to his attention, or sought his opinion. Was that betrayal? A frisson of anger arrived to accompany her doubt. What right had he to demand that she try to conceive immediately? How could he expect her to stop her work so quickly? Surely he knew it would take time to fill and establish her apothecary, time for people to begin to come to her in larger numbers, time to gain a reputation and trust in this land where she was still so much a stranger. Was Bain the betrayer – not she? That thought fuelled her anger for only a few moments, then died with the honest scrutiny she turned on herself. No, Bain had done nothing to stop her work. In fact he had encouraged her, even accompanied her to help with gathering some plants and roots. But why was he so furious? Why had this revelation shocked him so? *I ought to have told him, made him aware instead of waiting for him to discover it on his own.*

She sank into her chair, miserable, lonely, and afraid this rift would haunt them forever. Would he rethink his reaction? Would he come back with an apology? Would he remain angry? Would he insist she stop drinking the tea? If he did, what would that do to her feelings for him? Could she refuse him her bed? Could he demand it? Would they grow to hate each other? With each moment her thoughts became more dire, more hopeless. What could she do?

She decided, for the moment, to do nothing. This was partly because she was numb, but partly because she could not think of any action that would make things better. The prospect of conceiving and then dying in childbirth haunted her. On the other hand the thought that Bain, and likely the others she had come to rely on, would see her as a traitor paralyzed her. There was no one she could turn to, no one who would understand, who could make Bain understand.

His accusation echoed in her mind, over and over. *"You have betrayed me!"*

A light knock made her look at the door. She heard herself say, as if from somewhere else, "Enter."

Mira poked her head in. "Milady, Kort is wondering if all is well. He expected you at the apothecary some time ago."

"I lost track of time." She rose and straightened the apron in front of her skirt. "I am on my way."

The quizzical look Mira gave her as she held the door for her barely registered ... Kort. Would he listen? Would he understand and remain loyal to her? *No, he will never die in childbirth. He will never wed. How can he begin to understand?*

She got through the rest of the day as in a trance, speaking only when spoken to, answering with only one or two words, avoiding eye contact.

Towards the end of the afternoon, Kort asked, "Milady, what is amiss? Perhaps I can help."

That brought her up short. Of course he had noticed. She turned to him and said, "It is nothing important. It will pass. Thank you."

Kort did not press her but the expression on his face made it clear he believed not a word. He turned his attention back to the liniment he was preparing. "I wonder when we can expect Nurias. She has offered to take me to some of her patients. I am eager to learn more about that part of this work."

Nurias. What would her reaction be? Nurias knew how Phaera felt, had heard her fear of dying in childbirth. Whose side would she take? Had Bain gone to her with his tale? He was her son. Would she side with him?

Phaera shook herself. "Yes, I hope she will ask for you soon."

Kort filled a small clay jar with the finished liniment, pressed the cork into the top, and wiped his hands on the cloth on the table. "Milady, it begins to grow dark. It is time to go in for dinner."

Phaera looked out the open door, allowing that information to register. "Yes, let us go."

She ignored the long look Kort gave her and headed out the door.

Bain had not returned as she dressed for dinner. Nor did he join them at the table. With each hour Phaera grew more miserable, more apprehensive.

When she returned to her chamber and prepared for bed Bain

still had not returned. Where could he have gone? By now she was certain he would not return with an apology. He was still furious with her. She tossed and turned most of the night, sleeping in short fits accompanied by lurid dreams of everyone turning against her, calling her traitor.

As dawn brought the early light into her chamber she dressed and opened the door to Bain's adjoining one, the one he never used as he always slept with her in her bed. It was empty. The bed had not been disturbed. She stared at it in abject misery. Was he so angry that he could not even bear to be near her?

At the morning meal she asked Lord Makin if there had been some duty that had taken Bain away. Lord Makin gave her a quizzical look, shook his head, and suggested, "No doubt he is attending to some matter that needs his presence."

Phaera was grateful that he did not press her as to why she did not know where Bain was. How would she have answered him? Telling him what had happened was out of the question. He, of all people, would not have understood.

Her only hope was Nurias. Could she go to her, explain, and hope she would find some support there? If so, Nurias might help Bain understand. If not, she did not know what she would do. Perhaps she would be sent back to Kinterron in disgrace. Perhaps Bain would set her aside and find another woman who would provide him with his heir. At last, tears broke through the desolation she felt. She sank into her chair and wept. Was this what she would come to?

When she had no more tears left she splashed water on her face, put on her riding gown and strode to the stables. She hoped her face would no longer betray her by the time she reached them. She sought out the stable master and ordered her horse saddled.

"Will you be riding alone, Milady? And will you be long?"

Under normal circumstances she would have answered civilly, understanding that he was merely doing his duty and showing care for her welfare. Today her answer was curt. "Yes, I will ride alone and I know not when I shall return."

The man's eyebrows shot up for a second, then he hurried away to get her horse. When he brought the mare and held her still as she climbed up he ventured, "If asked, Milady, where may I say you have gone?"

Her first impulse was to tell him it was none of his concern, but she caught herself. "I have business with Nurias and have gone to see her."

The stable master lost some of his wariness, relieved. "Thank you, Milady."

He handed her the reins and stepped out of the way.

CHAPTER FORTY-ONE

TO NURIAS

*B*ain's fury had not abated on the ride to see his mother. He had remained lost in thoughts of betrayal, anger – and yes, hurt.

His mount, familiar with the route, had needed no guidance. Once turned in the direction of Nurias' cottage Bain had given him his head. It left him free to simmer in his own dark mood. *She knows how important this is. Lady Flor could not give Father an heir. That is why he chose to make me his heir. Now it is my duty to produce a legitimate one. She knows this. How could she try to prevent it? How could she hide it from me? Did she think my blind love for her would excuse it? Does she believe she can do no wrong in my eyes; that I will forgive anything? Does my reputation mean nothing to her? After all I have done to make her happy, things that no woman in her position has ever been able to do – her work, her apothecary. Am I merely a pawn? No! I cannot let this go. How could she? She has betrayed me. I trusted her.*

Bain's mind circled in a loop that offered no way out. And with each repetition his rage and hurt grew, though he refused to acknowledge the hurt and fueled the rage to avoid it.

When his mother's cottage came into view the day had passed

unnoticed. Now, with his early home in sight, he realized that he had eaten nothing and it was now late afternoon. His stomach distracted him from his gloomy litany with a loud growl.

Nurias had spotted him as he approached and came to greet him. "Bread has just come from the oven. Come." She still held the dark fragrant loaf on a wooden board and used it to gesture toward the door.

When Bain sputtered about needing to talk she gave him a knowing smile and said, "It can wait until you have a full stomach."

The choice of chamomile for the tea had been hers. After a quiet meal Nurias led him outside to sit in the warm sun where he related his tale of betrayal.

"Discuss it? How could I. She was drinking the stuff before I returned. And she did not ask me, or tell me she was doing so."

"Hmmm. You misunderstand me. Have you and Phaera discussed when you both would like to have children, what is the immediate future you would like to see?"

"Why? We both have a duty to produce my heir." Bain knew his mother always had a reason for any question she asked but this time he did not want to follow her lead. "What can there be to discuss?"

"How old are you?"

Bain bristled. "You know I am twenty."

"Indeed. And how old is Phaera?"

Finding no easy retort come to mind Bain finally answered. "Eighteen. Why?"

Nurias looked out into the distance, her voice so low Bain had to strain to make it out. "And how many years do you think Phaera has before she can no longer produce a child?"

Bain had no answer for that. The only thing he could muster was a feeble, "But she betrayed me."

When Nurias remained silent Bain became annoyed with her. *She is doing it again. Her mother talk.*

But the "mother talk" was doing its work, making him stop to think, to question himself, to look beyond his rage.

The sun had sunk lower bringing a chill to their bench which now sat in shade. Nurias rose. "Come. Bring some wood in for the hearth and start a fire. I will make some warm milk and honey. It is too late to return to the castle. Your cot is ready, as always."

Bain stood and watched her back disappear into the cottage. The talk was over. It had been years since he had had this kind of conversation with his mother. It had not often been necessary. So he took a steadying breath and decided pursuing this further tonight was unwise. He knew from experience it would accomplish nothing. He could almost hear her words from the past. *"We can talk again when you have had time to calm yourself and think more clearly."* Resigned, Bain filled his arms with wood and followed Nurias into the cottage.

They spent a companionable evening, saying little. Bain watched his mother go about her homely bustle. The familiar routine and the warm milk had their desired effect. His rage seeped out slowly to a manageable level. Unfortunately that also allowed his hurt to surface. He felt desolate. By now the sun had disappeared. The only light came from the fire in the hearth and the candle Nurias handed him that would light his way into the low loft where he would find his bed.

"It is time to sleep, Son." She took his face in her hands and kissed his forehead, as she had done ever since he could remember. "Good night."

He pulled himself out of the chair with effort, his limbs heavy and movements slow. "Goodnight, Mama," and made his way up the ladder to his cot. *But will I sleep?* For a moment he wondered if his mother had added valerian to his tea, then shook his head with an inward smile at his foolishness. Had she done so he could not have missed the horrid smell and taste. He must just be weary indeed.

When Nurias still did not bring the subject up as she served him porridge and eggs the next morning Bain knew he had to be the one to speak first.

"You are right, Mama, that I must speak with Phaera. But now that this has passed between us I know not what to say. She ought to have told me about the tea, to have asked me what I thought of it."

"Perhaps. But you said it was in plain sight. Is it possible she expected you to know?"

"I do not know."

"Then, perhaps, that is where the discussion may start." Nurias turned to face Bain, leaning back against the table, hands folded in front of her apron. Bain thought she hesitated, as though wondering whether to say more. He waited, as he had learned to do when she was thinking. She did not keep him waiting long.

"You know the circumstances of Phaera's mother's death, that she died in childbirth and that the babe was also stillborn, do you not?"

"Yes, it is well known."

"Think. How old was she when this happened?"

Bain furrowed his brow. The question was simple enough so why did she ask it in that way? "Very young, I think, perhaps seven years only."

"Yes. And she was at the bedside as her mother took her last breaths. Now think carefully. What effect do you think such an early trauma might have on a young girl?" Her voice had taken on a tone of admonishment. "Remember that when you speak with her. I can say no more without breaking trust."

Bain felt the sting of her warning. He thought about what Nurias said and finally ventured, "She told me that it was her mother's death that prompted her wish to become a healer."

"True." Nurias had turned back to the kettle and replaced it on the hook with the one she used to make tea. She smiled over her shoulder at him as if this were the most ordinary conversation in the world. "Sage, this time, I think?"

Bain simply nodded. He had more important things to think about, not the least of which was how to open a conversation with Phaera after he had acted so rashly. He had made assumptions. Those needed to be acknowledged. And he had to listen, so that Phaera would trust him. Would she explain why she had not been more open with him? Had she always felt he would not understand?

When he finished his tea he knew he could delay no longer. "Mama, will you pack me some bread and cheese. I must go back and it grows late already."

Nurias raised an eyebrow at him. "Have you already forgotten how to do that yourself?" She smiled and reached for the cheese.

The smile took the sting out of her words. Bain sent her a rueful grin back. "It seems I am getting too used to being waited on." He took a knife out of its groove on the wall and pulled the bread towards himself.

With a low chuckle Nurias reassured him. "I will never allow that as long as you are in my presence."

"I hope not. I count on it."

Bundle in hand he led the way out of the cottage and to his horse. He put the food into the small saddlebag and turned to embrace his mother. "Goodbye, Mama. I am grateful, as always, for your wisdom."

"All will be well. But you must remember that lasting love can only grow where there is trust."

CHAPTER FORTY-TWO

PHAERA'S TERROR

It was late afternoon when Phaera spotted the smoke from Nurias chimney and urged her mare into a faster trot. *Thank goodness she is at home.*

Remembering that Nurias was already aware of her terror of childbirth had calmed Phaera somewhat. She believed that, at the very least, Nurias would listen, even if she did not approve of her actions. *What if Bain is there? What if he has already told her what happened?* Even so, Phaera trusted that Nurias would also wish to hear her side.

She rode up to the cottage just as Nurias had come out to see to her own horse before retiring. She looked up and waved when she recognized Phaera, and waited for her to ride up.

"My dear, it is good to see you. Welcome. Have you eaten?"

The answering growl from Phaera's stomach made her laugh. "Oh, I see. Well we must remedy that."

Phaera could not help but smile in return. The comical exchange helped to ease her anxiety.

Nurias insisted that she eat and finish her meal before speaking about why she had come. The food, the tea, and the warmth from the hearth added some distance to her distress.

Somehow her situation no longer seemed so dire. *This is what makes her so successful as a healer.*

Once the few dishes had been cleaned and put back onto their shelf Nurias set her chair opposite Phaera's and folded her hands in her lap, her 'listening' posture.

"Before you begin I must tell you that I know what caused you to seek me out. Bain has already been here. He left earlier today. You must have missed each other. Just as well, I think." She sent Phaera an encouraging smile. "Now, how can I help you?"

Phaera blurted out the only thing that came to mind in that instant. "I am not ready."

"You do not feel ready to bear a child."

"No."

"Can you explain?"

"I need time to set up my apothecary and people need time to trust me and come to me. I need time for them, especially those at the castle, and Lord Makin and Lady Flor, to see me for who I am. I am not like other lords' wives. I cannot be content with only that role. They need to accept that." Phaera's voice had risen and become more plaintive as she spoke. "I cannot have a child yet. I cannot."

"You think no one will accept that – even Bain."

"No. It has been made plain that my duty is to provide an heir. It seems that is all I am good for." Phaera leaned forward, rigid, fists clenched in her lap.

"There is more, I think ... more that makes this problem so important."

Phaera deflated, letting her body sag into the back of the chair. *Yes, there it is. I am found out. I am a coward.*

Her excuses all gone, she could no longer hold onto any show of strength. Tears began to flow freely. She did not try to hide them behind her eyes, or her hands. There was no point. She lifted her head, and opened her silent misery to Nurias. At last she ventured, "I am so afraid. I do not want to die. I need some time before I die."

Nurias rose from her chair and knelt beside Phaera, taking one limp hand in her two.

"I know child. But how much time do you think you need before you no longer need more time?"

Phaera broke down. Huge sobs wracked her body. Nurias said nothing but wrapped her arms around her and drew her close as she wept.

When the sobs had run their course and began to subside she whispered to Phaera, "This is the fear of a young girl who watched her mother die. You know, Child, from your own work, that it is highly unlikely to be your fate." She stroked Phaera's back and drew back a little so she could see Phaera's face.

"Are you brave enough to look at that with me? I am here. I will not shame you. I understand where that fear comes from."

"How will that change anything?"

"We will go back to that day – together. You will not see it alone. We will look at every small piece that frightened you, and we will face them together. I will be with you."

A fresh spate of tears wet Phaera's face as she clung to Nurias and tried to bury her head into her shoulder. That made her realize how uncomfortable Nurias must be. She managed to collect herself enough to say, "Forgive me. Perhaps we can sit on the bed together."

Nurias nodded and rose to move to the bed, not letting go of Phaera's hand. She sat on her cot and drew Phaera over beside her, placing an arm firmly around her.

"See how strong you are. Even in your worst moment you can muster compassion for another. You can conquer this fear, Phaera. I will help, and I daresay Bain will as well."

They explored every aspect of Phaera's phobia, every small thought that popped into her mind as they talked. A few hours and several mugs of tea later Phaera was spent. She had no more tears, no more objections or ideas, nothing left to drag into view. She was left with only a deep, lethargic calm.

"You may sleep in Bain's bed tonight." Nurias indicated the ladder to the loft. "I think you will have no trouble sleeping." She gave Phaera a quick hug. "Good night."

"Good night ... and thank you."

Nurias was right. Phaera fell asleep almost as soon as she lay her head down and woke only when she heard Nurias rustling about below her.

"Good morning sleepy head." Nurias' warm smile and cheerful tone was contagious and Phaera found herself smiling back. "What smells so good?"

"The hens laid eggs. I've mixed them with some stale bread, milk, and honey in the skillet, along with some raisins. I call it bread pudding. It was always a favourite of Bain's."

Phaera sniffed the skillet as Nurias moved it to the table. "Mmmm. Perhaps I shall pass this on to Velna at the castle."

"I am sure Bain would not think of that. It will be a welcome surprise to him."

Phaera found she had a good appetite. "I can see why Bain likes it. This is delicious." She poured herself another mug of the bitter chicory root brew. "And the bitterness of this sets it off. I had no idea you were a good cook as well as a healer."

They both looked up at the sound of a horse approaching.

CHAPTER FORTY-THREE

THE TALK

When Bain returned to the castle darkness had already begun to fall. The stable master met him to take his horse, looking as though he had been preparing to retire, pulling a clean tunic over his head as he hurried over, hair spiky and wet and hands still wet from washing.

"Milord, I am not sure if I ought to tell you this but ... Lady Phaera left early today. She was not herself. When I asked if I might say where she was going she said she had business with Nurias."

"You did well to inform me. Saddle a fresh horse. I will go there at once myself."

The stable master looked like he wanted to ask more but caught himself and simply said, "Right away Milord."

"Good. I will return momentarily."

Bain raced into the castle and had Cook pack some travel fare. While she did that he sought Lady Flor to inform her where he was going and that Phaera was likely there already.

At her worried question he answered, "No, there is no need for concern, Milady. You may expect us both by tomorrow evening."

He turned on his heel to hurry away before she could press for more.

By the time he reached the stables a fresh horse stood saddled and ready, reins in the hands of the waiting stable master.

"Thank you. If anyone asks you may say we will both be back by evening tomorrow."

"Yes, Milord."

Bain took the reins, jumped into the saddle and rode into the darkness. This horse did not know the way. Bain had to remain alert but he had ridden this route so many times since joining Lord Makin's household that he had no trouble traversing it even in the dark. A half-moon provided just enough light for him to avoid boulders and small bushes.

As he reached Nurias' cottage he spotted his mother emerging to see who might have come. He watched her turn to say something to someone behind her and breathed a huge sigh of relief. Phaera must be there. That was confirmed when she followed Nurias out.

Nurias reached him first. "There is bread pudding and brew on the table. I have work to do out here. Take your time."

Phaera had remained behind Nurias, looking uncertain. "Thank you, Nurias." She turned and led the way back into the cottage.

Bain sat on his mother's cot while Phaera set one of the chairs to face him, a cup of brew in each hand. She handed one to Bain and set hers on the table.

When it became apparent that Phaera would not be the one to open the conversation Bain took a breath. He decided not to hedge and asked his burning question head on.

"I did not wait for an explanation before I left. I need to know. Why did you hide the tea from me?"

Phaera shook her head, though her face was sad more than angry. "I did not hide it from you. I simply did not bring it to your attention." She looked up at him from her hands which she had been clasping and re-clasping in her lap. "I should have."

Bain could not hide the edge in his voice. "Yes, you should have. Why did you not? You promised me 'no secrets' between us. I trusted you. I thought you trusted me, too. It seems I was mistaken."

"I was afraid." She sent him a beseeching look. "I was afraid you would think me a coward, or selfish, or, as seems to be the case, as betraying you - or even my duty."

Bain bit off the angry retort before it passed his tongue, remembering his talk with his mother. He was going about this all wrong. It took him a long moment to collect himself.

"Let me start over. I came here to find you and to listen. I will try to be silent until I have heard you out. Tell me what I need to know to understand. Why were you afraid?"

Phaera nodded and resumed twisting her fingers as she spoke. "Nurias knew. I had told her some of it before." She proceeded to explain everything, just as she had with Nurias earlier, but without the tears. She kept her eyes on her fingers, not looking up to meet his until she ended with, "Bain, I have work to do before I die. I am not ready to die. And I fear that is exactly what will happen if I conceive right away. So many choices have been taken from me. I could not risk this one being taken as well, one that might cost me the rest of my life. I feared you would not understand."

Bain had leaned toward her the entire time she spoke. Now he sat straight, hands pressed, into the blanket on the cot as if to hold himself there. He sat, studying her for some time. When he finally spoke his voice was low.

"I knew you were afraid of childbirth but I had no idea your fear ran so deep. I never considered that you might die giving birth. That possibility never crossed my mind."

He studied her again before continuing, unable to keep his hurt and confusion from showing in his voice. "I thought that my support of your work, against, as it is, our traditions demanding how a lord's lady is expected to act, would mean that you ... well, that you would agree to try to conceive immediately, that you would support *me* in *my* duty to produce an heir. Does that mean so little to you?"

He watched her face crumple and a single tear find its way down one cheek. "I want to do that for you. Truly I do. But I cannot. Not yet. I thought I would know when the time was right. But Nurias has helped me to see that that will never happen on its own. I know I need to face my fear, to trust that I am unlikely to die." She buried her face in her hands, as new tears spilled over her eyelids, "but I am still so afraid. You must think me a coward."

Bain had never seen her weep before, never seen her so vulnerable. His hurt melted away. He knelt by her chair and drew her into his arms, where her tears wet his tunic. It took some time for her sobs to subside into sniffles and hiccups.

Finally, as he stroked her hair, he whispered, "Forgive me, my love. I wish that you had not been afraid to speak to me of this." He felt her nod into his shoulder.

Feeling his legs begin to cramp he half stood, put one arm under her knees and lifted her to sit beside him on Nurias' cot.

They sat that way, saying nothing, until Bain offered, "Perhaps my mother can help with your fear. She heals more than bodies."

Phaera sniffled into his shoulder, then looked up at him. "Yes, she has already helped me find the courage to tell you. But I will need some time. Can you grant me some time? Will you wait for your heir for a while?"

Bain hesitated before reaching up to stroke her cheek and lift her chin so he could meet her eyes. "Mama pointed out to me that we are both still very young." He held her gaze for a moment before adding. "I think we may have some time."

When she wrapped her arms around his neck and whispered, "I do love you," he knew he had said the right thing.

CHAPTER FORTY-FOUR

SPRING

*P*haera looked up to see the light frame a familiar figure in the open door of her apothecary. A gust of cold air swept across her ankles.

"Kort! I see the winter has treated you well." She hurried over to greet him with a hug as he closed the door against the spring chill. "Come warm yourself by the hearth and tell me all about your studies with Nurias."

Kort strode to the fire and bent to rub his hands together close to the flames. Phaera followed behind. He turned his head to look at her as she came to stand beside him, his face wreathed in a wide grin. "You will not believe it. Nurias, wonder that she is, convinced a birthing mother to allow me to watch, though the woman would not let me touch her. What a miracle birth is."

"No! Truly? The husband did not prevent it?"

"That is the other wonder. Nurias convinced him to stay as well – to protect his wife's honour, she said, but she had told me earlier she has long wished men would remain to see their children born. She thinks they would value their wives more if they could see what they have to go through to give them children." He reached up to remove his hooded fur cloak, folding it across the closest chair. "Ah, it is good to be warm again."

"What a baby you are. It is not that cold out any more." She winked at him and reached for the pot sitting on the brazier.

Kort anticipated her, grabbed an empty mug from the table and held it out so she could pour the tea, sage by the aroma. *A warming herb.*

They each took a chair facing the other in front of the hearth.

"I have missed you these two months. Tell me what Nurias has taught you. Tell me what you learned from visiting people in their homes that I could not teach you here."

No one interrupted them and they lost track of time as Kort regaled Phaera with all his adventures and she pressed him for details. Only when one of her candles sputtered and died did Phaera exclaim, "Goodness, we will be late for dinner. Come." She rose and blew out the other candles and the lamps, keeping only one burning in its glass to guide them out and into the castle.

As they passed through the back doors and entered the dungeon Kort remarked. "I see this is no longer guarded. You are no longer considered in danger."

"Yes, I insisted it was not necessary." She jangled a heavy ring of keys. "They do insist that I keep the doors locked, however." Once inside she relocked the heavy doors and hung the keys on their hook in a niche in the side hall, out of sight.

"No prisoners left either, I see."

"Yes, all the political prisoners have been dealt with. Bain convinced Lord Makin that it would be safer to confine prisoners in the brig at the barracks. He plans to build a separate jail this year behind the barracks, away from the castle."

As they entered the hallway that led to the sleeping chambers Phaera hailed a maid. "Look who has returned. Please see that a fire is lit in Kort's chamber and," she looked in Kort's direction, "I assume you will be wanting a bath?"

Kort nodded vigorously, grinning. "Indeed. I dare not appear at dinner smelling of horse."

"Do not linger in the bath. I already smell dinner." She left him at the door to his chamber and went into her own to change her gown.

Bain arrived to dress for dinner just as she finished. "The stable master informed me that Kort has returned. Have you seen him?"

"Yes, he will be joining us for dinner. He has had a good winter."

Bain drew Phaera into an embrace. "Good, I look forward to hearing about that." He studied Phaera's face for a moment, a worried frown creasing his brow but he said nothing. His expression cleared as he took her hand and said, "Come. Let us go. I could eat a whole sheep."

They joined Lord Makin and Lady Flor for a lively dinner during which Kort kept them entertained with anecdotes from his studies over the winter.

"The reactions of folk to seeing a man as healer have certainly been interesting."

Kort's rueful shake of his head told them it had not been as serious as he had feared. He confirmed that when he said, "The women seem to accept me better than the men, which I found surprising until I thought about it. It makes sense to me now. Women are less bothered by me. When Nurias explains what I am they understand I am no threat to them. The men have greater difficulty with that."

"But do they believe Nurias? Do they become less suspicious after hearing of your preference? Or do they remain angry?"

Kort looked sad. "It is hard to let them know what I am. So many get angry or try to turn away. If Nurias were not with me I fear I might not have returned in such a good state." He sighed. "But Nurias is very persuasive. I think she has made several people – women and men – think about - well, about what it means to be who I am, that I am no danger to them."

Phaera nodded. "I hope that grows, Kort. If you are to be a healer, and be on your own, that will be important." She gave him an approving look. "I know how much courage it has taken to be open. I also know it is necessary if you are to be accepted as a healer."

Bain nodded agreement. "But you must be careful."

"Thank you both. And I will. But I am open not only for myself but for all like me. Our lot is not easy and perhaps, in some small way, this will make it easier."

Lord Makin and Lady Flor had been mostly silent. Now they both nodded as Lord Makin said, "I hope so. I will admit, until Bain introduced you and stood up for you I was suspicious of you. I trust you now, but that has not come easily."

"I am most grateful that you do, Milord." The catch in his voice betrayed the depth of his gratitude.

CHAPTER FORTY-FIVE

LATE

With each day that Phaera counted her anxiety grew. By the sixth she was snapping at both Bain and Kort for no obvious reason.

On the seventh morning Bain found her huddled on the floor in the privy, arms hugging her knees, rocking back and forth. He began, "What is…" and stopped midsentence, regarded her a moment then followed with, "Oh" before crouching down beside her.

Phaera could not speak but she did not need to. She could tell that Bain knew, and that he knew better than to touch her.

"You will not die, my love. You will not."

When Phaera did not respond he said, "I will send for my mother. She will help you."

He reached a hand toward her, offering it for her to take. "Come, you cannot remain here. Let me help you up."

Phaera looked at his hand. Slowly his words reached her. *You will not die. My mother will come.* She unwound one arm from where it clamped around her knees and reached out to take Bain's extended hand. With great effort she uncurled and allowed him to help her stand before letting him wrap his arms around her.

As he rocked her from side to side he whispered into her ear, over and over, "You will not die. Mama will see to it. You will not die. It will be all right."

It took some time before his touch and voice soothed her enough that her paralyzed body would allow tears to flow. She took strength from his calmness, from his warmth, from the support of his arms holding her close, from his whispered mantra. She was grateful he made no effort to change what he was doing, that he just let her be, let her take all the time she needed.

As her sobs subsided she felt wobbly on her legs and unable to hold herself up. Bain tightened his grip and caught her, lifted her up and laid her on the bed. He lay beside her and pulled her toward him until her head rested on his shoulder. He still said nothing so she did not have to speak, did not have to answer. That felt good. When she began to shiver he pulled the blanket over them both.

It took a long time before she became fully aware that Bain was making no demands but as that awareness found its way into her perception her gratitude grew. As did her trust of Bain. As did her true sense, in body as well as in mind, that he loved her. He would not press her to be brave. He would not give false assurances. He would not expect her to pretend she was not frightened. She let this deeper awareness of his love infuse her. The burden was no longer hers alone. He shared it.

As this new awareness grew so did Phaera's love for Bain, this man who accepted her as she was, who did not fault her for her weakness, who would stand side by side with her, whatever happened. She was not alone. She finally believed it. And she calmed. She could now also accept herself. With him she had a sanctuary where she need not be brave. She wept anew, this time tears of release, of recognition, of relief.

When those tears were spent she was able to look at Bain. "Yes, Love, send for Nurias. I am ready."

When she made to get up he hugged her close again before releasing her. "We will get through this together."

Phaera nodded. "Yes, we will," and found she believed it. "I may still die but I know I will not be alone."

When Bain looked about to protest she put her fingers to his lips. "Do not make promises you are not certain you can keep."

She sat up, accepted a drink of water and discovered she could think again. "Do you think it possible to keep this to ourselves and Nurias for a time? Can we invite Nurias here on a pretense?"

"That may be difficult. People will talk if she is summoned."

"Then I shall go to her."

Bain looked startled. "Are you certain? I know you can but you will be alone. I can think of no excuse to go with you without raising suspicion."

Phaera thought for a moment. "I will take Kort. Since he is studying to be a healer, and has done so with Nurias, that will not look strange."

Bain nodded, looking relieved. "Then he will need to know."

"Yes, but he will say nothing."

"Good."

Kort seemed only mildly surprised when Phaera announced that they would visit Nurias but asked no questions until they stopped midway to eat the fare Velna had packed for them.

When Phaera leaned back against the tree that shaded them from the late spring sun and closed her eyes he said, "You look tired. I sense that this outing is not only for pleasure or for my learning."

Phaera let the unspoken question hang in the air before she opened her eyes and faced Kort. "You are correct, my friend." She felt the old fear rise as she tried to find the best way to tell Kort. She could tell by the growing concern in Kort's face that he saw it.

"Kort ... I am expecting a child ... and I am terrified that I will die as my mother did."

She watched understanding dawn on Kort's face. He became

very serious. "I see. And Bain does not wish you to be alone and Nurias must be informed."

"Yes."

"I know this is what you want. I also understand that it is what you fear most."

"Yes."

A silence hung between them until Phaera ventured, "You must tell no one – not yet."

"You have my word."

CHAPTER FORTY-SIX

WITH KORT AND NURIAS

"Come in out of the cold. That wind has turned raw." Nurias held the door open and waved her two visitors in. "The kettle is hot. It will take me only a moment to make tea."

Before Phaera could answer, Kort said, "Perhaps Phaera's ought to be raspberry leaf."

Nurias shot Kort a surprised look over her shoulder then turned to face Phaera. "So, it has happened, then?"

Phaera could only give a small nod and whisper, "Yes".

"And you have come without Bain." Nurias' raised eyebrows emphasized the unspoken question, *"Why?"*

"He was unable to come. And also we did not want to arouse speculation." Phaera found her voice. "Kort knows, as you see. He has sworn to tell no one."

Nurias acknowledged Kort with a quick nod before turning her attention back to Phaera. "Good." She indicated her two worn chairs and reached for some branches of dried herbs hanging from her rafters. "Raspberry and…" She eyed Kort. "Chamomile, I think, for both of you."

As Nurias bustled about making the tea and setting out a pot of honey to sweeten it, she kept up a light banter.

She is trying to put me at ease. Phaera smiled inwardly. *And it is working. I do feel calmer already.* Aloud she quipped, "So I am special. I get two kinds."

Nurias chuckled. "I think Kort has no use for raspberry leaf tea."

She turned and handed them each a steaming mug. "Add your own honey."

She pulled a stool out from under the table and settled herself facing them but directed her question to Phaera. "Do you wish that Kort remain as we talk?"

Phaera stiffened again. "I had not given it any thought yet."

"I thought you might not." She patted Phaera's knee. "May I suggest that he remain? It will have two benefits. As Bain must attend to other duties you will have someone near you with whom you can discuss things without wondering how much he understands…" As she spoke she leaned closer and took both of Phaera's hands in hers. "And it will be useful for Kort's training."

Phaera studied Kort. *Can I allow him to see me at my weakest? Will he understand?* She thought for a moment about all Kort had experienced; his loyalty, and his friendship, all the pain he had been through. And she had certainly seen Kort at his weakest.

"Kort may stay. He has proven his loyalty many times over. I trust him." She grimaced. "Though it will not be easy for me to…"

She felt Nurias give her hands a reassuring squeeze. "Good. You have never shied from what is best. And Kort will be a good support. He will be nearer at those moments when your fear threatens to overwhelm you. Those times may come when you least expect them."

Kort spoke for the first time. "You may rely on me … always." He leaned his lanky frame slightly forward, his face alert.

When Nurias released Phaera's hands and sat back so she could see both of them the warmth and reassurance lingered.

"Kort, you will listen. Do not say anything." She turned her attention back to Phaera. "Tell me what happened. I know you would not come here so suddenly without cause."

Nurias assumed what Phaera liked to call her listening pose, relaxed, attentive, and receptive, but with an underlying air of meditation. Phaera knew she would remember everything.

When Phaera finished Nurias once again took her hands.

"Now that you have accepted the truth of your condition you will be better prepared to deal with the fear. The worst is, perhaps, already over."

Phaera could only give a timid nod.

Nurias gave her hands a small shake and a squeeze. "You will not take this journey alone. You have three people who understand and will comfort you. I promise to see you regularly." She let go Phaera's hands and sat back on her stool.

"Here is the first thing you must remember. How many births have you assisted with?"

The question took Phaera by surprise. "Why, I don't know. Let me think ... Perhaps near thirty."

Nurias nodded. "Yes, that seems likely. Now tell me how many of those mothers – or their babes – have died."

"Two. It was terrible."

"Why did they die?"

"One had the cord around its neck. I could not remove it in time to save the child. The mother lived, though." Phaera took a deep breath. "The other was because the afterbirth sat too low, blocking the birth canal. The mother bled to death and I could not save the babe."

"Excellent." Nurias gave a satisfied nod. "Many healers have much poorer records. Your training must have been very thorough."

Nurias looked like she was waiting for Phaera to say something. When Phaera remained silent she went on. "I have delivered over 300 babes in my life as a healer. Some have been difficult, such as those in the wrong position that have to be turned before the mother pushes. But I have lost only five babes and four mothers. You were present during a very difficult birth. You know that even then both mother and child survived." Nurias bent forward and again took Phaera's hands in her own, holding her gaze intently.

"This is what you must remember. This is what you must continue to tell yourself. This is how unlikely it is that you will not survive a birth, or that your child will not."

She looked at Kort. "And this is what you must remind Phaera of."

She let go of Phaera's hands again, facing Kort and Phaera in turn. "Do you understand?"

Phaera glanced at Kort and saw him nod before adding her own. "Thank you, Nurias. It does help to know that. I know there are other midwives and healers with much poorer success."

Nurias smiled at her. "There is another advantage you have. As a good healer and midwife yourself you will know what to expect and what to do."

Kort piped up. "That is true Milady. And I will continue to learn."

The rest of the evening was spent in comfortable chatter. Phaera slept well that night, perhaps due to the valerian tea Nurias gave her. She left for home the next morning feeling much more relaxed.

CHAPTER FORTY-SEVEN

AN UNEXPECTED BIRTH

"Milady, come quickly. You are needed in the kitchens." The scullery maid stopped just inside the door of the apothecary, heaving to catch her breath, eyes wide with fright, and clearly distraught.

Phaera wasted no time. Even as she grabbed her basket she asked, "What is amiss? Has someone cut herself?"

"No, Milady. But…"

Phaera shooed her out with one hand as she pulled the door shut behind her. "Well, what is it then? Tell me so that I may be prepared."

"It is Nisha, Milady… she… she is giving birth."

Phaera frowned, trying to picture the girl. "Is Nisha the plump one with dark hair?"

The girl nodded, still looking frightened.

"She has not been to see me. I did not know she was expecting a child."

"No Milady. She told no one."

They had reached the door to the dungeons. Phaera unlocked it and pushed it open, carefully locking it again before commenting further.

"Then she will be very frightened."

"Yes, Milady." The girl scurried after her as she strode the long hallway and mounted the steps to the hall that led into the kitchens. Before she reached the entrance she recognized Velna's voice.

"Stop gawking and get back to work. All of you."

Phaera followed the direction of the voice as she entered. There, at the back, in a corner against the wall, Cook stood bent over, barring Phaera's view from what must be the girl in labour. She hurried over.

"Thank you, Velna."

Velna looked over her shoulder with a start, then straightened and backed out of the way. "Milady, I am so relieved you have come."

Phaera barely heard. She assessed the wretch huddled on the stool in front of her. A spasm took her and she cried out. Phaera waited until it passed.

"You are Nisha, I believe?"

The terrified girl, likely no more than fourteen nodded. Before Phaera could ask anything more she wailed, "I will be sacked!"

So. That is why she has not seen me.

"We will speak of that later. Now we need to help you bring that babe forth. Please stand and ..." Phaera looked around until she spotted a table behind her. To Velna she said, "Clear that table. Then find clean cloths, hot water, and a small blanket to wrap the babe in." She did not wait to see if her orders would be obeyed.

"Now, Nisha, I will help you up onto the table. Lie down. I must examine you to see how far along you are, and to check the babe's heartbeat." She placed a supportive arm under Nisha's. "You can walk. Do not fear. It will be well."

The girl calmed at her words enough to obey. By the time Phaera had helped her onto the table Velna had returned with the hot water, followed by a kitchen maid carrying cloths and a blanket.

I have never seen a girl so terrified while in labour. She is too afraid of what will happen to her after. This will not be an easy birth.

"Nisha, I want you to take slow deep breaths. Count to five with each one in, and six with each one out. Do you understand?" She took the girl's chin and made her look at her. "With me, now … one, two, three, four, five – yes, that's it – one, two, three, four, five, six." Phaera counted aloud with the girl for three more breaths, feeling her begin to calm as she concentrated on counting.

"Good, now keep doing that while I see how things are." Phaera spotted another scullery maid, hand still over her scrub brush, eyes wide. "You, come stand at her head and if Nisha falters, count with her again."

The child's eyes grew even rounder but she hurried over to obey.

Phaera nodded encouragingly. "Here, take Nisha's hand. Count aloud with her, quietly." She turned her attention back to Nisha.

"Your waters have broken." Phaera looked over her shoulder at Velna, who stood behind her, attempting to get a better view. "How long since her waters broke."

"Not long Milady. I sent the maid as soon as Nisha cried out and I saw the wet."

"Phaera lifted Nisha's skirts above her waist and placed her listening horn on the taught belly, the other end to her ear. *Good, the beat is strong and steady.* Aloud she said, "Your babe is strong. What do want? A son or a daughter?"

Instead of answering Nisha let out another anguished wail before clutching the edge of the table, half sitting as another contraction overtook her. Phaera watched the ripples under the girl's skin, waiting until it passed.

"Keep counting, Nisha. Good. Now spread your knees apart so I can see."

Phaera shook her head in exasperation. The girl had clearly not bathed in a while. She grabbed a cloth, dipped it into the bowl of water and wrung it out, then carefully bathed the girl's nether region. The water was soon soiled.

"More water. Quickly."

Another contraction passed by the time the fresh bowl arrived. Phaera repeated the washing. When she had finished she called for yet another bowl of fresh water. After washing her hands again, she spread the girl's knees wide and gently probed the opening of the birth canal. She removed her hand when another contraction hit and looked up at the girl with a reassuring smile. "All is well. The head is in position and you are opening nicely. Two fingers already."

As labour progressed Phaera coached the girl to breathe between contractions, and slowly got her to answer some questions, keeping up some reassuring chat in between. The girl panicked again when it came time to push.

"No, it will not be safe here. No, no, nooooo..."

"Yes, your child will be safe and so will you. But you must do as I say." As the first urge to push overtook the girl Phaera had Velna lift her shoulders. With no birthing stool available that she could sit on Phaera had her shifted to the end of the table where she could catch the babe.

"Small quick breaths, Nisha. No. Hold back as much as you can. There, good girl. I see the crown. Your babe has a lot of hair."

As the next contraction hit the girl began to grunt with effort. "Yes, Nisha, now is the time to push. Do not clamp your teeth. Make as much noise as you like – but push ... push ...."

Nisha let out a long guttural wail as the head emerged.

"Your babe is almost here. One or two more pushes."

Nisha gave a long, almost desperate push on the next spasm and the babe slid into Phaera's waiting hands.

"You have a strong daughter, Nisha."

When the cold air hit the little body the babe erupted with a lusty cry. Phaera let out a relieved sigh, and heard that the entire kitchen joined in. She set the babe on the waiting blanket, checked her breathing and made sure her mouth and nose were clear. She watched until the cord stopped pulsing before tying and cutting it. Then she wrapped the child snuggly and laid her onto Nisha's chest.

As she did so Phaera saw the girl's belly contract again and caught the afterbirth. Nisha had a small tear but did not need stitching. But if the mother was not to die of festering she would need strict instructions on how to keep the area clean. And decisions would need to be made about the pair's future. Phaera knew they could not be made by her alone. For now, Phaera ordered a cot to be prepared in the small closet where she had set up her first apothecary. It was just large enough and offered the pair warmth and privacy until better arrangements could be made.

Once they were comfortable and Phaera had shown Nisha how to get the babe onto her breast to nurse she gathered her basket together and made to leave. On her way out she gestured to Velna to follow her into the hall.

"Did you know of this?"

"I suspected, Milady, but she hid it well. I suspect she feared she would be sacked as soon as I found out."

"So you did not ask her?"

"No, Milady. I thought it best to let her have her secret as long as possible. Here she was warm and fed. She has no family and there seems to be no man about to care for her. If I knew, I would have been obliged to tell Lady Flor or Lord Makin and I did not know what they would do."

"That was well done. But I wish you had told me. Something could have been arranged and this would have been much easier."

Cook looked chagrined. "Forgive me, Milady. I was afraid. What will happen to them, now?"

"I will need to discuss that with Lord Makin, Lady Flor, and Lord Bain. But you may be sure they will not be sent out the door with no means to live."

"Thank you, Milady. Nisha is not a bad girl. She is not very bright and I suspect she was easy to take advantage of."

"Then I must make sure she gets the advice she needs to care for herself and her child."

Cook's shoulders relaxed and she gave Phaera a relieved look. "Thank you, Milady. I ought to have told you of my suspicions."

"It is done. Take care of them until tomorrow. I will return to check on them both and hopefully I will have a plan."

"I will, Milady."

With a nod Phaera turned and walked away. *The child was so frightened. And yet both are well. Will I do as well? I must.* Phaera shook herself. *I must.*

CHAPTER FORTY-EIGHT

BAIN'S ENVY

Once Kort had been given the position of confidant and helpmeet during her pregnancy Phaera included him, as a matter of course, in their evening meals with Lord Makin and Lady Flor. She had not asked permission. Bain understood that to her it simply made sense. Kort was a lord's son and thus merited a place as guest at their table even under normal circumstances.

Bain, while he could find no reasonable objection, and while he agreed with Phaera's unquestioning acceptance of Kort as her equal, found the arrangement rankled him. For several weeks he pushed his growing irritation away, ignoring his increasing unease. So when Phaera confronted him her question came as a shock.

"My love, something is amiss and I wish you would speak to me about it. You have grown increasingly silent, even when we are alone. What is it that bothers you so? I thought we had promised we would not keep anything from each other."

"You imagine it. There is nothing. I am pleased that you are feeling so well and have been able to continue your work." *But there is something. She is right. Why do I not know what it is?*

Phaera echoed his thoughts, though they belied his words. "There is something. I feel it, a hesitation, a distance that was not there before. And you have not asked about how our child grows, or how I am faring for several days."

"You have Kort, and even my mother, for that."

And there it was. The thing he had pushed away. He could hide from it no longer.

He watched Phaera's face change from one of concern to shock. She looked as though she had been slapped, though she said nothing.

Could she not understand that he, too, was struggling with the new revelation? Why not? His thoughts tumbled over each other, leaving him unable to grasp any one of them long enough to form a response.

After a few moments Phaera said, in a low voice heavy with sadness, "Bain, we need to talk this out."

Bain let his shoulders slump and gave a weary nod. "It seems we do," and turned to sit in one of the two chairs in Phaera's chamber.

Phaera took the one opposite, pulling it close enough so that their knees almost touched. She watched him with an intensity he had never received from her before. It was a look she reserved for her patients when they had something seriously wrong with them or when they resisted her instructions. The directness of her gaze made him squirm.

She said nothing for a time. Finally, she leaned slightly forward. "Speak to me. What has Kort to do with anything and why does that trouble you so?"

Bain fought back a flare of anger and clenched his fists in his lap to control it. *What has Kort to do with it? Kort, who spends all day with you, even our evening meal together, who knows your most intimate fears, who supports you through the growth of our child - my child - while I can do no more than stand by and hope for the best. Who is there to listen to MY fears? I fear I will lose you, lose our child, lose everything I hold dear. It is Kort who comforts you. That is my place. Do you not see that?*

Bain said none of those things aloud. Somewhere in the back of his mind, a small voice seemed to say, "Stop. Think. This is like facing a battle. Use reason. Do not act rashly."

Instead he took a deep breath and said, as calmly as he could muster, "I need a few moments to think."

He saw a little of the tension leave Phaera's shoulders and she sat back.

A sudden recognition, as he watched her, almost made him smile. *She has donned my mother's listening pose. She will say nothing until I have spoken, now.* It was just enough distraction to clear his thinking a little. Bit by bit his thoughts became less confused. Finally, he took a preparatory breath and began.

"My love, I am ashamed."

Phaera's eyebrows shot up and her eyes widened.

Bain carried on. "You know I can only spend most nights alone with you. Almost all your time is spent with Kort. He is the person you confide your fears to about the birth. He is the one who talks you through those fears when they overtake you." When Phaera began to shake her head in protest he held his hand up. "No, please hear me out."

She sat back against the back of her chair again, her expression troubled and bewildered.

"When I knew Kort would be with you I was happy to see him accompany you to my mother, relieved that you would have someone to turn to when I cannot be here. It felt good to know that someone with some knowledge of midwifery would be here all the time." He watched Phaera's face but saw no reaction there he could read.

"You see, that is why I am ashamed. My head tells me this is for the best. I know Kort is trustworthy. I also know that you do not confide your fears - or anything important - to your ladies. They would not understand in any case. Even Lady Flor is not told everything as a daughter might her mother. She has borne no children and so cannot understand much of what you experience. So, aside from the visits from my mother, it is Kort who lives each of those moments with you."

Bain leaned toward Phaera, hands spread wide, pleading. "I suspect that were it a woman who has your ear I might not feel as I do. But Kort, despite his preferences, is still a man. This is also my first child, possibly the heir we so desperately want. I am envious of the time Kort spends with you, the intimacy you share that I cannot, as I am away with my duties. Even were I here, my knowledge of midwifery does not have the depth that Kort's has."

Bain stopped for a moment, then added, feeling sheepish, "And Kort is even present during what little time we do have together."

When Phaera began to open her mouth he held his hand up again to prevent her from commenting. "Yes, I know he is of noble lineage and has every right to expect to dine with us. It is petty of me to resent it. I fear it has also come between Kort's and my friendship. He deserves better from me, too."

Bain sat back into his chair, ending with, "I hope you can forgive me, my love."

Phaera had sat upright again as he spoke and now regarded him with a bewildered shake of her head. "I hardly know what to say."

Bain watched the play of emotions on her face as she took in his declaration. *Will she think me a fool?*

Just when Bain thought he could wait no longer Phaera rose from her chair, knelt at his feet, took his hands and placed them under hers above her heart. "Perhaps the fault is not yours alone, my love. It never occurred to me that you might feel less important when I share so much with Kort." A small crease formed between her brows. "And I think I understand why it might be different if a woman were in Kort's place. It would never be questioned. It would be expected. Were he a woman you would take his presence for granted."

"Yes, just so." Relief flooded Bain's body.

"But you know he does only what that same woman would do."

"Yes, and that is why I feel shame."

Phaera squeezed his hands and kissed them before looking up at him. "So, my love, what are we to do?"

The question caught him by surprise. After thinking about it he found he could smile, almost wanted to laugh. "Why, nothing at all. Kort is welcome at our table. I am glad you have someone so trustworthy to care for you when I cannot." Now Bain did laugh, a light sound filled with relief. He bent down, pulled Phaera into his lap, and hugged her close. "I have been a fool, my love, but that is gone now. I should have spoken much sooner, but I did not know what it was that bothered me until now. Seeing it for what it is I am able to dismiss it."

Phaera snuggled her head under his chin and relaxed into him. "Sometimes we do not know what bothers us until it becomes spoken. That is what happened with my fear of giving birth. I never fully understood it until Nurias helped me."

She lifted her head to meet his eyes. "We must remember not to let such things come between us."

Bain nodded and kissed her before asking, "And is your fear less, now? And will you share it more with me when it arises?"

Phaera gave him a brilliant smile, just a hint of teasing twinkle in her eyes. "Yes. And yes."

Bain's hand had rested on her belly as she spoke. "I feel it. The babe. He moved." He pressed a little more carefully. "There. Again. My heir moved!"

Phaera laughed, the sound brushing away any lingering doubts about how she felt. "Or your daughter…"

"Ah, you have me."

More serious Phaera asked, "Will it disappoint you terribly if we have a daughter?"

"Not me, my love. Only that it means you must face this again."

Phaera stroked his cheek. "I think nature will take care of that."

"Hmmmm."

CHAPTER FORTY-NINE

BREAKING TRADITION AND CRISIS

"Yes, I want you to be there." The look on Bain's face at her request was so comical Phaera almost laughed aloud. Had the request not been so serious and not flown so far in the face of convention she might have. As it was she simply waited for it to sink in.

Bain's face grew serious and he sank slowly into the chair behind him.

Phaera joined him in the one opposite. "I suppose I ought to have had you sit before we began." She leaned toward him. "I know Nurias would approve. She has long felt that men would appreciate their wives more if they could witness the birth of their children."

"Have you mentioned this to her?"

"No, not yet. I thought you ought to be the first. And you do have some healer training, though not in childbirth."

Bain gave a thoughtful nod but said nothing.

"Nurias will be there as well, of course. She does not travel far from the castle now that my time draws near." When Bain still said nothing Phaera began to worry. Did he not want to be present? Did he not understand that she needed his support? "My love, you know how I fear this birth. Nurias does much to calm me but I need you there as well. I feel ... it is hard to explain ... but it feels like you will hold me here, tether me to this life, that you will not allow me to leave."

Phaera watched understanding rise in Bain's face.

"Ah, then of course, I will be present." He leaned forward to grasp both her hands. "Truth be told, this has been a secret wish of mine. I have not suggested it because I am concerned that the people will see it as weakness on my part – and that you have too much influence over me." He grimaced. "We have already broken with so many traditions this seemed like one too many." He gave a rueful grimace before brightening again. "As you know, Mother has been saying that husbands would appreciate their wives more if they saw the birth of their children." He took her hands. "But I already appreciate you as much as it is possible for a man to."

"So you want to?"

"More than you can know." The shadow lifted from Bain's face and he beamed at her as though making a new discovery. "To see my child brought forth. How wonderful."

Phaera breathed a sigh of relief until Bain asked, "And what about Kort?"

She shook her head. "No, my love, this is for us alone. I know he has assisted at three births, now, with Nurias, but I want this time to be ours, just ours."

"Then it shall be."

Bain grew thoughtful again. "My love, I know that my mother stays close by but it is always possible that someone may need her at the same time that you do. You have some time yet but if the babe chooses to come early she could be assisting someone. May I suggest that Kort remain available as well, in the event that my mother is called away?"

A shiver of fear ran down Phaera's spine and she whispered, her throat tight, "She must be here."

"I believe she will be, my love. But we need to be prepared." He drew her into his arms. "It will be well. I have no fear. And I promise to hold you here. I swear it."

"Even if they forbid it?"

"I will allow no one to forbid it. You have my oath."

Though Phaera was aware that he might not be able to keep that promise somehow she chose to believe it and managed to calm herself. "I will have Nurias prepare Kort ... for the possibility."

She felt some of the tension leave Bain.

"All will be well, my love, I truly believe it."

"As long as you are there."

"Yes."

A KNOCK ON THE DOOR INTERRUPTED THEIR CONVERSATION. They sat in Phaera's chamber though Bain was the one who answered.

"Enter."

It was not Mira who entered but one of the maids that tended to Lady Flor. Her eyes were wide and she stammered as she spoke. "You must come, both of you."

Bain had already risen from his chair with Phaera close behind him. "What is it, Grella?" They followed close behind as the maid hurried in the direction of Lord Makin's chambers.

"It is Lord Makin, Milord. Something has happened to him."

Bain ran past the maid not waiting to hear more. Phaera ran close behind.

Lord Makin lay in the great bed, Lady Flor weeping as she sat on its edge clasping his hand. Two attendants hovered near the door looking lost and worried.

Phaera acted first. "Send for Nurias. Tell her..." She approached the bedside, hesitated, looked at Lord Makin and then at Lady Flor. "Milady, what can you tell me?"

Lady Flor shook as she answered. "We were breaking our fast. He suddenly went limp, he couldn't speak ... Oh, please help him."

The maid Phaera had addressed stood waiting, wringing her hands. Phaera caught her eye again. "Tell Nurias that it appears Lord Makin has had a brain attack. She must come immediately."

As the maid hurried away she told another standing by, "I need willow bark tea – quickly. Get me hot water – now."

Phaera had grabbed her healing basket as they left her chamber. She now opened it and extracted the sac with willow bark in it. She gave Bain a sharp look. He got the message.

"The rest of you. Out." Bain stopped one maid, "You, inform Captain Reynce and Captain Raskir that Lord Makin is unwell, that Nurias has been summoned and we will send more information when we have it."

Phaera was relieved that Bain had taken control.

The maid dipped a terrified curtsey, "Yes, Milord", and hurried away.

When the maid had gone Bain sat on the side of the bed opposite Lady Flor and took Lord Makin's other hand. He leaned close and searched his father's face. It was lopsided, his mouth crooked and drooling. Even his right eye drooped. "Father, can you hear me?"

Phaera watched closely and thought she saw a slight squeeze. The one eye Lord Makin could still control rounded on Bain's face.

Lord Makin's expression was so distorted that Phaera could not make it out but a look at Bain's told her how distraught he was. It was well that in this chamber he need not put a brave face on it. She could imagine what must be going through his mind, aside from concern for his father. What if Lord Makin died? Bain would become lord. She knew he did not feel ready, that he believed he still had much to learn. And Lord Makin had appeared so hale that he expected him to be there for many years yet.

Phaera pressed down her own concerns and returned her attention of Lord Makin.

She placed a hand on Bain's arm. When he looked up she motioned him to stand aside so she could administer the tea. He nodded and withdrew so she could take his place. "Can you lift your head Lord Makin?... No? I see." She turned back to Bain. "Take Lady Flor's place and lift him so I can help him drink this."

She had put the tea in her cup with the spout, the one she used when people could not control their lips. *I hope he can swallow.*

Lady Flor had pulled away to allow Bain to take her place. He placed an arm under his father's shoulders in such a way that he also supported his head and lifted him just enough so that Phaera could place the spout between his lips and pour some on the tea into his mouth. She withdrew it when he sputtered and coughed but was relieved to see that some of the tea had been swallowed. Between the two of them they managed to get some more into him before it became clear that he had tired too much to swallow any more.

The door opened to admit Nurias. Bain stepped away to make room for his mother.

Nurias murmured to him as she took his place. "He is in good hands."

Phaera had forgotten about Lady Flor. Now she became aware of her standing at the end of the bed, wringing her hands, silent tears flowing down her face unheeded.

Phaera beckoned to Bain, indicating Lady Flor with her head. She was relieved when he seemed to understand.

He joined her and placed an arm around Lady Flor's back in comfort. "Milady, he has the two best healers in the land caring for him. If he can be helped they will do it."

"I cannot lose him."

CHAPTER FIFTY

WHAT NOW?

Nurias addressed Phaera. "Good, you have done exactly as I would have. There is nothing more to be done at the moment." She turned to face the others in the chamber. "Lord Makin needs rest," and shooed everyone out except Ashin, her apprentice, who had arrived only moments after her.

Later a grim group gathered around the table in the private meeting room outside Lord Makin's chambers. Lady Flor's silent tears kept stopping and starting. Nurias helped Lady Flor into a chair and sat beside her. Bain and Phaera had not yet taken chairs but stood facing them.

Phaera understood the depth of Lady Flor's fear and grief. The man she loved and relied on might never rise again, or even speak again. Phaera wondered about that, too. These sudden attacks were unpredictable, not only in when they would strike, but in whether, how far, and how quickly the victim would recover.

No one spoke for some time. Nurias was the one who broke the silence by telling Bain and Phaera to sit.

Phaera looked across the table at Nurias. She knew that she, too, had loved this man once, likely still did in some way. She was pale but seemed calm and in control. *And what do I feel?* She allowed herself a few moments during the silence to think about that. *He is a good man, the father of my husband. He has shown me kindness. But what will happen if he does not recover? What will that mean for Bain, for me, for our child?*

Nurias cleared her throat. "I think we all know how serious this is. You will all have questions. I do not have all the answers but I will be as honest with you as I am able."

Lady Flor leaned toward her, hands open, beseeching, in front of her, her voice cracking with emotion. "Please tell me he will live."

The sadness in Nurias voice as she answered said more than her words. "There is nothing I would like more to say but I cannot. A throw of the dice will tell as much as I can. The next day, two days are the most important. If he survives them there is hope that he will live."

Lady Flor sank back into her chair and wept again, her sobs no longer silent. Nurias, sitting to her left, put an arm around her shoulder but she shook it off.

Phaera also knew what could happen, so did not have any questions for Nurias.

Bain spoke next, his face ashen. "I know his recovery will be slow and that we will not know for some time how far that will go. What is it we must do to keep him comfortable and to help his healing?"

Phaera could see that Bain would not even consider that his father might not survive the night. When she felt the babe kick she understood only too well how important his survival was. She stroked her belly and murmured, just loud enough that all could hear, "He will live. He must. He will see this babe born."

She could only hope her words would prove prophetic. In any case they had the effect of helping Lady Flor staunch her tears and send her a grateful look.

Bain's expression mirrored that of lady Flor. He straightened his shoulders. "We need a plan, both for Father's recovery and care, and for what to tell Captains Reynce and Raskir. I will need to discuss with them how to proceed while Lord Makin is unable to act."

Nurias turned to him. "The mantle now lies on your shoulders, Bain. And it will remain there until Lord Makin can make his wishes known, or until it comes to you permanently. I believe you can do this, my son."

Phaera added, "Yes, you have been preparing for this for three years, now. And you trust Captains Reynce and Raskir to advise you. They will not fail you. Rely on them as you did when we were at war."

She watched Bain's shoulders come down minimally.

"That is so."

Though he had made the declaration with a firm voice Phaera could sense the worry behind the declaration.

Bain pushed his chair back. "I must not keep the good captains waiting. " He turned to Nurias and Phaera in turn. "I know Father is in good hands. Please tell me immediately if there is any change."

Lady Flor rose, too. "I must be with him. He needs me."

Phaera was about to prevent her, as Lord Makin needed rest, but Nurias intervened.

"Yes, come sit with him. It will comfort him. He will sense your presence. But you must let him rest."

Lady Flor sent her a grateful look and hurried ahead of Nurias and Phaera into Lord Makin's chamber. Phaera took one of the chairs there and set it by the head of the bed so Lady Flor could sit undisturbed. *Nurias is right. This is good for both Lord Makin and Lady Flor.* She silently chided herself for not seeing it, too.

Phaera asked Nurias to join her in her chamber. "I know there is nothing more to tell me about Lord Makin's prognosis. I do not know what it is I need or even if you can help me with that. I expect Bain is in shock and wondering what this bodes for him."

She pressed her hands together between her knees. "I must help him. Yet I am so afraid for myself and for our child."

Nurias gently pulled Phaera's hands out and held them. "The babe will be fine, as will you. Your duty is to take these last weeks and to keep telling yourself that. I am close by. Now, with Lord Makin so ill I will be even closer as he will need my care as well. I will not leave this to you. Your first duty is to keep yourself well for the birth." She paused a moment.

"Phaera, Bain is under a great, new, and unexpected burden. The way to help him is to keep yourself as calm as possible. Share your fears more often with me, or with Kort. Reassure Bain that you and the child are well. I am not asking you to deny your fear, only that you do your best to relieve him of caring for you so that he may keep his attention on his other duties. You are strong, Phaera. Show that strength as never before ... for Bain, for Lady Flor, and for Lord Makin. Let them see it. Breathe. Let yourself see your fear. Then see the strength you have to deal with it. Every time the fear seems too great ... stop ... breathe ... calm yourself. You need not always act immediately."

Nurias did not let go Phaera's hands when she stopped. She held them, calmly, and waited, holding Phaera's eyes.

The touch of Nurias' hands, the tone of her voice, almost a drone, seeped into Phaera. Her breathing slowed. Her body began to relax.

After several moments Nurias gave her a gentle smile and squeezed her hands lightly. The spell broke. "There, you see, you are calmer already. You can do this. It is a method that I have learned over long practice." She let go Phaera's hands. "Remember that I am never far away. Nor is Kort. Now I think some chamomile tea would not be amiss."

Nurias rose and began the ritual of making the tea at the brazier. When she handed Phaera her cup she sat and faced her again. "Let me see you breathe, now. Show me you will remember."

After several breaths Phaera recognized the pattern. "It is much like what we say to women as they give birth."

"Exactly, only deeper and longer. And with each breath in say to yourself, 'I can do this.' And with each breath out say, 'All will be well.'"

Phaera took several more breaths. Finally, her tea gone, she said, "Thank you, Nurias." To herself she thought, *"This is like magic".*

CHAPTER FIFTY-ONE

LORD MAKIN

Nurias, Kort, and Phaera spelled each the first three days. Lady Flor, however, could not be persuaded to leave his side. When it became apparent that she would collapse if she did not sleep Phaera suggested she be allowed to lie beside him in his great bed.

The suggestion proved a good one for both of them. Lady Flor slept, one arm draped over her beloved husband. Phaera noticed that her touch seemed to calm Lord Makin as well. His breathing evened and he seemed more at peace. He, too, slept more.

At times he woke with a start, his useful eye rolling wildly until he saw Lady Flor beside him. Then he relaxed.

By the fourth day Nurias had agreed with Phaera that he was not about to die and that he showed some signs of recovery.

That first question of Bain's, when Lord Makin had squeezed his hand in response, offered them a way to communicate. He could let them know if he wanted a drink or an extra pillow. On the fourth day, he managed to utter an unintelligible growl that indicated an attempt to speak. He stayed awake for longer periods and listened keenly whenever Bain told him what was happening outside the castle.

Bain visited every day and told him what was happening. "All is well, Father. The good captains manage the lesser matters of law as they have been trained to. They have shown themselves to be resourceful and efficient." He laughed. "I know you expected no less."

Was that growl a chuckle? It was a good sign.

"We also consult on all matters that require a decision. As for myself, I make time daily, as you did, to hear the complaints and petitions of the people. Thus far they make no protest over my decisions. You may rest in peace, Father. All is in order." Was that crooked expression one of pride? Bain hoped so.

More than that, Bain hoped his father would recover fully, though that seemed unlikely. He knew that some of the duties Lord Makin had carried would fall permanently to him. But he hoped his father would still be there to advise him and to share in some of the daily consultations.

By the seventh day Lord Makin could sit up for short periods, well propped by pillows. His swallow reflex had improved and he could hold a cup in his good hand and bring it to his mouth. Each day he worked to speak, though still could not form words they could understand. One thing was clear, to Bain's great relief. There was nothing wrong with his father's mind. It was a good omen.

When he began to be able to sit for short periods Lady Flor was finally convinced to leave long enough to bathe and to begin to resume some of her duties. The first time she was away Phaera ordered Lord Makin be bathed on the bed. She helped make his bed with fresh linens and blankets.

To Bain she explained, "I avoided this until now because I do not want Lady Flor to see how difficult this is and how weak he looks. It would upset her too much. He needs her to appear strong for him and he for her."

"Good thinking, my love. That is best."

The next day, when Bain came to visit and saw how much

better his father looked he asked, "Father, would you like Captains Reynce and Raskir to come and give their reports personally? I will interpret for you when they do not understand you."

Bain watched his father's expression brighten, at least on his good side, and took the growl to mean agreement.

Bain was buoyed by the response. "Good. I will have them begin tomorrow, one at a time at first."

When Nurias heard she added her approval. "Yes, it will be good for him to be involved as much as he is able." Pride crept into her voice when she added, "I am glad you are making these decisions. You have learned when to decide on your own and when to ask for advice, be it from me or from the captains and others."

"Even when it concerns his care?"

"Even then. You have eyes. You can see what he can manage."

"Thank you." That evening when they were finally alone in her chamber Bain studied Phaera for a moment. "My love, you have remained remarkably calm since this tragedy. I appreciate that this has freed me to do my work but," He gave her a quizzical look, "what happened? What brought this change?"

"Your mother." Phaera shook her head in puzzlement.

Bain's eyebrows rose, surprised. "But she has tried to calm you before. What is different this time?"

"After your father fell ill we spoke in my chamber." She gave her head another bewildered shake. "I don't know how, exactly, but it is as if she placed a trance on me. I feel normal but ... I cannot explain it. When the fear rises she taught me a breathing tool, much like we have women use in birthing labours ... yet somehow different."

"Aah, yes, I think I understand. Mother has a method she uses when all else fails. I do not know exactly how it works but something about how she speaks, her tone, and the way she holds the eyes has a sort of trance effect. I have seldom seen her use it but I know it can be very helpful."

Phaera stiffened and her eyes widened in alarm. "Does that mean I am entranced, that I am not in my own mind?"

Bain shook his head with a short laugh and drew her into his embrace.

"No, my love, only that she has given you a way to stay in your own mind when your fear threatens to overtake you. It is the fear that is not of your mind. This new control is just the opposite."

Phaera went silent for a moment. "Then this is something she must teach me. I must learn how to do that."

"I hope she can teach you. I know of no other with this gift."

"If it is a tool for healing fear then I will learn it."

Bain gave a low chuckle and hugged her tighter. "Then you will."

As the final weeks of Phaera's pregnancy flew by Lord Makin continued to improve. While it seemed likely he would never walk again he did begin to regain control over his speech and some movement in his right arm and hand.

Phaera was elated when, as she helped him sit so she could arrange his cushions behind him, he rested that hand on her belly. When the babe kicked he let out a delighted half laugh.

"He is a feisty one."

The words might not have been intelligible to someone unfamiliar with Lord Makin's garbled speech but she understood. The babe was particularly active at that moment so she sat on the bed beside Lord Makin and placed both his hands on her gown over her belly so he could feel all the movement.

"It seems he is eager to make your acquaintance Milord."

She let him enjoy the experience for a few moments, wondering if she ought to say what was on her mind. She decided not to hold back. He needed to be prepared. "Milord, this babe may not be the heir you hope for. It is equally possible I bear a daughter. I hope that will not disappoint you too much."

Lord Makin's hands left her belly and he took one of hers. "I know." His words came with difficulty but she could make them out. "You have more time." Then he gave that growl that served as his laugh, "But it is a son."

Phaera shared in his mirth. "Since you have declared it, then so be it." *I hope you are correct. You may not live long enough to wait again.* She felt a shiver descend her spine but brushed it aside. All would be well. She stood and placed a light kiss on his cheek before leaving the chamber.

CHAPTER FIFTY-TWO

BIRTH

"My love, you've been restless all night. Are you all right?"

Phaera felt more irritable than usual and that came out in her tone. "No. My back aches and I need sleep."

"It is very near your time."

The solicitous look on Bain's face did nothing for her mood. Could he not see she wanted to be left alone, that she did not want to engage in small talk? "The plug has not come away yet. And Nurias agrees I have several days yet. I am fine. Go about your day."

Bain studied her for a moment, gave his head a small shake and left, though the crease between his brows remained.

Phaera frowned after him as she rubbed the small of her back and stretched. She eyed the bed, wondering if she could go back and get some sleep. She decided it would be no more comfortable than it had been earlier. She might as well dress and go down to break her fast with Lady Flor as usual.

She went to the privy. When she wiped herself with the rags kept there for that purpose she noticed the mucous, streaked with blood, on it. *No, not yet. I have a few more days. Not yet.* She repeated the mantra as she went down to meet Lady Flor.

She was already later than usual. Only Lady Flor remained at the table. She looked about to leave. "Oh, you are here. I will stay a while, then."

"That is not necessary, Lady Flor. I am not good company this morning in any case." She winced slightly at a cramp in her belly.

Lady Flor noticed. "Are you all right? Perhaps I should send for Nurias to check on you."

Phaera shook her head as she sat down. The ache in her lower back was not subsiding. "No, Milady. My waters have not broken. It is not time yet."

Lady Flor's eyebrows rose and she looked slightly hurt. "I see. Of course I know nothing of these things."

Phaera felt a pang of guilt and wondered if her tone had been sharper than she intended.

When another twinge assailed Phaera she grimaced and rubbed the small of her back again. She looked at the food on her plate and decided she didn't want to eat. "I am not hungry. Please excuse me, Milady."

Phaera stood up to leave, and froze. A trickle of liquid ran down the inside of her thighs. She gasped and grasped the side of the table. "No! Not yet!"

Lady Flor, already on her feet, said, "I will send for Nurias."

Phaera could not answer.

Lady Flor returned almost immediately, alone. "Nurias attends a birth outside the castle. I have sent for her." She took Phaera by the arm. "Let me help you to your chamber."

"She thinks I have more time. Bain, get Bain." It was all Phaera could manage to say as she let herself be led away. She might have cried out for Kort as well but it had been decided that one man in the birthing chamber might be all the people could accept.

"Yes, as soon as I have you settled."

"No, **now**!" It came out as a shout cut off by a cry as a spasm caught her.

Lady Flor looked frightened but did not stop. She peered over her shoulder and accosted the first maid she saw. "Innis, fetch Lord Bain immediately. Tell him it is time."

They had reached Phaera's chamber. When Mira spotted them she went ashen and stopped in mid-motion, a pillow dangling from one hand.

Bain and Ashin, Nurias' apprentice, arrived together moments later to hear Phaera arguing with Lady Flor. "No, I will not get into bed."

Phaera held on to the back of her chair with one hand as she bent with another contraction, waving away the efforts of both lady Flor and Mira with the other.

Ashin said, "Lady Flor, Mira, I am here now. You may leave. Thank you for your assistance." She turned back to Phaera. "Nurias says you will be some time yet. She will be here before the birth."

Phaera searched until she spotted Bain. He seemed at a loss. That lasted only a moment.

"My love, it has begun, then." He strode to her side and placed his arm around her back. "Remember the breathing, my love."

The calmness in his voice soothed Phaera a little. When she felt Bain begin to massage her lower back she found herself counting her breaths, as she had taught so many women to do. When the spasm passed she straightened and faced Bain. "Nurias. She swore she would be here."

Ashin broke in, turning aside from where she prepared the bed with extra sheets and pushed the blankets away. "She knows and will be here. She attends another birth and knows you have just begun. I was closer by. You have time. All will be well, Milady."

Phaera began to protest but Bain cut her off. "My love, babes come when they decide. Ashin is here. I am here. All is well."

Phaera watched Ashin pull the birthing stool out from its

corner, where it had been waiting, ready, for some weeks, and set it in the middle of the floor. She approached Phaera just as a new contraction took hold.

"Breathe. That is right. Well done." When Phaera stood erect again Ashin directed Bain, "Take her other elbow in case she needs support. I will take this one. We will walk."

Phaera felt the confident touch under her left elbow.

"Now you must walk, Milady. We are here if you need us."

As her pains grew rapidly closer together Phaera alternated between a mild stupor, feeling both distant and inside herself, and bouts of panic when she cried out for Nurias. "Why is she not here? She swore to me."

They continued this way for some time, the pattern broken twice when Ashin directed Phaera to lie down so she could check her progress.

"You are doing very well, Milady. Things are progressing very quickly."

Ashin's cheerful tone and easy reassurances had the opposite effect she intended. Only Bain's calm repetitions of, "I am here. It will be well," kept her from total panic.

It struck Phaera as odd that when she looked out her window slit the sun shone onto the foot of her bed. That meant it was at its highest – only midday. It felt so much longer.

"Let me check your progress once more, Milady."

Before Ashin could lift her gown over her knees Phaera felt an enormous contraction. "No ... not yet! ... Nurias!"

Bain bent down and put his face close to hers. He took hers in his hands. "My love, let Ashin look." He held her gaze. "Just look at me. I am with you."

It took all Phaera's courage to allow Ashin to spread her knees apart.

"You are almost ready, Milady. You are fully dilated. Come and sit on the birthing chair now." She took Phaera by one arm. "Here, let me help you."

Phaera no sooner felt the stool underneath her than another contraction, different form the others, overtook her.

"Hold back, Milady. Fast breaths now. Hold back." Phaera felt her probing. "The babe is crowning, Milady. It will not be long, now. You are doing well."

When Phaera felt the next urge to push Ashin said, "You may push, Milady, but gently. Hold back a little. Short breaths again."

In the middle of the contraction Phaera lost concentration and wailed, "I want Nurias!" She kept her eyes squeezed shut.

Bain had positioned himself behind the stool and supported her shoulders.

As the pain subsided she heard Bain say, "Mother. Thank goodness."

Phaera opened her eyes to see Nurias exchange looks with Ashin and hear Ashin say, "All is well. The babe has crowned." She watched Nurias wash her hands and Ashin rise to make room for Nurias to take her place.

"So, you decided to surprise us." Nurias reached between Phaera's legs to probe for the babe's head. "Ah, yes, it will not be long now." She raised her eyes to Phaera. "On the next contraction you may push as hard as you like. You are ready."

Something in Nurias tone, perhaps the calm confidence in it, cut off Phaera's protest that she was not at all ready.

"You came."

"Yes, I did."

Something about the tenderness in her smile reminded Phaera of her mother's whenever she had comforted Phaera as a girl. The two faces blended and seemed to become one. *Mama.* Phaera forgot her fear. She held Nurias' gaze, taking strength from it as the next surge overtook her.

Bain had taken her hands when she arched and reached them beside her head. She felt his reassuring grip and heard him whisper in her ear. "I am here, love. I will not let you go."

"Push, Phaera. Hard now. Good." Nurias face, or was it her

mother's, loomed again in front of hers. "Well done. The next one will bring the head."

It did. Two more and the babe emerged. Nurias put her finger into the babe's mouth to remove any mucous, at which Phaera heard a lusty cry.

"You may give Phaera the news." Nurias beamed at Bain as she held the babe up for both Bain and Phaera to see.

"We have a son, my love." Bain's voice was so full of emotion Phaera almost couldn't make out the words.

She peered over the edge of the blanket. "A son? An heir?" She didn't know what to say. Yes, there it was. A penis. She had a son.

She heard Nurias as if from far away. "Bain, will you cut the cord? Here. Yes, just so."

Nurias drew the child away and wrapped the blanket more securely around him. Then she handed him to Phaera and guided Bain's hands around hers. "He is strong and healthy. A fine lad."

Phaera hardly noticed when a contraction came on and the afterbirth slipped out. She just stared at the face of her son, her babe. He stared back at her as if to reassure her. His eyes watched her face with such serenity "Artem. Your name is Artem" He seemed to understand.

Bain whispered in her ear. "Thank you, my love," but she hardly heard him.

She came out of her reverie only when Nurias said, "It is time to clean you up and get you into bed. Ashin, see to the babe and hand him to his father. It is time they met, I think."

When Nurias got Phaera into bed she kept the blankets down and massaged her belly. Phaera knew this helped slow bleeding. Phaera looked over at Bain to see him staring, rapt, into the face of his son. The babe had gone to sleep.

Nurias finished her massage and drew the blankets up over Phaera's chest. Then she reached for the babe and placed him in Phaera's arms. "Are you ready to make the announcement, Son?"

Bain seemed to shake himself back to the present and leapt out of his chair. "Of course." He strode to the door and into the hall to shout, "A son. We have a son."

A cheer went up in the corridors. When that ended Phaera heard someone ask, "And how fares Lady Phaera?"

Phaera could almost feel Bain's joy, not only hear it. "She is well."

Another cheer.

When it died down Bain turned to face into the chamber again. "My love, I hate to leave you but I must let my father know."

Phaera nodded. "Come back quickly."

When the door closed Nurias sat on the bed next to Phaera. "My dear, you have done well. This was an easy – and fast – birth. I think you need never fear childbirth again." She paused. "You are not your mother." Phaera felt the will of her gaze. "Do you understand?"

Phaera nodded, remembering her vision. "Mama was there."

"I do not doubt it." Nurias took her hand and they sat in silence together until Bain returned.

Nurias rose. "You will want to be alone now."

With that she and Ashin left, Nurias closing the door firmly behind them.

EPILOGUE

When a people, and also individuals, have endured crises, suffered losses, and celebrated hard-won victories, these peaks in the cycle of life are usually followed by periods of peace and predictable stability. This is true at all levels - in the cycles of history and in the lives of individuals, families, and groups.

It will not come as a surprise, then, to learn that the futures of Phaera, Bain, and those close to them, as well as that of the fiefs of Marston, Kinterron and their allies, settled into a similar pattern of calm, at least for the duration of their lives.

Lord Makin never recovered enough to resume regular duties but he lived another five years, during which time he acted as advisor and support as Bain took on the role of Lord. They did not always agree but their mutual respect made theirs a solid relationship. Bain, over time, was able to change some laws and customs in the direction of greater cooperation, consultation, and inclusion. He earned the respect and love of the people as a result, in spite of resistance from some of the older men who wanted to keep the old ways. Bain also had the support of Captain Reynce, a man who helped convince those reluctant to embrace his less authoritarian approach.

Phaera was able to carry on with her healing work. She gradually had Kort take over much of her practice as her court duties and motherhood demanded more of her time, especially after Lady Flor became less able to do so. Her influence at court, at least at Marston, led to an easing of some of the formality she hated. This was received with mixed responses, especially from the other fiefs when it was Marston's turn to hold the twice annual gatherings.

Phaera bore three more children, a daughter, Lena, then another son, Rilken, and lastly another daughter, Serin.

Serin was born with a large facial birthmark. She was headstrong like her mother and followed Phaera's footsteps to become a healer, as apprentice to Kort. She declared, almost with relief, that no man of high status would want a woman with a marred face and used that excuse to avoid marriage and to remain absent from the gatherings where young men would be looking for suitable matches. Like her mother she had no patience with protocol and ceremony.

Both Bain and Phaera supported those decisions.

Artem proved to be a strong, intelligent, and healthy lad. Bain and Phaera made sure his education, and that of his siblings, included involvement with the common folk, which taught them respect for all walks of life. All four were exposed to the art of healing as well as that of conflict and history. They made sure that their daughters were also taught classes in politics and strategy. When Lena wed it was to a man of her own choosing, though with the approval of her parents.

While the lords of their allies did not all follow in this pattern, the ones that took over ruling Belthorn and Exalon after the war proved to be good choices. They restored order and trust in both fiefs and became staunch allies and trade partners.

Human nature being what it is, peace did not last indefinitely.

The lesser conflicts still arose. Old attitudes do not change overnight but evolve gradually. Eventually, with the following generations, greed and the lust for power in the few led to the predictable greater conflicts again. But that cycle of history remains for another tale.

MEDIA LINKS

Amazon author page:
http://amzn.to/1nLWC3T

Amazon.com:
http://amzn.to/1rCd4ZB

Amazon. UK:
http://amzn.to/1nXAo3I

Goodreads:
http://bit.ly/1n6wc0T

Website/blog:
http://yvonnehertzberger.com

ALSO BY YVONNE HERTZBERGER

EARTH'S PENDULUM TRILOGY

Back From Chaos: Book One of Earth's Pendulum
Battle and bloodshed have upset the Balance, crippling the goddess Earth's power to prevent further chaos. Unless it is restored more disasters will ensue: famines, plagues, more unrest, and war.
Four chosen: Lord Gaelen of Bargia, Klast, his loyal spy and assassin, Lady Marja of Catania and her maid Brensa. Each is unaware of the roles they must play in restoring that Balance.
Most important of these is Klast. It is he who must rescue the kidnapped maid, he who must unmask and bring to justice the traitor who threatens all their lives. It is also he who must deal with the scars from his tormented and abused past before he can accept the final part he must play in Earth's recovery. And during it all he remains unaware of the role he is destined to play and why his connection to the maid is essential.
He is a most reluctant and unlikely hero.
Get your copy here: http://amzn.to/1yVu29P

Through Kestrel's Eyes: Book Two of Earth's Pendulum
Through Kestrel's Eyes, begins seventeen years later. The peace that followed the end of the Red Plague is shattered when the lords of Gharn and Leith are toppled by traitors, throwing the land into chaos.

Liannis, the goddess Earth's seer, her apprenticeship interrupted by the death of her mentor, must help restore the Balance. Until it is, Earth's power is weakened, preventing Earth from sustaining the rains needed for good harvests. Drought and famine result. Liannis battles self-doubt, the lure of forbidden romance, and deep loss as she faces tests that take her to the brink of her endurance.

But Earth sends a kestrel that allows Liannis to see with her eyes and a white horse to carry her, both with the ability to mind-speak.

Time is short. The people with starve if Earth cannot heal.
Get your copy here: http://amzn.to/1tSvDH9

The Dreamt Child: Book Three of Earth's Pendulum
Liannis, the goddess Earth's seer, can no longer deny the meaning of her recurring dream. She must join with Merrist, her devoted hired man, and bear a child – one with great gifts. Earth has decreed it. But the people resist the changes she brings, bringing danger to the pair and strife to the lands. Both Liannis and Merrist must face tests, sometimes without each other, to fulfill their destiny and bring The Dreamt Child forth into safety. They must succeed if they are to initiate the new era of peace and balance so desperately needed.
Get your copy here: http://amzn.to/1AlIFT5

Labyrinth Quest

When M'rain stops to rest in the mouth of a forbidden cave she is captured and help captive with a band of slaves in thrall to a madman. With the help of Glick, a spirit lizard, she escapes, only to have him charge her with restoring all yhe captives to their home village. Glick gives her magical sight for the ominous darkness of the caves and trails of light to follow so she will not become lost in the labyrinth of tunnels.

Get your copy here: http://amzn.to/1OgX1vv

READ THE FIRST CHAPTER OF BACK FROM CHAOS: VICTORY AND CAPTURE

Marja clutched her small jewelled dagger with white-knuckled fingers. She crouched in the corner, pressed tightly behind the door of the privy, willing herself invisible. The rough wood at her back pricked her through the light linen of her gown, and the muscles in her legs threatened to cramp from holding herself rigid. Her heart raced with terror. She knew if they found her she was dead, or even worse. She had heard what soldiers did to women, especially young, comely ones. Her beauty would not serve her now, nor would her rank as daughter of the ruling house. She gripped the dagger tighter. *They will not take me. I will not suffer that. I cannot.*

She suppressed the impulse to gag from the reek of burnt buildings and charred flesh. Even the usual stench of the privy was preferable to this. She tried in vain to blink away the smoke that filled every space and burned her eyes. Her nose tickled, and she fought the urge to sneeze or cough. Any noise might give her away.

Mercifully, she no longer heard the screams of the women and children. The last span or so had gone quiet except for the muffled sounds of men putting out fires. She could make out only the occasional shouted order from a soldier. She hoped to Earth that meant it was over. Perhaps she would escape after all ... if she could stay hidden until dark. She knew a back way out but could not safely get to it. They might see her crossing the hall if she left her hiding place now. Too many enemy soldiers still moved about. *Keep still. Do not give yourself away. Wait,* she repeated to herself, over and over, like a hypnotic chant.

Marja's body jerked in a spasmodic shudder as she recalled again the chaos that had wakened her at dawn. The Bargian army was well-trained and well-armed. They had successfully taken her father's army by surprise, by hiding in the forest only half a day's ride away and slipping close under cover of darkness. Had her father not scorned the advice of his advisors to guard the city more vigilantly, his people might not now be paying the price of his madness. The thought filled Marja with a moment of fury. Why had he not listened?

Marja wondered how Cataniast's informants had convinced him that the rumours of a planned invasion were false. Somehow they had persuaded the suspicious autocrat that the Bargians wanted to finish spring planting before coming to take Catania. Who had managed this clever misdirection? Had the Bargians bought off her father's informants?

Marja knew that many in Catania would be pleased to see the House of Cataniast fall. A pall of fear, suspicion and secrecy had hung over his court for years. She had watched many merchants and shopkeepers flee Catania, and she could not blame them. Some had gone to Bargia, the enemy who now bore responsibility for their defeat.

Only spans earlier, a servant had come running to Marja, crying, "Flee, my Lady. We must go now!" Marja had refused. At the girl's tearful request for permission to go, Marja had given it freely. She saw no purpose in keeping the terrified maid with her.

How could things have come to this so quickly? She had heard Northgate fall before midday. The sounds of clashing swords, the shouting of soldiers, and the cries of men dying had reached her even where she hid deep within the castle.

Marja knew that her father had fought at Northgate and had heard from the frantic shouts of the retreating men that he had been slain. After that, the invaders soon breached Eastgate and Southgate and overran the city. Those who had not been killed had fled. Now she waited alone for the death that surely awaited her.

When she could remain still no longer, Marja decided to venture into the main hall. If she could make her way to the hidden passage across the balcony it could lead her to freedom. She had just emerged from her hiding place when she heard the trudge of boots on stone and froze again.

"Looks clear. Klast, you take that side and I will check this one."

The words drifted up to where Marja stood rooted to the floor. Heart pounding, she found her feet and quickly shrank back into her corner. *Here they come*, she thought. *I waited too long.*

Marja made herself as small as she could as she listened to the man climb the stairs and check the room beside hers. Then his steps became louder as he entered her chamber. She held her breath as the steps went silent for a moment, then resumed in the direction of her privy. Her eyes went to the dagger still clenched in white-knuckled fingers. She could not have pried her hand open even if she had wanted to. Her fingers seemed welded shut. *Do I have the courage to do it? I must! I will not let them use me. I cannot.*

Suddenly, the door swung out and he stood before her.

Marja froze and caught a look of surprise crossing the soldier's face as he halted. She took in his air of authority, his broad shoulders and the wavy, straw-coloured hair, now lank with sweat and tied out of the way. He wore well-cut breeches, a tunic in the blue and yellow of Bargia, now stained with blood, and he carried a fine sword. Marja recognized her assailant. Here stood the son of

Lord Bargest, the spawn of the enemy who had brought this upon them.

He raised his sword for the killing blow. It felt like she watched from a distance, the motion slow and dreamlike, as if time had stopped. He halted, arm in midair, seeming to assess the woman before him.

What did he see, she wondered? Could he see her determination, her terror? Could he see past the dirt and smoke to her expensive clothing, the heavy gold chain still about her throat, the jewelled earrings and the hands unused to rough work? Would he understand that she was someone of rank? Would her russet hair tell him he beheld someone from Cataniast's family? Would it make any difference?

Slowly, he lowered his sword's point to the ground. Time resumed its normal pace. His face showed no signs of battle frenzy, but his eyes remained alert, and she knew he would not hesitate to use the sword if he needed to. Marja remained crouched, unwavering, dagger ready, defiance now faltering as confusion pierced her mental armour.

"I am Lord Gaelen of Bargia." He spoke formally, but she did not miss the weariness in his face and tone. "There is no point in resisting. My army has defeated you, and this demesne is now mine. Give me the knife. I will offer you my protection, at least until I decide how to proceed with the governance of this land. You will not be harmed. Surrender your weapon. Enough have died today."

This could not be true. He could not let her live. Marja smelled deception. "A daughter of the House of Cataniast will not be allowed to live!" she spat back. "You cannot take that risk. My people will rally behind me and continue to fight." Marja remained where she stood, knife just below her left breast, poised for the killing thrust. "I will not be taken to be used as a gaming piece and disposed of later."

She watched Gaelen raise one eyebrow slightly at her declaration. Then he rubbed his free hand across his eyes and pinched the bridge of his nose. "Lady, you mistake me for someone without honour. I have given my word that you will not be harmed, and I am a man of my word. Surrender your weapon." He hesitated. "I cannot assure you will not be injured if you force me to take it from you. But I have seen enough blood today and have no wish to spill yours. We will speak later on your fate. Unlike your lord father, I am not a man who acts in haste."

Marja did not miss the fleeting expression of anger at his mention of her father.

When she did not move, he added, "I gain nothing from spilling more blood. I swear, you and your people will be treated justly. Now give me the knife."

Something in his weary tone and the unwavering stance, feet planted apart, broke through Marja's defiance. What had he said? Honour? Justice? Her people? Could she trust him even so far? Could she yet effect some good for her people? A small flicker of hope ignited. With it, the iron will that had sustained her crumbled. Her arm lowered, and the dagger fell out of her hand to the floor.

Just as her knees buckled, he caught and steadied her, kicking the knife away in the same fluid motion.

Her legs responded woodenly as she let herself be led through the castle, his hand firmly holding her arm. His grip told her escape was out of the question. Marja's mind ran in useless circles, no longer able to hold a coherent thought.

As they emerged from the castle, she waited numbly in his grasp. Some part of her heard him hail one of his men.

"Argost, secure that dwelling to use as headquarters. And find two men you trust and have them report to me immediately." Marja felt more than saw him jerk his head in her direction. "We have a hostage, Cataniast's daughter. She must be closely guarded. She speaks with no one. No one must be told we have her. Have the guards find a defendable room upstairs out of sight. Take her there, and find her something to eat and drink. Find Sinnath and Janest. Set up a table and chairs in the front room. We will meet as soon as everyone can get there. Order must be established here without delay."

Later, she would remember and wonder at the ease with which Gaelen assumed the role of lord. It appeared as though he had been born to it, though she knew his older brother, Lionn, should have inherited. Gaelen was the second son.

Marja listened with only one ear. Then she remembered who she was and that her people were watching her. She forced her head proudly erect, squared her shoulders and took in the destruction around her. Anything made of wood looked burned or charred. Only stone remained unmarred, though it, too, had been blackened by soot. Windows stared empty-eyed, their glass and oiled skins broken or burned. Doors swung from broken hinges. Torn rags and broken crockery littered the near-empty square.

Struck by the devastation, her resolve faltered. She stumbled, momentarily overcome, when he marched her past a large group of women, children and old men standing silent. They waited, packed shoulder to shoulder like sheep, guarded by soldiers who held swords ready. She recognized defeat, fear and despair in the bowed heads and slumped shoulders. Eyes stared at her with the blankness of those who had seen more horror than they could comprehend.

Her people, or what was left of them. Earth, what would happen to them now? And what of her family? Her brother, sister-in-law and their three little ones? Had any survived? The questions screamed in her head, but her tongue remained silent. Now was not the time. She must assess her situation, must think carefully about her next move. Everything depended on it. Everything!

Marja put up no resistance. She let them march her into the mansion, up the stairs and usher her into a small bedroom.

Though she saw signs of scorching, the furniture here had not burned. She took in the sliced featherbed, empty of linens. No doubt they had been stolen. But a chair still sat intact, and with the last shred of dignity she could muster, she allowed herself to be lowered into it.

She watched dully as the guards checked the window and privy, determining that escape was impossible. They stationed themselves, one outside the door, the other inside, to watch her. In spite of their weariness, they appeared alert and ready to act. Neither spoke a word to her before or after the door closed. She eyed the guard who remained inside. He avoided her gaze, and she concluded that information from that quarter was unlikely.

After some time, a young soldier with a bandaged arm entered and set a tray on the small table beside her. Marja stared absently at the tray of stale bread and cheese and ewer of water, knowing she should at least drink, but could not find the energy to reach for the mug.

The sound of voices raised in anger seeped through the door, and she realized she ought to try to make out what they were saying. That, too, was too much effort. It occurred to her that she ought to be forming a strategy to deal with her captors, seeking a way to escape. Those thoughts warred with the desire to know what had become of her family, what the future would hold for her people.

Finally thirst won out. She put aside suspicions of poison and made herself drink. The water tasted fresh and cool and revived her somewhat. She forced herself to gnaw at some bread and cheese and take another swallow of water.

The enormity of her situation threatened to overwhelm her, but she knew her survival depended on staying focused. She recalled how she had recognized Gaelen. Just over a year ago an offer had come from his father, the now late Lord Bargest. He had sent a proposal of alliance. Part of the bargain had been a request for Marja to be joined with his second son, Gaelen. Gaclen himself had delivered the offer, and she had watched him from a curtained balcony. Her father had ordered her to stay out of sight, so Gaelen had not been aware of her scrutiny. Marja felt a moment of anger as she remembered that Cataniast had refused the offer. He had regarded it as a ploy, a way for Bargia to gain a foothold in Catania and subvert his authority. It had cost him his life and his demesne. A wave of rage washed over her, then as quickly ebbed. She had not the energy to sustain it.

Marja wondered if that information could be used to her benefit. So far Gaelen had kept his word. She remained unharmed and relatively comfortable. What plans could he have for her? Now that he had successfully taken Catania, would he see any advantage in keeping her alive? How could she convince him it would be prudent to court her goodwill? Could that be parlayed into concessions for her people? She knew letting her live would fly in the face of traditional thinking, which called for the deaths of all members of conquered ruling families. How would her position be affected if other members of her family still lived? If so, what difference would it make if they were still at large, or if they too had been taken prisoner? So many questions. So little information.

The spans passed, and eventually her exhaustion, coupled with the rise and fall of the voices below, lulled her into a fitful doze. Her chin dropped to her chest, her hands fell lax in her lap.

Get the rest of the story at: http://amzn.to/1yVu29P